Henry Bartle Edward Frere

Pandurang Hàrì

Or Memoirs of a Hindoo

Henry Bartle Edward Frere

Pandurang Hàrì
Or Memoirs of a Hindoo

ISBN/EAN: 9783337039417

Printed in Europe, USA, Canada, Australia, Japan

Cover: Foto ©Andreas Hilbeck / pixelio.de

More available books at **www.hansebooks.com**

PANDURANG HÀRÌ

OR

MEMOIRS OF A HINDOO

WITH AN INTRODUCTORY PREFACE BY

SIR H. BARTLE E. FRERE

G.C.S.I. K.C.B. D.C.L.

A NEW EDITION

London

CHATTO & WINDUS, PICCADILLY

1891

INTRODUCTION.

I HAVE been asked to write a short introduction, giving some of the reasons why I think the republication of this almost forgotten novel desirable at this present time. When "Pandurang Hàrì" was first published, nearly a half century ago, the book was received as a late and authentic picture of Native Indian society. I well remember my gratitude to a friend who recommended it to me, with "Haji Baba" and the "Kuzzilbash," as the only books he could find which gave any idea of what would now be called the inner life of Orientals. The works of Morier and Fraser have long since secured a permanent place in Anglo-oriental literature; but "Pandurang Hàrì" has been so completely forgotten, that when Dr. George Birdwood recommended its republication, the publishers were indebted to the liberality of Lord Talbot de Malahide for one of the few copies of the book which could be traced by Captain Meadows Taylor in any library, with which he was acquainted, in the United Kingdom. This neglect was not entirely due to comparative inferiority in literary merit. It is true that "Pandurang Hàrì" has no pretensions to the artistic skill and delicate sense of humour by means of which Mr. James Morier made the Persian adventurer a permanent favourite with all English readers. Pandurang himself can hardly be regarded in any sense as an interesting hero, and there are defects in the plot of the book, and in the slovenly execution of many details, which would interfere with its popularity as a mere novel. It possesses, how

A

ever, merits of a very rare kind, as a series of photographic pictures from the past generations of a great Indian nation. Its value in this respect would doubtless have been more permanently recognised, but for the circumstance that the pictures were, for the most part, taken from scenes of which Anglo-Indians in general had seen and heard but little. To most men who knew India in the Bengal or Madras Presidencies forty years ago, sketches from the life of a Maharatta adventurer could convey no true picture of Indian life and manners; but there are probably a few whose recollections belong to the Deccan or Malwa, and reach so far back as to include personal acquaintance with actors in the last Maharatta war, who will not fail to recognise, in the adventures of Pandurang, the general features of a mode of life and habits of thought, such as the Maharatta associates of their early days in Poona, Indore, or Hyderabad, delighted to dwell on. I had many opportunities of meeting men of this class in 1835 and subsequent years in the Deccan; and I can testify that there are very few of the scenes or stories contained in Pandurang's narrative, to which I could not find a parallel among the reminiscences I have heard related by old men, whose youth had been passed in Maharatta and Pindari courts or camps during the first twenty years of this century. But a traveller who might now visit, for the first time, the provinces in which the scene of the novel is laid, would meet little to remind him of Pandurang's adventures, or of such characters as he describes. I am convinced, from my own recollections of what I heard when I first knew the Deccan, that Pandurang's descriptions are remarkably faithful sketches of the time when the story was laid; and it is this fact which is one reason for my opinion that the republication of the old novel now will be of use to thoughtful Englishmen, as well as Hindoos, who interest themselves with questions relating to the progress, social, political, and moral, of Indian nations in modern times. The pictures drawn by Pandurang are by no means flattering or pleasing—they describe a state of society so hideously disorganised, and of morals so base, that they seem incredible as related of a period so near to our own, in which they would at once be condemned as enormously exaggerated or entirely untrue.

If then Pandurang's pictures be, as I believe them to be, substantially correct representations of the state of things in those provinces only two generations ago, it is clear that the country and people to which they relate, possess enormous inherent power of recovering from a state of debasement which would shock any educated native at the present moment. A knowledge of the greatness as well as the rapidity of the change which has taken place, may inspire fresh hope in those who are sanguine regarding the future progress of native society, while the same facts may moderate the self-satisfaction of some of our young native friends, who, not having any personal knowledge of the depth of degradation to which society had sunk during previous generations of anarchy and misrule, are apt to believe intelligent foreigners' estimate of their country and people to be tinged with prejudice or clouded by ignorance.

While, however, I can testify to the general truthfulness of Pandurang's sketching powers, I would by no means assent to his general estimate of Maharatta character. The author appears to have been a keen-sighted, quick-witted man, who readily apprehended the leading characteristics of what he saw and heard; but who shared, with the great majority of his official countrymen, in the difficulty of arriving at impartial opinions regarding the motives and feelings of his native associates.

The Introduction is characteristic of the manner in which but too many of our countrymen have always judged the natives of India. It never seems to strike the author that the irksomeness to Europeans of the society of natives of India may be as much due to our ignorance of what interests our native visitors, as to their ignorance of what interests us; and that, without some common topics of real interest to both parties, there can, in no country, be much pleasure in casual conversation.

His description of the motives of those natives who visit the European official in India, has no doubt some foundation of truth in every part of the world, as regards those who seek the acquaintance of men in power, and of those who are the dispensers of patronage.

In India, where for generations anything like purity in the

administration of justice or the distribution of patronage, had almost ceased to be expected by either the rulers or their subjects, the author's estimate of the motives which drew visitors to the doors of official men in India, fifty years ago, might be expected to be peculiarly applicable. Yet even there, the author admits that he found one bright exception to the sweeping condemnation which he passes on the general mass of his native acquaintance; and it is observable that, however severe may be the judgments pronounced by European crities on their native associates in India, the critic, if a man of any experience or real power of observation, rarely fails to check his condemnation of native society in general by describing "the only honest native, sir, I ever knew," or in some other form testifying to exceptions, which, even granting them to be as rare as such critics imagine, would suffice to prove that whatever the causes of presumed general depravity, the incapacity of the race for good was certainly not absolute nor universal.

The truth is, that, as has been long since pointed out by Shore and others, European critics of Indian society and social morality have generally laboured under such great disadvantages in their limited sphere of observation, as to render anything like judicial accuracy or impartiality a result difficult of attainment and rare in the extreme. How seldom, when we are ourselves judged by foreigners, do we find that they have knowledge of our language and customs sufficient to secure them from the most ridiculous errors. How still more difficult is the task when, as is usually the case in India, the man is the artist who represents his own contest with the lion. We know, in this country, how much allowance should be made in estimating the general standard of social morality from the official experience of those who see only the criminal classes of our great cities and garrison towns; and how badly we should ourselves appear, if some of the least prejudiced estimates regarding us were taken from the reports of ministers of religion, who habitually tolerate no standard short of absolute moral perfection. What large allowance must be made for defective powers and opportunities of observation in any European judgment of native Indian character, will be apparent to any one who reflects how little weight he would attach to unfavourable opinions of his own countrymen, expressed by foreigners of experience as limited in time, or extent of range, as we know must be the case with many Europeans who, from a brief tour, or a few years of official experience, pronounce *ex cathedra* very sweeping judgments on native-Indian society and morals. But, as already stated, the real merit of " Pandurang Hàrì " lies in the general truthfulness of incidental sketches and stories. The fidelity of some scenes and portraits may still be recognised by any modern sojourners in the Deccan, but there are others which already seem to belong to a bygone age.

I may instance, as one of the minor features of this kind, the position of the Gossein community, and the extraordinary depravity of some of its members. Modern visitors to Poona might have difficulty in discovering a genuine Gossein, or the habitations of any of the sect. But forty years ago, the Gossein warra, or quarter, filled with their semi-fortified and substantially-built houses, was one of the most conspicuous features in the old Maharatta city ; and any one who was fond of talking to the natives regarding the olden time, was, in those days, sure to hear endless stories of the wealth and the crimes of the original owners and inhabitants of those fortlaces, which a few years ago looked so palatial amid the meaner houses of the surrounding town. He would be told of the enormous influence of Gosseins in every grade of society during the reign of Bajee Row, of their secret springs of information, and of the doings, heroic or criminal, of the chosen band of desperadoes of this sect on which Bapoo Gokla, one of the few really patriotic advisers of the last Peishwa, relied in his last despairing efforts to retrieve his master's falling fortunes.

Again, except to a few adventurers, bear-hunters, or district police-officers, the robber's cave is probably now as obsolete in India as it is in England, or any other country where it has been relegated to the theatrical properties of melodramatic managers. But long after peace and uniform government had been restored to the Deccan, genuine robbers' caves, such as are described by Pandurang, were to be found in many remote districts. Some of the old Bhuddist cave temples, which are scattered so plentifully along the whole range of the Western Ghauts, were used as robber retreats to within a comparatively recent period, and thirty years ago robber-caves might have been found within a walk or ride of the now fashionable sanitarium of Mahabuleshwar, close to roads now frequented by English nurses and their infantile charges, and within sight of plantations of chincona plants brought from the Andes by Mr. Clements Markham.

One such cave in the laterite rock, overlooking the ancient road from Waee to the sacred sources of the Krishna and its sister rivers, just where the road branches to the fortress of Pretabghur and to the sea-port of Mhar, though now in the heart of the hill station, was pointed out to me some years ago by one of the elders of the Gaolees (hill herdsmen) as the place where, in his father's time, a robber band, with which the poor hill herdsmen dared not meddle, used to watch for pilgrims, merchants, or stray soldiers, and to pounce on any convoy which appeared, as viewed from their eagle's nest, to be incapable of resistance. The cave was spacious, well furnished with fireplaces and platforms for sleeping, and rude cupboard-like recesses; and could have comfortably sheltered fifty men unobserved, within watching distance of the ancient track over the hills. Similar caves are found in many parts of the same laterite range, which bounds the well-wooded and beautiful valley of the Koina, between Mahabuleshwar and the Chiploon Ghaut; and some of them as late as 1846, when the valley was still one of the most secluded in the Deccan, afforded permanent refuge, not often to active robbers, but to fugitives of society, who found in their recesses the shelter denied to them in more populous districts. Three or four such solitary outlaws, possibly the last of their kind, were coaxed into Satara by the head man of one of the little forest villages, and furnished with a safe-conduct from the Resident, securing them from molestation so long as they obeyed the law. All of these poor creatures had the quick observant glance, the attentive ear, and more or less the general air of wild animals rather than of men. One of them, who told me he believed he had lived in these rocky fastnesses for fourteen years, had fled from his home after slaying a man in a fit of jealousy; he described his life as one of almost unendurable suffering and privation, dependent for all necessaries of life (beyond what the roots and berries of the jungle afforded) on the precarious hospitality of the poor villages scattered along the banks of the river in the narrow valley. The villagers, partly probably from fear, partly from compassion, never denounced him, and at harvest time always left small offerings of grain, or a cast-off blanket, or pair of sandals, within his reach ; but they rarely noticed or spoke to him, and treated him much as one possessed by some evil spirit, whom they hardly dared to aid, still less to drive away. Occasionally a shooting party, in search of bears or sambur deer, would fill him with terror, as he watched them from the rocks overhanging the valley ; but the native beaters made a point of not noticing him, and he had never, till I saw him, confronted a white man close enough to speak to him. Forty years earlier I have no doubt these same rocks would have afforded refuge to such robbers as Pandurang describes ; and all the skirts of the Ghauts, and the Vindya and Santroora ranges, doubtless abound in similar valleys possessed of similar robber-strongholds.

Of detached pictures, such as might have been seen in the Deccan sixty years ago, and of stories such as might have been heard round the village peple-tree of an evening twenty years later, I have met no book which gives so vivid an idea as this almost forgotten and inartistic novel. The " Confessions of a Thug " incidentally refer to some of the social deformities of the same age ; but it relates merely to one class of criminal society, and that class limited in numbers, though not in range. The same graphic hand has drawn in " Tara " a charming picture of some of the most beautiful scenery and pleasing features of native life in the Deccan ; but for a truthful picture of Maharrata life, as it must have appeared in the latter and more corrupt days of the Peishwa's government, I have met with nothing equal to the dark bizarre sketches of " Pandurang Hàri."

Of the author, Mr Hockley, I have been able to learn little beyond the fact that he belonged to the Bombay Civil Service, and served under the Commissioners in the Deccan, and in the Judge's Court at Broach. He fell under a cloud and left the service, and of his subsequent career I have been able to trace nothing When I was first at Poona many stories were current of the practical and other jokes with which he exercised the patience of the older and steadier officers in the Deccan Commission; but this novel, which was published by Whitaker in 1826, is the only production of his pen which I have met with, and I have not even been able to verify the date of his death. No alteration has been attempted in the orthography of proper names—it is not uniform, or in accordance with any regular system, but is sufficiently consistent to satisfy the general reader, while any attempt to make it conform to more accurate transliteration would have involved other changes for which there is no sufficient warrant.   It is obvious, for instance, that some of the names could not have belonged to persons of the caste to which they are attributed; it is useless to attempt correcting them, and the reader must kindly take them, like the impossible names in old translations of the Arabian Nights, as belonging to the author's creation, and not to the age or people of which he wrote.

The modes of address, moreover, are of an English rather than native fashion, but to have carried out a correct translation of native expressions, would have involved alterations in style not justifiable in a reprint.

H. B. E. FRERE.

Wressil Lodge, Wimbledon, 1872.

INTRODUCTION TO ORIGINAL EDITION.

NOTHING can be more irksome to the European than the society of the inhabitant of Hindustan. His conversation is monotonous, and little calculated to relieve the tedium caused by that enervating indolence, which, in a tropical climate, overpowers the European, and is also a marked portion of the native character. If a native visit you, his call is not that of friendship, but always has some interested motive at bottom, or the hope of obtaining some personal benefit. The learning, talent, and virtue which a European may possess, are no objects of attraction with him; they are of no value in his eyes; and the crowd of natives who may flock around his door are drawn thither by the charm of his power, as agent of the Government, as Resident, collector, or judge. If they do not expect, through his means, to obtain some insignificant situation that they may turn to profit, the very circumstance of his admission of them as visitants gives them considerable consequence in the eyes of their countrymen, of which they do not fail to take advantage. Where the will of the ruler is regarded as law (which, from time immemorial, has been the case in the East), power is the great idol of adulation: to live in its shadow confers influence; its smiles are equivalent to the satisfaction of no very limited ambition; and this holds good, in its degree, as far as regards the lowest officer of the ruling authority. Such is a distinguishing feature of the natives of India, and of the Mahrattas more especially; and the characteristic is noticed here, in order to mark an exception to the general rule.

The editor of this work, in travelling through the Deccan, had the singular good fortune to meet with a native who possessed but little of the selfish character of his countrymen. His visits were disinterested in every respect, and they were uniformly met with that pleasure which, in European society, is always exhibited upon the reception of a generous friend. In his conversation there was nothing like deceit; for, ill resembling the generality of his countrymen, he left his mask at home. There was no affected humility in his manner, no servile and flattering epithets, so disgusting to European minds of any strength : he was, in short, the best specimen of the native character the editor ever saw; and his society was a thing of value, in proportion to its extraordinary rarity in that part of the world. The name of this native was Nanna, of the family of the individual of that name mentioned hereafter as the friend of Pandurang Hàrì. In the conversations which frequently took place—conversations which will be remembered to the last hour of life with pleasure—more knowledge of the people of Hindustan was gleaned than could have been acquired by the longest residence in the country, in the character of a simple observer. Speaking one day of the governments of India, and of the number of small states into which it was and is divided, my friend mentioned that the succession to the sovereignty was often a subject of quarrel and bloodshed. Usurpers, persons of the reigning family, and claimants distantly related to a defunct sovereign, by their disputes had occasioned much unhappiness to the people. Just claims had been made by individuals whose lives were spent in the lowest occupations in search of subsistence, or who had been driven into concealment and obscurity to secure their own existence; the reigning despot endeavouring to keep down all claimants to the throne, or one of them endeavouring to persecute to destruction another who might be nearer than himself to a musnud of which the speedy vacation was expected.

One day this native friend put into the editor's hand a MS., written in the Mahratta tongue, saying, "As you wish to be acquainted with some of the adventures of the better class of natives, and with the Mahratta character in particular, this will enable you to form your own opinion, and show them as they are. You will discover the shifts and modes of subsistence which even the higher castes may be driven to adopt, and the strange vicissitudes of life often occurring in a country where everything depends upon the will of superiors in power—where, except in religious observances and customs, there is a constant change, and the rajah of to-day may be the ryot of to-morrow."

After perusing the MS. of his friend, the editor thought a free translation of it into his own language would not be uninteresting to his countrymen ; he therefore set about the task, in doing which he has tried to render the language as simple and unpretending as the original, and to give the story as he received it, neither clothed in picturesque local description, nor heated by passion, beyond that which the languid temperament of the Hindoo will sanction ; for even love with him is little more, if anything, than a blind instinct. The reader must not, therefore, expect to revel in scenes of heroic or chivalric adventure ; but to peruse the history of a distinguished native individual, in its *vraisemblance* glance and characteristic simplicity.

To render the work as intelligible and clear as possible, advantage has been taken of an editor's license, and alterations have been made (but only such as appeared absolutely necessary) to Anglicise the narrative. Some of the editor's Indian friends will be able to confirm the truth of many of the leading details, because they must discover allusions to real facts, which have taken place, to their own knowledge, in our Eastern empire.

The editor is aware that a description of the Asiatic character has been before now given to the public, and he has seen the observations of travellers upon it. He knows that the secluded Brahmin has been regarded by the hasty visitant with admiration, and does not, therefore, marvel at the warmth of colouring in which it has been often the fashion to clothe his quiet, and therefore, as supposed, devoted and virtuous, character. It is with astonishment, however, that he has known persons, long resident in India, employ their pens in the same manner; and he wonders how men of talent can have resided years among this people, and have been so completely duped by plausibilities. Perhaps they never were at the pains to penetrate beyond the mere external picture, and judged of the truth by the appearance. Hindoo simplicity of character has been praised, and the virtue of the women held up as a model to the world (not regarding its powerful protection under a reign of castes); and a picture has been drawn, such as the world never yet saw, and never will see, of a pure, virtuous, open, generous people, inhabiting a country governed for ages by the most despotic barbarians, ground into the dust by a host of lesser native officials, and steeped in the most deplorable ignorance and superstition. Meanness, cunning, cowardice and self-interest are almost necessary, under such a system, to carry on existence, and these have been their resources, accordingly, for ages. The free mountain peasant of Switzerland is the pure and simple man, because he may live without the necessity of a recourse to such vices ;—the Hindoo never can. If the European, who has been deeply conversant with the Hindoo character in all situations, were to speak out, he would confess that the apparent simplicity and humility of the Brahmin is a garb of hypocrisy, to look well among the people and carry on his influence ; but that he is, in reality, selfish, vicious, and intent only upon blinding the credulous for his own ends. Let the Hindoo be seen at variance with his neighbour, or in any situation where his hatred is excited, and he will be found relentless in his anger, and cowardly in his revenge. Watch him at a moment when he has a chance of turning a single rupee, by almost any means, and let it be said, if his disregard of all but his object, his meanness and duplicity in pursuing it, can be exceeded ! Nevertheless, in a country where the law has so long been the strongest, it must be granted that the want of morality and principle is no great phenomenon.

Englishmen who have written so much in favour of the natives, it may be boldly pronounced, never mingled in situations where their private contests and private conduct with each other could be clearly observed. The editor went amongst them prejudiced in their favour : a few years undeceived him. From the rajah to the ryot, with the intermediate grades, they are ungrateful, insidious, cowardly, unfaithful, and revengeful. This much the editor thinks it necessary to say, to account for the colouring and acts of some of the characters in the ensuing narrative, without which its authenticity might be questioned by some who have read the eulogises of the natives of Hindustan; but, most assuredly, an Hindóo would hardly treat as matter of fact, without comment or apology, many of his own vices, as Pandurang does, if they were not commonplace to him, and inherent in the national character.

The editor apologises for saying so much upon this subject. It was needful to say something, and he has been as concise as he well could upon such a topic, and has now no more to do than to beg the reader's indulgence for the execution of his share of labour in the present publication.

PANDURANG HÀRÌ.

CHAPTER I.

HITHERTO it has been customary with those who write a history of their lives and adventures, to commence with a minute detail of all the circumstances connected with their earliest years—their family, birth, and education. I would most willingly follow preceding examples in this respect, had my history resembled that of other men ; but, unfortunately, I was a long period of my life in utter ignorance to whom I was under obligations for my introduction into the world; so that any information I may subsequently have acquired respecting my parentage, can hardly be said to belong to the first part of my history, as it would clearly do to that of the generality of mankind. This singularity, therefore, in the very outset of my existence, and the wish I have to adhere as closely as possible to the regular order of events, must be my apology to the reader for my not saying anything here upon these points, or even hinting just now who I discovered my parents to be ; I shall only thereby keep the public in the dark for a time on this subject, as I was once kept myself. Should any part of it betray an impatient curiosity as to these matters after I have begun, I must entreat it to keep my example in view, and practise a little Hindoo patience, trusting to my promise of disclosing these important secrets in due time and place.

My earliest sense of existence, as well as I can remember, was severely painful. I have a clear recollection of an Hindoo, advanced in years, stooping down and extricating me from the hoofs of a troop of bullocks and horses, where I had been left by some one who evidently made my safety a matter of small account. One of the animals, beneath which I was wallowing, had crushed my tender arm with its hoof, and set me, naturally enough, screaming and roaring with all my might. My deliverer took me to his tent, and bound up my bruised limb. I remember well his features and dress. He was a Mahratta, and a man of some consequence, travelling in the district upon business. On his head he wore a large white turban, tied under the chin : a stuffed coat, dirty boots, and a tremendous sword dangling at his side. He delivered me to a servant, who pestered me with questions which I could not answer; demanding who I was? whence I came? who were my parents? to which, of course, I was unable to make any other reply than *malla towak n,hae* (" I know not "). I then heard the servants disputing about my age. One said I was four years old, another five; at length the last number seemed to be decided upon. I next heard them debate upon my caste; and one of them perceiving the red mark upon my forehead, said I was a true Hindoo. It was to my good fortune he made this declaration, as I was deemed worthy of being noticed in consequence; for had I been of a different caste than I was—that of Choomar or Sudra, for example—I should have been left to starve, or been glad to herd with my old companions, the bullocks, once more. I was now taken into the presence of my deliverer, having been instructed by his servants to say, as soon as I came near him, *ram ram, Ma,ha,raj* (" your most obedient, my lord !") Whether I pronounced this salutation ill, or with proper confidence, I cannot now tell, but it was very kindly noticed by the Mahratta Ma,ha,raj. He ordered me to be clothed, and to have a red turban given me. I can even now remember the effect this treatment of me by the master produced on the servants: they immediately behaved kindly to me, styling me *baba sahib, Ma,ha, rag d,hunne*, as if addressing their lord himself. My young mind soon became elated by this attention, and my childish pride grew intolerable. I discovered that as long as I possessed the master's favour, I might act as I pleased among his interiors. In short, I at last considered myself his son, and he gave me the name of Pandurang Hàrì.

I will now pass over the term of my infancy, which was employed in learning to read and write—my preceptor being a *mahouhut*, or elephant-driver—and will take up my adventures from the period of my completing my sixteenth year. At this time Holkar, the great Mahratta chieftain, assembled his army, and a division of it was commanded by my benefactor, Sawunt Rao Gopal Rao. There was no expectation entertained that we should come to an engagement for many months, although preparations were at that moment deemed necessary. I had made a considerable proficiency in my studies, which pleased Sawunt Rao, and I soon found the advantage of my acquirements. My benefactor's chief *carcoon*, or clerk, allowed me to sort out and direct despatches to officers at a distance who belonged to the command of the great Sawunt Rao. The consequence this gave me in the eyes of Sawunt's dependants was wonderful. A boy soon came to offer his services as my *kullum dani*, or inkstand-bearer; another, as my *chitree burdar*, or umbrella-carrier ; and when I mounted on my *tattoo*, or pony, I could at any time have commanded the attendance of a dozen grooms—so many pressed forward to offer me their services. I accepted two and a slipper-bearer, but was greatly concerned to know how I was to pay them their wages. I consulted the carcoon, who laughed in my face, and demanded if I was mad to think of giving wages to those *nimuk hārām* (rascals). "No, no, Pandoo," said he ; "let them wait on you, and in a few years you may be able to provide for them under our government ; however, as you may want money, it will be a good plan to get Sawunt Rao Ma,ha,raj to grant you some to give these fellows, and you can keep it yourself. As to paying those scoundrels, it would be as absurd as flinging your money into the river." It will recur to the reader that I had now been some years with Sawunt Rao ; and having been gradually initiated in Mahratta roguery, it will not be matter of surprise that I entered into this scheme with true Hindoo delight. Success attended my first attempt ; and the carcoon pronounced I should soon make my fortune. He advised me to neglect no opportunity of fingering money; "for," said he, "Pandoo, there is nothing in this world equal to rupees. Get them, and you will get everything. We shall have rare plunder at the ensuing battle." I here ventured to observe that the tables might be turned upon us, and we ourselves get plundered instead of being the plunderers. "O Pandoo !" he replied, twisting his mustachios, "you little know the Mahratta valour ! In the field every man has the power of the many-armed Vishnu. No nation can resist us ; we are world-conquerors ! You will soon see whether I speak truth or not."

On the ensuing day we marched ; and when I observed the war-elephants in terrific panoply, and heard the roar of the nagarrahs or state-drums ; when I saw the long-drawn plain covered with soldiers, both horse and foot, all busy in martial preparation, I gave in my own mind implicit credit to the resistless valour of the Mahrattas, and began to plan how I should dispose of my rupees and plunder, as soon as I should gain possession of them. On arriving at our halting-place, I attended, as was customary, to make my obeisance to my master. He ordered me to wait in his tent while he ate his dinner. I seized this opportunity of sitting in a corner ; and sending for my inkstand and papers, I made a great show of business. During his dinner, Sawunt Rao never once noticed me ; but afterwards, when smoking his hookah, he exclaimed, "Ah, Pandoo ! what—can you write ?" I answered in the affirmative, and showed him some specimens, with which he appeared highly pleased. He dictated several letters to me, and sent orders by me to different officers outside the tent. He next desired me to admit to his presence any individuals who had complaints to make or orders to receive, as he was then at leisure to attend to business of that nature. I withdrew, and waited in a small tent through which all must pass before they could enter the presence of the Ma,ha,-raj. I had not been there long before a complainant[1] appeared,

---

[1] Chiefs like Sawunt Rao have in the East cognisance both of civil and military affairs.

and urged me to obtain an audience for him. I, of course, gave myself great airs, and roundly asserted that the Ma,ha,raj was sleeping, and would not be disturbed. The complainant seemed to know how to awaken both servant and master. Slipping a handful of rupees into my hand, he promised me double the amount if he succeeded. I now softened my manner and condescended to say, "I will see if I dare wake Ma,ha,raj, but I really fear for my life, yet for your sake I will risk everything." The Ma,ha,raj was still smoking his hookah when I entered, and I at once opened my business. I was ordered to admit the complainant, and was sent for presently myself, and desired to take down his business in writing. I did so, but was not yet as adroit as I should have been in putting my words quickly together, though I would not on any account confess my want of skill. I went on scribbling anything that came uppermost in place of the poor man's story ; and when I had done, I knew as little about it as before I began. Fortunately, I could see by my master's air and manner he was as indifferent to the merits of the case as myself, and therefore I felt very little uneasiness upon the subject. The complainant was dismissed with the assurances of receiving justice. I took care to follow him, and abuse him for his long tale, declaring my fingers were stiff with taking it down. The poor dupe had sagacity enough to discover there was one medicine which never fails to cure rigidity of the joints in such cases, and he accordingly applied his silver ointment to my hands once more. The cure was instantaneous : I promised him everything, and assured him his enemy should be trampled to death by an elephant if he desired it. I then ordered him to call at the carcoon's on the following day, when all should be settled ; but reminded him that this official must finger the rupees as well as myself, at least in equal proportion. So saying, I withdrew to count over my money. According to my advice, he did not neglect to appear at the carcoon's ; but that sagacious officer, having been informed of the petitioner's interviews with me, ordered him to quit his presence. He once more came to me, and I endeavoured, by assurances and promises, to keep alive hopes which I very well knew were doomed to be disappointed.

he took his leave of me, bowing so low as to knock his forehead on the ground.

Day after day passed over, and still Hybatty (such was the petitioner's name) remained unnoticed. He was even rudely treated by the official hirelings who lounged around the tents. Far from resenting such conduct towards him, I rather encouraged it; for Hybatty had become my second shadow whenever I appeared abroad. At length, losing all patience, I angrily bade him return to his village and trouble me no further as the Maha,raj would attend to the petition when it suited his convenience. Hybatty gave me a look that spoke stronger things than language could do, and hurried from my presence.

CHAPTER II.

AS yet there appeared no probability of a battle taking place; nevertheless, our army was kept up in full force and constant readiness for it. Our tents were pitched on the side of a river, while a majestic banyan-tree spread itself over a rising-ground at a short distance. Thither, in the cool hour of the evening, I was accustomed to go, and remain alone in reflection upon my dependent circumstances. "Unhappy being that I am!" thought I; "neglected by parents who still remain unknown to me, though destiny has flung me in the way of the good Sawunt Rao, what claim have I upon him or upon any fellow-creature? My very existence depends upon his— should he die, what will become of me? Should he frown upon me while living, adieu to all consequence with those around me! To obtain an honest livelihood is impossible: no trade is so unprofitable as honesty. It is very hard that, with the inclination to be just and upright, I should be compelled by the circumstances of my life to be a rogue. Could I but amass a few thousand rupees, I would lose no time in settling at Indore as a corn or grain merchant; and then," thought I, rising up with delight, "I will be honest for the rest of my days!" I had just finished making this notable resolution for conducting my future life, when I saw a little way off the figure of a tall man muffled up in shawls. He was looking everywhere around him, with a countenance full of suspicion, as if he feared lest his actions would be observed. He did not see me, it was evident; and I became very curious to know the cause of his extraordinary appearance, and the object he had in parading about in that spot in the dusk of the evening. I immediately climbed up into the banyan-tree, and hid myself among its luxuriant foliage. The person whose steps I had been watching now approached the sacred tree; and having performed *pija*[1] to a stone deity at its foot, proceeded to unmuffle himself from his shawls, carefully folding them up and placing them under the tree. He now squatted down, and began to grumble in a low tone, "Not here ! I am too early ! I can wait until he comes. I know my information is correct. He comes here every evening to meditate some fresh villany no doubt." Here he paused; and my breathing paused too, for he could have meant no one but myself, I having been the only constant lounger under that sacred tree at the evening hour. "Who can this man be?" thought I; "perhaps he is some one acquainted with my parents." On this idea suggesting itself, I was on the point of descending from my hiding-place, and begging him to satisfy my curiosity; but I was luckily deterred from my intention by hearing him again talking to himself, and saying, "Well, as I could not obtain redress, and was plundered for attempting to assert my rights, this dagger, thanks to *Hanoomān*,[2] has given me vengeance. My enemy is quiet enough, unless he has met with a god in the *mota bowrie*.[3] That young villain, Pandurang Hàri, shall keep Tulsajee company." There he stopped; and I almost fell from the branches of my refuge with fear when I discovered this man to be no other than the petitioner who so handsomely rewarded me on his coming to demand justice of my master. His case, notwithstanding his bribes, and the profuse way in which he distributed his *nugd*,[4] remained entirely neglected to that hour. Fancy may depict, but I cannot put into language, the fear I felt, and the breathless terror that came over me, when I reflected that the creaking of a branch or the rustling of a leaf might betray me. The evening was still and silent as the grave. A cold perspiration stood on my forehead. The insect that fluttered around me, whose wing at another time would have been

[1] Worship.

[2] The name of an idol in the form of a monkey.

[3] Deep well. [4] Ready cash.

inaudible, seemed now to fill my ears with its hum, so alive was I to the minutest sounds. I soon heard Hybatty mutter slowly to himself again, "The young villain! the young villain! to take my rupees, to neglect and insult me! Thanks to Siva and Brahma, I want not their help now; I am paid with the silver bangles[1] of my enemy, and his cash to boot!" A little while after this he arose, and went to a peepal-tree a short way off, where he appeared busy about something, I could not well make out what. He was delving in the earth, and, as I afterwards found, burying his ill-gotten treasure. He now halted, as if unwilling to leave the place while there was a chance of my visiting it. He returned to the sacred tree again, and I heard the words, "Pandurang Hàrì — dagger — his greedy heart," disjointedly uttered. He afterwards, raising his voice, said, "I swear by the holy *cow*[2] never to give up my revenge, though I pursue him to Oogein, and from thence to Delhi, and from Delhi to Cape Comorin; I will not rest till I have taken his blood." In a few minutes he muffled himself up in his shawls as before, and went his way. His departure was a reprieve to a condemned criminal; I seemed rescued from a suffocation worse than death. Once more my lungs got into full play, and my limbs appeared to be relieved from the heavy weight which oppressed them. When my enemy had disappeared, I descended from my hiding-place, and did not deem myself secure until I had joined my comrades in the camp. "It is well," thought I, as soon as I had gained a place of security—"it is well I can turn the tables upon my enemy. He has confessed a murder; and as I am to have no peace while he lives, I will try if I have not wit and interest enough to get him put out of the way. We shall see whether I cannot save him his journey to Oogein, Delhi, and Cape Comorin!"

When I reflected how corrupt all persons in authority were, I feared that, after all I could do, there would be but a small chance of beholding my foe dangling from a tree while he could command money enough to fee the farmer of the district, whose

---

[1] Rings worn about the wrists.   [2] A solemn Hindoo adjuration.

mercy was generally extended, even for the most flagrant crimes, to those who could purchase their impunity. The district farmers were compelled from necessity to raise money by every opportunity, and they never neglected their interests; for when a new one had not been a month in his district, he was every hour liable to be superseded by a successor, who had agreed to pay the Ma,ha,raj a higher sum for the office. On this account the actual occupant turned all robberies and murders to account, and never executed any who could purchase their lives, while the poor were sent into the other world without mercy. Thus justice was regulated, as it is in most countries, by individual caprice or expediency, instead of certain immutable principles, which should make it the same thing everywhere. I considered, therefore, that this mercenary principle in our government might tell against me after all if I appeared active in the business, and my enemy should afterwards escape by paying a fine to the farmer: for it was likely I should thus incur his threefold vengeance, and hasten my own destruction. What plan to pursue now became a matter of the utmost importance. "The tiger," I reasoned to myself, "must be deprived of his claws, and the lion of his teeth, before we can combat with them successfully. My enemy's treasures are his claws, and they are in my power. Fool that I am! are they not buried under the peepal-tree, where I saw him grubbing in the earth?" I accordingly set off for the spot, and pulling out my dagger, tried the earth around the roots of the tree for some time in vain. I was just on the point of giving up the search, when it struck against a hard substance, which I discovered, by the scanty light of the dawn (for I had taken no rest during the night), to be a brass pot, tied round with leather at the top. I could find nothing else; so closing up the hole and levelling the earth, I returned to my tent, lit my lamp, and proceeded to examine what I had found. First, there were the silver bangles of Tulsajee, the murdered man: these were worth two hundred rupees at least. Then there were gold *mohurs*[1] tied up in long narrow bags, which the victim of my foe

---

[1] An Eastern coin.

had, as is customary, bound round his waist for convenience in travelling, after the Mahratta manner. I then came to silver rupees, and women's ornaments of the usual kinds: the *nuth*, or nose-ring; the *boogrie*, or ear-pendants; the *toolsee*, or necklace; *kurrun*, *p,hool*, or ear-ornaments; the *bajoo-bund*, or armlets, with many rings all of gold, besides loose pearls and copper *pice*.[1] "Well, Pandoo," thought I to myself, "you have indeed made the most you could expect of your enemy!" I justly considered, from the rank of the fellow in life, that this must be all the wealth he had in the world, ill-gotten as it was. I calculated the whole to be worth two thousand rupees, and I dug a hole under the mat on which I slept, and there deposited my treasure. Having done this, I lay down to weigh what step should be taken next, and to fix upon the most certain and safe method of bringing my foe, Hybatty, to the gibbet.

[1] A small coin.

CHAPTER III.

THE next morning I bent my way towards the village where my enemy resided. The first step I took, consistently with the plan I had laid down for myself, was to wait upon the principal and heads of the village. These men of authority being aware I was a *hoogoric*, or one attached to the suite of a great man, received me with due respect. I longed for a good pair of mustachios to twirl about and exhibit my consequence; but, unfortunately, I was only eighteen years old, though in appearance at least four years more, and was obliged, for lack of length in those dignified appendages, to content myself with twisting about my shawl with an air of self-importance, and so as to exhibit my person to the best advantage. I then opened the purport of my visit, by stating that I was come to inquire into the complaint of a person named Hybatty against a man called Tulsajee, and desiring the complainant might be sent for. It will be easily guessed that this was my old enemy, who so pleasingly intimated his good-will towards me under the banyan-tree. He drew back on first seeing me, as if he had rather have not met me there. I appeared wholly unconscious of his harbouring any ill design against myself, and immediately addressed him, saying, "My good friend, you may now see I have not forgotten your cause, which would have been attended to much sooner could I have secured the ear of the Ma,ha,raj; but his time has been so occupied with political correspondence, that he has really had no leisure to think of anything else. You may now state your case, and justice shall be rendered you." Hybatty—for he it was—looked aghast at this unexpected condescension, and gave me a glance so peculiar in character, and yet so very far from agreeable, that I felt more than ever anxious to do him the kindness I had in store for him. It appeared as if he looked through my intentions, and suspected all was not as fair as it seemed to be, without his being able to fathom my designs. Hesitating a little at first, he soon launched out more fluently against his enemy, Tulsajee, as if the latter had really been in the land of the living! He repeatedly urged me to summon him, and see if he dared to deny any part of what he should urge against him. I replied, "I am sure he cannot deny any part of your assertions : however, let him be summoned." This devil Hybatty looked in my eyes more hellish than I thought it possible for a human being to do, on hearing the order given. After some delay, a message was sent from the friends of Tulsajee, saying he had left the village on a journey, and his family had not heard of him since he set out. "Oh, it is well," I replied (addressing myself to the village authorities) ; "we cannot help it ; when he returns assemble a *punchayet*,[1] and give this cause patient attention, seeing that Hybatty has justice." Having said this, I took my departure. The reason for my acting thus was, lest, upon conviction of the murder, Hybatty should accuse me of not attending to his complaint, and make my negligence a plea for the act which he had committed. I now proceeded to the *maamulut-dar*, or farmer of the district, and mentioned my suspicion that Tulsajee was murdered, and who the murderer was. "This affair," said I, " will put a few rupees into your pocket, as Hybatty, the murderer, has money, I am certain ; so you may fine him to the tune of five hundred rupees at least. He may plead poverty, but do not heed what he says ; and as he knows a fine will get him clear, he will not be at the trouble of denying the crime ; or should he do so, I can help you to evidence that shall bring it home to him." The farmer thanked me repeatedly for my consideration of him in giving this intelligence, and promised to proceed against Hybatty, without comprising me by mentioning my name. In a few days I heard of his apprehension, that the

---

[1] A court of jurymen, five or more in number.

farmer had charged him with the crime, but that he stoutly denied all knowledge of it. I immediately visited the farmer, had a secret interview with him, and desired him to tax the prisoner with the crime again, and to tell him he had flung the body into the mota bowrie. The farmer was astonished how I could tell him so much about it, and, I thought, almost regarded me as an accomplice. I told him he should learn all as soon as the affair was finally settled. Hybatty was then taxed with the crime again, and told the place where he had concealed the body. Upon this, and supposing the farmer knew everything, he confessed, and said he was the farmer's humble servant (meaning he would pay any fine the farmer might demand of him). I was not present, but had an agent at the trial. The fine was fixed at a thousand rupees, because, as the farmer afterwards informed me, there was a better chance of getting five hundred clear, by an appearance of lenity in remitting half of the original sum levied.

Hybatty, now completely in my toils, and little aware of his poverty, immediately consented to pay the rupees. Being in custody, he sent for his son, and on his arrival directed him where to find the money. The son set off; and I was malicious enough to wish I had again been in the peepal-tree, to witness and enjoy his disappointment. In the meantime, Hybatty sat smoking, confidently chewing his betel, and cracking his jokes. The body of Tulsajee had just been fished up from the well or mota bowrie, and was exhibiting to the populace, with the throat cut, and a stab in the heart; while, to enable the murderer to secure the silver bangles with greater expedition, both hands had been severed at the wrists. The culprit's son now approached, with rueful face and heavy footsteps, to the place of his father's durance. Being admitted, his tale was soon told; for he had not been a moment in the prison before a most dismal yell was heard from its interior—a more piercing shriek than ever struck a mortal ear before! Sobs and groans succeeded, then supplications; and when these were found of no avail, oaths and curses were dealt out liberally against those who had defrauded him. My name was on Hybatty's lips among the rest; but little did he think the plunderer of his property was so near him. The intelligence of his inability to pay his fine was speedily carried to the farmer, who before long made his appearance with a new rope and two *dheers*,[1] and in a few minutes Hybatty was a corpse. I then returned to my tent, reflecting as I went along on the events which had just passed. "What have I done?" thought I. "I have extorted money from an unhappy and injured man, under the false pretence of obtaining redress for him. I have neglected him, though I accepted his presents; I have driven him to desperation, made him a murderer, robbed him of his property, and betrayed him to death!" I now thought, but in vain, to ease my conscience by the consideration that my victim was deserving of death, having been a murderer. But the truth that, but for my neglect of him, he would not have stained his hands with blood, ever came uppermost. I contrived, however, to console myself that I had acted in self-defence. Hybatty had sworn to take my life; and I made that serve me as a justification. Besides, a great religious festival was at hand; and a dip in the river, with the offering of a cocoa-nut to the god and a trifle to the Brahmins, would purify me, and effectually remove my uneasy sensations.

Scarcely was the foregoing happy conclusion drawn, when a band of armed men surrounded me, and, without assigning a reason, hurried me away to a place of confinement, in a tent well guarded within and without. My terrified features must have condemned me, for I in vain attempted to assume a look of careless innocence, as I was not insensible of its value at such a moment. The commotion of my mind betrayed itself in my countenance. My tongue became parched, and fixed to the roof of my mouth; my eyes were cast down; if I attempted to speak, the faculty of language seemed to have deserted from my command, and I imagined every one around must regard me as a wretch, knowing (so fear led me to think) that my most secret thoughts and actions lay unmasked before them. When these feelings had subsided a little, I began to take breath, and consider what charge could be proved against me, and to hope I

---

[1] Low-caste men employed as public executioners.

should find no great difficulty in clearing myself. I determined to explain the whole affair to the Ma,ha,raj. I was well aware, however, that I must get over my first extortion from the unhappy petitioner in the best way I could, by softening or concealing the extent of it. The whole of the first night I was left, well guarded, to my solitary feelings and to repentance. Early in the morning I was awoke from disturbed rest by cries of *kis, kis* (clear the way), and ordered roughly to arise and appear before the Ma,ha,raj, who was sitting in his tent surrounded by all the tokens of Mahratta dignity. On my arrival before him, what was my horror on seeing the son of the murdered Tulsajee wringing his hands, beating his breast, and calling me at the same time his father's murderer ! Opposite to him was Hybatty's son, behaving in the same manner, and charging me with the murder of his parent. I was overwhelmed with their accusations; and perceiving the carcoon with his papers and inkstand close by, I begged him, for the love of Vishnu and Brahma, to inform me what was the meaning of such accumulated charges. Instead of a friendly reply from him, or even a recognition of his late deputy, he gruffly commanded me to be silent, and most consequentially passed by me. This was a dreadful blow to my hopes, and I fell to the ground insensible. When I recovered, I found myself on my own mat in my tent, guards being stationed without. I now considered what was best to be done to avert the impending storm. Could I not bribe the carcoon ? This I thought a happy expedient, and I would willingly have bestowed upon him all Hybatty's treasure if he would but ensure my safety. I then proceeded to examine the place where I had deposited this treasure,—but what was my dismay when I found it gone ! Bangles, pearls, money, ornaments—all had disappeared ! I cursed my ill-luck, and laid myself down once more to ruminate on this fresh disaster. " What a piece of retribution !" thought I. " Little did I dream, when wishing I could witness the disappointment of Hybatty's son at finding his treasure gone from under the peepal-tree, that I should so soon experience the horrors of the same situation." I recollected the yells and shrieks and curses of Hybatty, and even imitated him, though not quite as audibly. I groaned with internal anguish, and vented many a mental curse on my own avarice and folly. To be accused of two murders, also, was more than I could get over; I thought the guilt of one enough for any mortal, but the double charge almost bent me to the earth. I still imagined that, could I but get a hearing of the Ma,ha,raj and explain matters, I might escape the load of ignominy heaped upon me. But yet it was most probable I should be hanged without such an opportunity being allowed me, and I should perish with every imputation remaining upon my head. I had, however, no remedy but patience, and I made up my mind at last to await my fate calmly, be it whatever it might.

CHAPTER IV.

HE morning slowly broke; and when the sun had arisen, I was ordered to prepare for the eventful interview, which I pictured full of horrors. I was again ushered into the presence of my master. The Ma,ha,raj was smoking his hookah. He fixed upon me his dark eye, flashing with anger, and exclaimed, "Serpent as you are! instead of protecting the subjects of the world-conquering Holkar, you have stained your hands in their blood; you have committed outrageous crimes." I replied, "This, my lord, I deny. I am no murderer." "Do you dare deny being an accomplice in the murder of that boy's father?" said he, pointing at Tulsajee's son. "I do, my lord," was my reply again. "Think not to blind me by equivocation; you know the hand that inflicted the mortal wound—you were the accomplice of the assassin," said the Ma,ha,raj, his eyes flashing fire as he spoke; "mock me not: were not the man's bangles in your possession—buried under your own mat, in your own tent, by your own hand?" "This, my lord," I answered, "I do not deny." "You knew they were the bangles of Tulsajee?" "I had good grounds for thinking they were, and that the poor man was indeed murdered." "Then, wretch! you were implicated. Prepare yourself for the fate of your partner in blood, Hybatty." I attempted to explain and show my innocence; but the Ma,ha,-raj interrupted me, waving his hand and crying, "The bangles, the bangles! off with him!" All present—amongst whom were my old friend the carcoon and the two sons of the dead men, cried out, "Ay, ay! the bangles, the bangles! positive proof—all is clear!" I was now hurried away. At the door of the tent, the carcoon asked the attendants if any *dheers* or *maungs*[1] were at hand, in my hearing. Most fortunately for me, there were none, or this scoundrel clerk would have soon had me pendant from the next mango-tree. Once more alone, I gave myself up for a lost man, seeing no chance of escape. Having gone to the entrance of my tent to beg a little water, and ask permission to perform my ablutions before I left this world, I was rudely thrust back by my guards, but not before I had seen my late groom mounted upon my pony, with my slipper-bearer behind him, both in travelling order. They grinned impudently on seeing me, and in tones that cut me to the soul with mortification, exclaimed. "Ram, ram, Ma,ha,raj," at the same time spurring my pony, and scampering off—the bystanders relishing the joke. "Well, if I am to be hanged, the sooner the better, and then it matters not who has my tattoo," said I to myself; but I could not help taking a lesson from the conduct of these rascals, who, when I was in power, were grovelling cleaners of the beast which they now bestrode, and would have licked the dust off my feet! This had just happened when my inkstand-bearer made his appearance. "What!" said I, "are you not off also? I expect I shall see you march presently with my inkstand under your arm!" "No, no," he answered; "we must use the inkstand better, and save your life. Sit down, and draw up a petition to Sawunt Rao immediately. Keep not a single thing from him, as you value your life; and if you are not really guilty, there is a chance of your still coming off in a whole skin. The Ma,ha,raj would not have noticed this affair at all; but they who govern are desirous at this moment of conciliating all ranks of the people, and of giving them the semblance of protection." I thanked him, and inquired how this *toofan* or storm had arisen. "Why, you must know," said he, "the carcoon's boy is my friend, and I learned from him that the carcoon has been a long time narrowly watching you, and that he felt jealous of your influence. He also abused you for not sharing several presents you obtained with him. Your absence at the village for two successive days aroused his suspicion that

Low-caste men, usually employed as executioners.

C

you were making a harvest, and excluding him from the profits. His suspicions were strengthened by seeing the farmer's *hircarrah*, or messenger, bring a letter for you, which he unfortunately took to the carcoon's tent instead of yours. The latter ordered his horse, reached the farmer's house before you, and there gained some valuable information; for he returned before Hybatty was hanged, and went alone to your tent. In a short time it was rumoured that the murdered man's bangles had been found under your mat." I inquired if any other articles were mentioned to have been found there besides the bangles. He replied, none: the carcoon had reported that the bangles only had been deposited there. I now comprehended the motives of the carcoon. He thought I should deny the fact of the bangles being there, and that not a word of the treasure would proceed from my lips. Thus having got me out of the way by means of the dheers, he should be able to keep undisturbed possession of treasure worth eighteen hundred rupees, after he had restored the bangles to the son of Tulsajee. I also saw clearly not a moment must be lost, and instantly drawing up a petition to my late benefactor, I forwarded it by the faithful inkstand-bearer for presentation. In it I entreated the Ma,ha,raj, if he doubted my statement, to question Hybatty's son, and ask him if his father did not send him for money to fee the farmer, and particularly as to the spot to which he was sent, and it would be seen I had spoken the truth. I did not fail to state that with the bangles were many other articles of value, and I had reason to believe forty gold mohurs, in a small narrow bag, had been plundered from Tulsajee, and that the carcoon dare not deny my assertions. I represented that this man had a design to ruin me in his estimation, and also to take my life in order that he might enjoy the fruits of his plunder without molestation. I solemnly assured the Ma,ha,raj that I was only actuated by self-defence in depriving Hybatty of his ill-gotten wealth; and that, now he was no more, I had not the least objection to the son of Tulsajee having possession of his father's property. I concluded by referring the Ma,ha,raj to the farmer of the district, who himself heard Hybatty confess the murder, without implicating me or any other person as an accomplice.

When I had despatched this important petition I felt more at ease. The Ma,ha,raj read the paper, and instantly ordered the carcoon to be seized and searched. He was too old a hand at such matters to be found with the treasure upon his person; and nothing but the bangles were discovered. Tulsajee's son deposed to several other articles which his father had about him when murdered; and this, together with the suspicious circumstances of the carcoon going alone to my tent, induced all the country round to place credit in my assertions, especially as I consented to give up the treasure. I was now set at liberty; and immediately fell down on my face before the Ma,ha,raj, who really showed pleasure that he was able to let me go free. He severely lectured me for neglecting to bring Hybatty's case before him originally, which, had I so done, would have saved bloodshed to others and hazard to myself. The carcoon was ordered to restore whatever articles the son of Tulsajee could recollect his father to have had when he was murdered and plundered by Hybatty. The son gave in an amazingly long list of things, which I was well aware never formed part of the treasure I had brought away. After Tulsajee's son had given in this list, the son of Hybatty put in one still longer concerning articles buried under the peepal-tree, which belonged to his family, independent of what belonged to Tulsajee. Both these knaves had been suborned against me by the carcoon; and in consequence of his promise of reward and restitution of the articles of value, had consented to become complainants against me. They acted their parts as mourners with true Mahratta hypocrisy on the first day of my examination, as I have before shown. Now, when the tables were turned, they were anxious to become my friends. My evidence also was necessary to bear them out in their enumeration of the articles buried by Hybatty, which they sought to recover of the carcoon. On their making out their claims one said, "Was there not a nuth?" I nodded assent. "Was there not a silver beetle-nut box?" said the other; and again I signified in the affirmative. "And was there not a gold *chundun har?*"[1]

---

[1] Large necklace.

I responded, " Yes; worth, I should think, three hundred rupees."
The carcoon was all this while in a situation better to be imagined
than described. He found out that he had made a very uprofit-
able seizure in my tent, and at the rate we were going on we
must ruin him. I revelled in the anguish he felt at every nod I
gave. I knew his life's blood was not dearer than the treasure I
was drawing from him. His evident perturbation added to my
delight; and the thought of his endeavour to deprive me of
life for a few rupees prevented my having any mercy upon him.
As I nodded to every barefaced lie of his two tormentors, I felt
as if I partook a fresh draught of a cordial elixir that almost
made life perfect happiness. The list was at length swollen to
four thousand rupees instead of two thousand, the sum of which
the carcoon had possessed himself. He was ordered to make the
whole good to the last pice, and to be imprisoned until he had so
done. I was now dismissed from my service in a civil capacity,
and appointed clerk to a *paugah*, or corps of five thousand men,
and so removed entirely from Sawunt Rao. This was very mortifying to my pride ; but I was, after all, well off to escape with my
life, besides punishing my old friend the carcoon.

CHAPTER V.

I HAD just entered upon my new service, and presented myself to the Sudar, Khundeo Rao Baboo Rao, when despatches arrived with orders for us to march for Indore, Holkar's capital. We set out as soon as was practicable after the receipt of the order; and here it may not be amiss if I endeavour to delineate a Mahratta army the first time I saw it in marching trim. A Mahratta army consists in general of horse and foot of every neighbouring nation, religion, and costume. In truth, it makes a very motley appearance, as it is under no discipline, and destitute of a regular uniform. Few of the men in the same line, either cavalry or infantry, have weapons of a like form. Some are armed with sword and shield, others with matchlocks or muskets; some carry bows and arrows, others spears, lances, or war-rockets. Many are expert with the battle-axe; but the sabre is indispensable to all. The men in armour, of whom there are many to make up the variety, cut a very curious appearance. A helmet covers not only the head and ears, but protects the shoulders. The body is cased in iron net-work, or in a thick-quilted vest. They give the preference to a straight two-edged sword before the curved one used by the Persians and Arabs. They have no regular commanders, according to the rule of seniority. The principal officers are called *jummah-dars,* some of whom command five thousand horse; others, with the same title, but five hundred. Every rajah, prince, or leader is responsible among the Mahrattas to the Peeshwa, or head of the empire, for his general conduct. He pays tribute for his district, and attends, when summoned, with his quota of men, which is regulated by his wealth and the population. He is supreme in command over his corps, which is attached alone to him and to his fortunes, and adheres to whatever party he supports. The Mahratta camps display a variety of standards and ensigns. Each chief is distinguished by his own. Red is the prevailing colour, cut in the shape of a swallow's tail, and decorated with *zurree puttah* (gold and silver tissue).

After a fatiguing march we reached Indore, the capital of Jeswunt Rao Holkar, whose subject and servant I then was. Mulhar Rao Holkar, one of the commanders in the army of the first Peeshwa, was instrumental in extending the conquests of the Mahrattas to the northward; and, according to the usual policy of the Mahratta government, received a portion of territory in the province of Malwa for the support of his troops. This happened in 1736, and laid the foundation of the authority of the Holkar family; for as the oldest prince and family of the primary government declined, that of the principal viceroys, according to the usual custom, became independent. Mulhar Rao Holkar died in 1766, and was succeeded by his nephew, Tuccage Holkar. This prince governed until 1797, leaving four sons, Cashee Rao, Nuilkar Rao, Eithogee Rao Holkar, and Jeswunt Rao Holkar. The two first were alone born to him by his wife. Cashee Rao succeed Tuccage as the eldest. A dispute soon arose, however, between Cashee Rao and his brother Nuilkar Rao, who claimed an equal share in the inheritance; and they both repaired to Poona for the purpose of settling their dispute by the intervention of the Peeshwa. Dowlut Rao Scindea at that time exercised a despotic authority over the Peeshwa, and looked upon the opportunity as highly favourable for adding the possessions of the Holkar family to his own. Having made his terms with Cashee Rao, he surprised and slaughtered Nuilkar Rao and nearly all his attendants at Poona in 1797. The wife of Nuilkar being left in a state of pregnancy, produced a son named Khundeo Rao. Scindea obtained posses- sion of the infant, retained Cashee Rao in a state of dependence, and proposed to govern the Holkar dominions in his name. The other brothers, Eithogee and Jeswunt Rao, who had attached themselves to Nuilkar Rao, were at Poona when the latter was murdered. Eithogee fled to Kolapor, where he was taken in open hostility, sent to Poona, and put to death. Jeswunt Rao made his escape to Nagpore, and for some time found a shelter there; but the intrigues of Scindea at length prevailed, and the rajah placed him in confinement, from which he contrived to make his escape. He then fled to a place on the Nerbudda. Scindea, at that time too deeply engaged in securing an ascendancy at Poona, had not leisure to pursue the fugitive, and probably deemed his resources too contemptible to excite serious apprehension. This remissness gave Jeswunt Rao time to apply the means, which are always at hand in India, for collecting an army of adventurers by the prospect of plunder. It was not until 1801 that Scindea became alarmed in good earnest at the progress of Jeswunt Rao, and began to collect an army on the Nerbudda. In consequence of this determination on the part of Scindea, we were ordered to proceed to Indore.

Our preparations were now complete, and we were confident of success. For myself I would much rather have been allowed to stick by pen and ink, than be forced to handle the sword and shield; but all were required to do their best. Our cavalry was a strange rabble, mounted on tall and short horses of every kind and colour. Saddles were always slipping off for want of girths; strings, fastened to any old pieces of iron by way of bits, supplied bridles; old turbans served for martingales, and tent-ropes for cruppers. A most villanous medley of every clumsy shift under the sun was seen on all hands. The infantry were just as wretchedly accoutred as the cavalry; everything was wanting, and nothing regular. Here voices might be heard roaring out for ball, and there for muskets or arms. Those who were not fortunate enough to procure any weapon at all, supplied the deficiency by a bamboo-pole with a bit of iron at the top, which they dignified with the designation of *birchee*, or spear. It came to my lot to serve out to these ragamuffins the necessary accoutrements: but they who gave the order to me to do so, never calculated on the scantiness of the magazines; in consequence I was complained against a hundred times a day for what it was not in my power, nor in that of my superiors, to prevent. One said I would not give him a sword; another that I refused him a shield. This man said that "Pandurang" withheld a spear from him; and that asserted he could get neither weapon nor answer from me. In vain did I explain again and again that no more arms were left in the arsenal: I ended but to begin the same excuse again, and was wearied to death with my office. This was not the only inconvenience I had to encounter; I was in continual fear of being blown to pieces by the rascals who had the care of the ammunition, and went swaggering about, with their matchlocks lighted, amid piles of loose gunpowder, of which they took no more notice than if they had been heaps of sand or sawdust. As evening approached, I fancied I should obtain a little rest, when an order came out for me to pay the soldiers, in order to encourage them for the approaching battle. This I found a most arduous task. I had a list of their names, but it was so incorrect as to be useless to me. The rogues took advantage of several of their names being alike, and pressed upon me with such avidity that I believe I paid some of them twice or thrice over. At the end of the payment there was a deficiency of money, and I left many unpaid. More complaints were then made against me, but it was in vain I explained; I was ordered to make good the deficiency. This was just as possible for me to do as to raise a thunderstorm. The vagabonds, who were unfortunate in not getting their money, stuck to me like leeches, perfectly satisfied in their own minds that I had pocketed their pay. I walked off as fast as I could; but they dogged me about everywhere, muttering their dissatisfaction, and asking how they were to fight with empty bellies? One would fling away his cartouch-box, saying he wanted white powder, and would have none of the black. At length I determined to look big, and swore, by all the deities in the *Védas*, I would have them blown from a mortar; that they should await my pleasure; and that, if one approached my tent after the evening gun, they should see I would put my threat into effect. A dead silence ensued among them; but, every now and then, one of them would tap his empty belly, and point to his mouth, thus making their half-starved condition a plea for their boldness; and I must allow their complaints were but too well founded, and they were justified in their importunity. Pity was all I had to give them; and I cheered them with the hope of plunder on the morrow, and the certainty of a glorious victory. At length I left them as forlorn as they came.

Soon after the jummahdar sent for me, and inquired if there were sufficient arms and accoutrements for the troops, or rather for his own fifteen thousand men. "Is it possible there can be any deficiency, my lord," I replied, "in this glorious country? I could have equipped ten times the number if it were necessary. Never were men so well furnished with abundance of death-inflicting weapons as those of your paugh." "That's well, Pandoo," said he; "we have everything complete, you see." "Very true, my lord," I replied; "the whole world cannot exhibit such an arsenal as that of his Highness Jeswunt Rao Holkar." "Have we not a noble arsenal?" "You have, indeed, my lord," I replied. The jummahdar was much pleased at my flattery, while I laughed all the time the conversation lasted. On my taking leave, the jummahdar asked, in a low voice, and with a very significant look, if the pay were plenti-ful as the arms and ammunition. I told him every man had rupees enough to stuff his pillow with, if he chose, and that they were all in high spirits, eager for the hour of battle. He seemed highly delighted, and bade me be early at his side the next day, for Scindea might be hourly expected. It was now nine in the evening, and dark; not a soul of the half-starved unpaid soldiers was near, and I began to flatter myself with a good night's rest. I had just concluded my supper, when I heard an unusual bustle outside my tent, and was struck by hearing voices in all direc-tions, crying out, "A *jasoos*, a *jasoos!*" (a spy, a spy). "Put irons upon him immediately!" I exclaimed; and it was done. In the meantime, I repaired to the jummahdar to inform him of the discovery. He was half-asleep, and on hearing the purport of my visit at that hour, seemed angry at being disturbed for such a trifle. I asked his pardon, desiring to know what should be done with the spy. "Why, hang him instantly," he replied;

and dropped again into his doze. This was full authority enough for me. I went and issued the necessary orders, which were immediately carried into effect, and then retired to my bed, highly pleased at having so well completed my duty, and being perfectly satisfied with my own conduct.

The eventful day at length dawned. I awoke early, and opening my tent, looked abroad: all was dark and misty. I went to call a servant, and proceeded groping my way to his tent rather than seeing it. Between my tent and his was a mango-tree; and as I crept under its branches, I felt something touch my face, which, on laying hold of it, I discovered to be the body of the spy whom we had hanged on the preceding night. Fortunate was it for me I escaped being seen to come in contact with the corpse, for in that case I should have been deemed contaminated, and have had to undergo several troublesome purifications. I awoke my servant, and we talked of the spy, not being able to guess who he was, as, in fact, no examination of the unhappy wretch had been thought about. On leaving the tent, I saw my faithful inkstand-bearer, who had by his advice aided me in my difficulties respecting the murder of Tulsajee. He made a significant signal to me, the cause of which I did not understand. By this time there was light, and the sun was just showing itself, so that it was easy to distinguish the features of a human being. The inkstand-bearer approached me, and asked if I knew whom I had ordered to be executed the evening before. I observed that it was only a spy; and then it occurred to me that I had taken no steps to discover whether the man whom I had put to death were really a spy or not. "Do not be alarmed," said the inkstand-bearer; "we shall be all busy enough to-day, and no one will be able to enquire whether you have done right or wrong. I, for one, can answer, you have cut short the career of a villain, who has but met the fate he merited, a little earlier than he might otherwise." "Who can it be?" said I. By this time we were pretty close to the mango-tree; when my companion, without making a reply to my question of who it could be, bade me look up and see if I did not remember that long meagre face. "Good heaven!" I exclaimed

" the carcoon—it is Govindah, my old enemy!" There he hung, as cadaverous and ghastly as in his life, if it were possible; and yet I thought death had, on the whole, improved his personal appearance. "How can this be?" I exclaimed; "pray explain, my good fellow—tell me how it can have happened." I then hurried him with me to my tent, where, being seated, he proceeded to inform me that the carcoon had been closely guarded from the day he was ordered to restore the property of Tulsajee, valued at four thousand rupees; that upon his arrival at Indore, his family came to him, and advised him to pay the money and get out of confinement, but he persisted in declaring he had not a rupee in the world; in short, nothing except the two bangles. His uncle and family, including his mother, made up the sum with great difficulty, and brought it to him. He promised to pay the amount, and endeavour to recover his character. The greedy miser, however, reflecting upon the subject, deemed the four thousand rupees a singular mark of divine favour towards him, thanked his tutelar idol, and, securing the money about his person, contrived to give his guards the slip. He hoped to pass the camp under favour of the evening, and to go none knew whither, not even himself. He had not proceeded far before some of the troops who got no pay that day, and were prowling about for whatever they could lay their hands upon, surrounded and robbed him of his booty, which was sufficiently ample to compensate them for their loss of pay. The carcoon told them he should complain of them to the jummahdar; and seeing him go that way, they shouted out "A spy! a spy!" This artifice succeeded, and they who had robbed him, gagged him instantly in the dark, so that, I believe, he was suffocated before he was hung. Thus the carcoon, my enemy, by a singular concatenation of circumstances, suffered the very fate he was so ready in awarding me. Independently of this, I could feel no pity for the cold-blooded rascal, who accepted from his family a sum of money it impoverished them to raise, in order to restore his character, and then broke prison that he might decamp with it. The ingenuity of the drunken soldiers to prevent the carcoon's making a complaint amused me highly. With my little regard for the subject of their trick, I must say that, on the whole, I was rather gratified by it than otherwise. I therefore determined to pass the business over in silence; and, lest the family of the unfortunate man should hear of the circumstance, and make a stir at headquarters, I deemed it prudent to have the body cut down and buried without delay.

By this time it was all alive in the camp, which had been a little space before so deathly still. As the day advanced, clamour, turmoil, and preparation increased. The drums roared on every hand the call to arms. The war-elephants, caparisoned and ready, yelled with impatience, and towered loftily over all other living objects. The neighing of horses, the clash of arms, the buzz of impatient voices, the sounds of command, the march of the irregular and confused masses to their stations, was a new and impressive scene to my eyes, that now, for the first time, witnessed the bustle and excitement of the moment previous to battle. Soon the firing of guns, at first slow and irregular, then more rapidly, convinced me the work of death had begun in some quarter; and it seemed speedily extending itself towards the station of my troop, which I had joined well-mounted, and with which I remained with a fluttering heart in awful suspense. The current of battle now rolled close to me; and action soon took away all reflection, for we had enough upon our hands. Our men were all lean kine, and too scantily fed to be much heavier than skeletons. Our horses were in little better condition; and when Scindea's cavalry came down upon us, we were knocked off on the ground before we could strike a blow. In vain I tried to rally and remount my men. I succeeded in prevailing upon a few only to rally; the best part of them turned tail and fled, without once looking behind. Thus the division to which I was attached was speedily disposed of. Our infantry getting mixed with the cavalry that had been driven back by Scindea, was taken by it for the infantry of that chief instead of our own; and the sabre began to cut away upon them as if they were a field of *joanee* (standing corn). I laboured in vain to rectify the mistake, and stay the carnage of our own men; my voice was lost in the scene of death and discord, the rush of rockets, and the groans of the dying. How long this scene might have continued before it could have been put an end to I cannot tell, if the attention of the cavalry had not been drawn to something which, even in the heat of battle, was truly appalling to the sight, and made them, even there, think of self-preservation. A wounded elephant rushed in among them. Mad with the pain of a ball he had just received, he rolled his unwieldy bulk through and over the slashed infantry, and among the terrified horse. Beast and rider were overturned and crushed beneath his tread, and all that lay in his path became victims to his fury. This effectually put a stop to the havoc the cavalry had begun, as the horses took fright and bore their riders off the scene of action, leaving their own broken infantry to be trampled to death by the enraged beast—at least that part of it which they had not kindly mangled themselves. At this moment the cavalry of Scindea charged our artillery, and captured it all, together with our baggage. This was decisive. Jeswunt Rao Holkar saw his world-conquering heroes disperse in every direction; and the battle terminated in leaving Scindea no enemies in view, the pursued soon leaving their conquerors far in the rear, the virtue of leanness, which served us so ill in the battle, being now of singular service in making our escape.

In this my first battle I escaped unhurt; but I was sorry to find this was not the case with my old benefactor: he was not expected to survive the severe wounds he had received more than a few hours; and when we halted, which, finding our enemies pursued us but a short distance, was not a long time after the battle, I went to see him. He had received three musket-balls in the shoulder and a sabre-cut in the neck, while a spear had been driven through his thigh. No one knew what to do, or how to treat his wounds. He was perfectly cool and collected, recognising me immediately, and pointing to a small box, which he ordered to be opened. From this box he ordered a silver *kurdoorah*[1] to be taken. This, he said, had been found upon me when I was rescued from among the bullocks. "You may some

---

[1] A chain for the waist.

day find out by it, Pandoo," said he, "who are your parents." I kissed his hand, and my tears flowed fast upon it; I recollected the protection this best of all the Mahrattas had afforded me in the most helpless circumstances of life. His family arriving at that moment, I withdrew with a heavy heart. The Brahmins prayed, his relations uttered loud lamentations, and the doctors prescribed; but Sawunt Rao died.

As soon as the grief of Sawunt Rao's relatives had somewhat abated, I visited his widow and her brother, to condole with them; and before I quitted them, I begged they would take charge of the kurdoorah left me by the deceased. They readily promised me it should be preserved with the family valuables. This was highly to my satisfaction; and giving it to them, I respectfully bade them "farewell!"

CHAPTER VI.

HOLKAR, after his disaster, so quickly repaired the losses he had sustained near Indore, that he found himself, early in 1802, able to commence fresh operations. He determined, however, to change the scene of action from Malwa to Poona. Cashee, his brother, who had been allowed to repair to Kandeish, had for some time shown symptoms of a disposition to join in making war upon Scindea. In order to preserve the dominions of the Holkar family, Jeswunt Rao determined to liberate, if possible, the infant Kundeo Rao; and as Cashee Rao was, from natural imbecility, unable to govern, he determined to proclaim the infant head of the family; and, accordingly, as his uncle, demanded possession of his person. He likewise stated that he should himself take the administration of the government, and should march upon Poona to obtain justice of the Peeshwa, who had long been in a state of the most abject subjection to Scindea. Before the middle of 1802, Holkar, according to his threat, took the field with a well-disciplined force, compared with that which had so lately been beaten by his enemy. Soon after we commenced our march to the south.

Scindea was fully alive to the danger which threatened his interests at Poona, and detached a large portion of his army, under one of his most able generals, towards that place. This force arrived in the vicinity of Poona in time to effect a junction, unmolested, with the troops of the Peeshwa. I took care, having learned something from my past experience, that I would not want money and ammunition again. Our army was indeed a formidable one: our last defeat was a sad scene of confusion

51

and disgrace, and we had to regain our credit. The day of my second battle approached, and we were far more efficient than on the first, and everything was in the best order. On this occasion we commenced with a smart cannonade, which was continued for three hours, until my jummahdar, with his cavalry, supported by the rest of the sirdars, charged Scindea's line of infantry, and putting them to the rout, obtained a decisive victory. We then pushed on for Poona; but, when only a few miles from its walls, the Peeshwa sent to propose terms of accommodation, which Holkar at once rejected: we had, therefore, another battle to fight. We lost no time, and our cannon again roared over the plains, to the Peeshwa's discomfiture. He fled from the field, leaving in the hands of his minister certain engagements he wished to effect with the English. Holkar followed, in hopes to get the Peeshwa into his power; but we were too slow in our motions to cut him off. Our leader wished to get the Peeshwa, to make the same use of him as Scindea had done. Holkar, the Peeshwa's minister, and the English at Poona, held consultations, and endeavoured to bring about an accommodation between the two parties, the particulars of which I could not learn. Holkar and Scindea, however, again became friends, and united themselves with the Berar Rajah; while, during these amicable arrangements, the English escorted the Peeshwa back again to Poona, and placed him upon the musnud once more. This happened about seven months after our victory. The object of Holkar, Scindea, and the Berar Rajah entering into this confederacy, was to subvert the alliance formed between the English and the Peeshwa. It was now evident we should have to encounter the *Topee Wallas*,[1] who would give us more trouble, according to report, than we had had yet, and in a way to which we were unaccustomed. Scindea and Holkar being united, I was put upon a new footing, and had the command of two hundred cavalry, following Scindea's army in its march. At Assaye we opposed a great English general. He attacked our left wing, and we changed the position of our guns and infantry.

---

[1] English troops.

The English advanced to the attack ; our fire was dreadfully destructive to them, and we so thinned the right of their line that a body of our cavalry was induced to charge it, of which number I was one. We thought ourselves to be doing business pretty satisfactorily, until we found that the enemy's cavalry was in reserve to intercept us. They repulsed us with great slaughter. Those English are large powerful men, and the weight of their sabres almost annihilated my poor troopers. They unhorsed numbers of us merely by riding against us. I was so served for one, and, with many others, feigned myself dead. Our army being routed, fled, and the English pursuing them, left the guns they had captured in their rear. These I proposed to turn upon them ; we got up and did so with great effect. It was clear we made our shot tell pretty well, for a body of the Topee Wallas, with their general at their head, rode up to put a stop to the firing. The general had his horse killed under him. At this time our troops still hovered about one part of the English line. At length we fled, leaving ninety-eight pieces of cannon and seven standards in the hands of the English, with twelve hundred of our men killed.

After this fatal defeat nothing prospered with us. Assyghur and Burhampoor were taken, and everything seemed lost. Scindea at last sent Goparrah, one of his officers, to the English, and the latter selected me to accompany him. We proceeded to the English army, and had a conference with the general, who was dressed in a long red coat, covered with gold. Many of his sirdars were equally well arrayed, and were attending him at the time. This was the first time I had ever been so near a white person. The general sat on a throne,[1] and we upon the carpet, as usual. It struck me as most extraordinary to see them wearing shoes and boots when walking on a carpet, just the same as if they had been on the open plain. I saw one of the sirdars filthy enough to spit in his handkerchief and then put it into his pocket again, which nearly turned me sick. Goparrah felt full as much disgust as I did at the sight. The general first demanded

---

[1] The natives so call a chair.

our credentials, but we had none to produce; and this made us liable to be turned out of the camp disgracefully; but we were suffered to remain until the time necessary for sending to our master for them had elapsed. These documents were necessary to verify our powers to treat; and without them we ought not to have been sent. In the interim Scindea despatched a letter, stating that he had determined to forward another commission, and disavowing Goparrah and myself. This was a most cruel trick to play us, as we might have been justifiably hanged up as impostors; but the English commander was well aware of the tricks of our sovereign, and believed our assertions, adding he was fully convinced the master and not the servants were to blame. He informed us of our dangerous situation and dismissed us.

More battles succeeded: that of Argaum was the next, where we lost thirty-eight pieces of cannon, and finally scampered off, as at Assaye. I now thought fortune had for ever forsaken us. Gewilghur, a strong fort, was taken from us; and I clearly saw the English had every advantage, and nothing was left us of which to boast. The rajah of Berar made a separate treaty with the English, and we were left to sustain the conflict alone. Scindea, at last, was obliged to make terms with his enemies: he ceded Broach in Guzerat, Ahmednugur in the Deccan, and other strong places, together with a vast extent of valuable territory. My old master, Holkar, though he engaged to join the other chiefs, had hitherto abstained from active operations himself in the war against the English. I had become quite a partizan of Scindea; for Holkar had no objection to letting his officers help Scindea's cause, though he himself deemed it prudent to keep aloof. He always pretended great friendship for the English. He was, however, discovered by them; and intelligence reaching them of his having murdered three persons on a false accusation, they determined to take away his dominions and give them to Scindea. The latter was of course delighted at this prospect. I was, in the meantime, obliged to devote my services to the defence of the fort of Deeg. The English are perfect war-tigers; they drove us out, and we fled to Bhurtpoor, leaving our cannon behind us. The loss of Deeg was a sad blow to Holkar and the rajah of Bhurtpoor, who had joined us, and still kept the city. This place was eight miles in extent, and surrounded by a mud wall of great thickness and height. A broad ditch filled with water was at the foot of the wall, and the fort was situated near the eastern extremity, mounted with a numerous artillery. The whole force of Rungeed Sing was thrown into it, while we were forced to entrench ourselves under the walls. The English opened their batteries, and fired on the fort for two days. At night we stockaded the breach effected during the day. At length they advanced to the storm as if nothing could overcome their perseverance. They crossed the water that lay between them and the walls, and gained the foot of the breach, surmounting every difficulty. Here they made many wonderful efforts without success. Again and again they boldly but ineffectually attempted to mount. We tumbled them back again, and made dreadful havoc, which we rejoiced exceedingly to witness. Their chief sirdar was killed in leading them on. Day after day, with unabated perseverance, they attempted to gain their object, and as often failed. Once they were very near it, for the colours of one of their native regiments were planted within a short distance of the summit of our walls. We repulsed them, however, with terrible slaughter. On the following day they renewed the attack; and we discharged grapeshot, logs of wood, and pots of combustibles upon them, killing and knocking down all who attempted to ascend. They were at last forced to retire; and we, enjoying our victory, feasted ourselves day and night. But, notwithstanding our brave defence, we were ultimately obliged to come to terms with our foes, and peace was concluded between Holkar, Scindea, and the English. We now returned to Indore, where my services were no more wanted, and I was ordered to go about my business; but I was not singular in being treated thus, and therefore could not complain.

I had now to consider what was to be done; Sawunt Rao no more, and not one being in the world with whom I could make interest to get a situation. My stock of cash hardly amounted to a hundred rupees—a very small sum to begin the world with again. I parted with my sword, but retained my *kuttar* or dagger, and muffling up my head in a white shawl, I took my departure from Indore. About five miles from the city I reached the hut of a Gossein,[1] but hesitated about going near its miserable inhabitant. These scoundrels are the pest of the neighbourhood where they reside. Their habit is the only thing from which they can claim a semblance of virtue. They profess poverty, but grasp at every good thing they can lay their hands upon wherever they go. They are clothed in a ragged mantle, and carry a long pole, and a *mirchal*, or peacock's tail. They never leave off importuning every class and order of people they see, and even threaten, if they find it will best answer their purpose, in case their rapacious demands are not satisfied. I was anxious to inquire my way to Poona, and reluctantly tapped at his wicket, calling, " *O Baba, O Ma,ha,raj!*" No one replied; and opening the wicket, I discovered thick smoke issuing through the roof and over the doorway. I felt alarmed lest the hut should be on fire; and thinking that if I entered I might be of some service in extinguishing the flames, I crawled in; for so small was the entrance, it even required dexterity to accomplish the getting through it. I could not see nor breathe for the smoke, though I could not discover any flame. At last I perceived a spark or two of fire; and on approaching to extinguish it, I stumbled over something that seemed to be the body of a man, dead or alive. I lost not a moment in putting out what fire was there, and examining further, found a body, covered with ashes and dirt, apparently lifeless. I dragged it into the open air to ascertain the truth, and found it was a wretched Gossein, the probable inhabitant of the hut. The air, assisted by a little water, restored the body to animation. He opened his eyes, exclaiming " *árry, árry!*" an exclamation of surprise, and then relapsed into insensibility. More cold water flung in his withered face revived him; and he asked " who it was that thus disturbed his slumbers?" I explained to him his danger, and that but for me he would have been suffocated or burned to death. He made no other reply than

---

[1] A religious mendicant.

a demand for alms. I dared not discover all my wealth, but gave him a few pice, pleading my poverty for not bestowing more. I saw he had been eating *bang*,[1] and this readily accounted for his insensibility and heavy sleep. He made no inquiry as to the safety of his habitation, nor once inquired if the fire had gone out of itself. I demanded the road to Poona. He heeded me not, but continued mumbling to himself as if counting money. I repeated my questions; and he answered by asking what I wanted at Poona. He could not have put a more puzzling query to me at that moment, as I could not tell my business there myself. I spoke the truth, therefore, when I said, "I do not know; I have been turned out of Holkar's service, and am searching my fortune elsewhere." He ruminated some time, and then said, "Holkar is mad, Scindea is a fool, and Badjeroa, the Peeshwa, is both foolish and mad at the same time. Cringe no more to them or their underlings for bread. Have you not Brahma the creator, Vishnu the protector, and Siva the destroyer, for masters — ay, better masters than they? Throw aside all your notions of pomp and parade, and take up your mirchal, your pole, and your wallet, and follow me. If you must go to Poona, I will accompany you: there are fools enough there, and we may reap a pretty harvest." On saying this, he produced those emblems of religious mendicity—the peacock's tail, the pole, the wallet, and leopard's skin to swing at my back.

I had often heard that these Gosseins realised great sums of money, and thinking, in my destitute situation, it might lead to some good, I determined to try the advice given me. My religious friend now equipped me in the proper way, but first stripped me, and in so doing discovered my hoard of rupees tied tight around my waist. He made no remark whatever on seeing them, but proceeded to grease me all over from head to foot, and then covered me with ashes and dirt. My hair he tied up on the crown of my head. Then I had the staff of my order put into my hand, together with the peacock's tail; the wallet and skin were slung over my shoulders; and thus arrayed, I

---

[1] A preparation of opium.

followed my preceptor to Poona, he being equipped in a manner similar to my own. I found on the road that my tutor's name was Gabbage Gousla, and he appeared to be a character pretty well known everywhere, each traveller we met calling out, "*Ram, Ram, Gabbage!*" upon which Gabbage always bellowed forth some bitter complaint of hunger and poverty, and generally cheated the credulous traveller of his rupees. He remarked to me how callous the people were become, since the war, to his warnings and invocations of Ram and Seeta; "therefore," said he, "we must cut ourselves, and let the blood flow plentifully; for it is considered as much as their lives are worth to be the cause of spilling our blood." "True," said I; "but I really hope we shall not be obliged to have recourse to this severity." "Well, let it be prepared at all events," said he; "here is a very sharp knife; you need only draw the edge across your arm and the business is done." We entered Poona through a street of banyan shops. "Here is a harvest for us!" said Gabbage. We then stationed ourselves opposite a shop where grain was selling, and Gabbage began singing out pretty loud, "*Ram, Budjunta Ram, Sadjoo Budgelis Seeta Ram—Ram, Ram, Seeta Ram.*" No money coming, he repeated the same words again, adding, "*Rass, Pandoo, rass!*—cut, Pandoo—cut." I must own I did not relish this business at all. It appeared I was to have all the pain, and very little of the profit; so that, when he repeated the words, "Cut, Pandoo—cut," I said, "Certainly, Ma,ha,raj," and gave him a slice on the arm. He instantly set up a dreadful howl, scarcely equalled by that of Hybatty when he found his treasure and life lost together irrecoverably. The old villain charged me instantly with attempting his life. He told the people we had saved a few rupees between us, which I carried about with me; that being our joint property, I wished his death, that I might possess them all myself. I was immediately surrounded, my rupees taken from me, and I was carried before a great Brahmin, who was at the head of the police of the city. There I was stigmatised as a murderer, and had great difficulty in persuading them I was not one. The sanctity of my profession, however, saved me from condemnation or long imprisonment; but I was ordered to quit

Poona directly, which no inclination of my own was wanting to second, as quickly as I could get away. I had thus the comfort of being parted from the old impostor Gabbage, and his profession, which was some consolation in my heavy misfortune; I had seen quite enough of both to disgust me. But though I had the world all before me, I knew not where to go, naked and destitute as I was. My first step was to wash myself from the filth in which I was covered, and to clean my hair from the matted dirt Gabbage had plastered upon it. For this purpose I proceeded to a large tank near the road, and bathed myself deliciously—never did water seem so grateful to me. Hunger now was my next inconvenience, and I determined to combat it as long as I could. But I was in no long time obliged to resign the contest, and lie down under a tree to rest,—I felt so faint from want. I had not lain long when I heard a jingling of bells, by which I knew bullocks were approaching, and I determined to supplicate their driver for a morsel to relieve my suffering. He drew near, and on my telling him my state, he slowly unloosed his wallet, sat down beside me, and shared between us his coarse brown *aps*.[1] He then asked me whither I was going. I told him it was a matter of perfect indifference to myself; I cared not where I went. On this he told me he was going to Bombay; that he was employed by a shopkeeper of the Topee Wallas to drive bullocks with goods to the Englishmen at Poona, and was then returning; that if I chose, I should go with him, and he would advise me to look out for some employment at that place. He also assured me that wages were good, and regularly paid.

I now considered within myself, and asked the driver what I could do there, and what employ I could get. He told me I might become a palankeen-bearer, and get seven and a half rupees a month—a rate of wages not to be refused; or I might labour at the cotton-works, where I might get ten rupees in the same time; or at the wet-docks; or be a gardener. I might else be a peon, wear a badge, and have some little authority in the bazaar; or turn Sepoy in the Company's service. To the last

[1] Coarse bread.

proposal I at once put a negative; I had lately seen enough of fighting. The driver said he had left me to my choice as to employment; and I replied that if he could get me the situation of peon, or messenger wearing a badge, I should prefer it. He said he thought he could, but I must not expect to be a Government peon at once, and I had better begin by serving his master, the shopkeeper, first; that I should have little to do, and it might lead to promotion. I instantly agreed to the proposal. I had a good chance of success; for his wife's brother was chief packer in the warehouse, and the chief packer was on good terms with the head carpenter, and the latter was related to one of the under-clerks, who was very intimate with the head-clerk, as the latter was with the Topee Wallas, all of whose business he managed for them, and such interest could not fail. I could scarcely suppress a smile at the ladder by which the fellow designed I should mount to a peonship. I told him it *must* succeed. He then asked me what I would give him in that case. I told him half my month's wages. "Say three months," he replied, "and I am your man. My name is Nursoo, and you may put up at my house. I have no place but the verandah or the cow-shed for you to sleep in, but this you must not mind—do you agree?" I answered, "Certainly," reflecting on my miserable lot. We then proceeded to Bombay, and I assisted him to drive his cattle along the road.

In the course of our journey I inquired who this Company was of whom we heard so much. There were the Company's territory, the Company's Sepoys, and Company's hookimis or orders, talked of wherever I went. He said that, according to some accounts, he had heard the Company was an old English-woman, aunt to the king of the Topee Wallas, and that she had got so much money as might buy the whole world, were she not over-anxious to have our country first. Then again he told me that some of the Topee Wallas say "John Company,"[1] and he knew that John was a man's name, for his master was called John Brice, but he could not say to a certainty whether "Company"

---

[1] For joint company—a corruption.

was a man or woman's name. Finding he could give me no account on which I might rely, I asked no more questions on the subject, as Nursoo seemed to possess but a scanty information respecting it.

At last we arrived at Parwell, where we left our bullocks and took boat for Bombay. In a short time we saw the city and fort. The vessels surprised me by their size; they were indeed a fine sight—such flags, and standards, and guns, and tall masts, and white sails, as I had no idea of before. The fort struck me much by its beauty; but when I got inside it, I could not help expressing my astonishment at finding the large square filled with bales of cotton. "Why don't they take them away?" I asked, with some surprise, of my companion. Nursoo answered, "Remove them, indeed! they are the very heart and soul of the Topee Wallas; they get their rupees by them—let them alone for trading, my friend." I was going to say it was wrong not to keep the fort clear for resisting an attack; but I checked myself, as it might not be prudent to show too much military knowledge. At length we reached Nursoo's house. I spread my mat in the verandah, and having eaten some rice-bread, soon fell asleep.

Whilst my friend was making interest for me with the packers, carpenters, and clerks, I had abundant leisure to make my observations upon the country and its inhabitants. Bombay is an island containing every description of human beings: Hindoos, Parsees, Musselmen, Jews, Turks, Armenians, Arabians, Portuguese, and Englishmen. The Parsees were very numerous, and very fine men; ingenious and enterprising, but extravagant, fraudulent, and the most abominable liars in India, or second only to the Mahrattas. The English had a governor, whom I saw, together with a general and judge, who wore dresses made differently one from the other. The first a blue coat, cut with two tails; the second a red coat; and the third a black, save when on the seat of justice, and then he had a red loose gown like an Arab, and covered his head with white ashes, which recalled my friend Gabbage Gousla to my mind again. The shops abounded in the most beautiful things in the world for sale. Many of these were quite new to me, and I never had a knowledge of the use of them; all was grand and beautiful in my eyes, the more when it is considered that I had just emerged from amid tumult, strife, and misery. I lounged at the barbers' shops, drank toddy with the Mahrattas, talked with the Musselmen, and finally went home to learn my fate from Nursoo, and whether a place could be obtained for me. I found that, in a few days, I should have a chance of succeeding; and I borrowed eight rupees of him upon interest, on the strength of my prospects. I agreed very well with Nursoo and his family, the latter consisting of a boy and two girls. I even blessed my good fortune that had conducted me to a place of quiet and rest, such as I had never before enjoyed.

CHAPTER VII.

AFTER a delay of a few days, Nursoo informed me he had secured the situation I desired. I therefore got in readiness to take upon myself the duties of my new office, and accompanied him to the place where the goods of my employer were kept. I had not been there long before I saw the Topee Walla shopkeeper, who, to my surprise, was in a constant bustle, angry with all around him, and talking in bad Hindustanee to one, and in his own language to another. His face was quite pale, and he appeared much distressed by the intense heat. I was introduced to his notice by the head-clerk, M,hadaje Sinor, between whom and my new master some conversation passed in English, the purport of which I did not comprehend. I was then invested with a red belt, having a brass plate attached to it, on which some Topee Walla or English characters were engraven. My business was to wait at the door, carry about notes, and accompany the coolies from house to house with articles from the shop. I had not been more than a year in this situation when I became heartily sick of a service in which there was no chance of profit beyond my wages, and very little of promotion. The Topee Walla seldom spoke to me, and when he did, it was as if he were addressing a dog. It mattered not, however, as I could never make out a syllable of his bad Hindustanee. I could perceive by his manner, notwithstanding, that he thought me a butt against which he might vent his anger with impunity. One day, after he had been in one of his angry and insulting fits, I began to consider how I should quit a service I detested, when the clerk gave me a note to take to "the gentleman who lived in a tent on the esplanade." I did as I was commanded. The

Topee Walla Sahib read it, and his countenance changed with anger, which, I could see, was about to fall upon me. I waited patiently, till he furiously asked me how I dared stand at his tent waiting an answer. He darted from his seat upon me like a tiger would upon his prey, struck me with his fist on the side and face, and finished by kicking me out of the tent. I was so surprised, I could not strike him in return nor defend myself; but I returned to my master, and told him of the usage I had received. He told me he would have the officer punished. My master did so; and I learned that the officer was fined a hundred rupees. The note I bore him contained a bill, as I afterwards found, which he could not then pay; and instead of venting his rage on the money-lender, he chose to do it upon the bearer of the demand. I determined not to forget the usage I got from this man.

In a short time my master was obliged to reduce his establishment, and discharged me; but, at my request, obtained a place for me as peon in a house of agency. Here I found one of the best and kindest masters, and most generous and liberal men I ever saw. His name was K——n. He kept race-horses, carriages, and dogs; gave great dinner-parties, and seemed to have everything money could command. I could not, however, make much profit here, nor did I feel I was made of consequence enough in my own opinion. I was still unsatisfied; I wished to get into a police-office, and become a government peon. I at length made friends with the clerk in that office, and on the first vacancy left Mr. K——n, and took upon myself the badge of my new place. Here I felt myself more at home. I could hasten or retard the business of a complainant in proportion to the rupees he put into my hand. Then, when in attendance to superintend the punishment of the rattan, I could mitigate or increase the pain, in the execution of the sentence, according to the sum given me. At night, none were so zealous and attentive as I was in apprehending rioters and thieves who could not pay; but those were sure to be let off who could. The Parsees will find money to prevent any of their caste being disgraced. When any of this tribe were implicated in a crime, I failed not to exact pretty high fees for their escape. By these means I laid by a few hundred rupees, and hired a house and an old woman to cook for me. I buried my money in an inner chamber, where the old creature was not permitted to enter.

There were so many persons implicated in various irregularities, that my master had plenty of business falling to his share in the morning, and I had constant opportunities of bringing myself to his notice. He thought all was going on excellently well in his department, and I did not undeceive him, as I was certain the state of things could not endure long. This consideration made me the more exorbitant in my exactions. Month after month passed away, and still all remained calm. I converted my cash into gold bangles, necklaces, and silver rings, that I might be in readiness to decamp with my wealth about my person, should a storm arise. I even now applaud my caution; for in a short time a storm did arise, though not in our office, and by a chain of events it implicated us. The person at the head of the treasury was in the habit of intrusting the keys of the money-chests to the chief clerk, named Shackje, and simply contented himself with reckoning the balance remaining every Saturday. Shackjee was too much of a Mahratta not to turn this confidence to account. As soon as the treasurer was gone, having counted his money previously, Shackje and others concerned admitted the merchants and shroffs of the town, and let them take the Company's money, paying interest for the use of it to Shackje & Co., under promise of bringing money for an hour or two to replace what was wanting on the following Saturday, when the treasurer counted the cash again. Some person, who was dissatisfied with his share of the plunder, informed the treasurer of these doings. The latter kept the whole a secret, nor once allowed the clerks to guess he was well acquainted with their proceedings. Saturday approached, the money was counted, and found right, as the books showed it ought to be; and when it was locked up again, the treasurer took away the keys saying that in future he should keep them himself. A thunderbolt striking Shackje could not have stunned him more; he well knew the consequences. His master did not appear to notice his confusion at all. In an hour or two the unlucky clerk was surrounded by banians, soucars, and shroffs, as numerous as flies settling upon a carcase. No money could be had. In the bazaar, houses failed, shroffs and soucars stopped payment, ruin appeared everywhere, and trade was stagnant: the merchant-borrowers and money-lenders all were aghast.

The management of the Topee Walla treasurer, in securing to his employers all their money, was excellent; any other line of conduct would have rendered the loss irrecoverable. No Mahratta could have done better, or exceeded in ingenuity and sagacity this English treasurer. Shackje was an intimate acquaintance of Filchajee, the head-clerk in our police-office, and at this time was frequently at his house. Both these specimens of Mahratta virtue sent for me. They gave me a paper mysteriously folded, desiring me to find out a *Byraggee* or religious mendicant, famous for his skill in magic, and deliver it to him. I found him accordingly, but had previously thought proper to read the communication. It enclosed a request that he would bewitch the treasurer, and put him to death by a charm; and if common conjuration could not effect the object, the *magic of the sword* was to be practised. If successful, they agreed to give him two hundred rupees. The Byraggee was nearly in darkness when I entered his cell. Giving him the letter, he went to a window to read it; and the light falling on his countenance discovered, to my surprise, the old vagabond Gabbage Gousla. It was he whom they had bribed to commit murder, and a better man could not have been selected for such a purpose. I muffled myself up as well as I could to prevent detection. He returned no written answer, but desired I would tell my employers their business should be done, but they must send the rupees. I left him and reported his reply. They had a long consultation; at last the rupees were produced, and I was despatched with the bag. I thought it would be a sin not to pocket fifty of the two hundred, and trust to my ingenuity to deceive the old villain. Arrived at his cell, I told him my masters had determined on sending him only a hundred and fifty rupees, until the business was done.— "What business?" said he, with a peculiar quickness. "How should I know?" I replied. "I only gave their words." "Well," he observed, "it shan't be long ere I get the remainder." On repairing to the office the following day, I found all in confusion. Gabbage had been seized, and the papers found upon him. Shackje was apprehended, but he stoutly denied all knowledge of the matter. The police-master was assiduous in endeavouring to find out the conspiracy. The treasurer, whose life was implicated in the affair, was no less so. Gabbage was silent, and was remanded. On the following day the affair was pursued still further. The head of the police talked very lightly on the subject, and seemed to wish to impress on the public that he looked upon the whole affair as a jest, or as a nonsensical Hindoo conjuration, scarcely worth notice. Gabbage was again examined; and, to my dismay, stated that I had brought him the note, mentioning my name, and thus implicating me. I now found he had recognised me, when I little suspected it. I was immediately seized, imprisoned, and left to my own reflections. The day of trial arrived, and Shackje was brought before the court; but when they came to the cell of Gabbage, he was not to be found. The cunning old rascal had effected his escape, by what mode could not be discovered. The Mahrattas attributed it to his skill in magic; and so prepossessed were they with this notion, that not one of them would attempt to hunt for him, believing it an utter waste of labour. The place of trial was crowded; Shackje, Filchajee, Gumbiah, and myself, were charged with conspiracy to murder the treasurer. The two first were found guilty, and sentenced to imprisonment and to public whipping. Gumbiah and myself, being considered as ignorant tools, were acquitted. The police, however, had orders to ferry us across the water to the Mahratta country; and we were threatened with punishment if we ever showed ourselves in Bombay again. Previous to our sailing from Bombay, we heard that the police-master had been committed to prison on the charge of receiving a bribe from Shackje to screen him from the storm raised against him. How this matter terminated I never learned.

Gumbiah, who was ordered to be sent away with me, was a peon in the treasury office, and as well as Shackje was now ruined. We looked very foolish when placed in the boat that was to convey us away. Nursoo, the bullock-driver, my old friend, was absent, so I could not take leave of him. When we arrived at Parwell, my companion and myself proceeded towards the Ghauts, intending to go to Poona, where I hoped I should not now be recognised. I had about eight hundred rupees on my person, which I concealed from the sight of Gumbiah, who made several attempts to discover if I was as poor as himself. " I know," he said, "you had money as well as all the peons in the police office, who were reported to be rich !" I said in reply, " It was true; but all were not as unfortunate as myself." He then wanted to know what I had done with my money. I told him I had buried it in my house, from which, being so suddenly removed, I had not time to take it. He said I was very unlucky to lose my money, and that whoever found it would be very fortunate. No further conversation took place respecting it. On arriving at our halting-place we found a lodging, ate our rice, and retired to rest, intending to proceed early the next morning on our journey. On waking, I missed Gumbiah; he was nowhere to be found ; and I did not doubt he had retraced his steps to Bombay for the purpose of trying to get at my buried treasure. I enjoyed a hearty laugh at the fellow's avarice, and figured to myself his disappointment, and the risk he incurred on entering Bombay again. "Vishnu protect him," said I to myself, " though he be gone on a fool's errand." I began to ascend the Ghauts, and had already proceeded some distance, thinking how I should dispose of my wealth to the best advantage, when I beheld a body of horse approaching. Now, whether they were Pindarees or regular native troops—friends or foes—I was equally sure of being plundered. I had not a moment to spare,—to conceal my person was impossible, and the concealment of my treasure was nearly as difficult. I proceeded, however, to the foot of a mango-tree, and there dug a hole and deposited my little all, keeping no ornament but one silver ring on my person. I had good reason to applaud my foresight; for the horsemen were Pindarees, who, when they came up, stripped me, searched me for plunder, and finding nothing, ordered me to be their guide to a particular village. 'Alas! my poor treasure ! And must I leave it, and in such a dangerous place, too, hardly earned as it was? I shall be again moneyless!" I was thus inwardly complaining, when the stroke of a sabre on my shoulder stopped all further thoughts respecting my lost treasure.

"Scoundrel," said the fellow as he struck me, "where are you leading us? By the holy cow, if you go wrong, I will make you a head shorter!" I again pleaded my ignorance in vain, and we pursued our way until we arrived near a fort. The Pindarees declared I was playing the part of a traitor; and some of them proposed to hang me lest I should betray them to the English. I swore no English were near, and that I detested them. They renewed the cry, "Hang him! hang him!" and I certainly was never nearer execution before. We were now between two deep ravines, and just turning a corner, when a hundred muskets were opened upon us at once. Down dropped the Pindarees and their horses with them; there was no escape. Those who did not fall on receiving the first volley galloped off, some from, and others into, the jaws of the enemy. Among the latter I was one, though fortunate enough to escape with a wound in my shoulder, which gave me great pain. The enemies who thus attacked us were the English garrisoning the fort ceded to them by the Peeshwa. Spying us first from the battlements, they had lain in ambush for us in the ravine.

I was taken care of and attended by a doctor, who extracted the bullet and dressed my wound. The doctor's mild behaviour and tolerable knowledge of the language induced me to explain to him that I was no Pindaree, as he might observe, and had not even a sword with me, nor any offensive weapon. He promised to represent my case to the commander, and did so. I was summoned to attend the officers of the garrison, when I told them the truth as to my falling in with the Pindarees, and how rejoiced I was at their being dispersed. The commandant promised to let me go when my wound was healed, and, in the meanwhile, sent me among his own servants. The family of the officer in command consisted of himself, his wife (an English lady), and one daughter, whom we called Jane Bebee. Her real name was Juliana; but Jane being more adapted to the pronunciation of the Hindoo, we always knew her by that appellation. Her father had a number of horses, among which I almost lived. I paid so much attention to their department that he took a great liking to me. Among his stud was a small pony of a jet-black colour, on which the lovely Jane used to ride, but in a very strange manner, having both her legs on one side of the horse. The poor animal was accustomed to it, and so the young lady and pony agreed perfectly well. I took great pleasure in cleaning or superintending the cleaning of this pony, or tattoo, as we call it, and gave Miss Jane high satisfaction, which her beautiful eyes never failed to display. Never were features more regular and beautiful than hers; I could gaze upon them from sunrise to sunset, and still admire. Jane Bebee spoke Hindoostanee a little, and frequently praised me for the care taken of her pony, or, as she called it, her dear *Mottee*. At such times I would bow to the earth, lay my hand on my heart, and say I was her slave. In short, so much did I think about her, and so little of my buried gold, that when I recovered of my wound I forgot to demand my liberty. I had only recovered from one wound to receive another more severe. " O Jane Bebee !" I exclaimed to myself, " thy fetters bind me here stronger than those of thy father !" Fool that I was to cherish such notions—a poor Hindoo vagabond like me ! All I could do was to curse my destiny, and admire in silence my beautiful mistress. One day she had gone out of the fort to ride, and remaining longer than usual, her family became alarmed at her absence. I was despatched to find out the cause, when (I never shall forget that moment) I met her at the gate of the fort, bleeding and insensible, borne on a litter. The pony, her favourite, had flung her off upon rocky ground. I was eager to learn whether she was dangerously hurt. I found her arm was broken, and she had received several bruises on the head. I ran to the doctor, followed by a second messenger, crying, " Doctor, doctor, Jane Bebee is no more !" and he proceeded to the assistance of the lovely sufferer. Many days elapsed before she recovered the effects of her accident; but when she first made her appearance, I eagerly embraced the opportunity of making my salaam, which she acknowledged by a most gracious smile.

At length, wearied and despairing from the hopeless contemplation of an object that could not live for me, I deemed it best to separate myself from the spot, and bury, if possible, all my remembrance of her.

I now began to direct my thoughts to my buried treasure, and was ruminating on the first step to be taken to obtain leave to depart from the good commandant, when some of the sepoys, with whom I had contracted an intimacy, informed me that they were going to be relieved and marched back to Bombay. The commandant and his family alone were to remain. The new corps that came to take their place before they departed, I saw march in; and among the officers was the man who had treated me so ill on presenting him a letter from my master on the esplanade. I felt all my Mahratta spirit of revenge burn within me at the sight; and I determined to remain longer in the fort, to enable me to carry my threat of vengeance into execution. How I should accomplish it, I left to destiny. This officer seldom noticed any of the native men; and if he had condescended to cast his eyes upon me, I should have little feared a recognition. I observed that he went very frequently to the commandant's, and this made caution on my part doubly necessary. I soon found that Jane Bebee was the star of attraction there, and it quickly became rumoured that he had demanded her in marriage of her father, who had declined the proposed honour. I rejoiced at his disappointment, as it saved me much trouble, for I had secretly determined she never should be his. I knew not how I should have been able to prevent it; but to do so I was resolved, cost what it would. I swore by the holy cow, that the lieutenant, of all other men, should never wed her. Whether Jane felt much disappointment I cannot tell; I could not perceive that she did, or that her health or spirits were at all affected by her father's decision. The lieutenant's visits were now less frequent than usual; one day, however, he came and continued a long time, and on leaving the house I observed him slip something, which I doubted not was money, into the hand of the *ayah*, or serving-woman of Jane. Significant nods were exchanged, but not a word spoken; and the officer went his way. "Well," thought I, "good fortune attends me indeed. This must be looked into narrowly. Now or never is my time for revenge." My first step was to make friends with the ayah. For this purpose I purchased some fresh betel-nut and pawn-leaf, which I folded into the shape of a cane tipped with gold leaf. Thus furnished with the key of intimacy, I soon found an opportunity of seeing her alone, and began my attack by praising her beauty and presenting her with the gold-tipped pawn-leaf. This was to be plastered over with fine chunam, and the preparing it conveniently rendered it necessary for the ayah to squat herself down, which action was the prelude to a confidential chat. I presented my silver chunam-box, the contents of which she readily devoured when she had spread them on the leaf. I began by praising her mistress, and touched upon the proposals she had received from the officer, lamenting the father's refusal. "Ay, ay," said the ayah, spitting out her pawn-juice, "lovers don't mind what fathers say." "But in this," I said, "they *must* mind." "Not if I can help it," said the ayah. "I would I could help also," said I, hypocritically. "You can then," said she, "and be rewarded, too, into the bargain." "You know I would do anything for Jane Bebee." She replied, "I think I may trust you;" and I swore by the holy cow to keep her secret. She then commenced a relation of the plans determined upon by the mistress, though first suggested by the lieutenant and supported by the ayah. "You know," said the ayah, "that the drawbridge on the north side of the fort, when lowered, brings you to the sally-port?" I nodded assent. "Well, then, the sally-port being open, you enter the commandant's garden." "True," said I; "go on." "Into the garden, you know, Jane Bebee's window looks. Now, if you can get a ladder into the garden, the lieutenant will mount it, take away his mistress, proceed to Seroor, and there marry her. Her father will see the propriety of consenting when they have been so long together, or at least of forgiving them when the marriage is concluded." "Get me the key," I said, "and I am the man you want. Success is certain: but when is the time fixed?" "To-morrow night, at twelve o'clock," was the reply. "If we can get the keys of the drawbridge and sally-port, no other difficulty remains." " If you succeed," said I, " when will you give them to me?" She replied, " At eight o'clock the next evening." We then agreed I should meet the lieutenant at the stables at eight o'clock, going there before gun-fire, and not approach the fort again until twelve; then suffer him to ascend the ladder, await his descent, take away the ladder again and conceal it, lock the sally-port, swim the ditch, and enter the fort early in the morning. For this, three hundred rupees were to be mine. I agreed to everything, and I left her.

I had now to consider how I might best take my revenge on the officer. I did not wish to touch his life, but only to involve him in some serious trouble for the insults and disgrace he had inflicted upon me. After turning over the matter for some time, it struck me at last that the best method would be to suffer the lieutenant to mount the ladder, and then remove it; lock the sally-port, and, retiring, give the alarm of thieves: the commandant must then, I imagined, discover the lieutenant in his daughter's room. No better plan appearing practicable, I determined to enforce this. The evening came, the gun fired, and I was at my post. The ayah came trembling with the keys, and I set off before the gates were closed, the lieutenant following my steps in silence. I proceeded to the spot where the ladder lay, and we sat down opposite each other, the lieutenant every now and then enquiring how time went. The first bell tolled twelve. Up we went, he helping me to carry the ladder. The drawbridge was unlocked by the ayah from within, and the sally-port unclosed. We then entered the garden, placed the ladder, and the lieutenant mounted to the window. He had no sooner entered than I, eager to accomplish my plans, began to lower the ladder, without in my hurry reflecting upon its weight; while bending under it my foot slipped, and down it came with a loud crash, breaking a lower window in its fall. Aware of my danger, I arose quickly, but only to fall again, for the sentinel on the ramparts seeing me, levelled his musket and shot me in the leg. The alarm was given —blue lights burned—and I, nearly unable to move, knew that to remain was certain death; I therefore made shift to hobble off on one leg, shutting and fastening the sally-port, and crossing the bridge as expeditiously as I could. I had scarcely reached the other side of the moat when I saw lights, both outside and inside the walls of the fort. I heard hammering at the sally-port from within, and voices calling in every direction. Alarm-guns were firing, and everything seemed in confusion. My leg was in horrible pain; and creeping among the bushes, I at last found a hollow tree, into which I got and hid myself, half dead with fear, and hardly venturing to breathe.

CHAPTER VIII.

SCOUTS every hour passed my hiding-place, and I heard them mention my name as being the only one absent from the fort. At last a party of sepoys rested themselves close to the tree where I was concealed. "Here is a pretty toofan!"[1] said one of them. "Ay," said the other, "a greater one took place in the Buna Sahib's house!" "What was that?" said the first speaker. "Why, the commandant rushed through the house with his pistols, and firing was heard in his daughter's room. The women screamed, the men scuffled, but how the poor lieutenant got off I cannot tell." "Lieutenant!" said the first, "was he concerned?" "Why, yes, to be sure; he wanted to carry off Jane Bebee: but her screams led her father to suppose he was an unwelcome visitor; and he must be shot, I think, for I heard them call out for the doctor. A pretty toofan indeed has been raised!"

I was really concerned to find that the poor lieutenant had come off so badly in his beloved's apartments. The sepoys were soon hailed by their companions, and left the spot, to my great joy. My wound now gave me exquisite pain, which was notwithstanding hardly severe enough to quell the pangs of hunger. All being quiet, I emerged from my hiding-place, and set off, without knowing whither to direct my steps or how to travel, for I could not walk without great difficulty. What with hopping and limping, I contrived to reach a brook, on the banks of which

---

[1] Storm.

75

I rested and quenched my thirst, which was increased by my wound. Though bound up in the best manner I was able, it did not abate in the pain it gave me. I had not remained there long, when I perceived a poor man driving some asses laden with firewood and bricks. I asked him for something to eat, and he produced his humble fare of bread, cold rice, and onions, which seemed to me a most delicious repast. He told me he was going to Poona, and seeing I was lame, offered me one of his asses to help me on. The good-natured creature was anxious to learn by what accident I was necessitated to walk in such circumstances: but it may be supposed I was not very eager to satisfy his curiosity, particularly as I had been residing with the English; we therefore journeyed on in mutual silence. I found, to my great joy, we were travelling on the road where I had buried my treasure, and fallen in with the Pindarees. I was sadly perplexed how to get rid of my companion, or how to search for my treasure without his discovering me. I thought of several plans to leave him for a short time, but of none that were likely to be successful. At length we approached the spot; and I begged the man to rest a little, as I felt much fatigued. He acquiesced, and sat down under the tree on the very spot where my treasure was concealed. I did not dare to satisfy my curiosity by searching for it. At length the driver proposed we should proceed. I begged him to do so, and I would follow and try to overtake him. "No, no, my friend," replied the provoking fellow, "I cannot allow you to be racing after me; you could not overtake me, and then would be obliged to remain all day and night in the open air. If you are determined to rest another hour, I will do so too." I thanked him for his kindness, but heartily cursed his untoward conduct. His good-nature was most ill-placed at that moment. We sat another hour, and my curiosity increased irresistibly to know whether my riches were safe. The ass-driver insisted on helping me upon one of his beasts, and I refused as civilly as I could, saying that I had determined to retrace my steps whence I came. I then bade him adieu, with many thanks for his kind assistance. "What!" said he, "will you return to the place where you were wounded, and rush into the very jaws of destruction? Impossible! you must do no such thing."

I assured him I should do so, upon which he offered to lend me an ass, and to accompany me, saying he would drive the laden beasts to a village about one coss distance, and accompany me when he had secured them there. This was music to my ears, and I immediately thanked him, acquiescing in the arrangement. The moment he was out of sight I began to dig for my wealth; but had only turned up a few handfuls of earth when the neighing of a horse struck my ears, and turning round, I saw a company of sepoys, headed by an officer on horseback, approaching slowly towards the tree. My fears told me no time was to be lost, and with difficulty I clambered up among the boughs, which, on account of its being the rainy season, were very thickly covered with foliage. The party came close to the tree; and I discovered that the men wore the same uniform as those in the fort whence I had escaped. "I am very certain," said one, "I saw a fellow near this tree." "So did I," said another. "It must have been a ghost," said a third. "Let us wait and see him rise from the earth," exclaimed a fourth. They were on the point of marching away, when, to my terror, up came the ass-driver, inquiring of the sepoys if they had seen a man near the tree, or met him on the road. They inquired what sort of man; on which the ass-driver described me with the most mortifying accuracy, not forgetting the wound in my leg. The officer and men asked him a hundred questions respecting the lame man, all of which he answered with a strict adherence to truth. Surely, thought I, this fellow was destined to be my ruin. The soldiers consulted together, and it was resolved a party should remain there, in hopes of discovering the fugitive. My feelings cannot be described. Evening came, and still they kept their post; the ass-driver alone made his bow and separated. I now execrated the officious fellow, whose unaccountable perseverance in aiding me had drawn me into this scrape. The sepoys were still sitting beneath the tree, when one of them amused himself with digging up the earth with his bayonet close to where my deposit lay. How my heart beat! I trembled and perspired at every pore. Digging deeper and deeper, the rascal at length hooked up a gold bangle. They quietly divided the spoil between them to the very last article, and could hardly contain their joy. To see my treasure thus stolen before my eyes was too much. But for the pertinacious ass-driver, I might have found it safe as I left it. To think that there I lay skulking up in the tree like a stupid owl, to witness such a scene, quite overcame me. Losing all presence of mind, I vented my anguish at the sight in a loud continuous groan. The sepoys started up and cried, " *B,hooh, b,hooh! arry, arry!*" This cry of " a ghost " reached the ears of the officer, who bid his men fire into the tree, and that would bring him down, if there ; but if in the ground he must be left to himself. The sound of the ramrods clanking in the barrels of the muskets seemed my death-warrant. I cried out instantly, " *Sahib, Sahib!*"—Sir, sir!—" spare me!" On this he laughed heartily, and said to his men, " I told you we should soon bring down the ghost." I descended immediately, and was surrounded by the sepoys, who, with loud exclamations of surprise, pronounced me to be the very Pandoo who had given them so much trouble at the fort. My arms were immediately pinioned, and a file of men ordered to guard me with unceasing vigilance.

I now bitterly repented my selfishness in not discovering my treasure before the ass-driver. Had I done so, and given him a ring or two, the rest would have been still my own. I now attributed the fellow's care of me to his curiosity, or suspicion of something at my wanting to get rid of him on that spot. He might have easily judged I had something in view which I did not wish a second person to witness. Had my avarice not prevented my making him a confidant, everything would have been well ; but it was now too late to derive any benefit from the discovery, except as to the lesson it afforded me for the future.

I determined to explain to the officer my unfortunate condition, and beg him to release me and restore me my money. I told him I had been promised money by the lieutenant to aid him in his plans of elopement with the commandant's daughter—that the fear of my life on having been discovered in the garden of the fort induced me to abscond, and that I had no other design or designs in view; finally, that I was an unfortunate man, who had been taken by the Pindarees, and captured with them, and that before meeting them I had buried my money under the tree. The officer told me that he believed my story about the fort, as the lieutenant and ayah told exactly the same; but as to the money and ornaments, I told a wilful lie. I solemnly asserted the truth of what I said, and enumerated the articles which I saw the sepoys take away. "Point me out the two men," said the officer. I told him I thought I could, and they were ordered before me for the purpose; but their similarity in dress and appearance so perplexed me I could not succeed; I looked at them, one and one, without success. He then told me he had no orders to detain me—that he and his party were going to Seroor for the pay of the battalion — but that he must keep me till he could write and obtain an answer from the fort how to act. As to the tale of my money, he said it was too much like a Mahratta lie to be believed, particularly as I could not recognise the men who took it. Saying this, he ordered me away, and bade the party proceed to Poona that night. I was hurried along well guarded.

We reached Poona at the time fixed, and on passing over the wooden bridge, I again saw my tormentor, the ass-driver, quietly driving his animals into the town. "So," said he to the sepoys, "you have caught him. Is he a thief, a traitor, or a murderer?" "Neither," they replied, "only a jungle-fowl we caught at roost." The ass-driver grinned, and cast a look at me, which said, "You had much better have trusted me." I did not speak, but with downcast eyes followed my guard in silence. In a day or two we marched for Seroor, where having received the money for pay, we returned again to Poona, and here the officer received instructions to release me. I in vain renewed my supplications respecting my money; they were disregarded, and I was turned adrift in the vast city of Poona, with no means of existence and no employment.

When I entered Poona the first time, in company with the villain Gabbage Gousla, I passed through Ahmednugur, Seroor, Louce, Corygaum, and Shikarpoor, a road barren and waste, having only a few wretched hamlets scattered over the extensive plains which we crossed in our route. Milk bushes or prickly pear surrounded the hovels of poverty and wretchedness, that, erected of posts and mud, afforded little or no protection against the heavy rains of the monsoon. On entering Poona, therefore, after crossing the river at the Sangam, or junction of the Moota and Moola streams, the contrast was remarkable between the misery of the former habitations and the splendour of the city. These my adventure in the Gossein character allowed me no time to observe, and now I had unfortunately too much leisure for the purpose. Upon the hill to the left of the city I saw the ancient temple of Parvati,[1] encircled with trees, its summits glittering in the rising sun. The deep solemn sound of the najarrahs from among the recesses of the sacred enclosure, proclaimed that the hour of worship had arrived, and I felt a strong desire to lay my humble offering at the foot of the holy altar. Few people were to be seen in the bazaar at that early hour, and I continued to make my observations on the buildings around me. They were far more magnificent than any in the part of India to which I had been accustomed. Beyond the bazaar the houses were lofty, and erected part of the way up the walls with stone and strong cement to repel thieves, who easily effect an entrance into mud or plaster-built dwellings. These houses were terraced; but many close to them, being tiled, gave the city a look of great irregularity. In the central part I came to an immense reservoir of water, with an ever-flowing fountain in the midst. To live in Poona, near it, must, I thought, be happiness itself. The houses here were large, but had a dull and heavy appearance when they were not white-washed. They were constructed of a solid wood framework, filled up with hewn stone, generally granite. The woodwork was beautifully carved after various devices, together with the ends of the beams. The windows were neatly closed with chutters to keep out the heat; but nothing cheerful appeared to be going forward within. A lazy Mahratta peon squatted at most of the doors, and here and there a Brahminee woman was

[1] The wife of M,hadeo.

employed drying clothes on the terraces. Some of the buildings had not a single window next the street, but were built round a small, square, and gloomy court, from whence all the light and air entered. The doors were folding, low, and substantial, and led to staircases so narrow that only one person could mount them at a time.

In the centre of the city stood the palace of the Peeshwa, who was named Bajee Rao Pundit Purdhaun Behauder. It was fortified with regular bastions, curtains, and towers: between two of the latter were enormous and massy gates. It seemed to me as if the place must be impregnable to the most formidable enemy. The palace itself I had not an opportunity of seeing, until a curious concatenation of circumstances, which shall by-and-by be unfolded to the reader, introduced me within its precincts. On many of the walls around me were drawn figures of Gunputty,[1] of elephants, and peacocks with tails of most enormous expansion. In a short time the streets were peopled with Gosseins and Fakirs; women with copper vessels fetching water from the reservoir; Brahmins proceeding to the temples to perform their sacred offices; horsemen prancing about with well-trained animals; and porters and labourers carrying goods to market. The pavement of the street being rough, the carriages or waggons, drawn by bullocks with bells around their necks, must not be unnoticed; their noise almost deafened me; but I had no place of refuge to fly to from their distracting sounds.

Night arrived, the evening gun fired at ten o'clock, and I was still a wanderer in the streets. I went on until, turning a corner, I was laid hold of by two rough fellows, who ordered me to give an account of myself. What I said was not deemed satisfactory, and I was hurried to the Habeshee Kotwall, the Abyssinian police-master. This man instantly demanded of me a hundred rupees, as a fine for being in the streets after gun-firing. In vain I pleaded ignorance of the laws. Finding I could not pay that

---

[1] Gunputty, or Ganesa, a favourite idol of the Mahrattas. That captured by the English from the Peeshwa in 1819 was of solid gold, with diamonds for eyes, and covered with jewels. It was valued at £50,000.

sum, he ordered me to be instantly flogged, and turned into the suburbs. This cruel sentence was carried into effect, to my surprise and indignation, and I secretly vowed revenge.

One day a circumstance occurred, which gave me a glorious opportunity of wreaking my vengeance on him, and providing for myself at the same time. Disconsolate and miserable, I was prowling about the suburbs, and had sat myself down on a stone at the back of a solitary and mean-looking dwelling. The night was dark, and everything still, when fancying I saw a light in the house, I kept my eye on the window in which it had appeared. It was now gone, and a strange bustle attracted my attention from the interior. I heard a scream—a groan—and then all seemed hushed again to the stillness of the grave. I determined to see whether anything further arose out of this unaccountable disturbance. The clock struck eleven, and I had heard nothing more—twelve, and all was still silent. At length I observed the shutters of the old window grate on their rusty hinges. I changed my position, to be less in danger of observation, and kept anxiously watching the motions of the inhabitants within. I distinctly heard a person say " *Noko, noko,*" or, " No, no ; don't, don't," and voices of several persons mumbling in so low a tone as to preclude my comprehending a single sentence. At length a heavy substance was thrown out, and fell on the ground not many yards from where I stood. It seemed to be a body—whether dead or alive I could not tell. I thought that presently some one would come out of the house to remove the victim, to do which a circuit must be made. To be caught there, I was sure, would in such a case be dangerous to me ; yet I was anxious to know if the body were lifeless, and whether that of man or woman. I felt the head, and the length and the quantity of hair convinced me it was a woman's, and I fancied it breathed. All this was the affair of a moment. Lifting up the body, I threw it across my shoulders, and hastened to the river. There, by applying water to the temples, and wetting the mouth and lips of the unfortunate creature, I found to a certainty that she breathed, and rejoiced greatly at my success. I was again taking up my burden to get to some place more secure, when I saw lights in the direction of the house

I had just quitted. Not a moment must be lost. I boldly dashed into the river with the suffering female, and succeeded in gaining the opposite bank in safety. There was a straw stack near, and implements of husbandry. I conveyed the sufferer to the further side, to secure the less chance of discovery from her pursuers. I made the easiest bed I could for her with such materials, laid her on it, and crept cautiously round to observe the motions of the persons in search.

I now saw lights approach the river, and come down immediately to the bank opposite me. These lights, far from being of service to those in pursuit, only served to exhibit them to the pursued. I plainly saw some of them were Gosseins, and more than once fancied that one of them was the wretch Gabbage Gousla. "Surely earth never before bred such a fiend!" thought I; "his life seems spent in deeds of crime the most atrocious!" They were now close on the opposite bank of the river, and I could distinctly hear them speak. "She must be dead," said Gabbage; for it was he in truth. "If strangling did not destroy her, the fall from the window must have done so," said a second voice; "and even if she plunged into the river, after being able to reach it, she is drowned." "But what must we tell Trimbuckje Danglia?" said Gabbage. "Why, tell him the deed is done!" "But if she appear again?" "Why, then," said Gabbage, "woe be to us! But we stay too long here dallying: some one may discover us. Vishnu save us from Habeshee Kotwall, the police-master!" They then moved off, and I sneaked back to my charge, who seemed getting to herself rapidly. I dreaded the approach of day, but did not deem it prudent to rest until I had found some hut where I might deposit the woman whom fortune had thus flung in my way. I proceeded to the first village, and tapped at the door of a hut, when a voice within answered, "*Koun hue?*" Who is there? I requested succour for a poor half-murdered woman, assuring the speaker he should be rewarded if he admitted her. The owner opened the door, and begged I would not saddle him with my difficulties—that he had no money to bribe his way at court should he be accused. I assured him there was no danger, and he reluctantly consented to accompany me to the place where the unfortunate female lay. We lifted her up, and conveyed her to the cottage, where he promised he would take every care of her, and if possible keep it a profound secret that he had such a charge under his care. I gave him a rupee, not having more than five for myself, and promised him I would return in the evening, directing him what to do for the female, and to keep her on a soft bed, by which means she would recover quicker.

I hastened back to the city, that I might be there before the morning dawned. I reached it long before the shops were opened, and sat down outside a grain-dealer's shop. He opened his house soon after sunrise, and accosted me with "Holla, brother! what! so early in the markets!" "Indeed," I replied, "it is from necessity; not having eaten anything yesterday, I am famished, and require a *pylee*[1] of rice." He eyed me in a curious way, measured out the rice, took my money, but said not a syllable. I cooked my rice in a shed not far off, and then proceeded into the heart of the city. On arriving at the palace, I perceived a woman bathed in tears, beating her breast, and crying aloud for justice. I inquired of the bystanders what she wanted, and why she was so overwhelmed with grief. They replied "that she was crying for justice, as her niece, there was good reason to think, had been murdered; she was at any rate carried off, and robbed of her ornaments." It immediately struck me that her niece was the unhappy girl under my protection. I considered it impolitic to approach the old woman, but waited for more information as to the particulars of the transaction. It appeared her cries had reached the ear of the Peeshwa, who was informed of the cause. Habeshee Kotwall was summoned to his presence, and while so closeted I thought I would take the opportunity of asking something about this just and able superintendent of police at Poona. Habeshee[2] Kotwall was so called from his birthplace and police situation combined. He was born an Abyssinian, and a most

[1] A Measure.

[2] Abyssinians are called in India Habeshees. Habesh is the native name of Abyssinia. Habeshee means a native of Habesh, or, for shortness, Habshee.

ferocious villain he was in personal appearance. He had once been a jummahdar in the army, where he had signalised himself by brutal courage. At the termination of the war he was provided for by having a civil situation given to him, and was reported to be in great favour with the Peeshwa, over whom he had at one time a great ascendancy. How far he would have gone in this respect it is not easy to say, had he not been supplanted by a still greater villain than himself, Trimbuckje Danglia, who, from the meanest court office, pushed himself into the place of slipper-bearer to the Peeshwa, which situation he held for ten years, and then rose to be sword-bearer. From this time, he, being constantly about the person of the imbecile Peeshwa, contrived to supersede Habeshee Kotwall. Between these rivals the bitterest hatred existed, though it was a hatred mixed with mutual fear. When they met in the street, they eyed each other with deep venom. One stood for ever in the other's way to preferment. Insinuations were constantly poured into the Peeshwa's ear by Trimbuckje against Habeshee, and in the reverse way by the latter. But both being considered useful men, little attention was paid to their mutual malice and its results. Habeshee was the dread of the whole city; a herd of wild beasts could not cause it more terror. The woolly-headed Trimbuckje was little less feared than Habeshee. The only difference was that the latter carried on his nefarious practices at a distance, while the former did his in the very eyes of the Peeshwa. Habeshee was an open and avowed rogue: Trimbuckje was sly and designing; a cool, relentless murderer. He had been employed, as some said, in that very capacity by the Peeshwa himself, who often found it convenient to get troublesome subjects out of the way.

While Habeshee was closeted with the Peeshwa, the "*aswary*," or suite of Trimbuckje, arrived at the palace. He himself was informed ere he alighted from his horse that Habeshee was closeted with the Peeshwa. His anger, as if not conspicuous enough in his face, made his fingers tingle till they grasped his sword-hilt. Had Habeshee been near, he could hardly have escaped. I learned afterwards the cause of his anger on this occasion. Proclamations were issued and rewards offered for the disappeared. The police and Habeshee were on the alert. I could not fathom the reason why the Habeshee evinced such extraordinary zeal on the occasion. I was also more at a loss to account for Badjeroa, the Peeshwa, taking up the affair so seriously as to interfere personally. But why did Trimbuckje evince such anger on finding Habeshee with the Peeshwa? I could only at last solve the doubt by recalling the words of Gabbage the night of the intended murder; and I became convinced that Trimbuckje was implicated in that black affair. The Habeshee might be aware of his rival's guilt, and desirous of bringing it home to him, and working his downfall.

It soon struck me that all my conjectures might be verified or falsified by Sagoonah herself; and I proceeded to the village where I had left her; for Sagoonah, I had no doubt, it was that I had rescued. She was still senseless; and I removed from her throat a small bead-necklace, the only ornament remaining upon her, in order to relieve her throat, which bore the marks of the fingers of those who had attempted to destroy her. Suspended to the necklace was a copper box or talisman, in which a gold rupee was probably deposited, or some other trifle, as is customary among Mahratta women. Of this necklace I took great care, as likely to afford a cue to the elucidation of the affair. In the evening the female recovered her speech, but not sufficiently to relate her story. She was a most beautiful girl, and I became much interested in her restoration.

I now went again to the city, and found that Habeshee had gathered together, from all quarters, magicians, conjurors, and astrologers, offering high rewards, in the name of the Peeshwa, to any one who should discover the murderers of Sagoonah. The idea of personating a magician instantly struck me; but, first, it was necessary to know a little more myself before I could pretend to give information to others; and, secondly, to choose what party I should serve—the Habeshee or Trimbuckje; so that I might turn my art to the best advantage. I also became more anxious for Sagoonah's recovery, and returned to her immediately; I found her better, and able to speak. Her first inquiry was how she came to the cottage. I explained every minute particular to her, and impressed upon her mind the danger of appearing in

Poona, and that her enemies would now, more than ever, seek to destroy her. She was convinced by my reasoning; and I begged her to inform me how she got into the hands of the villains from whom I rescued her.

She sat up, and began, as well as her strength would permit, to state as follows:—"My name is Sagoonah. My father was a merchant, who failed, and shortly after died. My mother followed him as a *suttee*,[1] from which nothing could deter her; she died on the funeral pile. I had been betrothed several years before my parents died; but the boy who was to have been my husband left Poona with his father, and was never again heard of. I was, therefore, excluded from entering into any new alliance; and have lived ever since with my aunt, my father's sister, in a retired part of the city, near the Motee Baugh or Park Garden, where there is a pleasure-house belonging to the Peeshwa. One day Badjerao came to the garden; and I, being anxious to see the royal cavalcade, exposed myself at the window, not thinking the misery I entailed upon myself by so doing. As the Peeshwa returned he looked up at the window, where I was again posted to see him return. Evening arrived. I had thought no more of the Peeshwa and his elephants. My aunt was unfortunately absent, having gone to a village at some distance to remain two days. While I sat alone, a man, muffled up, entered the house; and, after flattering me, declared he came from the Peeshwa, who, having seen me, had become enamoured of my person, and was anxious to place me in his harem. I refused the honour, and said I would rather die than consent to it. He then left me, saying I should soon hear more. The following morning Trimbuckje Danglia came. I was aware of the purport of his visit, and knew he was the pander for his master, so I covered my face with my shawl. He began proclaiming his master's liberality, the number of ornaments his women wore, and which he had bestowed upon them. I refused the offer sternly, as before, and in my earnestness let fall the covering from my face. Trimbuckje gazed a moment in silence at me, and then audaciously made the same kind of proposal for himself. He offered to convey me to his village in Kandeish, and to deceive the Peeshwa by a report of my flight from Poona. I replied scornfully, 'The Peeshwa shall know this before sunset; I will expose you to his resentment. Leave me!' He went away, muttering curses. I determined to inform the Peeshwa of his conduct; and in the evening was proceeding to the palace for the purpose, when a boy overtook me, and inquired if my name was Sagoonah. I told him yes; and he then said, 'You must come with me; your aunt is dying in a house in the suburbs, and has sent me for you.' This scheme answered too well. I followed him to the dwelling whence you took me, and was surrounded instantly by four Gosseins, who attempted to strangle me, having robbed me of all my ornaments, and then threw me out of the window; the rest of my story you know. I have not a doubt but the Gosseins were agents of Trimbuckje, who wished to prevent my informing his master of his conduct."

In return, I told her I thought she was mistaken; for I had motives for not agreeing in her too correct opinion. It was dangerous for me to let any one know of what I was informed; and, next, I had not determined whether Habeshee or Trimbuckje should be the victim of my magical skill. I had settled in my own mind to enter the service of the survivor; and I had therefore to consider who was likely to remain longest in power. The inhabitants of Poona, I well knew, only waited for an opportunity to ruin Habeshee. If, then, I could make it appear he was directly or indirectly concerned in the murder of Sagoonah, that crime, and the other complaints that would pour in upon him, must effectually crush him. To ruin him, I must have access to Trimbuckje, and secure half the reward offered, and a promise of being retained in his service. The disguise I should put on to act the magician would, when removed, prevent any recognition of my person. Before I proceeded in my plan, I thought of Sagoonah, with whom I was deeply enamoured, and determined, if possible, to sue for her hand. "But will she consent," thought I, "if I am in the service of the villain Trimbuckje?" These considerations induced me to shake her opinion that he was her persecutor, and to fix it upon Habeshee, who had inveigled her to the house that he might rob her of her ornaments.

CHAPTER IX.

I NOW entered Poona again, and proceeded to Trimbuckje's residence, begging a conference with the owner, as having something important to communicate. I was desired to wait in the verandah. At length I was informed Trimbuckje would see me, but that I must submit to be disarmed. I readily assented, and gave up my dagger. I then followed a servant up and down several very narrow staircases, one after another, until I came to a door half open; and saw Trimbuckje sitting cross-legged on the floor, with papers before him, and a large figure of Gunputty, with the elephant's trunk, fastened to the wall over his head. His hookah stood beside him, and he wore a sort of skull-cap, with a muslin coat and short breeches. His two-edged sword lay near him, and before him an unsheathed dagger. I bowed to this "prince of darkness," whose complexion was of the colour of his heart. He desired the servant to withdraw, and told me to shut the door and sit down. Having obeyed, he began by saying he supposed that, having pushed my interest with Habeshee Kotwall and failed, I was come to solicit his assistance to aid me at court. I replied, "No, my lord; I am come to make proposals for crushing this Habeshee so effectually that no one will ever apply again for *his* interest there." Trimbuckje's eyes brightened as he looked me full in the face, and doubtingly inquired if I could really accomplish what I proposed? I told him I could, and he desired me to name my terms. I told him four thousand rupees were offered to bring home the murder of Sagoonah to the guilty party; and I

89

ought to have double if I bring the charge home to a man innocent of it. "Innocent!" said he; "is not Habeshee guilty of the crime?" "I know he is not," I answered, looking him full in the face at the time; "and I know who is." Trimbuckje cast down his eyes, and could not face me, but seemed inclined to anger. I bade him be calm; I did not intend to betray him; but I whispered in his ear "Gabbage Gousla Gossein;" from which he was convinced I knew more than I ought. "Well," said he, "you require four thousand rupees if you fix the charge on Habeshee?" I replied that I did, and a promise that he would provide for me about his person or in his village. I then represented how impossible it would be for him to deceive me; when, to show he was in earnest, he opened a chest and took out a thousand rupees, which he gave me in part payment of the reward. He next asked me how I proposed to act. I told him, in the disguise of a magician; that I should get introduced to the Kotwall; and if, by such means, I should establish my accusation, I intended to be allowed to pronounce the result of my conjuration before the Peeshwa himself. I did not fail to urge that, before commencing operations, as many petitions must be obtained as possible by him, Trimbuckje, from the inhabitants, complaining of Habeshee's conduct; so that, together with my accusation, his disgrace and punishment must be certain. I also bid him mind, that when the Peeshwa gave orders to search Habeshee's house, a durbar, or police-officer, should have men in waiting, and a confidential person be employed to search the Kotwall's *gardee* or pillow, where he sits in his durbar, and bring to the Peeshwa's presence whatever may be found there; and that no other proof would be necessary; for, though not actually guilty of the crime imputed to him, he had been guilty of a thousand equally bad, and the public good required that he should no longer oppress the city. Trimbuckje was highly pleased with my cunning stratagem, and promised to fulfil all my instructions. I took care to carry away the rupees given me, and to take and lodge them in the cottage to which I had conveyed the lovely Sagoonah.

I must confess I felt some hesitation at first, and feared I was going rather too far in fixing on Habeshee the horrible crime of murder: but I reflected on the infamy of his character, his universal conduct, and his cruel usage of me, who had committed no crime: this removed every compunction from my mind respecting him. Taking, therefore, the necklace of Sagoonah with me, I proceeded to Poona early the following morning, having previously provided myself with a magician's dress. I put it on in a field, that the owner of the cottage might not witness my metamorphosis. It consisted of a long white coat of muslin, hanging down to my heels, and gathered in at the waist, so that the upper part appeared like an abundance of petticoats, and, being new, rustled as I went along. On my head was a high stiff red cap, with snakes painted all over it. A red shawl, in the shape of a belt, was tied with a high knot on my left side. A long Persian kuttar was stuck in my belt, and a brass chain around my middle. I wore high-heeled shoes, and had a bell in my hand to imitate the Jungum priests.

Thus accoutred, I entered Poona, and sat down at a barber's shop, as if fatigued with long travel. The people that came in stared at me: as they well might, for I must have cut a most singular appearance. The barber asked me if I wished to be shaved. I replied, "Magicians, my friend, must nominate the day of shaving, not the barbers. If you would take my advice, my friends, do not allow a hair to be removed from your heads to-day." Saying this, I rang my bell, and cried out, "*Arry, arry, kuhea tegasta leta tula set buradia chugnhum set phraw aguhum;*" words in which there is no meaning at all. "Pray, sir," said the barber, "is that Sanscrit, or what language?" "May be it is *Jadoo,*"[1] I replied, in a solemn and deep voice. The poor barber's customers took the alarm, so superstitious were they all, and glided out of the shop, one by one, leaving myself and the barber there alone. The poor fellow did not much thank me for depriving him of his customers, and begged me to leave his shop, or he should be ruined; adding, "If you are a magician, there is plenty of work for you at the Kotwall's

---

[1] Magic.

chowry[1] in the market-place." " Fellow," I replied, " let those who want me seek me." "*Arry, arry,*" said the barber, " I did not seek you, and why did you come to my shop ?" " Dolt !" I answered; " do you think I came hither from choice—that chance led me ? No; it is written in the great *Pudubmishtah Veebeeshunah,* long ere you or I were born, that we this day should meet. Your face was described in those mystic pages as accurately as if a skilful painter had drawn your features, and doubtless destiny ordained this day for our meeting, that I might prevent the havoc you would otherwise have made on the chins and heads of misguided men. Shave but another man, and you will surely die." The terrified *n,hae,* or barber, put up his razors and quitted the house, leaving me sitting and mumbling nonsense in the middle of the room. Thousands of people came in all directions to look at me. Even Brahmins were confounded. At last I heard a cry of " Make way !" and the barber entered, bringing with him a jummahdar of police. I felt alarmed, fearing my schemes would get me another flogging, instead of heaping riches and honours upon me. The jummahdar, however, to my great joy, made me a profound bow, and begged me to accompany him to his master's office, he having heard of my arrival, and having a matter of great difficulty in his hands, which required my skill to explain. " Friend," I replied, " let thy master come himself; I rise for no hireling." Away went the jummahdar, and soon returned with Habeshee Kotwall himself in a splendid palanquin, with trumpeters, sword-bearers, and *chobdars,*[2] running before him. The air resounded with the vociferations of " Make way for the eater of mountains and the swallower of rivers—the mighty and merciful Habeshee Kotwall, Buchardar !" I could scarcely refrain from laughing at the last epithet bestowed on the most merciless of vagabonds. In came the most merciful, when, in a moment, awestruck at my appearance, he bent down to the earth, and begged me to exert my skill in the divine art of magic in an affair of great importance. I informed him the day was not propitious—but in vain; he

---

[1] Police-office.   [2] Bearers of silver sticks.

implored me to come to his house or to the chowry. "To the latter, if you please," said I. " I cannot go to your house ; you are an Abyssinian." A *palkee*[1] was got ready, and I was placed in it with great pomp and parade ; and Habeshee, not thinking how he was aiding the work of his own destruction, arrived at the office. I was led to the seat of honour, the magistrate's own gardee or seat. It was a carpet with a pillow to lean the back against. The office or chowry was crowded to excess. I felt alarmed at my own impudence ; and still more, lest one of the many eyes present should discover my manœuvres yet. I took an opportunity of slipping the bead necklace of Sagoonah into the covering of the pillow, and felt certain no one saw me. I then demanded the reason why I was summoned there. The Kotwall placed himself near me, and explained the case, taking care to hint that Trimbuckje Danglia had been seen at Sagoonah's house on the morning of her disappearance. " This indeed looks bad," said I, "as respects Trimbuckje. What am I to receive for my pains ?" The Kotwall said four thousand rupees were offered by the Peeshwa. "Give them to me," I said ; but he refused, yet had no objection to give me half, the remainder to follow when the business was done. I stipulated that I should be allowed to report to the Peeshwa personally the result of my incantations. The Kotwall agreed to this, and asked me where I would perform my magic rites. I informed him that any room in the chowry would do, provided I could be alone, and furnished with the necessary articles. I demanded a chafing-dish, charcoal, eggs, ghee, a living black-legged fowl, limes, and two needles, with hot and cold water, and some earthen pots. The collection of these articles caused some delay, and no little surprise, in the bazaar. I thought that a peep at the sun would help the mystery ; so, whilst the articles were procuring, I begged to be allowed to go into the open air. Room was made for me to pass ; and then, standing on the verandah, I made an observation of the sun through a bit of paper with holes in it. Now and then I shook my head in a grave and mysterious manner ; then I sud-

[1] Palanquin.

denly appeared to see something delightful, and muttered some sentences of gibberish. The populace appeared as if they could worship me, and numerous were the exclamations and praises of wisdom which saluted my ears. At length the articles I required came, and I went to work, killed the poor black-legged fowl and swallowed the raw eggs, burned the ghee and stuck two needles through the limes. I then gave notice that the business was complete, and begged to be allowed to proceed to the palace to report it to the Peeshwa.

As I left the Kotwall's office, the Habeshee took the opportunity of whispering in my ear, and asking if I had borne in mind the circumstances of Trimbuckje having been seen at Sagoonah's house on the day of the supposed murder. To mislead him the more, I said, "Trimbuckje is a sad man," shaking my head. The Habeshee's eyes sparkled with pleasure at this, and showed he enjoyed the idea of ruining his inveterate foe. A numerous suite prepared to accompany me to the palace, and we sallied forth in great pomp. Arrived at the royal residence, the Habeshee descried his enemy Trimbuckje, and exclaimed in his hearing, "Now let the guilty tremble!" Trimbuckje grinned a horrible smile, but did not deign to utter a word.

The Peeshwa, after some little delay, summoned me to his closet, and having bowed seven times, he ordered me to be seated. His highness had commenced conversation, when a door, which I had just perceived, directly behind the Peeshwa, opened quickly, and was again quickly and cautiously closed. The shutting caused the Peeshwa to turn round his head, and ask "*Koun hùe?*" who is there? No answer was returned, and the Peeshwa arose, and, opening it, became satisfied no one listened. He desired me to report on my incantations, and truly inform him of the result. I could have wished for an hour's delay to collect myself, and summon resolution to relate the mysteries of my pretended conjuration. I had entered the closet with unshaken impudence, and, with unheard-of effontery, was perfectly ready to answer all questions, and tell as many lies as were needful, when the opening of that door unmanned me; for, before it closed, I caught the wrinkled visage of Gabbage Gousla, though it was but a hurried glance. I could not be deceived; such a face could not be forgotten when once seen. Conscious of the deceptive part I was acting, I concluded some counter-plot was laid for my ruin, and began to repent the crooked path I had taken to arrive at promotion. The idea of treachery on the part of Trimbuckje, or a discovery by Habeshee, placed me in such a state of tremor, that, instead of conducting myself like an arch-magician, I must have seemed an arrant fool. The Peeshwa was impatient at my long silence, and urged me to disclose the name of him who had murdered Sagoonah. "Ah !" I thought to myself, "that is the question; I must give an ambiguous answer." I therefore entered into a discourse on the science of magic, taking care to bring up frequently that, after the most diligent study during one's entire life, cases would occur wherein we erred; that magicians were sometimes deceived by the cunning of worldly men ; and the study of the art was considered in those days extremely precarious. Too much was expected from students, whose occasional failure was by capricious persons construed into wilful deception. This often placed the character, and even lives, of magicians in jeopardy. All this time I was weighing the policy, or otherwise, of ruining the Habeshee, and whether it would not be better to accuse Trimbuckje. I feared, however, that the latter would exculpate himself, and put me to death for the false imputation I had thrown upon him. I had no doubt Gabbage was listening at some crevice, probably deputed by Trimbuckje, who was naturally suspicious, and dreaded treachery on my part ; so that if I accused him, some counter-plot would be ready to work my ruin. Perhaps the visage of Gabbage was thrust upon me as a warning, to beware of my conduct as respected his employer. I every minute felt more perplexed. My joints weakened, and my limbs trembled under me ; my head was in a maze, and I perspired at every pore. So much was I agitated that the Peeshwa could not help seeing it, and asked me what was the matter. "Oh, your Highness !" said I, "the Habeshee knew this was an unpropitious day, for I told him so, but he insisted on my incantations being commenced, and these emotions are the result." "I tell you then," said the Peeshwa, "that if this is all the result of your labours, you may quake a little more, for by all the gods in the holy Védas, if you have made a dupe of me and the whole city, you shall be a clog for an elephant in half an hour, and this will effectually prevent your practising similar acts of deception again!" I said in answer, "Most high and mighty Prince, I have not practised any deception, neither dare I attempt a fraud on your wisdom, or brave your resentment; as well might the traveller fling himself into the jaws of the tiger, or the feeble mouse defy the indefatigable cat!" "Give a reply," said the Peeshwa; "who murdered Sagoonah? Trifle no longer, or I shall prove the more cunning magician of the two, and pronounce that you yourself did it." Not a moment was to be lost, and I summoned resolution to accuse Habeshee Kotwall in a very low tone of voice. "Wherefore," said the Peeshwa, "could you not have told me so an hour ago?" No answer could I make, but sat silent, in indescribable agony of mind and body.

The Peeshwa now said, "You assert that Habeshee Kotwall is the murderer; give us some proof, my friend, that what you say is true." "If your Majesty," I replied, "will send and seize Habeshee, in the first place, and then search his house and office, they will somewhere discover a bead-necklace, having a copper box or talisman suspended to it, containing a small piece of money. This was the property of the murdered girl, and may be recognised and sworn to by the aunt with whom she lived." "Where, or in what place will this be found?" said the Peeshwa. That I told him should be disclosed to the person whom his Highness deputed to make the search, but first the Kotwall must be seized, or he would escape.

The Peeshwa then rose, and demanded, opening the door, who waited in attendance? The officer of the body-guard appeared, and received orders to secure Habeshee; who was, as he well might be, utterly confounded. Instead of seeing the ruin of his enemy, he felt it fall upon himself. This was a reverse he little expected, and falling on the ground he uttered a deep mournful cry of anguish, which I confess pricked my conscience not a little.

The groans of poor Habeshee, though totally disregarded by his guards, were music to the ears of Trimbuckje Danglia. He gave me to understand by a wink, perfectly significant, that he had despatched a man to search the pillow. I attempted to give a nod of exultation in reply, but, from my dread and anxiety, could convey to him anything rather than the hope of success. Alarm was painted on his countenance, nor could he refrain from making through the crowd to come near me. Had I been really a magician, the first use I should have made of my art would have been to transport myself from this nest of villany. Trimbuckje having reached my elbow, whispered to me, " Beware how you deceive me!" and giving me no time to reply, mingled in the crowd. He had scarcely gone when the Peeshwa strutted by me, dressed in his durbar apparel, looking like a gaudy peacock. When sufficiently near to me, he also said, with a look of dreadful import, " Beware how you deceive me!" Never was real or pretended magician in a more awful predicament.

Time flew on, and the searchers of Habeshee's house did not return. I felt convinced some circumstances, which I could not foresee, occasioned this unexpected delay. At last I saw a man whisper something in the ear of Trimbuckje; who catching my eye, shook his head, by which I understood the officer had searched and found nothing—no necklace was forthcoming. When it was understood there had been a failure, the Habeshee party were rejoiced beyond measure, and vented curses on my head, styling me a vile impostor and murderer. The report was soon conveyed to the Peeshwa, who summoned me to his closet once more. " How dare you enter my palace to mock me?" said the enraged Peeshwa; " am I to be made the laughing-stock of the whole city? Did I not tell you to beware how you deceived me?" A crowd of persons were standing behind the Peeshwa, apparently enjoying my confusion. Not having a word to say for myself, I determined to confess the whole at once and throw myself on the Peeshwa's mercy.

I had just cleared my throat to begin a relation of the whole transaction, and all the circumstances of the murder, not fearing even Trimbuckje himself, when, on raising my eyes, I beheld the awe-inspiring visage of old Gabbage, thrust between the shoulders of two men who were behind the Peeshwa, and immediately in my front. I became speechless, and cast down my eyes, for the countenance of Gabbage seemed reading my innermost thoughts, and saying at the same time, " Do if you dare !" There was no resource, and I felt myself obliged to adhere to my first story. I therefore summoned courage to address the Peeshwa. "True it is, most puissant Prince, I have mistaken the spot where the proof was concealed, but you will remember I said this was an unpropitious day." "And so," interrupted the Peeshwa, "you shall find it. Guards, secure him. Ho ! there, let an elephant be in readiness; we will show the magician how to come to a decision without any long ambiguous harangues !" At this moment the Habeshee sent word, requesting he might be allowed to enter the presence. His request was granted, and in came the Abyssinian, who, after bowing to the earth seven times more than he would have done at any other moment, asserted his innocence of the murder, and ignorance of the person of the murdered, declaring I was an impostor of the worst character; that I had agreed to implicate Trimbuckje Danglia at first for a bribe of five hundred rupees; "but," continued the Habeshee, " I scorned to take so great an advantage of my enemy, and refused to give this pretended magician the money. I told him he might discover the guilty person, for him alone was our royal master anxious to punish." This barefaced lie of the Habeshee came upon me like a thunder-clap. Whatever hopes I had before entertained of pardon, they were after this utterly annihilated. Rousing myself, I exclaimed—" It is false ; the Habeshee himself hinted his wish to me that I should accuse Trimbuckje, nor did I seek any reward beyond that offered by your Highness."

An officer now whispered to Trimbuckje, and he again to the Peeshwa, when the latter addressed Habeshee as follows : "Habeshee Kotwall, in consideration of your military services during the war, I promoted you to a situation in this city, with a salary and emoluments sufficient not only to maintain you, but to enable you to accumulate wealth. You would then have supported my dignity, and have risen to still higher honours. I regret to say that your passion for acquiring money has been so great as to banish from your mind the regard which you ought to have had for my service. My subjects have been abused, trampled upon, and robbed even within the verge of the judgment-seat of the court built for their protection. Too true it is that I have now before me petitions from several hundred families which you have plundered and reduced to beggary. Your principal harvest seems to have been the ornaments of unoffending women, whom you have **forced into holes below your office and** stripped of their jewels.[1] Now it is too certain these accusations are founded in truth ; nor can you say that they arise from or out of the enmity unfortunately in existence between you and Trimbuckje Danglia. I say these charges are true : for though the articles we searched **for** in your house and office are not discovered, yet we have found chests containing gold ornaments and pearls, too valuable for you **to** have purchased in a fair and honest manner. In **the present** affair **you have** borne an active part, although none of the murdered girl's jewels were found upon you or in your house. There is a probability the bead-necklace may yet be discovered ; and before I decide on the fate of the magician, I shall wait an hour. Whether it be forthcoming or not, the sentence I shall pass upon you is, that for your unheard-of cruelties and robberies you be trampled to death by an elephant. To prevent your insulting me by a **reply** or extenuation, I command that your tongue be cut out on the spot."

This sentence **was no** sooner pronounced than executed. Habeshee was deprived of **his** lying tongue, and I trembled so much for mine that the bystanders could scarcely refrain from laughter.

It was arranged that one elephant should do the business for both of us, and the execution of Habeshee was delayed until the **expiration of the hour** allotted for the discovery of the necklace ; during which time, poor Habeshee lay groaning and bleeding

---

[1] There *was* such a character as Habeshee Kotwall in the East, who committed dreadful crimes.

like a half-sacrificed sheep at the butcher's stall. I must confess that when he made so bad a use of his tongue as to attempt an accusation against me of ruining Trimbuckje, I was not much grieved at hearing the order given to deprive him of it. He could not now utter a word, should the necklace be forthcoming; for he might have urged the possibility, as well as the probability, of my having concealed the trinket in his pillow for my own views. It was therefore fortunate for me he could not speak; nor had he (and what fallen courtier ever has?) one friend to speak in his behalf.

The hour had now nearly expired, when a noise on the stair-case drew my attention. "The necklace—the necklace!" was murmured around; and, to my great joy, I beheld Trimbuckje's messenger enter the room with the identical article. Sagoonah's aunt was in waiting, and we were again summoned before the Peeshwa. The aunt deposed to the necklace having been her niece's, as well as the talisman. The Peeshwa ordered the talisman to be opened—much against the aunt's will, who declared it would bring ill-luck and misfortune on her —— niece, she would have said; and then burst into tears. "She is dead," said the Peeshwa, "she can fear ill-luck no more; let it be opened." While this was going on, I sat a little more at my ease than I had done all the day before, and began a mysterious mumbling, to attract the attention of the bystanders. I drew circles on the ground with my fingers—cut one of them, and let three drops of blood fall on the copper talisman. Even the Peeshwa himself now wavered about opening it, and asked me if he should do so. I replied that, having sprinkled it with my blood, no harm could now result from such a step, and I would open it, if he gave me leave. He nodded assent. A gold rupee was discovered in it, and two grains of wheat wrapped in a scrap of paper, on which something was written,—this paper I concealed. I presented the two grains and the rupee. The Peeshwa desired to know how the necklace had been found at last. The officer of his guard came forward, and deposed that being commissioned to search the Habeshee's house, nothing was found there; and that he then proceeded to the chowry, and made the most minute inquiry respecting it. "At last I ordered all the household to be called, and explained to them that I was searching for a bead-necklace ; desiring, if any one of them had the same, to deliver it on pain of death. The deputy Fèrash bashee (carpet-spreader) came forward, and said he had the necklace, and could produce it ; that to-morrow being the festival of the *Til Sunkeraut*, he was ordered by the Kotwall to sweep or clean the chowry, and put on the best pillow-cases, and that he set about doing it the moment the Kotwall and magician were gone to the palace. In fitting the new case to the Habeshee's pillow, something fell to the ground : it was a bead-necklace, apparently of no value ; and considering his daughter would be pleased with it, he carried it home to her. On my application, he sent to her to deliver it up, which she did immediately, and it is the same I delivered to your Highness."

During the preceding account I sat puffed up with consequence, and begged permission to retire, having occasion to go into Cabul, and to set off the same night. The Peeshwa granted me leave to depart, though he seemed sorry he could find no ground for subjecting me to the same punishment as the Habeshee. I got away, however, as soon as I could, followed by a crowd of persons who looked upon me as a god. The aunt of Sagoonah wished to approach me ; and pushing through the crowd, fell at my feet, begging me to relate the particulars of the murder. I dared not undeceive her at this moment, and in public ; I therefore whispered her to meet me at nine o'clock at the Mottee Baugh, or pearl-garden : she assented, and I walked away, followed by the crowd. Where to go I knew not, but passing the barber's shop again, I thought I might as well sit there until the curiosity of the mob was over. "*Arry,*" said the poor shaver, "what again, in the name of Brahma, has brought you here?" Why *now*, I told him, I wanted to be shaved, as the sun had set, and no ill-luck could happen, unless he drew blood, when woe would befall us both. The barber now begged to be excused, saying his hand shook so violently he could not answer the giving a gash or two. This, instead of dispersing, but increased the crowd—all begging their neighbours to come and see

the barber shave the conjuror.   As I really needed shaving,
I repented of having so much alarmed the barber, and conceived
that if we could but disperse the crowd, the barber might still
operate without shedding blood.   I called out, "The consequences of drawing blood will be fatal to those who witness it, as
well as to myself and the operator.   Beware therefore my
friends!"   The rascals heeded me not at all, and there we sat—
the barber trembling in one corner, and I half dying with re-
pressed laughter in the middle of the shop.   The greatest
annoyance to me was, that it approached to eight o'clock, and I
was to meet Sagoonah's aunt at nine.   There seemed no hope of
the mob leaving the shop-door until gun-firing, which would
disperse them.   I therefore called to the barber, who came up to
me trembling.   I whispered to him, and inquired if he could direct
me any back way to get off, and I would not compel him to
shave me; that I could manage until the next day, and promised
not to revisit his dwelling again.   He told me that if I went into
his back-yard and clambered over a low wall, I should find myself in a lane which would take me into or out of the city, whichever way I was inclined to turn.   I followed his advice, he telling
the crowd I should come back again.   Heartily rejoiced at finding
myself at liberty and alone, I threw off my 'dress and tore it in
pieces, and also my cap, muffling my head up in my shawl; the
clock struck nine,[1] and I hastened to the garden.

[1] An English clock oa the top of the Peeshwa's palace.

CHAPTER X.

THE dwelling-house of Habeshee lay in my way to the spot fixed upon for meeting the aunt of Sagoonah. As I passed, I heard moaning and lamentation, from which I judged that the dreadful sentence pronounced upon him had been carried into execution. I hurried past the scene of woe, and proceeded to the garden. The woman awaited my coming. I took her towards the tank, and sitting down, informed her that her niece lived, and was recovering. I explained how I had found her, but did not inform her who was really the author of the outrage. Promising to be guided by me in the means to be adopted for shielding Sagoonah from the power of the Peeshwa and the villany of Trimbuckje Danglia, she was still most anxious to see her niece. I consented to their having an interview. She was overjoyed at the prospect of meeting her again, having concluded her dead, and she arose and followed me. We went towards the suburbs, and had just cleared the city when the night-gun was fired. We quickened our steps, and reached the cultivator's cottage. Sagoonah was much pleased at my return, fearing something might have happened by my long absence. When I informed her who was my companion, the poor girl burst into tears, calling me her preserver. She clasped her aunt's neck, exclaiming, "My beloved *mousee* (aunt), do I once more behold thee?"

Being weak for want of food, I begged the coombie, or cultivator, to give me some bread and rice, and I enjoyed the homely fare with a keen relish. The lovely Sagoonah offered me water which had been just fetched from the well, and that with a modesty of expression that charmed me beyond measure. She asked who had been discovered to be the guilty men in making the attack upon her. I told her, the Habeshee. She said, she had imagined it must be Trimbuckje; and I reasserted that the Habeshee was the person who caused her to be waylaid, but at the same time impressed upon her mind the necessity of concealment, for fear of the Peeshwa. I told both Sagoonah and her aunt that I expected to get a situation in Kandeish, and that the best way would be for them both to accompany me. I promised to protect them from all danger as far as I could, and that they had better pass for my mother and sister, as discovery would thereby be nearly impossible. The eyes of the beautiful Sagoonah showed how much she was pleased at my proposal, and told her acquiesence in the justice of what I said. Her aunt alone remained to be consulted, before the resolution was acted upon. In the morning we consulted the aunt, who approved the plan; and we agreed to set out as soon as I had secured my promised place.

I now went again to the city. I cut my mustaches close, and wore a white turban, intending to get shaved on my way. By doing this, wearing short breeches and a common white coat, I hoped to prevent any recognition of my late character of magician. While I was changing my coat, I found the slip of paper which had been concealed in Sagoonah's talisman. Neither Sagoonah nor her aunt could give me any clue to the mystery, for neither could read. The sentence seemed to me in a singular character. Neither aunt nor niece were aware that the talisman had contained anything of the kind. The former, however, recollected that the father of Sagoonah had desired it should not be opened until she attained her twentieth year. I took great care of it, determining to get some learned Brahmin to decipher the sentence, which was very short, and badly written. Taking leave of my fair friends, I walked to Poona, and passed into the city by the wooden bridge.

The first place I entered was a barber's shop; and, inquiring the news, the barber began to tell me all he had heard about the magician, to which he added a thousand exaggerations. He declared ten murdered women had been found in the cellar of Habeshee's house, and that the magician had smelt them when taken to the chowry; that the people thought the magician little less than a god, who had visited the city to rid them of so great a tyrant. He told me the particulars of Habeshee's execution; adding, that before he was tied to the elephant's foot, he made a full confession of his enormities. I was much amused at this addition, when I remembered the poor wretch had lost his tongue, and could not, therefore, conveniently make either confessions or denials. I pretended ignorance, however, of the whole transaction, paid my two pice, and departed. Trimbuckje was at home, and gave me an audience. "Indeed, my friend," said he, "you were nearly ruined by your plan of the necklace. Had it not been found, the Peeshwa would have condemned you to die." "But now we have succeeded," I said, "I am come to claim my reward. Money I do not want, but some situation by which I may obtain an honest livelihood." "Honest!" said Trimbuckje, with a grin. "Well, would you wish to be employed here, or at a distance?" I told him, for some time at a distance; but that I should hold myself in readiness to obey his instructions, whenever he should require them. He assented directly, and wrote a letter, to which he affixed his seal, desiring me to deliver it to Venkut Rao Bhugrunt, his collector of revenues on his estate at Kandeish. It conveyed the order for me to be enrolled as a sub-collector, telling me he could not then do more for me. In all probability, Trimbuckje, knowing how well I was informed of his villanies, was on that account more punctual in the fulfilment of his promise than he would have been otherwise.

My next step was to search out some learned priest to decipher the mysterious scrap of paper found in the necklace. I was informed that there lived in Poona a celebrated ascetic, renowned for his austerity and learning: his name was Purrum Teeshoo, Nowhauthge M,hadeo. I found him out, and paid him a visit at his residence. He was reclining on a bed of iron spikes reading a book, and returned my salutation, seeming perfectly at his ease —indeed as much so as I should have felt on the softest cushions. I showed him the paper, begging him to decipher and explain the writing to me. He took it and mumbled over the words several times. He then said, "It is Pudiha, or verse, and the language is pure Sanscrit;" adding, "Where did you get it?" This was a question for which I was not prepared; I feared either to deceive him, or refuse to give any account of it. At last I said I had found it in a copper talisman. "Aye," said he, "it may be so, for it mentions a talisman;" and repeated these words, which explained the meaning as follows:—

"Let her who doth this Taweey[1] wear,
Guard against the Gossein's snare."

I paid the learned personage five rupees, and took my paper, pretending to be disappointed. I informed him I had hoped it would have shown me where to discover some hidden treasure. He smiled, and giving me his blessing, I departed, pondering in my mind what could be the meaning of the warning, who wrote it, and why Sagoonah should be persecuted by a Gossein? It was indeed true that she had fallen into the hands of my friend Gabbage, and but for me would have breathed her last; but this could hardly be the object and final intent of the warning. I thought it my duty, however, to put her upon her guard against those wandering miscreants, but still I feared there was much evil in reserve for her from the hands of these men. At length I reached the cottage of the cultivator, and explained to the females the meaning of the words on the paper. They were much alarmed, and fear showed itself in their faces. The aunt said Sagoonah's father was ruined by these wretches, who had vowed to persecute his race; but until the attack on Sagoonah in Poona, they had not molested her. The threat which preyed upon Sagoonah's father, and brought him to the grave, had been too little heeded by his relatives. "What cause of offence," said I to the aunt, "could your brother have given the Gossein?" She replied, "He brought him to justice for some crime, and the Gossein was punished, on which he made the vow. Sagoonah was about three years old when her father brought her home the necklace and talisman, given him, as he said, by a dear friend for his daughter; desiring the talisman should not be opened until she had attained

---

[1] Talisman.

her twentieth year. The talisman has been opened, and she is but sixteen—I fear for the consequences." I now endeavoured to convince her, that as Sagoonah did not voluntarily open it, no blame could on that account fall upon her, and begged her to think nothing more about it.

I now proposed that we should set out on our journey to Kandeish, as I had secured a situation, and that we should not delay beyond the following morning. No opposition being made to the measure on their parts, I executed the necessary arrangements for travelling. I hired a bullock and ponies, and went to rest dreaming of happiness and Sagoonah; before day-break we quitted the cultivator's. Sagoonah and her aunt were mounted on *tattoos* or ponies, but I preferred walking until the sun had risen. The bullock accompanied the cavalcade laden principally with the driver's goods, having nothing of consequence of our own with us. I had previously made a long bag into which I thrust my rupees, and this was all the baggage with which I was personally troubled. The owner of the ponies and bullock walked with me, and seemed very anxious to enter into conversation. He asked several impertinent questions, and once or twice it struck me I remembered his voice, but could not bring at once to my recollection where—so much was my mind occupied with plans and views for the future. He evidently knew me, and his manner and my taciturnity made me very distant with the fellow: my reply in scanty monosyllables did not, how-however, seem to damp his eagerness for conversation. He jabbered away incessantly. At length, after praising his cattle, he said, " Do you know, I met with a very curious adventure not long ago?" " Indeed!" I replied drily. " Aye," he resumed, " and one I have often laughed at since, too, over and over again. As I was driving my asses close to the village of——." He need have said no more to recall him to my recollection, even in the strongest fit of absence. I at once knew my companion, and accounted for his impertinent curiosity. It was the very ass-driver through whose means I lost my treasure, after my escape from the fort. I now made no attempt to interrupt him in a tale that so deeply concerned me ; but was subjected to the mortification of listening to the wretch calling me all the opprobrious names, and they were not a few, that his native tongue admits of. He concluded by observing, "I knew the rascal was after something he wished to conceal from me, so I stuck to him like a leech." Here he burst into a hearty laugh at his own penetration and at the embarrassments of the poor wounded scoundrel. He clapped his hands in exultation, when he told me how the sepoys seized the villain, as he called him. He dwelt long upon the story, drawling it out to add to my mortification. I interrupted him by asking if he knew why the traveller wished to be left alone? He said, because upon seeing him come with his arms tied into Poona, he had questioned one of the sepoys respecting the vagabond, and the men informed him that he had money concealed under the mango tree, and that the soldiers had dug it up and taken possession of it. "At this," continued the ass driver, "I laughed immoderately, because, had the greedy miser confided the secret to me, I would have given him every assistance, trusting to his liberality for a reward. Instead of this he, in shaking off the cat, fell under the paw of the tiger. Was not the fellow rightly served? Was he not a covetous, greedy, mean, and ungrateful knave, after the assistance I had given him?" I replied he was certainly an over-cautious man, and inquired what became of him afterwards; the ass-driver answered, "He was flogged in Poona, and expelled as a vagabond, and I have heard nothing of him since. I should like to set my eyes upon him again to joke him for his cursed avarice." I said that perhaps he would not put up with such jokes and insults; he might carry a dagger in his girdle. "Then," said the driver, "I should be very careful to hold my tongue and make him a low bow—one would not be spitted for a joke, however good it may be." I told him he would in doing thus act very wisely.

To avoid further annoyance from this impertinent fellow, I mounted my tattoo and joined the women, begging them to keep their faces well muffled up. This caution was indeed highly necessary, for soon the troublesome driver came alongside of us riding on his bullock. He began to peep and peer at the females, and try to draw them into conversation. I here thought it time to put in a word, and bid him keep in the rear, his proper place, and when we wanted him we would call him. *Nuthoo Bhae nuthoo majee ghirrut teen tattoo*, or "what a great man I am !" he exclaimed, and sullenly obeyed my order. I determined, the moment we arrived at Ahmednugur, to discharge the insolent fellow and hire fresh cattle. I kept my intention to myself, and we jogged on quietly, the driver singing as he went, and often, for want of some one else to talk to, conversing with his bullock, which he called *heera*.[1] The aunt now and then spoke to her niece to quicken her pace, saying, "*chul pooree chul*," or, "walk on, hasten, my girl." On hearing which, the driver sang, "*Ding pooree ding kuppal ā che bing, bing gela p,hootoon pooree gela oothoon.*" Sagoonah would sometimes say, "*arry mousee !*" (oh, my aunt !) Upon which the impudent driver, who had a scrap of song—a cant saying ready for every occasion, would sing out, "*Mousee tooptousee, tooput, purlee arle mousee.*" This was as much as to let us know he heard all, and was fully aware of the relation-ship of one of the women with the other, and then he would chant the well-known song of "*Chota, Chota, Muchulee.*"

At last the aunt saying to me, *O Bĕta !* (oh, my son), the fellow vociferated, "*Ramje he bĕta dra so b,hee Musselman ka sheeree-pooree k,hata n,hue maungtee tokra nanka ;*" the meaning of which is, that a Hindoo woman was permitted by the god Ramje to bear a son, but it was a Musselman's, and the proof of its being so was, its refusing to eat the common *sheeree-pooree*, or Hindoo pap, and calling out for a lump of bread. This was extremely insulting to me, as it was intended to throw a slur on my caste ; indeed, he might as well have told me I was only half and half bred, neither Hindoo nor Mohammedan. I became irritated at the insinuation, and riding up to him, gave him a blow which knocked him off his bullock. He returned it, and this exasperated me beyond measure. At it we went, each pulling off the other's turbans, and belabouring each other like two demons; the women were screaming all the time as if murder was taking place. At length I threw the rascal down, and kneeling on his breast, bade him ask my pardon, which he

[1] Diamond.

did very reluctantly. Matters becoming more placable after this, we continued our journey, the ass-driver keeping a profound silence. I now determined to send him about his business at Seroor instead of Nugur, and pushed on for that place, where we arrived late in the evening. Seroor was a cantonment of the English; I was therefore under no apprehension of a renewal of our combat. I now proceeded to a house appointed for travellers, where I left the females, and then went to the Kotwall of the place, begging him to procure fresh cattle for us, to be in readiness early on the following morning. He gave me a promise of them, and I was quitting him after thanking him for his attention to my request, when up came the Poona ass-driver, bleeding at the nose, his coat torn, and turban off, and bellowing aloud for justice. He complained of having been treated with great barbarity. I inwardly rejoiced to see the fellow had been chastised well, as I supposed, by some one who had less mercy on him than myself. The Kotwall demanded who had beaten him, and to my astonishment he pointed me out as the person, and declared it was only because he sang and for nothing else, and that the two good-for-nothing women with me fell upon him also and beat him as he then was. *"Array, array basree,"* exclaimed he, or, "what will become of me? I shall die!" The fellow made me stare with surprise at this base fabrication. I proceeded to explain the truth to the Kotwall; stated how the fellow had insulted me, and how we scuffled a little; but assured him no blood was drawn, and that it happened two hours previous to our entering Seroor. I added that it was on account of the fellow's insolence I had determined to hire fresh cattle from Seroor. The Kotwall asked where I was going: I told him to Kandeish; that I was in the service of Trimbuckje Danglia, and the bearer of letters to his head collector or *T,hu seeldam* there. On hearing this the Kotwall treated me with the utmost politeness. When the ass-driver saw this, and that he was likely to be sent away as he came, or punished for his falsehoods, he cried out, "It's all false, your honour; that fellow is no more in the service of Trimbuckje Danglia than I am: he is a runaway prisoner escaped from the English. I will swear I saw him, not a month ago, in charge of the English sepoys, with his arms tied behind him. I tell the truth, and would advise your honour to deliver him over to the English general here; who will reward both you and me for so doing." I was now utterly confounded, as I fancied the fellow had not recognised me. Had I entertained a contrary idea, I should not have quietly put up with his insolence so long as I did. The Kotwall bade me give an account of myself, because, if what the fellow said was true, he must deliver me to the English. I assured him it was true, but that I did not feel myself obliged to give an account of the manner in which I became the prisoner of the English; but assured him I had been honourably released, and that I should have no objection to explain the transaction to the general himself. Upon this the Kotwall declared it was his duty to report the case to the bazaar-master, and let him act as he thought fit. I was helpless, and sat down in the chowry guarded by several peons, while the Kotwall went to the bazaar-master.

After some time the Kotwall returned, saying, "The bazaar-master was gone out to dine, and therefore nothing could be done before morning." This was an unexpected mortification, hoping to be well on my journey before the sun rose. I was alarmed too for Sagoonah and her aunt, and the anxiety they must suffer in my long absence. I cursed the malevolent ass-driver a hundred times, lamenting the ill-fortune that had thrown me a second time in his way, and a second time brought me into trouble. Patience was now my only remedy. I requested one of my guards to send a messenger to the place where I had left Sagoonah, to inform her I should be detained, but would meet her in the morning. The man having promised to send the foregoing message, I felt more at rest. The driver petitioned to be allowed to go at large: which was granted him upon getting a banian to be bound for his appearance the following morning. The Kotwall retired to his dwelling, and I was left well guarded at his office. The night seemed dreadfully long, and, though fatigued by my journey, I could not get an hour's sleep. The morning at length arrived. Hour after hour passed away, and still the Kotwall did not appear. I was out of patience, restless, and disquieted. When ten o'clock arrived the Kotwall made his appearance, and desired me to accompany him to the police-master's house. The driver was in waiting to prefer his charge. On the accusation being made and the ass-driver's examination concluded, I was called upon to make my statement. I did not deny the fact of having been in the custody of the English, and professed my readiness to explain every particular to the general. The police-master advised me to make the explanation to them, because, if satisfactory, there would be no occasion for troubling the general on the subject. I begged that the ass-driver might not in that case be present, as I did not wish all the world to know my private history and misfortunes. My request being complied with, I related all the circumstances that befell me at the English fort, with my escape and capture, and my release by the officer under orders from his superiors. The police-master laughed heartily at the obstinate perversity of the ass-driver, and the affair at the fort with Jane Bebee. He assured me he had heard all the particulars before from the officer who apprehended me, and was fully aware of the order having been given for my release.

My mind was now considerably eased of its fears of further delay. I asked to be allowed to prosecute my journey: the police-master consented, and ordered me to be set at liberty immediately. I then proceeded to the *durhm sallah*, or place where travellers put up, and where I had left the two females. As I went along, I began to think I was the most unfortunate person in existence; for that I never proceeded twenty miles, east, west, north, or south, without some unpleasant adventure— I seemed born to misfortune. I finally consoled myself with the hope of better times, and anticipated a quiet, uninterrupted journey for the rest of the way I had to go. On reaching the durhm sallah, I saw no one but an old Mohammedan, smoking his hoo-kah in a corner. I of course concluded that Sagoonah and her aunt would be found inside the building. I went in, and looked around, but could get no tidings of the females: I enquired, but they were not to be found. I returned to the Musselman, and asked if he had seen two females leave the place. He replied in the negative. I was, indeed, at a loss to comprehend the meaning of their mysterious disappearance. I sallied forth to the bazaar, making inquiries of all I met respecting them, but without success; not a soul could give me any information that might serve as a clue to discover my fair friends. It began, at last, to strike me that some treachery had been practised towards them while I was in confinement. My suspicions were naturally directed to the malicious cattle-driver having practised some trick upon them. I proceeded again to the Kotwall, and begged him to apprehend that scoundrel, mentioning my suspicions. The Kotwall immediately sent in search of him; but he was nowhere to be found, both he, his bullocks, and tattoos, having moved off. I imagined he must have placed the women on his cattle, and taken the road either to Kandeish or back to Poona, deceiving them with assurances of acting by my orders. The Kotwall furnished me with some horse patrol, and parties were sent off in every direction. I headed one that proceeded on the road to Ahmednugur. As we were crossing the ferry of Gornuddi, I asked the ferryman whether two women had crossed the river early in the morning. He answered in the affirmative, "very early," and told me that two men were with them, one of whom was a gossein. "A gossein!" thought I; "then all is lost." The boatmen told me they went on the Nugur road, and that they were on foot. I pushed forwards with my party till we came to a village, where I summoned the potail or head man, and inquired if two men, one of them a gossein, and two women, had gone that way? He replied, "No;" but that a gossein had come there very early, badly wounded. He related that he had been waylaid by robbers, but he was ignorant which way the gossein had gone afterwards.

I now felt convinced that the women were somewhere in the neighbourhood, and begged him to let me have some villagers to search the fields and ravines. He immediately complied: and, with six sturdy coombies, or cultivators, I set out in search: they were well armed with sticks and staves. After ranging the country for some time without success, on passing through a deep ravine, I fancied I heard moaning and cries of distress; my followers heard the same sounds, and we pushed forward to the point from whence they seemed to come. At the end of the ravine was a cave, from whence the cries issued; and what was my concern on entering it, to behold Sagoonah tied to a stake, together with her aunt, unable to move or extricate themselves! On seeing me, Sagoonah uttered a scream of joy. We speedily liberated them, and, bringing them water, recovered them from the effects of their fear and suffering, so much as to enable them to tell me by what means they came into that situation, and how they were left in such singular and painful circumstances. The aunt said, "We were greatly alarmed at your long absence; and I proposed going in search of you, when a peon from the Kotwall's chowry came to us, and told us you had sent him to say you were detained, but would be with us in the morning. We were quite satisfied on receiving this information, and ate our supper without suspicion of the mischief brooding over us. At four in the morning the cattle driver, and another person muffled up, so that we could not observe of what caste he was, came to us. The driver said, 'Mother, your son has sent me to tell you he cannot procure fresh cattle, and you must therefore travel on with mine. He desires that, to save time, you will cross the ferry, and he will meet you on the other side of the river.' I inquired who the person was that accompanied him? He told me only a *choomar*, [1] to show him the way, as it was not daylight, and he was afraid he should lose his road. Not suspecting any trick, we got ready; and, packing up our pots and pans, we accompanied the driver and his companion over the ferry. The latter was still muffled up, so as to prevent any observation of his features; he never spoke, and I should have judged him a young man. When we had crossed the ferry, I remarked there were neither tattoos nor bullocks with us; but the driver said we should find them at the village, about a coss distant. I thought this rather strange. We still walked on, but no village came in view; and I was hesitating what to do, when Sagoonah came up to me, and whispered that the driver's companion was a gossein. I immediately cried out 'Treachery!' and said I would not proceed one step further till my son came up. The driver then seized me in his arms, whilst the gossein did the same by Sagoonah; and they carried us into

[1] A low-caste man employed as a guide.

the sugar-cane fields, and from thence to this cave. We screamed and called in vain : it was too early an hour for us to be heard by any travellers. The driver then produced cords, and, tying us to this stake, began to plunder me of my ornaments. An altercation now took place between the two robbers about the plunder, the gossein saying the booty was his ; but if the driver would wait until we should arrive at the end of our journey (not mentioning the place) he should be rewarded. The driver said he was too old to be imposed upon by a gossein, and insisted on his reward upon the spot. The gossein refused to allow him even a copper pot. The driver then proceeded to take all the goods he could lay his hands upon, and snatched at my necklace. Upon this the gossein fell upon him ; but the driver escaped, and threw a copper pot at the head of his antagonist, which cut him over the temple, and brought a torrent of blood. 'Woe be to thee that hast shed my blood !' cried the gossein. 'Aye, aye,' replied the driver, 'that nonsense may do very well in Poona, my friend, but not here—here we are but man and man. If you do not grant me all I ask, I will draw more of your precious blood ; for I know you mean to cheat me !' Then unsheathing a dagger he plunged it into the gossein's side, who fell, as I thought, lifeless. We screamed and shrieked aloud, whilst the driver packed up our baggage, tore off my ornaments one by one, and finally decamped. The gossein recovered in a little time, and found he could lose his sacred blood without dying. He at length got up, holding his side, which he tied round with a cloth, and walked away, saying, 'I go to a *vyd* or doctor, and shall be with you again in a few hours.' On his departure we continued to scream as loud as we could, but were nearly exhausted when you came to our assistance."

It appeared to me, from this account, that the driver had effected all this villany between the hours of four and ten in the morning, and had had the audacity to appear quite cool and collected at the police-master's to bear witness against me, hoping to revenge himself upon me most effectually—though he was a little out in his calculations ; and when I was set at liberty, he lost no time in absconding.

CHAPTER XI.

THE impression produced in my mind by the events detailed in the last chapter was, that the gossein had plans in view which were by no means developed. The seizure of a few paltry gold ornaments, or the pots and pans of the women, were not objects of sufficient account to interest him so deeply; he must have been the agent of some other person at a distance, who had employed him there, and to whom he would have conducted his prisoners. Who this was it was not easy to determine; but it became us to lose no time in returning to Seroor. Upon our way back, while making inquiries at the village, we learned that the gossein had again made his appearance; but upon hearing that we had been there, and had pursued the track leading to the cave, he had taken himself off, no one knew whither. I was angry with the potail for not detaining him : he urged in his defence, that he had no orders to do so. It might have been expected that, knowing we were in pursuit of the fellow, he would have acted on his own discretion ; but the fact was, the potail was awed by the sanctity of the gossein's character, and had no inclination to get into trouble on my account.

We reached Seroor at last, where it became necessary to rest that night. I first secured cattle, and then purchased a good two-edged sword and a brace of English pistols, which I well loaded, as I was determined to resist, to the last drop of my blood, any persons who molested us during our future progress. Thus armed, we left Seroor the next day, and reached Ahmednugur, without experiencing any interruption, either from the insolence of cattle-drivers, or the intrusion of gosseins. Remaining the night at Ahmednugur, we started the following morning for Kandeish. No event worth recording happened, until we were within an easy march of the place of our destination. The distance from Nugur to Kandeish being too great for us to make one march of it, we proceeded as far as we could, and halted—proposing to start the following morning, and thus terminate our journey. We stopped for the night at a village surrounded with trees, which gave it an aspect peculiarly retired and pleasing. Finding the carriage of my pistols about my person inconvenient, and not apprehending danger, as we were within ten coss of our final destination, I unloaded them, and gave them into the charge of the cattle-driver. We slept sound at the village till the chirping of birds awoke me, by which I concluded that it was daybreak, and therefore called to my fair companions, and to the driver, requesting them to get ready for travelling. Sagoonah hereupon observed that the night appeared very short; and but for the chirping of the birds, she could not have believed it to be already morning.

We very soon put ourselves in order for starting; and though it appeared unaccountably dark, we sallied forth from the village. It seemed as if the morning was strangely dilatory in making its appearance. Both Sagoonah and her aunt yawned, and were not at all refreshed with the sleep they had taken. I began, before we had got a coss from the village, to think of returning, and was opening my lips to propose it, when suddenly six men started from a thicket, and surrounded us so suddenly, that I had no time to draw my sword. The women screamed, and were terrified to death, and the driver fell flat on his face, begging that his life might be spared. The robbers soon got possession of my sword, and we now remained entirely at their mercy. Too late I repented bitterly the not having reloaded my pistols; but repentance was useless. They could take nothing from the women, who had been pretty well plundered by the gossein and his accomplice; but from me they carried away my long bag of rupees, being all I was worth in the world. Having got what I possessed, they next attacked the driver, who had only a pair of silver

H

bangles, and these they forced off his hands with such violence as to lacerate them terribly. Next they stole the bells from the neck of the bullock, and the driver's coat and shoes, which with my sword and pistols comprised everything we had worth taking; they then left us. We now returned again to the village. There was no appearance of daylight, though half an hour had elapsed since we first started: this was unaccountable to us all. I began to fancy the world was about to be for ever darkened, or that some mystery I could not penetrate had enveloped us. On reaching the village, I went to the potail's house. He and all his household were snoring aloud, as if it had been the dead of night; it was with some difficulty I awoke him. At length he came to his door, and I told him I was a traveller who had put up at his village the preceding night, and that, on prosecuting my journey, I had been robbed of all my property. He replied, "If you will be so rash as to set out on such a journey in the dead of night, you must expect to be robbed." "Dead of night!" I exclaimed; "what do you mean?—I heard the birds chirping in the trees, and felt assured morning was about to dawn." "*Arry!*" exclaimed the potail; "you have fallen in with the *T,hugs!*" Upon inquiring who they were, he told me a class of persons in that part of the country who lived by plundering travellers; and, to avail themselves of the darkness of the night, the better to conceal themselves and carry on their predatory schemes with surer success, they mounted into the trees and shook the branches. The birds at roost on them, being thus disturbed, begin immediately to chirp, as if it were near daybreak; and thus travellers, who are resting for the night in villages or farm-dwellings, are too often deceived and fall an easy prey. I told the potail I was sorry he had not given me that piece of information the day before, and I should not have been a sufferer. He remarked that it was then the middle of the night, and it wanted full four *ghurries*[1] before the birds would chirp, provided the T,hugs did not again molest them before their time. I apologised for disturbing him further; but I could not help asking him if I had

---

[1] Half-hours or near about.

no chance of recovering my property, to which he replied, "There was none, and he would advise me to go to sleep, and think no more about my money, but consider that I was well off in escaping with life."

I now returned to where I had left the females, and explained how we had been deceived by the T,hugs. Sagoonah observed that she had felt herself very little refreshed by sleep when I awoke her to proceed on our journey; and, in short, we talked so much of the deception and robbery, that to sleep again was out of the question. It was very fortunate this circumstance occurred so near our ultimate place of destination, otherwise I should have had no money to defray the necessary expenses of the road. When the birds again chirped, and we were certain it was dawn, we set out. Sagoonah advised me to go to the potail again, and as an additional precaution, to ask him if it were now really day :—she said this with a sly and arch look, of which I could clearly comprehend the import. We continued our journey further unmolested, and reached Trimbuckje's village in safety. I hired a house for Sagoonah and her aunt, and took lodgings for myself some distance off, saying that they were my mother and sister. I then presented my credentials to Venkut Rao, who received me very courteously, and appointed me under-secretary, or deputy-carcoon, in the revenue department, which brought me in a salary of a hundred rupees a month. I resolved to live as quietly as possible, get into no disputes, and make no extortionate demands from the ryots or inhabitants, and particularly not to cheat my master.

Everything passed away very well for the first month. I determined to make proposals of marriage to Sagoonah, to whom I was a constant visitor. The aunt saw but one objection, which was, that her niece had been betrothed when a child to another person. I urged the certainty of that person's death, but in vain; the fear of uniting her niece with me, whilst the fate of him to whom she had been betrothed was undecided, was an insurmountable barrier to our hopes. I say our hopes, because the sparkling eyes of my loving Sagoonah told me, as well as words could have done, the interest I held in her affections. I obtained, both from her and her aunt, a solemn promise that her hand should never be given to another; and that if, in three years more, no tidings of him to whom she had been betrothed were heard, the advice of some holy Brahmin should be taken, or a Shastree consulted as to the propriety of our marriage. With this I was obliged to content myself, very sorely against my inclinations, but there was no help for it.

I did not neglect to keep my fair friends on their guard against the "gossein's snare." I requested them never to admit one of the tribe into their dwelling, and never to be outside their habitation after sunset. They were also, even in the day-time, to be accompanied by my peons. They scrupulously obeyed my instructions, and for six months everything passed away as smoothly as I could expect or desire. At length it became my turn to go out into the district, to collect the revenue from the cultivators and inhabitants; and as we had lived so securely for many months, I had almost lost every apprehension respecting their safety during my absence. I informed Sagoonah of the necessity for my departure, and renewed my cautions, begging them to be ever on the watch to guard against treachery. I moreover informed them that I should not send even my most confidential servant to them, and that if they were summoned at all in my name, they must apprehend mischief. In case I should wish them to meet me at any time, a messenger should bear the ring I then wore. By these precautions, I trusted I should guard against the snares of our enemies—my fair friends promising to use every additional precaution that offered itself for adding to their security. I then took my farewell, with a foreboding heart; I fancied it was the last time I should ever behold my Sagoonah. The separation came over my heart like a cold blight; and, in despite of reason and everything I could urge against it, I was overcome with a degree of melancholy that seemed closely allied to the despair of hopes for ever extinguished.

After I left Sagoonah, I appointed a trusty person to give me immediate information should he observe anything occur to excite suspicion during my absence, and let me know, at intervals, how things went on. The hour of departure arrived, and I set off on my duties. Nothing worthy of record took place in the district to which I went; and I had the satisfaction of hearing all remained right at home some days after I had been absent. One month only, however, had elapsed, when a special courier came to me from Trimbuckje Danglia, demanding my presence instantly on a most important affair. So urgent was the business, that I deemed it necessary to set out for Poona from the place where I received the summons, fearing a return home first would occasion too great a delay. I despatched a messenger to Sagoonah, informing her of my summons to Poona, its urgency, and directing her to keep up a communication with me, if needful. On reaching Poona, I found Trimbuckje and his household in great confusion, and making preparations for marching. What most confounded me was, to see his house guarded by English soldiers. I soon learned that Trimbuckje had, since I left Poona, and at the instigation of the Peeshwa, murdered a Shastree on his way from the court of Guikowar in Guzerat, to Badgerao; that the English had taken up the cause of justice, as the murdered man was proceeding on political affairs in which they were concerned; and that they insisted on Trimbuckje being delivered over to them, promising not to take his life. Trimbuckje denied the crime; but I found that though he did not murder the Shastree, yet he employed a gossein to do it for him (Gabbage, no doubt), and that the Peeshwa had promised Trimbuckje land and a jaghire for life. Trimbuckje promised a thousand rupees to a gossein, and the latter employed a third party for five hundred rupees, and this third party, a gang of villains, who did the business for two hundred.

The Peeshwa was obliged to accede to the demand of the English, and to deliver up his minister, promising to look after his affairs, and to lose no time and spare no pains in effecting his speedy liberation. I found I was summoned to accompany Trimbuckje to Thannah, a fort in the island of Salsette, near Bombay. I was told I had come at a fortunate moment, as the prisoner was to set off that night. I should not probably have been required, but many of the sycophants who had surrounded him in his prosperity, skulked from him on the setting of his glory, so that only two of his retainers, besides myself, remained. Gabbage was left in the Deccan to carry into effect both his master's schemes and his own. I hoped he would have accompanied us to Thannah, and felt great uneasiness at learning he was not to go. Trimbuckje was much pleased at seeing me, and appeared to be in good spirits, though, being guarded by two sepoys, he durst not be as communicative as he would perhaps have been otherwise. I assured him I was ready to attend him anywhere, and vowed everlasting fidelity to so kind a master. In the evening we set off for Thannah, proceeding at the slow rate of ten coss only in a day. The names of the other two attendants who accompanied Trimbuckje, were Nanna and Juntoo, both old and tried servants.

As we proceeded on our journey, I felt miserable at the thought of what would become of Sagoonah during my absence. I dared scarcely suffer the thought to cross my mind, and had great difficulty to console myself with the reflection, that, if I did not like Trimbuckje's service, which, as he might be a prisoner many years, did not promise to be either agreeable or profitable, I could at any time quit him, and proceed where fortune might lead me. We reached Thannah on the day fixed, and were delivered over to the commandant, an aged and worn-out man, but very affable and good-tempered. He placed European instead of native sentinels over us, at which we were much pleased, as we could enjoy uninterrupted conversation without being understood. I found Trimbuckje not without hopes of effecting his escape, and he frequently said he relied on my cunning to accomplish it. We were allowed to walk in the fort every evening, at which time the commandant's horses were led out to exercise. I should have previously mentioned that the old commandant had been removed, and was succeeded by a younger and more active man. His horses, then, they were that I saw led about the fort. One evening, being near his horse keeper, I recognised in him my old friend, Nursoo, the quondam bullock-driver who procured me the peon's situation at Bombay. The recognition was mutual, and productive of mutual surprise. I dared not appear too intimate with him, lest the European sentries should entertain suspicion, which might frustrate all my plans for effecting my master's liberation. Day after day I met and conversed with Nursoo, and I hinted to Trimbuckje my acquaintance with him. I said I hoped, through Nursoo's means, to accomplish our object, and set him at liberty. He was highly pleased, and vowed to reward me most liberally, if it could be accomplished.

I found, upon sounding Nursoo, that, like most Mahrattas, he was very ready to finger the gold; and without being understood by our guards, we comprehended each other pretty well before we separated. I saw that a better man than Nursoo could not have been discovered to assist in such a scheme, and I speedily reported to Trimbuckje how ready and necessary a tool he was. Trimbuckje praised my ingenuity highly, and rang the old changes of flattery and reward. I conceived it would be desirable, nay, absolutely necessary, to obtain the co-operation of our friends in the Deccan, and to apprise them as soon as possible of the chance we had of effecting Trimbuckje's escape. He himself thought it would be easy to send a letter through Nursoo, who must be trusted in the affair, and could easily find a messenger to carry it; and he determined to write at once, until I told him the very day and hour must be fixed, that his friends might be ready on the other side of the water with horses, or means of rapid conveyance. Trimbuckje acquiesced in my plan, which I contrived to mature with Nursoo, who agreed to serve us for five hundred rupees; two hundred and fifty to be paid down on the spot, and the rest when we reached the Deccan in safety. Nursoo was to accompany us. The two hundred and fifty rupees were raised and paid with difficulty, and a letter despatched to the Deccan to give notice to our friends.

The commencement of the rainy season had arrived, and Nursoo, as the nights were become dark, proposed that the attempt should be made then, and all was arranged accordingly. He told us we must be contented to remain behind, and that when our master was flown we should be released. I did not much like this part of the affair, but there was no help for it, and we acquiesced. Trimbuckje's bathing-place was upon the ground-floor, and he usually visited it every evening at seven o'clock. It was agreed that, instead of going directly into the bathing-place, he should strike into a passage on the left, where there was a low window through which he might get out. On the outside, Nursoo would take care to leave a long bamboo basket-work covering, composed of leaves used by the cultivators of rice during the rainy season. Trimbuckje was to divest himself of his clothes, and using this covering, walk out of the fort before the eight o'clock gun fired, after which time the gates would be shut. To prevent the immediate discovery of his escape, I was to arrest the attention of the sentinel (who never intruded into the bathing-room, but remained at the end of the passage) by singing some Hindostanee songs, and conversing with him in that language as well as I could. Nanna and Suntoo were both informed of the plot, and Trimbuckje duly initiated into the part he was to take. The day arrived, and Nursoo found means to let me know he had met with a man in the bazaar, named Gabbage, a gosscin, who drew him into conversation, and asked him his name. On hearing it was Nursoo, and that he was in the service of the commandant of the fort, he called him on one side, and told him all was in readiness on the other side of the water. Nursoo desired him to be on the look-out before eight o'clock, and then left him. That this was no invention of Nursoo's I knew by his mentioning the name of Gabbage. It gave me great pleasure, also, to find that he was not playing his tricks in another quarter, where I had reason to fear him more sensibly. Evening came, and Trimbuckje went to bathe as usual. The sentinel and myself were left at the end of the passage, and I amused him with some of the songs I had heard from the ass-driver, whom the reader cannot have forgotten, clapping my hands to mark time and to make a noise. In a little while the sentry began to be anxious respecting his prisoner. He said he thought he was unnecessarily long in the bath. I said it was not wonderful, for the morrow was a great holiday, and therefore it was necessary to perform long and frequent ablutions. The sentry, however, was not to be so deceived, and pushing past me into the bathing-room, he gave the alarm of his prisoner's escape. Presently came officers, soldiers, servants, and lights from all quarters; but in vain—the prisoner was off. We were examined and re-examined ; but we declared we were ignorant of the means by which Trimbuckje effected his escape ; we were alternately threatened and coaxed to no purpose. I was immovable ; but Nanna mentioned that Nursoo, the horse-keeper, was implicated. Parties were sent in search of him, and all the shops in the town were unsuccessfully ransacked to find him out. The prisoner had, indeed, effected his escape beyond the reach of pursuit. It was discovered that he must have actually passed the two sentries at the gate ; though when they were questioned they stated that no one but a poor black cultivator had gone that way, little dreaming that he was the prisoner in question. His covering was found not many yards from the gate of the fort. Farther search was then made along the ramparts ; and a rope fixed to a gun, and a pair of shoes were found, which were proved to belong to the horse-keeper. Still opinions were divided as to the manner in which Trimbuckje effected his escape ; for, on searching the ramparts the first time, no ropes or shoes were discovered ; so that whoever they belonged to must have lowered himself, and disappeared, just in time to get clear.

The circumstance of a state prisoner quietly walking out of the gate of a fort is almost an unparalleled incident, and certainly shows the great laxity of those on duty, or it could never have happened. There seemed to me to be a want of the following very simple precautions — namely, the providing every conveniency upon the same floor that the prisoner lodged ; having guards of an equal number of sepoys and Europeans, and causing the gates to be closed sooner as the evenings drew in, instead of doing so at a fixed hour. None of these precautions being observed, it is not wonderful plans should be laid, and a prisoner walk off over the same road that other persons travel. In the meantime, our scheme had succeeded to the fullest extent we could desire. Unfortunately, myself and the servants were still detained ; but Trimbuckje was safe. In two months afterwards we were released. But my profits in the transaction were yet to come, and I had a long journey to travel before I could expect my promised reward—a reward, indeed, such as I little apprehended.

When the orders were received, and we were at liberty—

Nanna, Suntoo, and myself—we found ourselves pretty nearly in the same circumstances of destitution, and agreed to travel in company: we, moreover, were all bound to the same destination at Kandeish. We had not long set out before we deviated from the high-road, and travelled amid jungles and ravines. Being on foot, our progress was but slow. It was still the rainy season, and we were frequently drenched to the skin before nightfall. One night Suntoo called me aside, and proposed that we should again deliver Trimbuckje into the hands of the English, as great rewards were offered for his apprehension. Though I spurned the idea of turning traitor, I dared not express my indignation, lest Suntoo should watch his opportunity, and get me out of the way, to prevent my informing against him. I therefore appeared to come completely into his plans, but urged several reasons for delay before we put our scheme into execution. I said, "In the first place, let us get all we can for delivering Trimbuckje from prison; this done, we may enter upon our plans for obtaining a reward of the English, and get him in again." "An excellent plan!" said the traitor; "let it be so; and mind we agree to share the profits between us."

We arrived at last within three days' march of Kandeish, and were plodding through jungles and ditches, when we heard the sound of horses' feet, and had soon cause for alarm, when a horde of Pindarees rushed towards us. In an instant they began searching our persons, and not finding any plunder, we indulged the hope we should be suffered to depart, when the chief of the party ordered our arms to be tied behind us, and bade us follow the troops. Resistance was vain, and Nanna, Suntoo, and myself, were led like three malefactors by one of the troopers. They now penetrated a very thick bamboo jungle. A dreadful storm arose while we were in the midst of it. The thunder rattled and roared over our heads, and the lightning, shedding for an instant an intense brightness, left the darkness between every flash tenfold more deep. Now it seemed to run along the furniture of the horses, or from rider to rider, hanging about their arms, and standing on their sword-points. One man was struck dead, and another lost his sight. The rain came down in torrents, and the violence of the wind caused the tall bamboos to bend almost to the earth, creaking and cracking with a singular and at times a mournful sound, which added to the impressive effect of the scene. There was but one path through the jungle; so that to mistake our way, even under these circumstances, was not easy. After a long exposure to the fury of the storm, we arrived at the gate of a low and ruined fortress. Our party hailed its inmates, and we were answered by the sound of a large *nugarrah*[1] placed over the gateway. The doors were quickly opened, and we entered into shelter. The horses of the troop were tied up in sheds projecting from the walls of the great court-yard, and we were led up a narrow staircase, until we reached a spacious apartment illuminated by a single iron lamp. A fire was immediately kindled, and supper got ready. The troop consisted of one hundred; fifty of these constituted the party with which we unfortunately fell in. To gratify the appetites of the band, a large wooden bowl filled with rice was brought in and placed in the midst, from whence all fed indiscriminately, and without ceremony in regard to caste. We were consequently obliged to wait until the Pindarees were all satisfied, and then we were told we might devour what they had left. To us, who were totally unaccustomed to such impure feeding, the idea of touching a dish from which an indiscriminate rabble had fed was inconceivably disgusting. We therefore refused the proffered honour, begging to be allowed a little raw rice, to cook as we pleased. Some of them made objections to our request, as being too indulgent. At last a young man, of a somewhat better appearance than the others, came up to me and said, "Be patient, and you shall have all you desire." I thought I remembered his person, though I had not a full view of his countenance when he spoke, and the chamber was gloomy and ill-lighted. I thanked him for his attention, and he went away promising to procure us the rice. On his return he had a lamp in his hand, and I saw, to my agreeable surprise, that it was my old inkstand-bearer, who had been of such service to me under my early protector, Sawunt Rao. He did not know me at first, nor did I give him to understand that I recognised him. He said that he and two of his comrades were appointed to guard

[1] Kettle-drum.

us, either within or without the fort. He told us we were expected to enlist in the troop and become Pindarees, and endeavoured to persuade us to agree, as a contrary course might perhaps cost us our lives.

"When you have eaten your rice," said the inkstand-bearer, "I will give you an account of the kind of life which I have led here." We occupied one corner of the great room, where we cooked and soon devoured our rice. The storm had abated without, though the rain continued to beat against the walls of the building. The horde seemed well supplied with liquor, which we learned was a prize lately seized from some bullock-drivers of Bombay. Orders were given by the chief of the troop that we should be secured in a small room, and that our three guards were to sleep in the apartment. We were accordingly conducted thither without delay by our guard, consisting of the inkstand-bearer and the two who attended us before. Both the latter seemed in bad health and low spirits. When we were placed in security, I made myself known to the inkstand-bearer. He was much surprised, and particularly anxious to know by what strange vicissitude of fortune I had become his prisoner. My history was too long, and contained too many important secrets for me to volunteer it in a public narration; but I assured my former friend that I would one day give it him in private. I asked who his companions were, and what made them appear so dejected. He replied he could give me no information respecting them; that they had joined the troop only a month before, and one of them had never been observed to smile, or even wear an aspect of cheerfulness. At this moment Suntoo exclaimed, "Were there ever such unfortunate beings as we are, to be caught and made Pindarees against our inclinations!" "Indeed," said Nanna, "we are the most unlucky men in the world!" "I will answer for it," exclaimed the inkstand-bearer, "your misfortunes fall far short of what I have endured!" "And mine," said one of our downcast guards, "exceed not only yours, but those of any other person in the world!" "Mine excepted," said our third guard. Here the inkstand-bearer observed, "that as each seemed to be of opinion that he himself was the greater sufferer from adversity, the best way would be for each in turn to relate his adventures, and let the prisoners be umpires to decide the question. To this no objection was made by any of the parties, the most low-spirited of the two Pindarees saying he had no objection; and the other, that he hoped all who heard him would take warning from the follies he should show he had partaken in, and be cautioned against the villany practised toward him by designing persons. It was now urged, that as we were fatigued by our long march, and the night was advanced, we should first endeavour to gain some repose, and postpone the relation of the stories till the next evening; and to this all assented.

The following morning was cloudy and gloomy. I could only learn that we were in the Chandor jungles; but in what part, I was unable to discover. The buildings appeared to be of great extent; but as all the windows looked inwards, round a court, I could see nothing of the distant country. During the day my friend the inkstand-bearer, whose name was Mahadeo, told me that Scindia was befriending the Pindaree-hordes, and that, in short, a grand blow would be struck, by which the English would be driven out of India; that to enable them to effect this object, it was necessary to increase their numbers; and it was ordered that all persons that were met with should be pressed into the service, and be made to assist in attacking the common enemy of their country. My friend told me, in addition, that I had better make the most of the situation I was in; that my duties would be trifling, and very profitable; that I should only be expected to rob and kill, eat and drink. "A very honourable employment!" I said to him in reply. "As to honourable," he rejoined, "what is the practice of all our Rajahs and Mahal-rajahs, Peeshwas, and Sottans? Do they not call themselves the fountains of all justice? —rob, cheat, tyrannise over, and murder whomsoever they please; and that, too, when there is no necessity for such acts, when they can do without them, and possess means of existing honestly? Are not we now acting under their immediate sanction? Must we not live somehow? and what does it signify how? Were you deputy-carcoon again, you would spare no exertions to fleece a poor coombie of a rupee in a sneaking, underhand manner; whereas now, you may go to work in a noble and manly style, more worthy the manners of the East!"

The arguments of my old friend, I must confess, seemed to me to be unanswerable; yet, as is always the case with persons so situated, I attempted a reply in extenuation, by observing how repugnant my feelings were to the committal of murder. "Indeed! my old master," said he, "and who put Hybatty to death? who hanged the carcoon, under the pretext that he believed him a spy? Under the rose, I got into a scrape about this same hanging exploit of yours, as you will hear when I relate my history to you." "Well, but, my good friend," I answered, "the two instances you quote were not cool, unprovoked murders; the first I hanged because I heard him swear by the holy cow he would have my life; and the second, in the dark, agreeable to superior orders." "And these men's deaths preyed heavily on your mind, no doubt?" he interrupted. "Why, no; in truth, I cannot say I was much concerned at their fate; but I must at the same time say, that I will never commit cool, deliberate murder on unoffending persons." "Well, then," he replied, "you shall rob, and we will kill afterwards—you will then be the genuine Pindaree; or we will first run the fellows through, and leave you to plunder them. This division of labour will make the thing more easy, and save you any scruples!" "I imagine that division of spoil forms no inconsiderable part of a Pindaree's duty?" "Aye," said he, "fair division or actual separation is the law among them." I asked his meaning, as not clearly comprehending the import of his speech, and what he meant by "actual separation!" He, in reply, drew his hand across the back part of his neck with a very significant look, which altogether I could not easily misunderstand. The only hope I could secretly entertain of escape was, that if I turned Pindaree I must be furnished with a horse, which would afford me the means, when opportunity occurred, of decamping from the troop.

The second evening came. The troop, as before, partook of their mess like so many ravenous hogs. We were once more accommodated with permission to cook and eat by ourselves. When we retired to rest, I reminded the Pindarees of their promise to relate their histories; and my old friend, Mahadeo, the inkstand-bearer, immediately began.

CHAPTER XII.

"THOUGH I am at present but a vagabond Pindaree, I can assure you all, without any deviation from truth, that I can boast both of purity of caste and dignity of extraction. My father was brother to the Rajah of Satarah, though not the elder son; unfortunately another, far his senior, aspired to the musnud in case the reigning rajah died without issue. Nevertheless, my father was determined to assert his claims, and to dispute the right of his elder brother, by casting a slur upon his caste, and insisting that my uncle was the son of a Dobin, or washerwoman. His mother not being alive when he so sagaciously discovered this stain on his brother's title, she could not be appealed to, to decide the matter. Unluckily for my poor father's hopes, my uncle obviated the difficulty by producing, or procuring, at least twenty witnesses, who were ready to swear to his immaculate blood. This eldest brother had also a son, on whom my father did not look with a very delighted eye; he invariably styled my hopeful cousin the *Dobee-poora*, or washerwoman's boy. This youth I never had the felicity of seeing; for, though about mine own age, he lived a great way from my juvenile residence. My uncle frequently came to our town, and was for ever involved in disputes with my father; and so miserable did the latter contrive to make him, that at last he determined to quit the part of the country where we lived, and retire to live as far as possible from his brotherly torment. Before he took this step, he made a proposal to a high caste Brahmin to give his daughter to my cousin. My father hearing this, made similar proposals on my behalf. The Brahmin, fancying my uncle was nearer the possession of the sceptre than my father or my father's son, accepted my uncle's proposal in preference. This so enraged my father, that he vowed the most dreadful vengeance on his brother and the boy his son. The ceremony of the betrothing was performed between my cousin and the Brahmin's daughter, during which time my father remained at home, and kept me with him, not willing that we should be seen after he had sustained so great a mortification. After the ceremony, my uncle and his son went afar off to reside, as they had previously determined.

"About this period, I discovered that my father passed much of his time rapt in meditation, and I often heard him muttering to himself things which I could not comprehend, his arms folded, and brow heavy and clouded. He frequently absented himself from home all night, and on one occasion remained away three successive days. Upon his return, I perceived he was wounded. He gave out that he had been at Indore for the purpose of meeting his brother Sevaje, who had requested him to do so by letter; that, returning together, they were waylaid and furiously attacked by robbers; that he escaped, but that his unhappy brother and nephew had been assassinated. My father pretended to grieve over his brother's fate, and declared he would become a *sunyasse*,[1] and retire from the world. As soon as he recovered from his wounds, he was impatient to set out; and one day, taking me by the hand, he led me out of the back door of the house. We proceeded through lanes and crooked streets into the fields, walking at a rapid rate, and never looking behind us. We continued our journey until night came on, when we penetrated a thick jungle, in the heart of which we discovered a cave. On entering this gloomy abode, my father vociferated, '*Ho! Babagossein Baba!*' upon which a weak, but hollow voice, answered, '*Hah b,hae,*' or, 'What, brother?' My father then uttered some words wholly unintelligible in my ears, on which an aged gossein opened a small wicket, and let us in. Immediately on

---

[1] Persons who leave their families and friends, and pretend devotion to some particular god upon the least misfortune. They are clothed in red, and wear high-heeled wooden shoes. They are also styled gosseins.

entering, my father fell down prostrate and kissed the feet of the venerable sunyasse, and made me do the same. The old man raised us up and gave us some rice to eat, which he had by him ready prepared; from this I guessed that our arrival was not unexpected by our host.

"This sunyasse was indeed a strange being. He seemed a living skeleton, without teeth, and bent double from age and hardship; his hair was long, matted together, and stained purposely of a dirty-brown colour; his nails were as long as the talons of a bird of prey, and his toes were bowed inwards, while their nails furrowed the earth deeply at every step he took. One hand and arm remained erect over his head; in fact, the arm was no longer a living member, owing to disuse and the fixed position in which he had kept it for years, having vowed never to allow it to resume its natural, nor indeed any different position again. Pointed upwards from the shoulder to which it belonged, with its shrivelled look, it had the effect of giving its owner a character not belonging to the race of men—strange and supernatural. Not a rag of clothing covered his frightful anatomy, and his shrivelled and dried skin was smeared from head to foot with dirt and ashes. By these mortifications, he fancied he should propitiate the deity. My father beheld him with reverential awe, and I myself with inexpressible disgust.

"In one corner of the sunyasse's cave was Gunputti the idol, large, with an elephant's trunk; and *Mahadeo*, and *Parvati* his wife, were carved in the rock immediately opposite. I concluded that the purport of my father's visit to this miserable fanatic, was as much to gain instruction as for security. Having eaten some rice, the old man began to mumble prayers in a sepulchral tone; then to fall on the ground before the god, and keep dabbling in water. My father imitated him with the utmost exactness, and made me follow the example. I was heartily glad when these numerous ceremonies, and their still more numerous genuflexions were ended, as the stones on which they were made I found painful enough to my bones. A dead silence now took place for a full hour, the old gossein first breaking it by crying out, as loud

I

as his crazy voice would permit, '*Sudasheo!*'[1] and then desiring my father to say, '*Bōm Mahadeo.*' My father did all he was desired, and then they continued for another hour calling out, one of them 'Sudasheo,' and the other, my father, roaring out 'Bōm Mahadeo,' until they were both exhausted. As soon as the gossein had recovered a little, he rang a small bell, trimmed his lamp, and bade us follow him. We now entered an inner cell, where stood the figure of *Siva.*[2] The gossein desired us to do as we saw him do: this was to fall down nine times before the idol. This troublesome business being over, and when I hoped there was nothing more left for me to do, the old wretch presented us with a copper vessel filled with blood—whether human or not, I cannot say to this day. We were directed to take each of us a mouthful, and squirt it out into the idol's face. My father obeyed with great gravity; but when it came to my turn, I was in such haste to get rid of the filthy mouthful, that I let the whole go, not into the face of the idol, but into the eyes of our preceptor. My father immediately felled me to the ground, apologising a thousand times over to the gossein for my conduct. I yelled, cried, and begged forgiveness, promising to hit the mark better next time. My father was told to repeat the disgusting oblation sixteen times, and I was ordered to follow his example. I succeeded, from fear, in getting nearly through with the total number, in despite of my stomach's repeated warnings. At last I was no longer able to subdue its rebellious impulses, and Siva received, not the contents of my mouth alone, but both together. Indeed, nature had effected wonders in enabling me to resist so long the horrid doses of blood, which would have disgusted a tiger. The gossein now set up a frightful yell; and my father, to appease his wrath and satisfy his own anger, once more levelled me with the earth. Siva, the destroyer, had been defiled, and it became necessary for the sunyasse to purify his godship. For this purpose he fetched water, oil, sandal-wood, and red ochre, muttering a prayer between each application. Sundry cocoa-nuts were then offered, with prayers and moanings;

---

[1] The name of an idol.   [2] The destroyer.

and after another hour spent in purifying the idol from the con-
tamination I had cast upon him, the sunyasse conducted us back
to the outer apartment. He now produced a cauldron, lit a fire,
and poured into the vessel water, blood, resin, oil, ghee, and
rice; he then sprinkled brimstone into the fire, the blue flame
of which, shining upon his countenance, gave me a full view of
its cadaverous hideousness. So horrible and ghastly a being till
then I had never beheld. Terror crept coldly over me; my
heart was chilled with secret fear, and the hue given to the
gossein's face by the brimstone impressed me with the idea of
his not being a creature of this world. Even my father's hardened countenance bore an expression, if not of terror, of awe and
wonder, at the sight. The sunyasse next produced a string made
of horse-hair and fine cotton, which he dipped in his infernal
cauldron, muttering blessings or curses, I could not tell which.
He then, with a pair of tongs, drawing it from the cauldron,
bathed it in blood, drew it through his toes, and then soused
it once more in the charmed pot, where he suffered it to remain
about half-an-hour. Then taking off the cauldron, he poured its
contents at the feet of Gunputti, leaving the string at the bottom
of the pot, which he cut in two pieces, one longer than the other.
After this, he formed the sacred string worn by the Brahmins,
gosseins, and many Hindoos. One of these strings was designed
for my father, and one for myself. He desired us to take off our
old strings and cast them into the fire; and this being done, he
invested us with those he had just consecrated, telling us that as
long as we preserved them pure and entire, and never removed
them from our bodies, we should rest in perfect security, safe
from the attacks of enemies, and unhurt by the shafts of malice, or
even the incantations of witchcraft. He then presented my father
with some of his own hair, consecrated in the same manner as the
string had been, and he ingeniously, with his one hand only, wove
it into my father's locks. This, he told him, was an additional
security; and as long as he wore it interwoven with his own,
all his schemes, objects, and desires should prosper. We now
stripped, by his order, and were rubbed over with ashes from
the fire over which the cauldron had been heated. My father's

eyebrows were scored with red ochre as well as mine, and this, with large daubs of red paint on our naked bodies, finished at length our consecration, of which I was heartily tired. We were now told we might go to rest, and depart on the following morning. I was indeed happy to find a quiet corner anywhere, in which I might obtain a few hours of comfortable repose.

"The morning again dawned; but my sleep had not refreshed me. Horrid dreams annoyed me through the night. Idols, Brahmins, devils, and sunyasses, visited my slumbers by turns. I was flung from rocks and down precipices; now lifted up to the sky, and whirled about with surprising velocity—or thrown into black gulphs, where I appeared falling amid thick and bottomless darkness; now I was held in the hands of Siva, or grasped in the talons of a mis-shapen demon. One time I fancied I was boiling in the sunyasse's cauldron, and then swimming in a river of blood. These terrors, caused by hurried imagination from what I had seen, combined with an empty stomach, prevented the refreshment commonly arising from rest. Well or ill, however, I was summoned early enough to attend my father, who had taken leave of his tutor, and now bade me to do the same. He ordered me to make my salaam to the holy man, and then we set out on our travels, completely metamorphosed from what we had been on the preceding day. I was much concerned to see my father in his present circumstances. Before, he had a manly, warlike appearance; now he looked a most mean, abject wretch, covered with filth and ashes. His hair straggled wild, stained brown, and his body was bedaubed with paint, while he had only a rag to cover him. I could not see myself, it is true, but I could fancy how I looked. The more I did so, the more I detested myself, and the profession on which my father had forced me to enter. We had not proceeded many coss on our journey before I formed the resolution of decamping, and leaving my wise father to enjoy the pleasures and profits of his new mode of life alone. It was not long before an opportunity occurred favourable for carrying my resolution into effect. We were met by a gang of gosseins, who invited us into a cavern, where they ate opium and smoked ganza, until they were all stretched insensible on the ground. Finding how profound their sleep was, I lost not a moment in carrying my intention of decamping into effect. Arising softly, I unbarred the wicket, sallied forth, and from that hour to this have never seen nor heard anything of my sagacious father.

" The first thing I did on gaining my liberty was to proceed to a tank, and wash myself clean from the paint and ashes with which I was plastered. I took care, however, to preserve the sacred string ; and thus purified, and in appearance a poor cultivator's son, I begged my way to Holkar's capital, Indore, where I served in his Highness's stables. I next entered the service of a banian, and then of a tailor. From them I went as boy to a carcoon, hoping through this last service to obtain a footing in the royal durbar. My court speculation, however, served me to little purpose. One of the carcoons, to whom I had made myself useful, promised to get me made deputy-foujdar or under-runner in the police department. I bowed to the earth before him upon having this kind offer, but still lingered month after month in idleness. At length the place became vacant, and I entertained reasonable hopes of success. I never omitted an opportunity of standing in the way of the head carcoon, but to no purpose. I smiled and bowed, and bowed and smiled, in vain ; he seemed to have forgotten both myself and his promise. I determined to remind him of it, and proceeding through the bazaar towards the palace for that purpose (for he transacted his business there), I saw a procession attended by the peons of the police department, and on inquiry learned, to my great mortification, it was the newly appointed deputy-foujdar, who had been presented at court, and was just installed into his office. This was a cutting disappointment to me, and with downcast eyes I sauntered towards the palace, in the hope some other place was in reserve for me. I could not gain admittance ; but was obliged to wait outside all day till the carcoon appeared. The only notice he took of me was to desire I would get out of his way, and I was forced to obey the command. Presently all my friends, who heard me speak of my promised good fortune, called me *boor ke luddoo,* or the great man's sport.

"Being now thoroughly disgusted with all around me, I went to my lodging, which was at a baker's shop. The baker's wife was scolding and rating him about money matters; and I soon discovered that I was the unfortunate cause, the wife insisting upon the propriety of his compelling me to pay. I approached them, and promised to settle the next day; how, or by what miracle I was to fulfil this promise, I knew not. The woman now lowered her tone, and the man proceeded with his business. I was additionally mortified by this accident, and sought my forlorn garret with no very enviable feelings. I now began to consider what I should do, or how evade my promise of payment. After much cogitation, I made up my mind to decamp; but to effect this with success, it was necessary I should avail myself of the present moment. Softly, therefore, unbarring the door of my room, I groped my way down the narrow staircase which led to it, and found myself close to the baker's chamber. I distinctly heard him and his wife conversing. Money was the subject; and I heard the woman say, 'When we get the ten rupees from the lodger, we shall have a round hundred, you know.' 'Aye,' said the husband, 'but I fear we shall have no chance of getting them.' 'No chance!' replied the wife, 'if he does not pay us the first thing in the morning, I will claw his eyes out—that I will.' 'If,' said the baker, 'his eyes would sell for five rupees apiece, I would help you; but as they are not saleable articles, let us be content with the gold buried in the hole in the inner room, and send him about his business.' 'No, it shan't be so,' said the woman; 'if he must go about his business, he shall go with a dozen rattans on his back, for I am determined to get him punished as an impostor.' This agreeable piece of information determined me not to await the tender mercies of the baker's wife. I immediately descended the stairs, and cautiously entering the inner room, I groped about in search of the treasure, and I believe examined every hole until I came to one where I thought the money must be concealed. I thrust in my hand with great eagerness, but withdrew it again with still more; for I had thrust it into a heap of burning ashes, which caused me intolerable pain. It was, in fact, a small oven, where the baker's wife prepared the

light cakes, which were her exclusive manufacture. The pain I
suffered was so great, and my right hand so utterly useless, that,
though inclined to search further, I had not the **power**. With
my left, therefore, as softly as I could, I unbolted the door, and
reached **the** verandah, where I thought I was beyond the reach of
danger, entirely forgetting the dog that carefully guarded the outside. On my stepping out, up he sprung, and commenced hostilities by a dreadful barking; and set a whole pack in the street at
the same unwelcome noise. **I had** not a moment to repent of
the mode by which I had so thoughtlessly attempted to abscond.
I stood still a moment, not knowing which way to turn or what to
do. The baker, aroused by the barking, vociferated, 'Who is
there?' Waiting a moment, and getting no reply, his wife began
to scream out, 'Thieves! thieves!' upon which I made a bolt and
ran down the street. The night rounds, alarmed at the noise the
dogs made, and the cry of 'Thieves!' rapidly approached me,
I dared not pass them, lest suspicion should attach to myself;
but, with tolerable presence of mind, I called out to the patrol,
'Come within, my friends, there are no less than twenty thieves
broke into Mahadaje, the baker's shop; for Heaven's sake,
come and help **us**!' Off they went, thinking I was following
them; but I took care to turn down a narrow alley, and seek
refuge in a shed full of cows and buffaloes. How I longed to be
in the open **fields**! This was impossible until daylight; for the
city gates were shut, and would not be opened until then. I had
not long been in my **place of** concealment, when the night watch
passed, searching for the baker's lodger, who had stolen all the
money, and decamped. 'The rascal!' said one, 'I wish we
could find him.' 'Well,' said another, 'and if we could, what
should we do?' 'Do,' replied the first, 'why, take the baker's
money from him, and let him go.' 'And give the baker the
money?' 'No, no,' said the first, 'I warrant we should know
how to dipose of that amongst ourselves.' 'That's right,' exclaimed three or four voices at once; 'but how has the fellow
escaped us? It must have been he who called to us to assist the
baker.' 'He is a cunning fellow,' said another, 'he quite
deceived me.' 'He made fools of all of us,' said a number of

voices together; 'but, if we find him, we will make him repent his knavery.' 'We shall never find him,' said a single voice; 'let us go on and search, however.' I now found, from the sound of their voices, that they were moving away from the spot where I had concealed myself, to my no small satisfaction.

"Before daylight appeared, a part of Holkar's army, commanded by Sawunt Rao Baboo Rao, passed by my place of concealment. Nothing could happen more opportunely for my deliverance. I waited until the camp-followers that usually flock in the rear should make their appearance. It was not long; and this class of persons being as numerous as the detachment it accompanied, I contrived, under cover of the dawn, to slip in amongst them without observation, and thus effect my escape from Indore. No one can imagine the joy I felt at being once more in the open fields. The detachment at length halted at a village about ten coss from the city; and when people had time to ask questions, I was repeatedly asked who I was, first by one, and then by another; and to every person I told a different story. First, I was the son of a soldier; next, of a suttee; and then, of a baker. I repented mentioning the latter trade; for one of my inquisitors, first looking hard at me, asked me if I knew a baker named Mahadaje. I replied in the negative; for that was the name of him from whom I had absconded. The fellow remarked it was somewhat strange I should not know the chief baker of Indore. I replied that I had never said I baked in Indore, as I was never there for more than one hour in my life. 'What!' said my questioner, 'did you not join us there?' I answered, 'No; I joined you at the village about four coss from Indore.' 'Indeed! then it was at the village you baked, was it?' he rejoined. 'No,' said I; 'I sold liquor there.' 'Well, my friend,' remarked the other, 'I think I never was in company with such a liar before, as thou art! It happens that my uncle is the sole liquor-seller in the village, being the only man licensed to do so by Government; and as to your selling a bottle there—you would as soon dare to mock royalty itself to its face! Thus, fully satisfied that your tale of being a liquor-merchant is false, I am justified also in doubting the correctness of your baking story.' I was now in utter confusion, and thought I could get out of one scrape by stating that I was a liquor-maker only, but feared detection in my brewing as well as in my baking. I could not tell what more to say to satisfy the inquirer, whom I heartily wished to the devil during the colloquy, when I perceived a Mahratta carcoon unhorsed, and the animal running away at full speed. I did not lose a moment in flying to the assistance of the fallen man, and thus put a stop to any further examination. I found the carcoon much hurt. He was sensible of my attention, and desired me to keep close to him; by doing which, I avoided a repetition of my brewing and baking conversations. My attention to the fallen man was not lost; for he appointed me his inkstand-bearer, and I remained in his employment: so that, whatever inclination my inquisitorial friend might have had to renew the conversation and prosecute his inquiries further, he was too much overawed by knowing I was one of the lowest of the low on the ladder of power. I kept my situation as long as my master retained his, which was about two months from that time, when he was turned adrift for reasons which I did not learn. Fearing my old enemy might annoy me again, I volunteered my services as inkstand-bearer to a young, acting, under-deputy assisting-clerk, named Pandurang Hári, and was accepted. Pandoo, though not high in office, ranked among the favourites of our Maharaj Sawunt Rao. This was, therefore protection sufficient for me, and I served without any hope of wages."—[During this part of the narration, the Pindaree gave me several looks, which no one but ourselves could understand, the other Pindarees not being aware we had ever before met.]—"I served this vagabond, Pandoo, for some time, until he also lost his situation by concerning himself too deeply in a hanging affair, and he narrowly escaped the halter; but the fellow's ingenuity saved him. It appeared that he had buried some ornaments under his bed belonging to a man who had been murdered. These ornaments his principal in office, named Govindah, had ferreted out, and got into his possession. Pandoo gave so good an explanation of the manner by which they had come into his possession, and expressed himself so ready to give them up to the son of the murdered man, that he escaped; and the carcoon was ordered to make good the amount, which exaggeration increased from two thousand to four thousand rupees—thus, Govindah was a loser. Pandoo was sent to a paugah, and I remained idling about. I was wandering I know not whither, reflecting on the fate of Govindah, whom I hated— because, but for him I should have reaped a golden harvest, having spent two entire days in persuading a client what a useful man of business I was, and what interest I possessed, and how much I had it in my power to assist him. The envious Govindah came up, just as I was about to finger the cash. He threatened to annihilate me, and ruin the petitioner; moreover, informing the latter I was a mere cheat, who could not give him the smallest assistance. I was, therefore, the enemy of Govindah; and it was by my means chiefly that Pandoo got off as well as he did. Previous to our first engagement with Scindea, while we were in camp at Indore, some soldiers, dissatisfied with the smallness of their pay, and others disconcerted at getting none at all, were idling about the camp; I joined them, and heard the detail of their grievances, as they were making their mutual complaints. At that moment, we saw a man stealing cautiously along, as if wishing to evade notice; he had a bundle in his hand, and his turban was tied under his chin—a sure sign he was going to run away. The hungry soldiers rushed upon him like ravenous beasts of prey, gagged and rifled him of four thousand rupees, which he had in a bag, concealed about his person. I came in for my share; and what was my surprise at discovering, in the unlucky wight we had pillaged, Govindah the carcoon! He had escaped from prison, although his friends had raised the money to pay his fine; but, instead of doing so, the mean villain was endeavouring to decamp with it in his possession. We were at a loss how to dispose of the fellow, when one of the soldiers, more ingenious than the others, called out, 'A spy! a spy!' This succeeded admirably; and, by a strange chain of events, Pandurang Hàrì was the person who issued orders for his immediate execution, not being at all aware who the man was. I took care not to undeceive him; for I saw the carcoon recognised me, and I should have to answer for being concerned in robbing him : the sooner he was removed, therefore, the better. I hastened the execution of the unlucky wretch, and he was hung up without loss of time. On the following morning, early, Pandoo was moving about the camp, when I unfolded the circumstance to him of the pretended spy being no other than Govindah, whom we had both such good cause to detest. He desired me to conceal the body as quickly as possible, lest inquiry should be made into the matter. That very day was the day of the battle, and I did not anticipate any very active search for the dead man, nor any outcry at seeing a corpse dangle from a tree, when there were so many to be seen everywhere around. I neglected Pandoo's advice to bury the body immediately, thinking that, if necessary at all, after the engagement would be time enough."

The Pindarees here growing sleepy as well as myself (for it was after three o'clock in the morning), we agreed to defer hearing the remainder of the tale until the next evening

CHAPTER XIII.

THE next evening, being all seated together as before, the first Pindaree continued his story as follows:—

"As soon as the battle was over, I hastened to the camp, and from thence to the tree where Govindah hung, and removed the body. Having no assistant, and being too lazy to dig a proper grave for it, I threw it into a deep pit or hollow, covering it over with stones and rubbish. To conceal the corpse effectually, however, I found it necessary to decend into the pit myself; and I completed the operation, and was about to ascend, when I saw a woman turn the corner of a rock that hung over the hollow. I had committed no murder, but to be seen employed in such an affair filled me with terror; so that my whole frame shook violently, and rendered all my efforts abortive for reaching the upper earth again. I was paralysed with unknown fear, and my limbs refused to perform their accustomed offices. By great exertion, and using every mental and bodily energy I could summon to aid me in the task, I climbed about half-way up the rugged sides of the pit, and made sure of reaching the top, when, happening to look up, I again saw the tall female figure I had before observed; she was bending over the brink. I averted my eyes, and, having a tolerable footing, kept my position. I ventured to look again, and her form was gone. I now gathered courage, and was getting towards the brink slowly but steadily, when the haggard visage of the woman again met my gaze. Her eyes were fixed sternly and fiercely upon me. I continued to hold fast by the stump of a tree, growing from the almost perpendicular side of the hollow, for a moment or two. At once my knees began to shake under me, my hands relaxed from their hold, and down I fell to the bottom of the pit, upon the dead body of Govindah, which I had deposited directly under the place where I attempted to climb up. The covering of rubbish I had laid upon it was but scanty, and the body served to break the violence of my fall. I did not escape, however, unhurt, having sprained my right ankle violently, and received several slight bruises. Evening approached, and I still lay helpless in the pit. A thousand times I cursed my folly in again going near the hateful body of Govindah. Had I but buried it, in obedience to the wishes of Pandurang Hàrì, all would have been well. My approaching it the second time must have arisen from the fiend conscience gnawing my heart, and telling me I was indirectly a murderer! I felt this was the cause that actuated me in concealing the body; and thus the step I took to evade detection might end in being the means that should discover me. As I lay, or rather sat (for I had raised myself up a little), I fancied I saw the flash of a lamp on the opposite side of the pit; but how it could come there I was at a loss to discover. Now it flashed upon my sight, and then disappeared, leaving all around as black as night. I never shall forget the horrors of that infernal den!

"The light now appeared again, and I could distinguish a tall figure, muffled up in a dark dress, approaching with that solemnity of step which indicates energy and power. The figure now came close, and I could distinguish that the light was borne by the tall woman whose appalling countenance had so struck me when it looked down upon me in the pit. I felt cold water run through all my veins again at the sight of her; I was as lifeless, as bereft of power, as the corpse on which I was seated. My joints seemed dropping asunder with fear; and a blow, like that of a strong man's hand, struck upon my heart, when a deep, hoarse voice said, 'Rise, accursed murderer! rise, I say, or dread my vengeance!' Had terror not paralysed me before, the authoritative tone of this command must have done so. I attempted to obey, but fell back again; my sprained ankle rendered the effort fruitless. The woman, seeing this, grasped my wrist with the strength of a giant, and pulled me upon my feet. She bade me follow her, and I hobbled on a few yards, until we came to a strong wooden door, not three feet high, through which she crept, and ordered me to enter after her. I obeyed, for I had no resource but to obey. She led the way to a miserable and damp cell, and, pointing to a mat in one corner, bade me sit upon it. She then placed herself opposite me, and, after a short pause, addressed me thus :—'What punishment is due to remorseless murderers? What should I not do to the villain who has robbed me of a son?' Here she fell into a paroxysm of rage that relieved itself in tears. 'Govindah, whom you, miscreant as you are, have murdered, was my son—my only tie to this vile life—the being for whom I dragged on a miserable existence, which the sight of him alone made tolerable to me. Thou hast basely slain him, and dreadful shall be the vengeance which I will inflict upon thee for this crime. Here, on this earth, I swear'—— 'Stay!' I cried; 'I conjure thee, stay, and hear me! I am not thy son's murderer!' Speech, that had been taken from me by fear, now seemed restored by the dread of encountering something more terrible than I had ever yet done. I prayed her to hear my story before she imprecated the vengeance of hell upon me; and as she made no attempt to deny my request, I related to her how I came to appear under such suspicious circumstances, asserting that I told her only the truth. I went into my whole history, as I did here yesterday evening, and swore by the holy cow I had kept back nothing from her.

"When I had concluded, she remained some time silent, musing and muttering something unintelligible to my ears. At length she said, 'Boy, I will be satisfied—it must be so! yet, Heaven forbid!—bare thy left arm!' I did as she commanded me. Taking up the lamp and examining my arm closely, she fell to the earth with a frightful shriek. I crawled towards her, and proffered assistance which I had no power to give; when she arose, crying, 'Who can war with fate?—the witch's words are verified! I have fostered a viper, and it has stung me!' I requested her to explain herself, and excused my own conduct as to having willingly injured her. After some further time spent in lamentation and weeping, she said, 'There was a time, young man, when I loved you as my own dear son, who now lies cold on the outside of this cave; but for him you would never have lived to be the cause of the death of your preserver. This was predicted before you were two days under my care.' 'My preserver!—Govindah, my preserver!' I exclaimed. 'You were abandoned, young man, by those who stole you from your friends; you were put into a basket, and sent afloat in the wide river. Your father had scarcely overcome the loss of your mother, who died in bringing you into the world, when he was again thrown into affliction by the news of his child having been stolen. We found you, and he whom you have destroyed rescued you from the waves; he plunged into the river, and bore you to the shore—thus, at the risk of his own life, preserving yours. I caressed you, and gave you food and raiment. My son Govindah, on entering the city the following day, made his discovery of you public, or rather of finding a male child floating on the surface of the stream. Your father heard the report, and had an interview with my son, who conducted him to my cottage; and he brought with him persons who identified you, and claimed you as his child. I had become so foolishly fond of you, that I begged, with tears in my eyes, as you had lost your mother, that I might be allowed to supply her place. Your father consented, and left you under my care for a year, at the expiration of which he intimated his intention of calling for you. He then departed, after liberally rewarding both me and my son. A few days after, Govindah set out in quest of employment, and being an excellent writer, entertained sanguine hopes of succeeding in the Mahratta durbar. The day preceding his departure, as we were sitting at our door enjoying the coolness of the evening breeze, Govindah smoking and I employed in nursing you, an old woman came and begged alms. I gave her a few pice, and, in return, she blessed me, but prophesied that the infant in my arms should one day cause me unutterable grief, and prove the destruction of my son. I ridiculed the prophecy, when she repeated, 'You foster a serpent in your bosom, who will return your kindness with his venomous sting!' I begged to know how I should avoid the evil, when the old woman told me to give her the child, and she would deliver it to its father. I now suspected the witch was an emissary of your father's enemy; and, refusing her offer, I bade her depart. She did as I commanded, and went away muttering, 'You foster a serpent!—you foster a serpent!' How true she spoke! That serpent is now before me; he has destroyed his deliverer with his venom—he has stung his benefactor—he has made childless her who nursed his orphan years—he has made the widow desolate! O Govindah, my son! here is thy murderer!'

"The woman then gave way to a violent paroxysm of grief, while I sat the image of amazement and regret. After a little time had elapsed, she again resumed her story. She said that at the end of a year my father called to take me away, and she never saw me again after that time; that, from the circumstances I had narrated to her, her suspicions were confirmed that I was the infant that she fostered. On examining my arm, she knew me by an indelible mark I bore upon it, and her suspicions were confirmed. She told me, moreover, how she discovered her son. Many years had elapsed before she saw him after his departure from the cottage on the banks of the river, where he found me. When she first saw him, it was but for a short time, he having succeeded in getting employment, being made chief carcoon to Sawunt Rao Copal Rao, who was about to take the field. 'He brought to me,' said the woman, 'two thousand rupees to keep for him, and five hundred for myself; he then departed again. The next time I saw him he was a prisoner, confined unjustly, and a fine of four thousand rupees was set upon him. I gave up the two thousand he left with me, as much of my own as I could spare, and some of our relations made up the rest. With what joy did I take the money to his prison, and how my heart rejoiced at the hope of beholding him on the following day at liberty! Alas! I was doomed never to behold him again alive! a report reached me that he had absconded. I have no doubt of his having bribed his guards, and that he was proceeding to me, in this my concealed habitation, to restore me my money. On this journey it was that he was surrounded, as you inform me, by the rapacious soldiery, and executed as a spy. I wandered about when I heard of his escape, hoping to meet him; but what was my horror on seeing him lifeless! At the very time the armies were engaged, he was suspended from a mango-tree. I had scarcely recognised him, when I fell to the ground in an agony of grief. Mine was a mother's sorrow; there is none that cuts so deep. A thirst of revenge mingled with my grief; I vowed, if I discovered the author of his shameful death, to visit him with a parent's vengeance. It struck me that those who hanged my son might again visit the spot where his body was suspended. I kept watch, not far off, behind the rock which overhangs the pit, and commands a view of the fatal tree. I saw you cut down the body; but I need tell you nothing more; you will not easily forget it. I can only say my determination was to keep you at the bottom of the pit until I could get you apprehended, being certain, from your last fall, you could not escape. I descended to the bottom by a passage known only to myself, and thus we met; may we never meet again! Go, and let the reflection that you destroyed the life of him who preserved yours, be your punishment, and embitter your days in this world! Go, and let the great *Dum* dispose of you as he sees fit, when your lot is cast to die!' I was overpowered by the awful manner in which she spoke. I never heard her speak again. She arose, and, beckoning with her finger, I obeyed as well as I was able. She led me up a narrow stone staircase, between two rocks, which brought us to the surface of the pit. She waved her hand to me to go away; I fell at her feet and embraced them, expressing the anguish I suffered for having caused her so much misery. She again waved her hand for me to depart. After I had gone but a little distance, I turned round and looked, but the woman and the light were no longer to be seen.

"The night was dark and gloomy. Lame, forlorn, and unhappy, I walked or crippled along, I knew not whither, until the morning broke, when I was surrounded by a party of horsemen, who forced me to accompany them. These, it will be readily conjectured, were the Pindarees with whom we now are. I soon after embraced their mode of life, and have remained with them three years. Now, my friends, it strikes me you will agree that it is impossible any one can have been rendered more unhappy than myself, in struggling for subsistence through this world of misery."

Here my old inkstand-bearer concluded, and we all agreed fortune had dealt hardly with him. The other two Pindarees, although they were of the same opinion, yet declared he had far less reason to complain than themselves. It was proposed on the following night the second Pindaree should relate his story. This being settled, we stretched ourselves on our respective mats, and were quickly lost in a profound slumber.

CHAPTER XIV.

THE second Pindaree began his story on the following evening as follows:—" My name is Fuzl Khan, and I am a true Musselman. I was born at Broach in Guzerat. My father was a Shiekul-ghur, or sword grinder; my mother earned her pence by selling in the open streets the most dainty *kabobs*[1] in the town. These luxuries were retailed hot to passengers and afternoon loungers; and so excellently did the good woman roast and fry them, that several Musselmen of consideration would stop at her stall, and partake of her exquisite morsels. At the time I mention, Broach belonged to Scindea; at present, as you know, it is in the possession of the English; and I understand kabobs are just as much in fashion there now as ever. In my early years, I showed a disposition, or rather a talent, for stealing and deceiving, really wonderful for my age. Few excelled me in a stratagem for outwitting others, among youth of my own standing. But you will say that was not wonderful, considering I was the son of a sharpner, or sharper, to come nearer to the point. My father was occupied all day in grinding, and my mother in frying; they had not much time, therefore, to look after me. I generally passed my hours in idleness, wallowing in the dust in fine weather, and playing with the mud during the monsoon. In such a city as Broach, I did not want companions in my dirty amusements; and I was particularly fond of the society of a dozen young Mohammedans as idle as myself. I shall pass over my first years, and proceed with my history from the time when I was fifteen, about which period of my life I contracted a fondness for gambling. So eager was I in the pur-

---

[1] Pieces of roasted meat.

150

suit of my favourite propensity, that I stuck at no means of raising funds to enable me to indulge in my love of it. My father seldom interfered with me in my childhood. Instead of chastising me as I deserved, he did nothing to check my idle propensities, and would enjoy any sly trick of mine which came to his knowledge. Sometimes, to be sure, if I offended him, he threatened to cut off my head ; and as he was every hour of the day armed with an instrument well calculated for the purpose, I trembled for my safety upon such occasions, and kept out of his way.

"My mother was more indulgent to me than my father, and from helping her at twelve years of age in her daily avocation of cooking kabobs, I contracted an attachment to the culinary profession, in preference to the more dignified business of my father. The latter was extremely angry at my giving the frying-pan a preference to the grinding-stone, and tried every mode to obliterate my attachment for so degrading a business. He called it a 'beastly occupation to live by roasting and rolling in grease, fit only for old women.' My mother on these occasions would retaliate by abusing the mystery of the grinding-stone ; and these disputes, begun in jest, frequently ended in earnest. Volleys of abuse were let loose, and whenever exhausted nature afforded a momentary pause, though this seldom happened until they had mutually come to a standstill for lack of fresh epithets of vituperation, my father generally broke silence first, saying, 'It does not signify talking, Fuzl Khan shall grind.' 'He shall not grind,' my mother would reply ; 'he shall fry.' Then the storm would rage, till the words 'grind,' 'fry'—'grind,' 'fry'—were alone distinguishable ; but I found that my mother had invariably the last word. Perhaps this led me to believe that she was always right, and my father always wrong ; for the last word she always would have if life depended upon it : and as often as my poor father said 'grind,' 'fry' was sure to come after—the first growled out, and the last muttered, to avoid a concord of sounds. Thus, between grinding and frying, I led a very uncomfortable life, and often meditated a trip to Surat, and a disappointment to both my father and mother. My old companions, however, dissuaded me ;

and, for the sake of peace, I endeavoured to please both my parents—by grinding at times for the one, and frying a little for the other. Every pice I could raise I now staked at *puchees,*[1] *eki beki,*[2] and other games. This course of life, besides taking my money, led me into serious quarrels with my companions. A youth named Buxoo Bhæ invariably won my money, and I began at length to entertain suspicions of his unfair dealings with me. One day he fleeced me of every pice I could raise, and I proposed one game more of eki beki, in the vain hope of regaining my money. He assented, and we began to play. I was soon more and more a loser, and he insisted upon my giving him a small and favourite gold ring which I always wore, as a pledge for the debt. I threw it to him, and went away in no very enviable state of mind. It so happened, that when I reached home my father ordered me to turn his grinding-lathe for an hour or two; I consented with a very ill grace. After the first hour, my father was called away, and desired me during his absence to polish the sword he had just sharpened. It was a long Mahratta double-edged weapon, and consequently required double labour. In my then ill-humour, I polished away at a great rate, wishing to get through my job as soon as I could, and also to work off the remembrance of my ill-luck and the avarice of my antagonist. My father's grinding-shop was situated in an obscure alley, where few people were to be seen after sunset. This evening, unfortunately, just as I had finished one edge of the sword, I looked up and saw the greedy Buxoo, who, in a triumphant manner passing by, held up to my view the ring I had lost, and gave a smile of exultation as it caught my eye. This was more than I could bear; I rushed out of the shop with the two-edged sword in my hand, and cut at him with it. The blow fell over his shoulder; down he dropped, and away I ran as fast as my legs would carry me, leaving the sword behind me. I took refuge in my mother's kabob-shop, dreading the result of my furious conduct. My mother was not within, but I soon saw her return laden with sheep's heads, tails, livers, and trotters. 'Hey-day, son,' said she, 'what brings you here? I thought you were at the grinding-

---

[1] A sort of chess.   [2] Old and even.

shop ?' 'O, mother!' cried I, 'confound the grinding-shop, and all that belongs to it. I have brought myself into trouble. Would to Allah I had never touched a sword!' 'What now— what now?' said my mother. 'I have only killed a young man with the sword I was grinding, as he passed by the shop.' I then told her the whole tale, and of my loss at eki beki. The good woman loaded Buxoo with abuse, and did not seem to think I was much to blame. Whilst we were talking over the matter, some of the durbar police entered the cook-shop, and seized me without asking a single question. A crowd surrounded the door instantly, and thus was I led in captivity to the *chowkee* or lock-up house. My mother went weeping and wailing behind me.

" In the chowkee I passed the night, and in the morning was led before the chief magistrate of the city. Buxoo, with his arm in a sling, stood ready to bear witness to the assault made upon him; he stated the truth with a little exaggerated colouring. The *cazee*[1] was present, and bore his part in the consultation and proceedings. The chief magistrate was inclined to propose a fine only upon me ; but Cazee Shana, badeen, who never lost an opportunity of displaying his consequence, insisted on the propriety of applying the rattan, to which I was accordingly sentenced to the tune of two dozen stripes. The fine was thirty rupees, which my father and mother between them paid for me ; but no entreaties could prevail on the magistrates to remit the rattan. Fortunately, I had not hurt Buxoo so much as I had expected. Probably in my hurry I turned the sword, so that the flat part, or at all events the blunted edge, only fell upon him ; had I struck him with the edge which had been just set in order, I must have cut into the bone. All this was said after the manner of prosing judges from the bench, and mingled with admonitions to curb my passion for the future.

" The rattan was duly applied, and I roared with pain ; in addition to which my ears were assailed between every stroke with the piercing shrieks of my mother. The two dozen being unmercifully laid on, I was suffered to go home. My mother

[1] A Mohammedan official.

rubbed my back over with mutton fat, oil, ghee, and other greasy substances, and then put me to bed, where the agony I endured for a long time prevented the possibility of sleep. Time, the great healer of sorrow and sore backs, at length conducted me again into the kabob-shop. My mother employed me to go to the butchers' shops to buy sheep-heads and other materials for her business, and furnished me with money for the purpose. I was one day, I remember, to bring six sheep-tails to make soup with. I met some of my old companions, who persuaded me to have a game of eki beki, and I lost very quickly all the money which I was to have laid out in sheep-tails. In great perplexity how to account to my mother for the loss of the cash, I met Hoossein Bhaee, a very particular friend. He advised me to get some dog-tails, as they were plenty enough, and to boil them up. He added I might be sure the difference would not be found out by the greatest glutton in Broach. I hesitated at first, but there was no remedy for it, and begged him to help me; he very willingly lent me his assistance. Taking some meat with us, therefore, we enticed away into an obscure place several of these unlucky quadrupeds, and sliced off the tails of six of the best fed and most plump among them. Home I went, scalded off the hair, and popped them into the pot. I had scarcely done this when my mother came into the cook-room, and chid me for my long tarrying. I assured her I had made all the haste I could, and that the tails were actually in the pot: she commended my zeal, and seemed pleased at the skill I had shown in manufacturing the soup. At the usual hour in the evening the loungers began to call for their basins of soup, which I served out to them with great solemnity. Not one discovered any difference; they paid their money and departed. Finding I succeeded so well, I determined to pocket the money in future, and substitute dog instead of sheep-tails.

"In a day or two after the foregoing affair, I was again sent to the butchers' shops to buy some odd bits to roll up into kabobs, as well as more tails for soup. I again consulted with Hoossein Bhaee, who once more advised me, not however to slice off the tails of the unfortunate dogs, but to buy real sheep tails this time, as by so many dogs losing their tails we might be discovered; and to kill a puppy two-thirds grown for the kabobs. I followed his advice strictly, spent half the money given me in sheep-tails, and returning to the cook-shop, rolled up the puppy-flesh in ghee and threw it into the pan, and then made the soup all in such good time, that my poor mother over and over again commended my diligence. The customers dropped in as usual, and among them my late friend the magistrate, who got me rattaned. He called for kabobs, and I was in a panic lest he should discover the trick. He devoured them, however, heartily, paid handsomely for what he ate, and went away perfectly satisfied. It was a gratifying sight to me to see the old fellow's jaws working at the dogs' kabobs, and the grease from them running down his beard upon his magisterial garment. This fun and its profits were too good to last long. One day I applied to my friend Hoossein to get me more dog's flesh, and begged him to be very speedy. He surprised me by the rapid fulfilment of my commission. I took the flesh, rolled it up in balls, and fried it, according to custom. The Musselmen called as usual for kabobs; but, on tasting them, spit them out again, and declared they were poisoned. Some vomited, and others called for water. In the midst of the hubbub I sneaked off to Hoossein, leaving my mother to account in the best way she could for the nauseous taste of her kabobs. Hoossein said that our friends, the true believers, were so fond of grease and oil that he thought anything rolled up in it would go down; and not having time and opportunity to kill a dog, he conceived that a few slices from one already dead, near by where he lived, would do as well. I told him he had ruined me; for if the cazee should hear that he had been fed upon dogs' kabobs, he would have no mercy upon us.

"By this time it had got rumoured through the city that our kabobs were made of dogs' flesh. I crept into a large jar, used for keeping grain, which was placed at the back of Hoossein's house, during the hubbub. Several persons, quite infuriated, had come to search for the villain who had given them dogs' flesh for that of sheep, and I plainly overheard their conversation. One said the cazee was seized with violent vomitings the instant he heard of the imposition, although he ate his share the preceding day, and enjoyed it highly. This I deemed a good joke. The police, I heard, were in search of me. Hoossein declared he knew not where I was, and appeared as anxious as the rest to discover me. Then I heard several persons complaining that their dogs had lost their tails most mysteriously, and they had no doubt how they were gone; that it was evident the deception was systematic, and had been long continued. The worst thing I heard was that my mother had been confined; upon this I determined to deliver myself up, but would not yet leave my hiding-place, lest Hoossein should be implicated for concealing me.

"As soon as the crowd had dispersed from opposite Hoossein's door, I emerged from the friendly jar, and thanked my old acquaintance for the protection he had afforded me. I stated to him my determination to surrender myself to save my mother· He lamented my hard fate, but advised me to conceal myself a little longer in a shed opposite his house, while he went to make inquiry how matters stood. 'Possibly,' said he, 'your mother may not be confined at all, and is even now at liberty. Do not be too rash, and throw away a chance when you may yet escape.' I applauded his caution, and concealed myself in the shed. I had not been there more than an hour, when the durbar police made their appearance, and dragged me from my hiding-place. Hoossein stood outside with a face expressing great concern, though I afterwards learned that this hypocritical friend had betrayed me, for the sake of the reward offered for my apprehension. Had I known this, I should not have hesitated to implicate him as an accomplice in the act; for I then easily guessed why he recommended me to seek a shelter in the shed, instead of under his own roof. I was now hurried to the durbar,[1] and, to my astonishment, found my mother at liberty, and spoke to her, by which I learned that she had never been involved at all. I told her why I did not abscond,—that it was entirely on her account, and on my hearing she was imprisoned. She caressed me for my kind consideration towards her, and bade me be of good cheer, that I should not be very heavily punished. I

---

[1] Court house.

must acknowledge that the thought of another two dozen rattans raised no very pleasant sensations in my mind. Being summoned to the court, I perceived the cazee in the plenitude of his power, talking very seriously to Scindea's soobahdar, a Brahmin of consequence and chief of the city. He appeared both disgusted and amused with the cazee's serious deportment on the occasion, and could not refrain from smiling as the recollection of how the dirty Mohammedans had been duped crossed his mind. The charge was read against me, and I confessed the crime. The soobahdar, and all his Brahmin and Hindoo associates in the durbar, enjoyed a hearty laugh at the account I gave of the transaction; whilst the cazee and the Mohammedans were mortified to the quick, and deeply repented having given publicity to the affair. At length the soobahdar said, ‘Fuzl Khan, this is the second time you have been brought before this durbar. It appears you have indulged in gambling, from your own account, and for that I shall punish you. In respect to your soups and kabobs, if people will eat such beastly fare, I cannot but think they are well served. The present case should be a lesson to them in future to be less eager to swallow all that comes in their way, and make them a little nicer in the examination of what they eat. It is still my duty to prevent your frying any more kabobs in this city; and your sentence is, that you be imprisoned one month, and then expelled from Broach; and severe shall be your punishment if you are ever caught within the city walls again.’ I bowed to the ground, and was conducted to prison, well pleased at my back's escaping the rattan, and happy at not being fined. My mother visited me in prison, as did my father, who failed not to hint to her that he knew what would be the end of my frying. ‘Peace, peace,’ said my mother, who, as usual, would have the last word, ‘I knew what would be the end of grinding; for remember, but for that destestable occupation, Fuzl Khan would not have been punished the first time.’ My father could not reply to this home-thrust at his reasoning, and he sheltered himself in silence from the pending storm.

CHAPTER XV.

"THE term of my imprisonment having expired, I was led out of the city, accompanied by my mother, who, as her trade had been ruined, determined to quit the place, taking me with her. We followed the road to Surat ; and as we trudged along, she gave me a severe lecture for my dissolute manner of life, blaming my father for every bad action of which I had been guilty. I now first learned through her the duplicity of Hoossein. She abused him in the strongest language when I told her he was the person who had sliced off the dogs' tails, and had first initiated me into the trick. 'Aye,' said she, 'that dead dog was the ruin of us; good fresh dog-flesh, for all I know, might have passed for ever.'

"My mother had provided a bullock to carry all she was worth in the world. This animal was grotesquely laden with frying-pans, kettles, pots, and baskets. A sheep's-head and trotters hung dangling at the tail of all. My mother bought the latter to save money on the road, or, as she said, 'to secure a cheap supper at Kim Chowkey,' the half-way house between Broach and Surat. Nothing worth mentioning happened on our journey, and we reached Surat in safety. This town belonged to the English, and everything there was conducted with the utmost regularity. Walking one day in the street, a man very civilly asked me to carry a basket, which he had in his hand, to the durbar, to be given to the English judge. He gave me half a rupee for my trouble ; and being thus paid beforehand, I set off briskly. On my way, I felt very curious to discover what the basket, which was of an extraordinary shape, contained. I accordingly took it home, and, entering a room at the top of the house, took off the cover. How was I terror-struck at beholding the head of a man covered with blood ! I trembled to think what an escape I had met with. If

I had presented the basket, I should have been in all probability hanged, as no one would have credited my receiving it in the street. To keep it a moment in our own house was dangerous, and I consulted my mother as to what had best be done with it. She replied, ' Anything but to make kabobs of it, you young rascal !' I assured her I had no such inclination ; that my last experiment in that line was amply sufficient for me. She then advised me to roll the head down the staircase of the next house, which was terraced as well as our own ; and then the owners of that house, who might be more ingenious than we were, would perhaps be able to give a better account of it. These people were Jews, and lived by usury ; they were consequently disliked by most of the inhabitants around. My mother's advice, whether given in jest or earnest, seemed to me the best which I could follow under the present circumstances ; and therefore, at night, when I was pretty certain there were none of the tenants in the upper apartments, I climbed over a low party-wall, and very deliberately rolled the head down the staircase, having carefully repacked it in the basket. This being done, I went out for a ramble, leaving my mother at home. All was quiet in the Jew's house when I went out ; but, on my return, I found a crowd around the door, and the foujdar, or native master of police, with all his train, was approaching in the full plenitude of his self-sufficient authority. The poor Jew was naturally in great terror and alarm. His family were in tears ; and in spite of their protestations and supplications, he was arrested and borne away. The head, too, was taken to its original place of destination,—to the judge of the durbar. Inquiries were now set on foot everywhere, and rewards offered to any who would throw light on the mystery that hung around the affair, for it was acknowledged that mystery enveloped it. The Jew was very naturally believed innocent. It was not probable, if he had committed a murder, he would suffer so easy a discovery of it to be made ; and then, where was the body ?

" It happened that, on casting my eyes over the crowd, I saw in the midst of it the very individual who had first put the head into my hands. He was an Abyssinian by birth, and of gigantic stature. I was so curious to know the history of the head, that I determined to inquire the particulars from the man himself. If he refused, I had made up my mind to bear testimony against him; and for this purpose I forced my way through the crowd, and, placing myself beside him, whispered him to accompany me to a more secluded spot. It was by this time quite dark. He followed me, and I opened to him the purport of my business with him, threatening an immediate disclosure if he withheld from me a single circumstance connected with the murder. He soon settled my curiosity by drawing a dagger from his waist, and plunging it into my side, saying, 'Take that as a reward of your curiosity!' I fell, and he ran off, no doubt believing that he had sealed my lips in eternal silence. I should have perished but for the night patrol, which was attracted to the spot by my groans and lamentations. They carried me to a house close by, where I fainted from loss of blood, and became utterly insensible. How long I lay in this situation I cannot tell; when reason returned, I found an English doctor by my side, together with my mother. My wound was bandaged, and every care had been taken of me. As soon as I was recovered sufficiently, I was carried home, and then ordered to give up the name or describe the author of my sufferings. The first I could not do, from my utter ignorance of it; but the second I described so well, that I soon learned he had been apprehended and imprisoned. The Abyssinian was now brought to trial, and great stir was made in consequence of the public curiosity being excited respecting him. The fellow possessed a great deal of cunning, and guessing that I should relate the whole truth, took care, previous to his trial, to be beforehand with me. He stated that he met me one evening, and that I desired him to carry a basket containing the head of a dead man to the police-office, but that he shrunk back in abhorrence from the employment. Upon this I wanted him to promise not to divulge the circumstance, and that I would find out another mode of getting it conveyed there. My house adjoining the Jew's, where the head was discovered, naturally made his hearers give his story more credit than it deserved. He had still, however, to account for stabbing me; and this he contrived to do by informing the magistrate, with the utmost composure, that he had threatened to accuse me on the night the head was discovered, and that I first attempted his life; upon which, in his own defence, he had drawn and used his dagger. My depositions, on the contrary, were deemed artful and ingenious fictions; so I was transferred to the gaol myself, and the Abyssinian made the witness against me. After a long imprisonment, my trial came on before a different judge from him who had committed me; when, after a tedious process, I was acquitted of murder. The Abyssinian was also set at liberty, the proof of the crime of which I was accused being utterly inefficient. The witness against me was suspected, after all, to be guilty; but the trial, though postponed in the hope of further evidence being obtained, was concluded without unravelling the mystery of the head. No one recognised it, nor was any trunk ever discovered. I could not myself account for it, why the Habeshy should wish it sent to the judge of the court.

" It was but justice towards me that I should now be released, but you see how unfortunate I have always been. I was in the present instance saddled with strong presumptive proof of murder: then I was stabbed, and confined a long time in durance, and finally brought to a public trial. In fact, I suffered more in the present instance, in a case in which I was innocent, than at Broach, where I pleaded guilty to every charge on which I was arraigned. My mother, as usual, was overjoyed at my escape, and conjured me to think seriously of some employment, she declaring that her roasting and frying could not maintain two of us. I tried hard to get made a police peon, but I had neither money nor interest to back me. At length I became a sort of undergroom to a rich Banian, cleaning his horse and running errands for him wherever I was commanded to go. My chief employment, however, was to carry about a large bundle of goods, consisting of clothes and linen. In this I was accompanied by one of my master's under-shopmen, named Sewchund, a Marwarry. My master's name was Lalchund Doorgadas, a man of wealth and consequence. Lalchund was a perpetual suitor in courts. If he had no just claims, he invented them to suit his own purposes; and, nine times out of ten, succeeded by means of false evidence and fabricated documents. I was frequently called upon to bear witness to facts that never came within my knowledge, and required to sign my name as a witness to deeds, the contents of which were never explained to me. It was fortunate they expected nothing more of me, as to scrawl my own name was the utmost stretch of my acquirements; and this I learned at Broach. I succeeded so well in my new calling, and got so familiar with the iniquitous business, that I no more hesitated in taking a false oath, than in swallowing one of my mother's kabobs. Lalchund invariably rewarded me when he gained a cause. I was frequently admitted to the midnight manufacturing of deeds and mortgage-bonds. The greatest nicety was to make the paper bear the appearance of age; to do which, some of my master's council advised him to rub the paper on a bullock's back, which would deprive it of its gloss, and give it a dirty hue at the same time. This was recommended also to me by one of the court-vakeels or pleaders, who encourage as many suits as possible for the sake of their individual profits, each being allowed certain fees for every suit brought in. These men, being intimately acquainted with all government regulations, are the very best persons to be employed out of court in the manufacturing of causes, and in court to plead in their support. I have been kept up a whole night by them, learning my lesson for the next day.

" I must now proceed to a case of great importance to me and my employers, which ended in no very honourable way. In a cause of great consequence, in which my master's interest was very deeply concerned, I had been drilled for three successive nights. Lalchund and several of his partners were present the whole time. These wiseacres did the thing too well, and they over-drilled me. On the day of trial I became so confused, from the quantity I had to remember, that I forgot half my cue, and upon a sharp cross-examination, contradicted myself so often, that they threatened to send me to gaol for perjury. I shall never forget Lalchund's long visage on this occasion. He might well look confounded, as he lost his suit, his money, and his character at the same time,—all this, too, through my over zeal in his service; for I forgot to mention before that I told many more lies than were required, in addition to and by way of mending matters. Prudence had wholly forsaken me. I was committed for my perjury, and Lalchund was under horrible fears lest I should let out, on my trial, the whole of the frauds in which he had employed me, and so ruin him. The truth is, I was pondering whether I could not by this means save myself from punishment, and whether it would not be best to relate all my nocturnal drillings; not that, if convicted of perjury, I should escape, unless I showed I had important revelations to unfold, which might be a matter of convention; but then Lalchund would be undone, and I did not wish this. While meditating on the best policy for my own interest, and how I might in the safest way get clear, or lighten the cloud hanging over me, my mother entered the cell where I was confined. 'In prison again !' said she ; 'what a hopeful son I have ! How long will this continue ? You will be hanged in the end to a certainty !' 'Well, mother,' I replied, 'the knowledge of this is some consolation, for then I shall find an end of my troubles.' 'Now, then, my boy, listen to me,' said she. 'I know all your present difficulties, and think we may yet turn them to some advantage, although you must prepare to get severely punished.' My reply was, 'Well, mother, there is nothing very new to me in punishment; show me what advantage will accrue from it, and here is my back ready for the cane, if it be worth purchasing at such a price.' 'Why, you know you are to be tried for perjury, boy.' 'I know that too well, mother,' said I. 'Well, and what do you mean to say in your defence ?' she observed. 'Why,' I rejoined, 'I mean to criminate Lalchund.' 'Then you are a fool,' she returned, 'if you think that will save you. Are you not equally culpable?' To this I answered, 'Yes, I allowed that; but whether I accused him or not, the judge must know that he bribed me, or at least that I had been bribed by some one ; and who would he fix upon as soon as Lalchund ?' My mother agreed to the justice of this. 'But then,' said she, 'the system of drilling, the disclosure of their midnight meetings, and the conduct of the vakeel or government-pleaders, need not come out. Would you bring ruin on them all ?' 'What ruin have they not brought upon me ?'

I answered. 'The more fool you,' said my mother; 'you know I always told you that eki beki would be your destruction. Listen, however, I have received an offer of five hundred rupees from Lalchund, and five hundred more from the pleader, if you will hold your tongue.' 'What! one thousand rupees! Why, my dear mother, you may cut my tongue out for that sum. I will be mute, never fear—silent as a dead dog.' 'Pish! no more of dead dogs, if you have one particle of love left for me; recollect what I have suffered by them. But, son, this is a serious affair—one thousand rupees, recollect!' 'Ay, ay, mother; you may fry away long enough before you will make that sum: lying is, after all, a more profitable thing than cooking kabobs.' 'Silence,' said my mother, 'is more profitable than either, just at present.' 'Then,' said I, 'my dear mother, get the money. Make them believe I am determined to blab all, and they will come down with the cash at once, depend upon it. Let me know when you have it, and then set off with it to Broach as fast as you can; for if you remain here when they have got all they want, and the trial is over, rely upon this, that they will never rest until they get the money back from you again.' 'Impossible, child! impossible! they cannot do such a thing; there is no law to help them.' 'My good mother,' said I, 'you do not know them; they can frame a bond as quickly as you can roast a kabob; and as to evidence, there is a regular set here who live by the trade of swearing.'

"Our dialogue continued some time longer in much the same strain. It concluded by her inquiring what would become of me? and telling me that I should be terribly punished, and by my observing that they could hardly flay me alive; that one thousand rupees was an ointment of great virtue for sore backs, far better than her mutton-fat; and that if I was imprisoned in addition, as she said I should be, she would always know where to find me; and also, that I should be certain to get into no new scrapes for a time at least. On taking leave, she wished God might protect me; and I begged her to hold out, and try and get a hundred or two of rupees above the thousand. She left me, promising to do so, and to see me the following day. Never, thought I to myself, was man so well paid before for holding his tongue. The payment I shall get will be in a different shape, but it will be dealt to me whether I remain dumb or not. One thousand rupees! charming!—two dozen rattans! terrible! thought I; and, stretching myself on my mat, I fell asleep.

"My mother visited me the next evening, and reported the improbability of gaining more than one thousand rupees, and not even that sum, without considerable demur. They even talked to her about drafts and bills of exchange for the amount. Thus it had appeared as if they designed to evade the payment. I declared I would blab out the entire of their nefarious proceedings, unless the cash was paid down in good coin. My mother was as anxious as myself for this mode of doing the business, and departed once more to demand prompt payment. On the following day she came to me again, but brought no good account of the rupees, and what was as bad, told me that the gaoler refused to admit her any more after the present day, and that, therefore, if she got the money on the next, she should send me a letter. She had forgotten that I could not read, and so was cut off from any advantage I might derive from her correspondence. She then told me she could contrive to scrawl some symbol of success on paper, and affix her mark to it, which I thought was a scrawl to resemble a skewer, but she told me it was a spoon. 'Well,' said I, 'mother, I thought it was something in your trade; explain exactly, that all may be clear.' 'Well, boy, it shall be a large bag, tied at the neck,' said she; 'by which you will understand that the money is secure in my hands. Your trial will come on the day after to-morrow, and if you do not receive this sign from me, you may be very certain the cash is not in my hands as it should be; you must then do the best for yourself.' 'I'll ruin them all if you are not paid,' said I; 'and so, my good mother, adieu!' 'In that case, as you please, my dear son. Farewell!' 'Farewell, mother!' I replied; 'if you get the money, hasten to Broach with it—not half a moment's delay!' 'Trust me for that,' she replied, and departed. Never were son and mother more sympathetic in disposition, more congenially connected!

"Another long night passed over my head. Morning came, and a letter was delivered to me by the gaoler. Full of hope I tore it open, and, to my indescribable joy, discovered the picture of a bag tied at the neck, and a mark at the bottom, which my mother no doubt intended should resemble a spoon, but it looked more like a staff with a round head, so dreadfully ill-managed were the proportions. I destroyed the paper, and waited most patiently my fate. On the following day the court was opened, and I was led up to take my trial. The judge being anxious to discover the midnight-manufactures of the bonds, offered to pardon me if I would put the court in possession of all the particulars of the transactions truly and faithfully; seeing, with the keen-sightedness of a man of his profession, that I was merely a tool of men whom he already suspected of crimes, but respecting whom he possessed no proof by which to obtain their conviction. He informed me, with a sternness not to be witnessed by one in my circumstances without tremor, that if I kept back or varied one minute point from the truth, I should not escape severe punishment even then. I now began to reflect on the effects of the rattan and a long imprisonment; and as I had, I thought, pocketed the cash, I was not inclined to set at nought a sore back, as I had done previously, when the money was only viewed by anticipation. I begged an hour, therefore, to consider, and was allowed to retire into a small room by myself. On my way to the entrance of it, among a crowd of persons I recognised the pleader and a clerk of Lalchund's. They gave me a significant look, and placed their fingers to their lips to remind me of my promise of secrecy. I drew my hand across my throat, as much as to say they might cut my throat if I criminated them. This produced a nod of satisfaction from those scoundrels, who separated or mingled among the crowd with revived hopes of their security. Left in a small chamber by myself, I turned over and over again the offer of the judge to pardon me. The more I thought upon the subject, the more eager did I feel to avoid the rattan, and the less consideration did I feel for Lalchund and his associates. I apprehended no violence from them, in return, towards my mother, as I felt certain she had decamped to Broach; and I could have nothing to apprehend, as the associates would all be seized the moment I mentioned their names, and I should have nothing to do but to set off to my mother; for, though I dared not be seen in Broach, I could enter her house by stealth, and keep close, and get away again in the same secret manner. Then I urged to myself that I had promised to be silent if they paid me, and that I was about to break my word. But the rattan! the rattan! This fearful instrument of punishment drove from my mind all ideas of honour, and I had determined to avoid, if possible, its direful smart. At length the hour allowed me for consideration expired, and I was once more placed before the judge, to whom I related every particular, and implicated by name Lalchund, Hurry Bahae the pleader, Sewchund the Marwarry, and many others whose names I need not relate. No sooner were the syllables out of my lips, than orders were given to apprehend the whole gang, and I was released, being obliged to find security to appear against them. An enemy of Lalchund did me the kindness to be my recognisance on this occasion, and I found myself once more at large.

"At the very door of the court, as I was passing out, who should I see, to my great surprise, but my mother, who I expected was long before at Broach, and settled in her old kabob-shop again. 'Why, you look astonished at seeing me,' said she, the moment she saw me. 'Indeed I am,' I replied. 'Why are you not gone to Broach?' 'Why should I?' she rejoined. I then made a sign to be silent, and whispered her that this was no place to talk over our secrets, and that we had better proceed to her house; for it was difficult to make my poor mother keep quiet or talk low in public; and, in spite of all I could do in the present instance, she continued to mumble in a low tone as she walked beside me. 'I am glad you impeached the rogues—the villains! it serves them right.' I longed to ask her what she meant, but dared not do so in the public street. We arrived at her lodgings, and having locked the door of her room, she again began. 'Serve them right, the villains! the scoundrels! the rogues! serve them right, I say. How glad I am you gave them up! Were you not sadly disappointed in not getting a letter from me?' 'Not getting a letter, my good mother!' said I; 'why, I did get a letter, marked with your bag and spoon!' 'O the crafty villains!' observed she; 'it serves them right—they are done for!' 'Explain yourself, my dear mother; pray explain!' I answered. 'Did you not send me a letter? Were not the bag and spoon drawn on it? Have you not received the money?' 'O the crafty dogs!' she answered, 'you have served them right! they are ruined, as they deserved!' 'My dear mother,' said I, pettishly, 'tell me whether you did or did not get the money and send the letter?' 'Neither, boy,' she replied. 'Money—letter, indeed, not I; but I see through it all now. Sewchund, the clerk of Lalchund, called upon me to talk over the matter, promising to bring me the money almost immediately; but, understanding I had been refused admission to the gaol, asked by what means I contrived to convey intelligence of the money having been paid to you. I told him all that was arranged; that I had agreed to send you a letter, signed with the mark of the spoon. He then said the money should be forthcoming very shortly, and he should soon see me again. Now, instead of bringing me the money, they forged a letter to you, with the mark of which I told them. Serve them right!' repeated my mother; 'the rogues! the wretches! the villains!' I then observed, 'My dear mother, your conjecture is very just; they nearly succeeded; for I thought the money was safe in your hands.' 'Then how came you to implicate them?' said my mother. 'Alas! my dear mother; had you ever felt the rattan, you would not have asked that question; had you known what its smart is, you would have acted as I did; for, making sure of the money, I felt anxious enough to avoid the cane upon any terms.' 'O the villains!' cried my mother; 'it serves them right! Trying to deceive, they have been deceived; it is a proper punishment for them, the knaves! I should have been broken-hearted had you borne the punishment, and not gained by it a single rupee to help us out of our difficulties and cure your wounds.' 'I was very nearly so situated,' I remarked, in reply. 'You see, mother, the necessity of writing; had you been able to sign your name, no forgery could have taken place.' 'Why, dolt,' said my mother, angrily, who felt her hieroglyphics arraigned by the observation; 'could you have read it if I had been able to do so? You may see the necessity of learning to read from the same cause.' 'Ay, true, indeed,' I answered; 'we are neither of us scholars, and the more the pity!' 'Scholars enough to outwit men who are no conjurors!' she answered. 'Thank Allah and you, my lad, we shall see the greedy villains well punished! Serve them right, the rogues! the scoundrels! the scapegraces!' A hearty laugh now burst simultaneously from us both, when we reflected on the way in which the biters had been bit. On the strength of our good fortune, my mother went out and bought a sheep's head and some odd bits, which were twisted into kabobs without loss of time, and we enjoyed a hearty supper.

"After our supper was over, I retired to my mat in high spirits at having escaped the dreadful rattan, and soon fell into a soft slumber. From this I was speedily awoke by hearing a noise in my room. Looking up, I saw two men with canes and a lanthorn standing by me. 'Alas!' thought I, 'it is not decreed that I shall escape the cane, after all—caned I must be! Who are you?' I demanded. 'That we will speedily answer,' said one of them; and I discovered him to be the Jew who lived next door to us. 'We will teach you,' he cried, in bad Hindostanee, 'to throw heads into my house, you Musselman dog! We will give you a lesson for this trick, which you shall well remember!' So, dragging me over the floor, they began to lay on me in a most furious way. I heard my mother screaming outside the door, which the Jews had taken the precaution to fasten. She could not, therefore, afford me any kind of protection. The infuriated son of Israel applied the cane as long as he could stand over me, and then departed, my mother giving him and his companion a volley of abuse, to which no reply was made, other than by pushing her down stairs, they effecting their escape over the terrace into their own house. The caning I received at Broach was a flea-bite compared to the present. I bled very profusely, and mutton-fat was this time found to be of no avail in healing my wounds. I was not at all prepared for such a punishment; for in my more recent troubles, I had forgotten all about the head, the Jew, and the Abyssinian. My mother, fortunately, received no injury, although she rolled from the top to the bottom of the stairs. She was, therefore, able to administer to my wants, and assist me, as far as she could, in healing my wounds. It was, indeed, a lesson I shall never forget, as the Jew said it should be ; and full severe enough to prevent my ever rolling bloody heads down my neighbours' staircases again.

"The following morning my mother, without my knowledge, repaired to a magistrate to lodge a complaint against my punisher. Persons were sent off in every direction to apprehend them without avail ; they had packed up their goods and departed. When I recovered, I could never leave the house a moment without being watched by the emissary of the man who had stood security for my appearance as a witness against Lalchund ; and this I found at last so unpleasant, that I confined myself entirely within doors. After three months had elapsed, I took my station in court, and had the pleasure of seeing Lalchund put to the bar. He and his associates all pleaded not guilty ; but my testimony soon proved to the contrary, and Lalchund was sentenced to pay a fine of two thousand rupees, and to be imprisoned for a year. Sewchund, the office-man, was to be paraded through the city on an ass, with his face to the tail, and to be publicly flogged ; the pleader was fined five hundred rupees, and dismissed from his office ; and the clerk was to accompany Sewchund in his ride through the city, and receive one dozen rattans. Thus was the gang disposed of ; and being myself at perfect liberty, I returned home to my mother's house. When she heard the sentence, she took her station at an upper window, and determined to see the culprits ride in disgrace through the streets, saying, 'Serve them right ! serve them right, the villains ! the rogues ! the wretches ! the forgers of my marks !' I was with her when we heard the trumpet and drum, which in mock ceremony led the procession. First came the Marwarry, the office-man or shopman, with his face to the tail of a lame ass, looking miserable indeed. The clerk followed him, and was so ashamed that he covered himself over with a cloth. My mother, observing this, called from the window, 'Take off the cloth ! take off the cloth ! serve them right, the forgers !' It was with difficulty I could restrain her. Most fortunately no one heard her, or if they did, paid her no attention. She waited at the window to see them return, and then went to behold them flogged. She told me the crowd was so great she could not get near enough to see anything; but she heard the cry of the knaves, and it was music to her soul—concluding as usual with, ' Serve them right, the villains !'

" I now began to consider whether it would not be hazardous for me to remain in the city, where I must have many enemies. I therefore told my mother I should enlist as one of the Company's sepoys. She made no objection, but lamented the separation which must inevitably ensue between us. I cheered her with the hope of one day meeting again, and that I would not fail to let her know from time to time how I succeeded. Everything being previously arranged, I enlisted in a battalion then at Surat. Now I had to undergo discipline of another description. My instructor enforced his lessons with such frequent applications of the rattan, that I began to think I was born for no other purpose than to be caned. I had scarcely learned my duty, when we were ordered to march for the Deccan. I took leave of my mother, promising to send her a letter whenever I could get some one to write for me; she made the same promise to me, and we separated. We arrived at Seroor fatigued to death, and the duty soon became so severe, that I deserted with one of my comrades, and hearing of this horde of Pindarees, I volunteered among them. I have been here two years. Just before I deserted from the English, I heard from my father, by a letter, the melancholy news of my poor mother's death at Surat. I have now concluded my story, and leave it to you, my friends, to say whether you do not think with myself that I have been more hardly used and worse treated than my friend, whose tale you have already heard. What my other comrade may be able to relate (alluding to the third Pindaree), I know not, though I remain to be convinced that his misfortunes are equal to mine."

We all laughed at his " misfortunes " as he called them, instead of commiserating him, when we recollected their nature, though we verbally stated that he had been hardly used. One of us asking him if he ever heard anything more about the bloody head, he replied that he was not over anxious to appear busy in his inquiries respecting a thing which had involved him in so much trouble.   He said, "I heard that the Abyssinian was an agent of the Nawaub's, who had employed him to despatch some fellow that had contrived to get access to his seraglio. Instead of rewarding the man, the Nawaub dismissed him.   This induced the assassin to screen himself by trying to fix the murder on the Nawaub, without implicating himself.   Whether this was the real fact or not, I have never had the power of deciding." Here the second Pindaree concluded his story.

CHAPTER XVI.

THE tale of the second Pindaree entertained us much, and not the less from the fellow's belief that, because he was unsuccessful in the nefarious transactions in which he had been engaged, he was entitled to pity. His ill success at eki beki he seemed to think a ground for receiving the compassionate consideration of others, and demanded pity almost in proportion to the knavery he had exhibited. This was like a true son of Mahomet, who always aspires to honour and riches, be he ever so great a vagabond, or sprung even from the lowest of the low. We humoured the foolish rogue, however, by affecting to condole with him, and by telling him how much he was to be pitied, and how hard it seemed that one with talents such as his, superior to those possessed by persons of his years in general, and with such kind dispositions and amiable propensities, should be unsuccessful at eki beki, lose his rupees as often as he did, and suffer so much from the rattan. He thought we condoled with him in good earnest, and impressively lifting up his eyes and hands, exclaimed, "It is the will of Allah!" to our great entertainment.

The third Pindaree now offered to relate his history, and with a melancholy countenance began thus :—"I was born in Kattywar. My father was a merchant of great respectability. His word was considered as good as his bond, and his neighbours all looked upon him as one of the most honest and upright merchants in India. His name was Lalldas, and mine is Gopaldass Lalldas. At fifteen years of age I was placed in my father's shop, and at seventeen was made a partner in his trade. We dealt in grain, and my father had the repute of being a very rich man. I know myself that he advanced loans to the Rajah of Kattywar. Notwithstanding all this, I could never finger a single rupee; but I was well provided with everything else I could wish at home. My father carefully checked every disposition to extravagance on my part, and set me such an example himself, that I soon saw the advantage of keeping a close fist. My father, however, might have spared his lessons on economy, if he had reflected that he took care I should not have an opportunity of being wasteful or extravagant, by never allowing me to call a rupee my own. We were also sahoukars[1] and granted bills of exchange upon Bombay and Madras, and we advanced money on interest. This business kept my fingers in contact with piles of money; but I made a secret vow never to do a dishonest act, and I adhered to it. Perhaps one reason why I more easily adhered to my resolution was the certainty of discovery taking place, in case I was guilty of dishonesty. My father was continually counting his rupees, and adding them up, calculating interest, and comparing the balances in his different books, and he would have very soon discovered the smallest deficiency in the money that he kept by him for business.

"I was betrothed at eight years old to a girl named Gopee. Upon my arriving at seventeen years, neither I nor my father contemplated the engagement with much pleasure. Gopee's father had been a Sirdar of some consequence, and in possession of a considerable degree of power; he was now reduced to a mere nobody, bore a bad character, and his wife was reputed to be a witch. An alliance with such a family was by no means desirable; for, independently of the character of my intended wife's parents, some one had put it into my father's head that the old woman would cause her daughter to bewitch me, and that together we should conjure all his money out of his strong box. This was full enough to determine my father to break off the match if he could, and to issue his commands to me for that purpose. Such a step as this was a very singular one, not only in Kattywar, but in every other place in the neighbourhood; for, after the betrothing, who ever believes it possible to get off from marriage? A Brahmin was consulted upon the subject, and he

[1] Bankers.

told us that a release from our contract could not be obtained in any way. Thus I was obliged at length to marry Gopee, the witch's daughter. My father, however, would not suffer my bride to enter his house, or set her eye upon his strong box, although he had emptied it, and taken the precaution to keep his money buried in some secret place, together with his bonds and papers. I hired a house for my wife, who often visited her mother, and spent a great deal of time with her. Both wife and mother used to attack me early and late for money, constantly asking for rupees. When they found I had none in my possession, they proposed I should rob my father, and at last even desired me to murder him. I was horror-struck, as may well be imagined, at the atrocious character of these two hell-cats with whom I was so unfortunately connected, and I rushed out of their presence upon their making me the horrible proposal.

"Thus time passed away, and found me miserable enough. One day, upon entering my father's office, I found the family in great fright and grief, my father being stretched upon his bed unable to move. The servants were struck dumb with fear, and looked like statues. Upon inquiry I found, after great difficulty in questioning and cross-questioning, that a lime with two needles stuck into it, and laid on two copper pice, had been placed the night before on my father's threshold; that he as usual first opened the door, and first beheld the dreadful omen. I was too well aware of the bent of my father's mind to doubt the effect upon him, or that the act was intended to produce mischief, whoever the party might be that did it. I guessed at once who had done it, and fixed the act immediately on the shoulders of my wife's mother, who was enraged at not being the better for the riches which my father was known to possess, and of which she thought she might easily get a portion through her daughter's marriage with me. My father recovered from his fright, but never regained his former state of health. From that time he seemed to fail rapidly. I am not sure, however, whether my marriage was not the main cause of his decline, which the circumstance now related tended to increase. At last he became incapable of transacting his affairs, lingered on a little time, and died without informing me where he had concealed his money and valuables. My mother-in-law was thus not a whit the better as to rupees for my father's decease. I begged her one day to tell me (I spoke ironically, as she was reported to be able to pry into all things) the spot were my father's money was deposited. She replied, 'She would find it;' and she did so, took it all away, and decamped with it, leaving her daughter to console me in place of my father's property. My consequence and credit now ended very soon. I could not honour bills, or pay the debts incurred since my father's death; and I had gone on as usual, hoping by the discovery of the property to settle everything. A prison was the next step; but my creditors, finding it was inability to pay that kept me from doing justice, soon released me.

"I now found myself reduced to a state of absolute want. I had difficulty even to preserve myself at times from downright starvation. My old acquaintances avoided me; some affected to pity me, none offered to do more; and I soon knew that no earthly condition is so miserable as his who has nothing but the sympathy or charity of his fellows to rely upon for existence. To add to my misery, my wife came back to me, having had a quarrel with her mother. How to exist myself was a consideration involved in great difficulty; but at such a moment to have to provide for a wife, and a wife like mine, was a burthen almost too overwhelming for me to sustain. It appeared that my mother-in-law had refused to give a single rupee to her worthy daughter, and the latter, on this account, according to her own representation, came again to me. I explained to her that, owing to her mother's machinations, I was a ruined and destitute man, and that therefore she had better try and get some employment, which was the step I intended to adopt myself. 'What!' said she, 'you would have me beat rice, I suppose?' 'Yes,' I replied, coolly; 'or beat out your own brains, whichever you prefer doing.' This enraged her terribly. She assailed me with volleys of abuse, and called me pitiful, sordid, and cowardly, that I thus submitted to be robbed and pilfered by an old woman. When a pause in her abuse came, I ventured to ask what she would have me to do. 'Do! you whining, whimpering wretch!' she exclaimed; 'why, do anything, rather than sit down and starve quietly here. Oh, if I were a man, I would raise heaven and earth before I would submit so quietly!' I saw that she was endeavouring to stir me up to the commission of some violent act, and to urge me to vengeance on the wicked plunderer of my money. It even seemed as if nothing but a proposition for me to kill her mother would appease the violence of her anger. I hereupon asked if there was any possibility or probability of our getting part of the money from her mother. 'The witch,' she answered, 'is only successful against fools; but still, if you are not quite unmanned by poverty, if you have a grain of spirit left, we may recover some part of it.' I inquired what she had done with the papers. 'I know nothing about the papers, and very little about the money,' my wife replied; 'most probably they are together.' I then inquired how her mother had found the treasure, and she said, 'By the same means which you yourself might have made available had you been possessed of wit, courage, or perseverance. She watched your father (who was foolish enough to empty his box and bury his cash) to the spot where he used to visit it. There lay the glittering treasure; and, mistress of this secret, she frightened your superstitious father to death with the lime and needles. Now, will you consent to make an effort to recover your property?' I replied that I would; but before I proceeded I would know, whether I was required to stain my hands with blood to succeed, because, rather than commit murder, I would relinquish everything. 'You will defend yourself if you are attacked, I suppose,' she observed, 'and you will also stretch forth an arm in my defence?' I answered 'I would.' 'Yes,' said she, 'because I shall be useful to you in finding your money, otherwise you would much rather aid in taking than defending my life.' I assured her of the contrary, that I bore her no enmity, that I pitied her for the way in which she had been educated, and that I should be highly delighted to find in her a companion and a friend. She then observed, that she could be both, and asked me if I knew where her mother lived. On replying in the negative, she said, 'My mother lives at Bhooj, in Cutch. My father is also there. To gain access to them is impossible, without incurring the most imminent danger. They dwell in the ruins of the palace which was lately destroyed by the earthquake, and there also is the money.' I inquired if she was certain of this, and whether we should be able to get it. She said, 'she was not so sure of that;' and I then asked if any one besides her father and mother lived among the ruins. She informed me there were a hundred freebooters there, of whom her father was commander, and they were always ready to protect his treasure. 'Surely,' I observed, 'the Government does not sanction this. Why does it not put them down?' She answered, 'she did not know; there they were, and against them we should have to contend.' I told her, in that case, our scheme was perfectly hopeless; two against a hundred were fearful odds to contend with. 'Courage,' my wife replied; 'artifice and perseverance will work through stone walls. Keep a firm resolution, and follow me.'

"My wife led me into the open fields, and through ravines, until we came to a small hut, which she entered, and desired me to put on the habit of a gossein, while she arrayed herself in the dress of a boy, with a guitar in his hand. She said she preferred the dress of a gossein, because her mother was strongly bigoted in favour of these religious mendicants, and would not dare to turn away one from the door of her habitation; and that having thus obtained a footing, we might indulge in the hope of succeeding at last. I ought to have seen through the shallowness of the artifice, if I had reflected but a moment, and that the knowledge of our persons rendered such a plan out of the question, as to success, were it even undertaken in good faith. The idea of recovering my property closed my eyes to all other objects. I left my crafty wife to manage all, and proceeded in silence to Bhooj, which we reached after two days' journeying on foot.

"The ruins of the palace at Bhooj presented a most awful appearance; shattered, riven, tottering, the vast fragments were a chaos of appalling objects. The heart thrilled on approaching the confusion of ruin on every side; nor could I bring myself to believe there were any human beings who would dare to inhabit such a terror-stricken solitude. My wife halted without the ruined place until evening. About an hour after sunset, I followed her into the thickest part of the fallen buildings. She stopped at a small iron door, and began to tune her guitar. In a few minutes the door slowly opened, and a man in a hoarse voice demanded our business. I began bellowing out something in the true gossein style, and the man begged my blessing, which I granted, and then demanded admittance. This he dared not permit, until he had consulted his superiors within. He went away, and in a short time returned and beckoned us to follow him. We obeyed, and were led through archways and narrow passages, until we found ourselves in a spacious apartment, at the upper end of which sat my mother-in-law. I approached her with trembling steps. She was a singular-looking being. She immediately began by a string of interrogations, demanding whence I came, and whither I was journeying. To these, and a number of similar questions, I gave suitable replies. She then began to question me respecting some points in my faith, and inquired the nature of the penances I had undergone; if I had subjected myself lately to any mortification, such as half-hanging, or half-roasting myself. I answered I had not, and she then said she supposed I had contented myself with a slight flagellation only. I replied that there was no necessity for my so suffering, as I had been very strict over myself. 'Well then, holy man!' the hag screamed out, 'a touch of the rattan at present would be grateful no doubt. What, ho, there! who is in waiting?' Upon this two stout fellows came into the room provided with rattans, and notwithstanding all my prayers and entreaties, began to strip me. I looked round for my wife, as much as to say, 'What shall I do now? what is the meaning of all this?' when she burst out into a loud laugh, in which she was joined by her mother. I now perceived how I had been duped and inveigled by the daughter into the mother's clutches, and that my wife had been sent after me for the purpose. The two fellows, in the meantime, proceeded to obey their orders, and beat me most cruelly, while between every stroke I heard the loud laugh of my wife and her demon of a mother. When I had received about forty strokes, I was ordered to follow the two men, who took me down a narrow staircase, at the end of which was a strong door studded with spikes.   This being opened, they thrust me within it, locked it fast, and left me in utter darkness."

.   .   .   .

We were suddenly interrupted at this moment by the sound of a horn, and the third Pindaree broke off abruptly.   The report of a matchlock succeeded, and all around seemed to be on the alert in a moment.   A loud knocking at the door of the chamber in which we were was now heard, and on opening it a messenger from the chief of the troop entered, and told us that the English were within two miles, and we must instantly decamp.   "To horse! to horse!" was heard in exclamations from all quarters, and in less than an hour we were mounted and clear of the fortress.

CHAPTER XVII.

T happened, most unfortunately, that upon leaving our place of refuge in the old fortress, in our too great haste to avoid the enemy, we rushed into his very jaws. A warm, indeed a heavy fire was poured in amongst us from a small but well-placed body of infantry, upon which we could not make an impression. Our men and horses dropped fast. The friendly party which had with me occupied the story-telling-chamber agreed to keep together in the skirmish, and we all fought desperately. Early in the action, a ball struck Gopal das Lalldas, the third Pindaree, who had not been able to conclude his story; and, falling from his horse, he was run through the body by one of the enemy's Havildars. Even at such an occupied moment, the poor fellow's unfinished story flashed on my memory like a momentary light, as he fell and ended his misfortunes for ever. Soon everything decided itself against us, and we had no time to indulge a thought but for our own safety. To protract the contest was useless, and to turn our backs to the foe seemed the best policy. We followed it, and soon left the English infantry far behind us. Nanna and Suntoo, my companions, who had been servants of Trimbuckje, proposed to take this opportunity of deserting. Nanna knew the country well: and, crying to us to follow him, he rode off, Suntoo and I keeping close at his heels. We galloped hard until we reached a village, through which it was necessary to pass. Nanna proposed dashing through at full speed (for our appearance and dress gave us the character of Pindarees, though we were not), since we knew explanation with the villagers would be useless. The latter were so oppressed by the roving Pindarees, that we should inevitably be the victims of their revenge. We used our spurs, jaded as our horses were, and dashed on at full gallop. It being early in the morning, the guard alone was up at the chowkee, or guard-house, situated in the principal street. As we passed it, a dozen matchlocks were fired at us, and Suntoo fell dead. Nanna and I escaped unhurt ; and attaining again the open country, congratulated each other on our lucky escape, lamenting the death of Suntoo. " It was his destiny, though," said Nanna at last, very coolly ; " Suntoo could not outride that."

In our flight our horses bore up surprisingly. They had, I have no doubt, been fed with opium, a method adopted by the Pindarees when they expect them to encounter any extraordinary fatigue, or they find it needful to force them through long journeys. Some of their horses, so treated, will travel eighty coss in a day, and enable their masters to elude pursuit most effectually. We arrived with our jaded animals on the borders of Kandeish, and then determined to proceed on foot. We turned our horses loose in the fields, pulled off our Pindaree boots and wadded coats, and having washed ourselves in a tank, walked like two honest travellers into the first village we came near. We learned there that war had commenced at Poonah between the English and Badjerao, the Peeshwa, and that the whole of the Deccan would soon be involved in confusion. We found also, by chance, that Trimbuckje Danglia was near the very village in which we then were, and we thought this a most fortunate circumstance, as we needed his assistance in our present destitute condition. He received us with apparent pleasure ; but I thought he eyed me in a manner so singular, though I was at a loss to account for it, that I did not feel quite comfortable. He seemed to have forgotten the reward he promised for effecting his escape, and was in a very bad humour. The potail of the village had reported to him that an English officer with some men were arrived in the village, and Trimbuckje had given him orders to watch the strangers narrowly. The potail, however, thought proper to proceed to the officer's tent, surround it with several Bheels whom he had in his employment, and murder him in cold blood. He sent the head to Trimbuckje, who blamed the potail, and asked him who gave him power to kill the officer ?

The fellow made some excuse, and his offence was thought of no more.

After a few days spent with Trimbuckje, I asked leave to proceed to the village wherein I had held the official situation. Trimbuckje answered that I might go to the devil if I liked, by which I well understood I had nothing to expect from him. Being anxious to see Sagoonah, I set off as quickly as I could, and in two days' time arrived at the place where I had left her. The house in which she had dwelt was standing, but its external appearance gave me but too faithful an impression of its forsaken state. The doors and window-shutters were torn off their hinges, and all was desolate. The reflection that I could hardly expect to find my fair friends in the same spot where I had so long ago left them, prepared me in a certain degree for the disappointment I experienced. The state of the house, however, I could not pass over, as it evinced marks of violence exerted against it by other hands than those of time. Perhaps Sagoonah had been murdered! The idea that it was so began to haunt me; it made me feverish and restless. "Why, my lovely Sagoonah," I said a hundred times to myself, "why did I ever quit you? Why were you doomed to be so persecuted, and why am I for ever to suffer disappointment?" Thus I bewailed my lot, until my feelings became so excited, that I was very near ending my days on the threshold of the house where I had once been so happy—over which she had passed or been taken lifeless; she who was the sole object that made me bear the multiplied calamities of my wandering life with patience, and who alone reconciled me to human existence! I knew not what it was that prevented my carrying this desperate purpose into effect. It was some casual or passing thought, to which hope clung, that led me aside from the deep dark pit into which I was on the point of falling. It was not impossible Sagoonah might even now be alive, and be requiring my protection. I must live to rescue her from the hands of villainy again, and be once more repaid by her kindness and love. "I will live," thought I, "and search throughout India for one who is so linked with my own being."

With the foregoing idea in my head, and with a full heart, I repaired to the house of the collector under whom I had been formerly employed. I was informed he was asleep, and must not be disturbed. I then inquired if I could be informed what had become of my mother and of my sister? "Your mother and sister," one of the servants exclaimed, with a look that expressed he knew the contrary far better than I chose to suppose he did, "are not in this village." I told him I knew that as well as he, but asked where they then were. "In the first place," replied the fellow, "I can't tell, because I don't know myself; and in the second place, if I did, I would not tell, because "——— "Because," I interrupted, "because why?" The man significantly tapped his stomach, and then pointed to his mouth, signifying it was more than his place was worth to do so. I saw directly I should get nothing from him, and, sufficiently dispirited, I went away. When I conjectured the great man had finished his sleep, I repaired a second time to his residence, and was told he was at his meals, and could not be spoken with. It was evident he did not want to see me, but still I determined to wait an hour longer. At the expiration of that time, I again made my appearance at his door; and, that I might neglect nothing, I presented two rupees to a peon, begging him to give my name to his master, and inform him I wished to speak with him on business of importance. The peon went up-stairs, and soon returned, saying his master was engaged over papers of consequence, and would not be interrupted. This was proof sufficient to convince me that an audience was denied me, and that I might spare myself the trouble of any future applications for an interview. I felt persuaded that the collector himself had aided in the outrage which I apprehended had been committed. Passing by the chowkee, or guard-room, a little time afterwards, the fellow whom I had addressed on my first visit, beckoned me aside and whispered to me, "The sooner you are off the better." "Why?" I answered. He drew his finger across his throat, and said, "Be wise." I thanked him, and was about to ask another question, but he turned on his heel, and I saw no more of him.

It was now very clear that I must provide for my own safety. To what point I should direct my steps I knew not, but I wandered again by instinct, while considering the subject, to the deserted house where Sagoonah had lived. It was the evening hour. The interior of the building was dark and gloomy; not one article of furniture remained in it save an old couch with three legs, upon which I sat to finish my meditations on the best step to be taken to solve the mystery that hung over the fate of my fair friends, and the cause of the desolation I saw around me. It seemed strange that the house should be so totally deserted. It was not in ruins; why did not some one inhabit it? why were its chambers left empty, be the fate of its former tenants what it might? Perhaps a murder had been committed within its walls, and it was shunned as a place of horrors; and who knew but the victim might have been my Sagoonah? This, one moment, I thought must be the case, and I even sobbed aloud until the bare walls echoed back my lamentations. I never felt so wretched. After a little time, I recollected the caution of the man at the chowkee; and, summoning the aid of reason, I descended the stairs with the intention of leaving the place, when I saw a light issue from under a door on my right hand at the foot of the staircase. What it meant I could not conjecture. "Some one must inhabit that room," thought I to myself, "and I will find out who it is, even if my life be hazarded by my rashness." With this determination, I crept softly down to the door whence the light issued, and laid my ear close to it. I now heard whisperings and chinking of money, which made me think they were thieves who harboured there; and I judged that they could not be of that class of persons from whom I could learn anything to my advantage. With this idea I was going softly away, leaving the house to its secret tenants, when the talking became louder, and I again listened, but could only hear disjointed sentences and scattered words, such as "money," "services," "Trimbuckje Danglia." It now struck me that if I knocked at the door, and demanded admittance as a traveller desiring shelter, I might possibly learn something of advantage to myself; I therefore gave a loud knock. The light was immediately extinguished, and I heard the chink of money very audibly. Not a word more was uttered; and fearing the persons might rush out upon me, I slipped into a recess at a little distance from the room they occupied, where I was well concealed at that hour of the night. I had scarcely got into it when a pistol was discharged from the head of the staircase, and a bullet passed through the outer door. Had I been in my former post, I must have fallen, and my fortune been at once settled for ever. I was now convinced there was more than one person in the house, or I should have immediately followed the man who fired. Uncertain of the number or force under the roof, I conceived it would be madness to move out. There could be no doubt the men, whoever they were, had a perfect knowledge of all the passages of the house, even better than I had. Notwithstanding, therefore, the danger I incurred in remaining longer, curiosity chained me to the spot until I saw a light flash from the head of the stairs. The person who held it was perhaps the villain who had fired. Seeing no one, he retired, and all was again still and dark. Soon after, I heard the voices again in the room below, and one of them distinctly say, "'Twas a false alarm, there was no one there; or if there was, he is there no longer." "No, no," observed another, "my shot sent him about his business; but we must not waste time here. Farewell! we meet again at Asseerghur." "Ay, ay," said the first, "there is work enough for us there." They then made their exit, by what means I cannot tell; but I felt no small pleasure at their departure. I looked into the street soon afterwards, but could see neither of them, which makes me imagine there was some secret passage of which I knew nothing. With an eager but faint hope that these men were privy to the removal or present situation of Sagoonah and her aunt, if they were indeed alive, I determined to follow them to Asscerghur, a very strong fort situated on an immense height of rock, which renders it impregnable; it is therefore considered the most important place of defence in that part of the Deccan. I left the village accordingly, and took shelter for the rest of the night in a cowshed, where I obtained a few hours' sleep, and in the morning set out for Asseerghur.

Comfortless and hungry, I kept my journey onwards, until I reached a small village, where I sat myself down in the durhin sallah, or place for travellers. There were two men within, of most savage countenances, busied in lighting a fire to cook their rice. They appeared like myself to have only just arrived, and I, having no rice to cook, had plenty of time to examine the countenances of these ferocious-looking personages. No two men ever existed more unlike each other. The one was very tall, with a thin, emaciated face, enveloped in whiskers and mustaches, so that his small, black eyes and the tip of his nose only were visible, except when his mouth opened, and then a splendid set of the whitest teeth I ever beheld illuminated his gloomy countenance. The indices of age in man and horse convinced me that the object engaging my attention, though apparently past fifty, was in reality scarcely thirty. He wore a white coat, long white trousers, with a red shawl over his shoulders, and a black leather belt round his waist, in which were a brace of pistols. On his head was a dirty green turban, twisted in the form of a Madras nuthkhut's, or conjuror's, so that I was much puzzled to discover either his country or his caste. The other was a short, mean-looking villain, with no hair on his person save his mustaches, which were mere stubble, and of a very light colour; he was fair, and had two small grey eyes and a snub nose, with very thick lips and a miserable set of black broken teeth. A large scar on his forehead showed me he had been no stranger to broils, and knew how to fight his way through life. He had a red turban, which looked as if it had been daily worn time out of mind, without its being reformed or newly arranged since it was made. He bore a common kuttar in his girdle, but was encumbered with no other weapons. Previous to eating, the tall man withdrew the pistols from his girdle and placed them by his side on the ground. By this time it was highly necessary that I should think about something to eat, for I was in truth almost famished. To have begged either of the tall or short man would, I could clearly see, be as idle as to beg of the stones under my feet. These men might perhaps have thrown me their scraps, which my caste would not admit of my accepting. I therefore required money, or if I

could not obtain that, a little raw rice would have been acceptable. The short man seemed to have a good supply of this last
commodity; and, impelled by want, I ventured at last to beg the
loan of a *jeen* of it, assuring him I would repay him when I
reached my journey's end. He looked very hard at me, and
then asked if I really thought he was fool enough to be cheated
out of his rice by such a man as I was. "Repay me, indeed!"
said he, "you know that must be a lie. Pray, in the first place,
where is your journey to end, because we may going different
ways?" "Why," replied I, "my journey lies towards Asseerghur."
"This means, I suppose," observed he, "that you are going to
Asseerghur?" "Certainly." "Then what need was there of
your saying your way lay towards Asseerghur? Do you think it
likely I shall bestow my rice on one who equivocates so much as
you do!" "He is a liar," observed the tall man; "give him rice,
indeed! here is something would suit him better" (taking up one
of the pistols)—at which the short man laughed most heartily. I
began to augur that no rice would now fall to my share, and I
sat suffering the torments of hunger, until the two fellows had
finished their repast. The tallest man having washed his mouth
and cleaned his white teeth, approached me as I sat on a stone in
the doorway, looking down upon me as he would do upon a
reptile which he had half a mind to trample upon out of sheer
wantonness. I did not dare to raise my eyes to gaze upon this
formidable personage, but sat perfectly silent, suffering the keen
pangs of hunger. After some time had elapsed, the fellow said,
"Who are you, and what is your business at Asseerghur?" This
was indeed a perplexing question. I knew if I told the real
truth my life would be in danger, if these men chanced to be
connected with Trimbuckje's schemes; and if I replied I had no
business there, I should be looked upon with suspicion. If I
made myself a person of no consequence, I should be despised;
and if I made any pretensions, I should be deemed a liar with
very good reason. Never did I before feel my nothingness so
much as on this occasion. At last I ventured to say, "And who
may you be that thinks yourself authorised to question another
respecting his objects in travelling?" "Oh, what!" said the

fellow in reply, "you are going to vapour, are you? You would make us believe you are a great man, would you?" "No," I answered, "I have no such design ; I am no great man, nor am I quite so great a fool as you would consider me." "Poh," said he, "I don't know that—it is not very polite for beggars to be saucy." "Who begged?" I asked. "Did you not beg rice of us?" said he. "I requested a loan," I replied ; "which, had my request been granted, should have been repaid, provided we travelled the same road ; but since you are so supercilious, pray keep your rice to yourselves. Keep away from me, I am not accustomed to associate with people of all castes." "What, impudent villain !" said the tall man, "do you pretend to be of a higher caste than a choomar?"[1] "I shall not dispute with you," I answered ; "I know my caste, and how to preserve it unspotted." "Let us hang the fellow," cried the short man ; "he will be a high caste fellow, a high caste Hindoo then, in truth."

This wit amused the two fellows greatly, and they prepared to lie down after their meal. They had endeavoured to provoke me into abusing them or striking them, and now, though they were both inclined to sleep, they indulged themselves in scoffing at me. The tall man said, "Hollo, you choomar, get out of the durhm sallah ; no Hindoo will enter it if you sit on the threshold." "*Arry M,ha,raj,*" cried the short man, "what is the matter?" "*M,ha,raj a che pōt b'hooh lāglē,*" replied the other, meaning that his majesty's belly was hungry. They shouted with laughter at this joke ; but I still sat silent, obliged to hear all and bear all with patience. They continued their jeers until they dropped asleep.

As soon as I was certain it would not awake them, I crept softly to the side of the tall man and took up one of his pistols to see if it was loaded ; but what was my surprise on discovering them to be the pistols stolen from me by the T,hugs, when on my way to Kandeish with Sagoonah ! I knew them to be mine by a particular mark on the stocks. One was loaded, the other appeared to have been lately discharged, as the pan bore marks of powder having been recently inflamed in it ; and the position

---

[1] One of the very lowest caste.

of the lock proved my conjecture to be correct. Could these fellows have been inhabitants of the forlorn residence which I had left not long before, and where I was so nearly paying a high price for my curiosity? Perhaps it was my own pistol which had been fired at me, and the tall man was the person who did it. I became convinced I was right in my conclusion; for they said they were going to Asseerghur, or they should meet at Asseerghur. Perhaps only one of them was in the house, and he had been subsequently joined by the other on the road. That they were all united in one common league of interest appeared evident. I now laid down the pistols, and left the place in search of food.

CHAPTER XVIII.

I WAS reduced by hunger almost to the last extremity consistent with the power of action; and I succeeded at length in relieving my necessity by applying to the potail of the village, and pawning my turban to him for rice. Thus I was obliged to bare my head to satisfy the cravings of my stomach. Fortunately I had a worn-out red shawl around my waist, which I transferred to my head; so that my appearance at present bespoke my real character, as to the state of my finances. I was now a mere *shack*—a penniless vagabond. My white coat was loose, for want of a *kumberbund*, and my head looked of an enormous size; because, instead of a neatly-folded turban, it was covered with my loose shawl, the end of which sometimes flapped down over my eyes. My beard had not been smoothed with a razor for many days; my shoes were worn out at the toes, and my trousers torn at the knees. Thus may some idea be formed of the wretched plight in which I appeared.

On returning to the durhm sallah, the tall man was awake, and sitting upright examining his pistols. " English," said I, alluding to their make. " Ay," said he; "and hard work I had to get them. I should think I fought at once with four or five English troopers before I got them." " Four or five !" said I. "Ay, four or five !" he replied; "but I conquered them, and these are part of my spoil !" "You let the women go, then, I suppose?" "Women ! how should you know there were any women present ?" he rejoined. "I happen to know it well," said I. "Oh, then, you have met with one of the English troopers who got away?" "Not I," I replied; "I have met with no runaway Englishmen; they are not so often put to flight, as we know to our cost." "Then how could you know about the women?" he observed. "Why," I replied, "because I happened to know the women themselves." "So do I," replied the fellow. I then asked if he had seen them since; upon which he said he had a great mind to blow my brains out for my impertinence, and wondered how I could suppose him fool enough to answer my queries. I assured him I had no wish to pry into his secrets; and moreover I would assist his memory, if I could. "Why, you hypocrite," said he; "do you think I did not recognise you as the fellow who was with the women?" "Oh, then, you did not contend with five English troopers at all, I find!" said I. "Why, I must own that is a lie," he remarked. "Do you think, then, I did not recognise you as the man who forced my pistols from me?" "Ay, that may be," said he; "but I still think you lie!" "Well," I rejoined, "as you were candid enough to confess you had deviated from the truth, I will confess that I had no recollection of your person; but I could swear to my pistols." "What! at this distance of time?" he observed. "Yes, my friend," said I; "because I examined them while you were sleeping." "You are, then, the most audacious vagabond I ever met with!" said he. I told him that might be; for, at any rate, I always possessed a good share of curiosity; which he told me to take care I did not pay too dearly for, some time or other. He then wanted to know how I came with the women, and if I was related to them. I replied in the negative, in a very careless manner, that I was only hired to protect them as far as Kandeish; and that, between ourselves, I had robbed them long before he enticed us out by making the birds chirp. He inquired if they never suspected me; and I said they did not, for they could not; as I could answer for it, they believed everything I ever said, even to this day. The fellow then observed, that now perhaps they were more wary. I said, that probably they were so now, since their fate had led them among strangers; and then as I recollected, I used to observe they were very suspicious. "But what now signifies it, my friend," said I, "where they are, or what they are?"

While the tall man was thinking what answer to make to this, his companion awoke. The latter evinced no little surprise at

discovering his comrade in earnest conversation with me—the choomar, as he had, not long before, thought fit to designate me. The tall man then bid me cook my rice; and he would talk to me again after my meal. I turned away, wondering where all this mystery would end, and from what cause this sudden civility arose. While cooking my rice, the two men whispered together in a corner, and appeared to be very earnest upon the subject on which they were engaged. The tall man was trying to persuade the short one to join in some new arrangement, and in so doing he encountered considerable opposition from his comrade. That their conversation implicated myself I did not doubt, both from the manner and tone in which they argued, and the way they occasionally regarded me. When I had devoured my rice, the tall man beckoned me to take my seat beside him. "My friend," said he, "we need your help in a difficult, and even dangerous affair. You shall be liberally rewarded, and shall succeed to some lucrative situation under Scindea's government "——
"That is," interrupted the short man, "if you are successful, and play no tricks; for you must beware of treachery towards us. Death will be your fate, if you attempt to deceive us !"

Having considered a little while, and urged by the hope of gaining a clue to the discovery of Sagoonah, I consented to enlist in their service, provided they would inform me of the true character of the duties required of me. I told them I demanded this not from motives of curiosity, because their business could not interest me in any way except in aiding in effecting their objects; that I entered their service from necessity and sheer want, and that I demanded these particulars, and an account of the service I was going upon, and the individuals concerned therein, because, as I was to proceed by artifice and cunning, the least blunder might cost me my life; and even if I escaped evil from the party opposed to us, I might find it difficult to persuade those in whose service I embarked, that I was innocent of things they might impute to me—perhaps charging me with treachery instead of mere error. The two fellows now consulted together again, and came to a determination to confide to me the particulars of the business in which they were employed. They observed, however, that the place we were then in was too public for commencing a narrative of what they wished to communicate, and bade me follow them, and they would lead me to a retired place for the purpose, which no one knew but themselves. "Stop," said I; "how am I to be certain of being safe in your company?" "Dolt," said the short man; "what good will your death do us? Think you your old rag of a shawl and those handsome trousers are worth our killing you for? Here, take this pistol, and if we attempt to harm you"—— "Enough," said I, accepting the weapon; "lead on." They did so accordingly, and I followed. I asked the tall man his caste as we went along; he told me he was a Goud, and one of the twelve hundred horse that infested Souduana; his comrade was a Bheelalah,—and both formerly served Trimbuckje Danglia, until they quarrelled with him about pay and left him. "That Trimbuckje!" said I; "he is a most ungrateful villain!" "You know him, then?" was the reply, "and have suffered, too, from his ungrateful conduct?" "I am, in truth, a sufferer from him," I observed: "but for me he would still have been a prisoner. I effected his escape from Tannah; and, instead of rewarding me, he left me to beggary and want." "You would, then, like to be revenged upon him?" observed the tall man. "I should, indeed," I replied; "for I owe him a deep grudge." "You will have the opportunity, then," said the short man, who, till now, had been silent: "the very service we are engaged upon will, if we succeed, make Trimbuckje mad with rage; and not merely that alone, but will withdraw his attention from affairs of a more serious nature, and thus ruin him beyond redemption;—but we approach our secret halting-place."

My guides now led me a most intricate road, among hills, deep valleys, and impenetrable woods, until we reached a cave, wherein was an idol, such as I had never before seen, nor could my companions afford me any information respecting it. Behind the idol was a door, which opened by a secret spring. Through this door we passed, and, having reclosed it, found ourselves in a small square stone chamber. Here, then, was the place where my curiosity would be gratified, and I hoped to obtain tidings of Sagoonah. This chamber, I could clearly perceive, had been before inhabited by my companions, or probably resorted to by them when necessity compelled them to seek shelter behind the friendly god. Mats, pots, pans, and oil, with lamps and cocoa-nuts, bespoke a secret haunt of desperate villainy. One of my companions lighted a lamp within; when we entered and seated ourselves.

Upon the present occasion, as, indeed, for the most part pre-viously, the tall man was spokesman. He began by saying that, before he entrusted me with the motives that prompted both him and his **companion to their** present objects, and before he mentioned the name of their employer, it was proper to state that they had pledged their lives to perform the duty they had undertaken. When they first agreed to embark in this service, they did not apprehend the difficulties that now stared them in the face : and, in truth, circumstances had arisen which had con-tributed to thwart and counteract all their attempts. Chance had now thrown in their way the person of all others who could render them assistance, and that person was myself. He then stated that, if I succeeded in what I should have to undertake, I should receive two thousand rupees as a reward, besides employ-ment under a Government where we should all enjoy lucrative **situations.** That it was not too late for me to decline the service required of me ; and if I did so, I was at liberty to go away wherever I pleased ; but if I behaved treacherously, my death was certain : they could be with me when I least suspected them, and escape would be impracticable. Here I signified I knew that was likely to be true, and that I was ready to do my best, but could not promise success, as I did not know what was expected from **me.** "**True,**" **said my** tall companion ; "all we ask from you is fidelity, and a firm attachment to the cause you have undertaken **to support.** Accidents and disappointments may render all your attempts abortive in serving us ; but nothing besides the most determined treachery can prevent your doing your best, and being secret and firm to the cause you undertake." I promised to be faithful, fully determined, if Sagoonah were involved in their objects, to thwart them by every means in my power. The shortest man of the two now bade me recollect that it was no trifling affair in which I had engaged, of which I said I was fully aware; and the tall man then told me that he and his companion were employed by Gunput Rao Mahadeo, the lawful successor to the musnud of Sattarah. I observed here, with some surprise, that I thought he had long ago bade adieu to the world, and having become a sunyassee, had never been heard of since; that he had a son also. They said he had, and that he was now in search of him, having had the most positive assurance of his existence. "He is alive," thought I to myself, "and there is little doubt but Mahadeo, the first Pindaree, is the son the father is seeking after." Of this, however, I did not say a word to my present companions, nor show any marks of surprise at feeling that it must be so. My informant now assured me that Gunput Mahadeo was alive, as well as his son, and that the father was searching for the son, to complete a marriage between him and a female, who, if united to him, might be the means of elevating the father to the Government of Sattarah; and, after his death, his son also. "But how, my friend," I interrupted, "can an alliance with the girl raise both father and son to the musnud?" In reply, I was informed that "the uncle of the girl was at Sattarah, immensely rich; that the deposed rajah was imbecile, and for a good round sum would not hesitate to declare Gunput Rao his lawful successor to the crown; nay, in all probability, would resign the musnud in his favour before he died: or if not, he would, for a large sum, secure the throne to Gunput after his own demise; for money was his god, as it is the god of all feeble minds. Now, the uncle of the girl could raise a crore of rupees, if needful; and, distressed at the absence of his niece, he had had an interview with Gunput Rao, who prowled about in the habit of a gossein, and was reputed to be very skilful, and to render great assistance to those who consulted him. While asking advice of the gossein, the uncle little thought he was consulting the pretender to the throne; nor would he ever have known it, had not the gossein himself discovered the secret, at the same time promising to find the girl about whom the rich man was so anxious, and then to try and discover his own son, and marry them. Thus the girl would become queen of Sattarah, if the rich man would consent to the match. The latter was overjoyed at the prospect of seeing any one of his relations raised to govern a kingdom, and promised Gunput Rao, if he could discover his niece, to consent to her marrying his son as a reward; and that he would spare no money or pains to raise him to the throne, which, after his decease, the young couple must naturally occupy. It appeared that Gunput Rao inquired by what means he might recognise the female of whom he should go in search; and he was informed that her name was Sagoonah,"—(here I could scarcely conceal the emotion this intelligence produced)—" and that she wore round her neck a bead-necklace, with a talisman, which the uncle authorised Gunput to open. The contents, he said, were three grains of corn, a small antique coin——'The coin was of copper,' the gossein observed. 'How can you know this?' asked the uncle. The gossein then related a story about the alleged murder of such a girl at Poona, and that every person there supposed she was actually no more, but that he knew the reverse to be the truth. The inquiry respecting her death, and the examination of her necklace, took place in the open durbar; and he himself said he saw the grains of corn and money. The uncle then inquired if he saw no writing contained in it? The gossein replied in the negative. 'That is fortunate,' said the uncle, 'because my wife, knowing the girl's father was ruined by some gosseins, feared Sagoonah would also become a victim of this class of persons: and therefore she enclosed in the talisman a written caution, warning her to beware of such people. Now, your present character is one best suited to gain admission to the girl, provided she has not been pre-judiced by this warning: wherever she be, I authorise you to force her hither, if stratagem fail. Of me,' continued the uncle, 'she has no recollection, nor her aunt either; and a letter to her would be most likely looked upon as a forgery.'

"Thus authorised, our employer was still of opinion that the warning against gosseins might have got into the hands of Sagoonah, as he recollected that the person deputed to open the talisman was her avowed protector, and that no time was to be lost in following his footsteps. He took leave of the uncle at Sattarah, and journeyed to Poona, where he employed a gossein

N

to hunt out Sagoonah, and a man who accompanied her, named Pandurang Hàrì. The latter, if it was necessary, might be despatched out of the way; but Sagoonah and her aunt must be conveyed to the spot where we then were, and final orders would be given respecting them. By some unknown means the plan miscarried; and the gossein entrusted with its management was dangerously wounded, and lost all traces of the females. It was I," said the tall man, "who informed Gunput Rao's messenger where to find the two women, whom I recollected I had robbed near Kandeish, and that they were accompanied by a man, whose person I could not describe on account of the darkness. There was also a second man, I supposed a bullock-driver, in company. After being robbed, I imagined they all went back to the village from whence we enticed them. You were the man, then, it seems, who accompanied these women. Are you Pandurang Hàrì?" "Not I," was my reply, with boldness; "my name is Ramje Goobie. I was employed, about the time you mention, to escort the women to Kandeish. I believe they placed great confidence in me." "Who employed you?" inquired the tall man. "That I cannot tell you," was my reply, "because I do not know his name—I was well paid, however." "Do you think it was that Pandurang Hàrì, of whom I spoke before, who employed you?" "Perhaps it was," I replied; "but I have never troubled my head about it since. I was more grieved at losing my money and pistols than anything else. But did the gossein ever catch the women?" "He never did, though he made many attempts; they were too well on the watch against the arts of that class of people."

"Having left the service of Trimbuckje," continued the last speaker, "I have been employed since by the gossein, who, though still in Trimbuckje's service, is his decided enemy. It appears that Trimbuckje having conceived a passion for this very girl, determined to seize her, and place her in his harem, and had given orders to that effect, when he was arrested and escorted to Thannah. The man to whom he issued orders for this purpose, was the collector of the village where Sagoonah resided. He obtained possession of the women by force, and has concealed them somewhere that none of us can discover; but we have strong suspicions they are in the fortress of Asseerghur. The gossein, who had actually been dismissed from Trimbuckje's service, upon finding his plans differ so much from those of his master as far as respected Sagoonah, thought it would be still highly advantageous to himself to get on the same footing as formerly in Trimbuckje's family. Having been applied to, therefore, to aid his escape from Tannah, he acceded, and again entered his employ. The gossein, however, has never been able to find out where Sagoonah is concealed, and he has engaged us in the attempt to discover the secret. We have learned that there are two women in the fort of **Asseerghur**; but whether they are those we seek we should not know if we were to see them, our employer himself not being able to give us any very accurate description of their persons. **Now, then,** we ask you to enter the fort, see the women if possible, claim an acquaintance with them, and persuade them to accompany you from the fort. This must be achieved by bribery and artifice; and when done, you have only to deliver them up to us." "But is it likely," I said, "that Trimbuckje could get the women into Scindea's fort?" "Trimbuckje," said one of my companions, "is a great friend of Bassoo Scindea's, one of the generals of whom you may have heard, in the history of the Scindea family, as commanding large but insubordinate armies. **This** Bassoo keeps the women in close confinement, from which it will be your duty to release them." "Are there no orders to give him about the goatherd in the glen?" observed the short man; "he may as well "—— "Peace!" said the tall man; "we can manage that. We have no more work for you at present, Ramje," said he, "but what you already know."

Much as I wished to ask some other, and to me highly important questions, I dared not do so. I only enquired, in the first place, the nearest way to the fort. They directed me to go through a thick jungle, and then across a plain, after which I should enter a second wood. On emerging from thence, I should find myself in a deep glen, in which was a goatherd's cottage. This I was not to enter, but to proceed until I reached the open plain, when I should see Asseerghur at about three coss distance

from the border of the glen.   I ventured to inquire whether Gunput Rao, the employer of my companions, did not occasionally
pass by the name of Gabbage Gousla?   They asked how I knew
this.   I had a reply in readiness, and told them that when I was
employed to guard the two women to Kandeish, my employer
told me a person named Gabbage Gousla was to be particularly
avoided, and that he was a gossein.   This seemed to satisfy the
two men ; but they again declared that if I acted treacherously
towards them, my life should pay the forfeit ; and they asserted
that the previous knowledge I possessed of the persons of the two
women alone induced them to confide in me.   My duty was to
persuade the women I was a messenger from Pandurang Hàri,
who awaited them without the fort, but for certain reasons dared
not trust himself within the walls.   I ventured, without appearing
too anxious, to ask how Gabbage discovered his son to be in
existence.   They informed me that a servant of Trimbuckje's,
named Nanna, had fallen in with a troop of Pindarees, one of
whom related his history, and, from the peculiar circumstances
he narrated, Gabbage became convinced it could be none other
than his son.   I was much surprised at this piece of intelligence,
as I was at the singularity of Nanna's relating the son's history in
presence of the father.   I wished much to discover how Trimbuckje had found Sagoonah to be alive, after understanding that
her death had taken place at Poona ; but I dared not put further
questions, and left it to chance to gratify me with this important
piece of information.

CHAPTER XIX.

Y wallet being replenished, and ten rupees paid me in advance, I prepared to set out for Asseerghur. It may be considered certain that if I succeeded, I had no intention of bringing the women to the place agreed upon, though I had made a promise of so doing. Yet I well knew the consequences that would follow this treachery, and that as long as I lived it must be in a state of prepetual anxiety and terror, lest either the meagre form of the tall man or the squab figure of the little one should cross my steps; nevertheless, I set off on my enterprise. While creeping through the small iron door for that purpose, I saw that a strong bolt was affixed on the outside, and as soon as I was clearly out and the door closed again, I drew it across into its place, and consigned the two men to a lingering and terrible death! There was no other egress from the chamber. They heard the grating noise that sounded their knell of destruction. They attempted in vain to open the door; they screamed, and were then silent for a time, then burst out into louder curses on my head and on their own folly. Then they quarrelled, and ended their altercation with deep and bitter groans. Theirs was a horrible destiny—to be eaten up by famine, to waste into death! But were they not plotting against others? and those, too, far dearer to me than mine own existence? Was not my Sagoonah to be their victim? and were they not scheming mischief against the poor goatherd they spoke of in the glen— perhaps to murder him? These considerations, and the consciousness that to frustrate the schemes of such men by such means was fully justifiable, bore me up, and afforded me consolation in respect to the justice of what I had done.

Night had now come on, and I feared to enter the first jungle at that season, though I kept as near it as I could, to avoid the groans and maddening screams that came from the cell in which my victims were immolated. I could not get beyond the hearing of them. At times I was almost tempted to go and seal my own destruction by unbarring the portal, the cries of suffering so softened my heart! When I recollected they were still men like myself, a chill of horror came over me; but reason after many struggles resumed her seat, and the memory of Sagoonah's security again fixed my tottering resolution. The owl and the bat flitting across my face, added to the impression of that terrible hour. The wild beasts howled in the jungle; once more I went to avoid them towards the cave, as I had done several times before, but the yells of the miserable captives drove me away. Again I reached the entrance of the outer cave, through which their groans echoed and almost palsied my heart, and again I returned towards the jungles. At last I summoned resolution to fly from the damps of the frowning rocks, in which the cave was scooped, for ever, and to leave my prisoners to die. A friendly tree, as far off from the spot as I could venture in the darkness, gave me shelter in its boughs for the night from beasts and men, and at dawn of day I pursued my journey through the first jungle.

The entrance into such a place, and at so early an hour, was highly dangerous; yet I longed to remove myself as far as I could from the neighbourhood of the cave, and to get nearer Sagoonah. As I went along I shook the limbs of the lower kind of under-wood, and disturbed the birds of prey roosting among them, that fluttered away with shrill shrieks. The roar of a tiger not far from me made me hastily conceal myself behind a large tree on the opposite side whence the sound came. A second roar appeared to be very close by, and I lost not a moment in ascending the tree before the eye of the savage should flash upon me. It was then the hour of grey dawn, rendered more obscure by the forest foliage; but I could still see objects very distinctly for some distance around me. I had not sat long on a huge overhanging branch, when two enormous tigers issued from the thickest part of the jungle in a violent struggle for some heavy body in which their fangs were plunged. They came directly under where I sat, and I perceived they were contesting for the body of a man that appeared completely lifeless. "Who could the unhappy victim of these animals have been? where were they dearly united to him in life—the wife, the children, or the parent—who would never know his fate?" This thought crossed me rapidly when I saw the body between the two animals, which neither dared to feed upon for fear of his antagonist. They stood glaring frightfully at each other, then growling furiously, and lashing their sides with their long tails in the utmost rage. At last one of them went off, and the other appeared for a considerable time to be sucking out the blood of the unfortunate man; he then slowly left it, as if gorged to satiety with the fluid of life. The ornaments and part of the man's dress lay on the ground by the body, and I determined to descend and secure them, when I could do so with safety. It was with no little pleasure I saw the creature walk away into the dense part of the wood to take its repose, as is the habit of these animals in the day. I then descended from the tree and searched the body of the dead traveller, which had been sucked till it was dry and light; not a bone was touched, nor the flesh anywhere very deeply torn. I found what I searched for tied round the loins of the corpse; it was a silver waist-chain or *kurdoorah*, which I transferred from the dead to a living body. There were also two massy silver rings for the wrists, and a chain round the left ankle, which I secured with no great difficulty. I found no money upon the body at first, and I therefore concluded it might have fallen on the spot where the tiger first seized the unhappy man, a little distance off. I tracked the place by the blood, where the progress of the traveller had been fatally arrested. There I discovered a red turban, shoes, and some other articles which had belonged to him; but above all, a bundle of letters or papers, which I placed in the folds of the turban, and planted the latter on my head, hoping to pry into their contents at some more convenient opportunity. I also found an hircarrah's staff.[1] This convinced me that the unfortunate man had been a courier in the service of some great person, whose correspondence I had a strong inclination to peruse.

[1] A small javelin borne by couriers and messengers.

Fearing to remain longer on that spot, lest I should encounter a fate similar to that of the hircarrah, or, what was worse, fall into the hands of the men whom I had bolted up in the cave, if any chance should effect their liberation, I pushed on through the jungle as fast as I could, and did not once venture to look behind me. Having gained the open plain, I sat down under a large tree, and there indulged my curiosity by examining the directions of the letters. What was my surprise to find two directed to Trimbuckje Danglia Behauder, at Poona! These I broke open directly, and one of them was as follows :—"To the illustrious, mighty, benevolent, and just Trimbuckje Danglia Behauder, the source of all justice, this letter from the friend of his heart Bassoo Scindea, killehdar of the world-towering fort of Asseerghur, conveys the melancholy news that the two females, Allaya Bhae and Sagoonah Bhae, being guided by the star of destiny, have, by means unknown to the friend of the merciful Trimbuckje Danglia, unfortunately made their escape from the fort. In the hope of retaking the fugitives, horsemen have been despatched different ways, besides many hircarrahs and spies in disguise, to all parts of the country, who have returned without success. By the aid of Ishwur, this attached friend has determined to move mountains and to drain rivers, in attempting to find their place of concealment; which, having done, an hircarrah camel, swift as the wind, shall be sent off to Poona to the illustrious Trimbuckje Danglia, to give him the joyful intelligence. May glory, honour, fortune, and wealth attend his footsteps !"

Thus terminated the first letter, and thus ended my hope of finding Sagoonah at the fort of Asseerghur. Though I rejoiced at her escape, yet it was a sort of disappointment to me to have lost the only clue by which I could trace her footsteps, and to have all to begin over again. The second letter I opened began thus :—"To the beloved and most friendly Trimbuckje Danglia, the writer of this letter, Bassoo Scindea, gave, in a heartrending despatch, news of the escape of two females placed under his care ; he now begs leave to remind his attached friend, that the captives, having been in the fort for two months, incurred these the following expenses, for which a *hoondie*[1] from Poona, in favour of this firm friend, will be most acceptable.

	R.	Qr.	
Rice and ghee, from 1st kastick to the present date, for one captive, Allaya Bhae,	15	2	63
Do. Sagoonah, rice only,	11	3	0
Dhal, onions, carrots, &c.,	6	2	75
Firewood,	9	3	0
Two old beds, and mending one,	20	0	0
Two mats, one old,	5	2	0
Tobacco for Allaya Bhae,	6	3	0
Hookah,	2	2	0
Red Sarry for Allaya Bhae,	30	0	0
Chowley for ditto,	10	0	0
Sarry green for Sagoonah, gold border,	45	0	0
Chowley, red, for ditto,	12	0	0
Shoes and slippers,	4	0	0
Paid for servants and attendants, &c.,	15	0	0
Rupees,	195	3	38

"The hoondie for this account may be despatched as soon as convenient.   Farewell."

I was much diverted by this "firm friend's" disinterested kindness, and the strong love of Bassoo Scindea for Trimbuckje Danglia. The latter would, had he been circumstanced in a similar way, have done precisely the same thing, and would have had as little chance of getting repaid as the kind Bassoo Scindea had now, especially since his letters had got into my hands. These accounts were no doubt base fabrications on the part of Bassoo; a very small part of these expenses was really incurred by my dear friend and her aunt. There was also a third letter, addressed to a Brahmin, Succaje Punt, containing nothing that could interest me.

I now arranged my dress in the best way I could, and by the aid of the hircarrah's red turban, silver bangles, and waist-chain, I cut a very respectable appearance. I began to consider where I should bend my steps. I had now no business at Asseerghur, nor in any place in that direction. I wandered undetermined

---

[1] Bill of exchange.

on, until I found myself in the second jungle, into which I entered with trembling steps. I passed through it without meeting with either tigers or men, and soon found myself in the glen described by the tall man. It was a place fitted to enact the most bloody and pitiless crimes in—in every respect a den for murder. On all sides arose lofty dark rocks, topped by the majestic peepal trees, the branches of which, meeting above, cast beneath them a darkness that one almost shuddered to be involved in. Torrents pouring down deep gulfs, rugged rocks, and broken masses of fallen stone, rendered it extremely difficult to find out the proper path, which continually wound around or between them. Having proceeded onwards for some distance, I saw a miserable cottage perched on a point of rock close below a wooded precipitous height, which I concluded must be that of the goatherd. I clambered to the door, and knocking, it was opened by a venerable aged man, who demanded my business. I apologised for interrupting his quiet, and begged he would allow me a corner of his verandah in which to cook my rice, and give me a few sticks to light my fire. He pointed out a place to which he told me I was welcome, and I began my cooking, though I had much rather have had nothing more to do than to converse with the old man. As I proceeded, he examined me closely, and inquired at last whence I came, and whither I was going, the old questions which all the world seemed privileged to ask me. I told him my first destination was Asseerghur, but —— "But what?" interrupted the old man, in a sharp tone. "Why, nothing," said I. "Which means," observed he, "that you do not choose to inform me your reasons for deviating from your original intentions." "There have unexpected events happened," I replied, "which have prevented my going to Asseerghur. What these events are, my short acquaintance with you does not warrant me in disclosing." "I admire your prudence, my friend," he remarked; "in this world of misery, one has need to keep one's own counsel." "I intend to keep mine," said I, "I assure you." "Then I would advise you not to wear that silver chain so openly around your waist, especially as blood tells tales." "Blood!" I exclaimed. "Ay, my friend, blood!"

he replied; "is it possible that you have stained your hands with murder?" "Indeed," said I, "you wrong me by the unjust suspicion." "Wrong you!" he observed; "it was but yesterday I saw that silver chain round the waist of an hircarrah of Asseerghur, and, if I mistake not, those bangles also; and now you wear them, spotted as they are with blood! You also tell me you were first going to Asseerghur, and then that circumstances led you another way; I hope I am wrong in supposing those circumstances are robbery and murder." "You never were more wrong in your life," I rejoined; "I am no murderer." I then explained to him all the particulars of my witnessing the tiger scene, and of my picking up the ornaments of the man who was killed, and that I would give them to any of the relations of the poor man if I knew them, or should ever chance to meet with them.

There was an openness in my manner which seemed to please the old man, and he gave credit to my story; but advised me not to wear property so obtained in that open manner; it might be recognised by friends or relatives of the dead; and there were plenty who were always disposed to give the worst colouring to a circumstance of the kind, when I might have a hard matter to persuade them into a belief of my having uttered the truth: a tiger would be made of me, and plenty of guns would be levelled at me. I thanked him for his kind advice, and promised to be more cautious. Having now eaten my rice, I deemed it to be my duty to warn the goatherd of his danger, and of the means I had taken to screen him for the present from his pursuers. "It is impossible," he exclaimed; "no one is pursuing me, nor have I now an enemy in the world; I had once, but those times are past." Here he wiped away a tear from his eye, and seemed oppressed with the remembrance of some heavy sorrow or bitter recollection. His appearance spoke care, blended with a manly firmness of character. I admired his countenance; and it seemed as if I was drawn towards him by some extraordinary kind of sympathy, some unaccountable partiality. Both of us appeared anxious that we should know each other's situation, and unburthen our miseries. This was so strong a feeling with me, that I felt unable to account for its arising so suddenly, and the reflection of treachery, or fear of mischief to myself, alone restrained me from unbosoming; yet, if ever I felt certain that my confidence would not be misplaced, it was at that moment.

The goatherd appeared very anxious to have the persons of the men described who were meditating the interruption of his peace, and perhaps conspiring to deprive him of his life. That either of these things was the real object of the men whom I had placed in durance, I could not positively assert; I could only state that his name and place of abode were mentioned in a very mysterious manner by the two men whom I trusted would be soon no more. By degrees, as the kind disposition of the goatherd unfolded itself to me, I related more of the conversation I had heard in the secret chamber of the idol, and I informed him of the plans of a man named Gunput Rao Mahadeo, the pretender to the throne of Sattarah. On hearing this, name the old man grasped my arm, as if clinging for support, and then let his head fall on my shoulder as if he were insensible. In a short time, he recovered himself. The first words he uttered were, "Young man, you are in error, Gunput Rao is no more; or if he really exists, he is dead to the world." "Oh, then, you knew him?" I observed. "I knew him too well," he replied. Here he folded his arms, and remained perfectly silent for a considerable time. At last he exclaimed, "It is impossible—he cannot be alive!" "There is too much reason to believe that he has put on the garb of a gossein, and that he wanders about under the name of Gabbage Gousla." A heavy sigh from the goatherd interrupted me, and prevented my communicating further information respecting this mysterious person. "Young man, you have spoken the truth—Gunput Rao lives—I have myself seen him; but, when we last met, little did I think I entertained my inveterate foe within these walls!" "He has then been here?" I observed. "He has," replied the goatherd; "and, under the name of Gabbage Gousla, has partaken of my homely fare." He now described the face and figure of this arch-fiend so accurately, that I did not hesitate in declaring him to be the man who prowled about in the garb of sanctity, and, affecting to have resigned all worldly affairs, aspired to a throne. "He shall not succeed, by Ishwur, and all the gods in the Vèdas," cried the old man, with an energy and vehemence that astonished me. He perceived my surprise, and instantly composed himself, saying, "Excuse my vehement behaviour, my friend; I keep you from your food. Eat, and then pursue your journey; I will accompany you, for it indeed behoves me to provide for my safety."

The goatherd now retired into an inner room, and I went on eating my rice. It occurred to me that this old man was the brother of Gunput Rao or Gabbage Gousla, whom Mahadeo, the first Pindaree, supposed to be murdered, and by whose account it was evident he was the true and lawful successor to the Sattarah musnud.

The subject appeared to be of a nature far too delicate for any individual unconcerned in the event to touch upon; but I felt deeply the sorrows and injuries this unfortunate old man had undergone, and probably was yet doomed to undergo. He speedily returned to me, having a wallet at his back, and a few brass pans and pots in his hands. I lost no time in accompanying him, and we bent our steps through the lonely glen. The shades of evening approached, and cast a melancholy gloom around. We had proceeded but a short distance from whence we set out, when I asked my companion whither he intended to bend his steps. "Dost thou ask from an impertinent curiosity?" said the goatherd. I replied, "No, believe me, I ask from an ardent desire to serve you; and would guard you from the secret attacks of your enemies, if accident should ever enable me to be so useful." "I believe you to be sincere," said he, "and we may meet again. If you should by any chance become acquainted with the machinations of the man called Gabbage, you cannot serve me better than by communicating them to me."

To convince the old man how anxious I was to do him every kindness in my power, I related the plans of Gunput Rao, or Gabbage, concerning the marriage of his son with a girl named Sagoonah. The old man groaned inwardly, but said nothing. I inquired by what means I could convey to him any information I might chance to acquire respecting him. He desired me to write to him under cover to Shewdhut Wanee, Indore. "Is it possible," I exclaimed, "you are going to such a distance?" "Necessity compels me," he replied, "for there alone can I now expect a secure asylum." "Should I be permitted to visit you," I added, "by what means can I gain access to your place of refuge?" "Take this small silver ring," said he, presenting me with one of little value, on which was engraven a dove encircled by the word "*sulamut*" (health, prosperity). Show it to a wanee near the Motta Tullas¹ in Indore; his name is Shewdhut. He will conduct you to my place of abode, provided my enemies allow me time to retire to it in safety."

By this time we had entered the plain, about three coss only from the fort of Asseerghur. The old man now inquired my intentions, and whither I proposed travelling. I replied that I had wished a short time since to enter Asseerghur; but now that those whom I sought were no longer within its walls, I did not know where I should direct my steps. "Whom do you seek?" said he. I replied, "Two unfortunate women." "How dost thou know they are not now in the fort?" I stated that I had read the despatches of the killehdar to Trimbuckje Danglia. "Those despatches contain the truth," said the goatherd; "the two women are really fled. Six nights ago, at the hour of twelve, my cottage door was assailed with a violent knocking. I arose, and demanded why I was thus disturbed, and a female voice begged me, in most moving terms, to admit two unhappy women, whose lives depended upon my acquiescence with their wish. I could not be deaf to such an appeal, and ascertaining that they were alone, I opened the door and let them in. They called blessings down upon my head for my kindness to them; and, in the course of conversation, I learned that they had fled from the fort of Asseerghur. One was a very young woman, the other more advanced in years. The face of the latter I could scarcely see, and that of the former not at all, it being carefully veiled. I informed them that it was but too probable persons would be despatched in quest of them, and that if they were found in my cottage, ruin would fall upon us all. They told me that they

¹ Great Tank.

intended to pursue their journey as soon as possible, and requested a small supply of raw rice, which I presented to them, at
the same time urging a longer residence under my roof, or at
least until morning dawned. They acquiesced in this arrangement; and when I arose in the morning, I found they were gone.
This includes every particular I am acquainted with respecting
these females and their escape, nor do I know whither they
directed their steps."

The goatherd, hinting that no time must be lost in effecting his
security, turned into a narrow path, and bade me "Farewell."
As we parted, he said, "We may meet again; if we should not,
remember thy promise to convey to me any intelligence thou
mayest think can be of importance to me." After his departure,
I stood several minutes in silence, reflecting upon the old man's
conduct; and at length I sauntered on, dissatisfied, I knew not
wherefore, towards the fort of Asseerghur. As matters had now
turned out, and the women were secure, I repented seriously the
having immured the two men in the secret chamber of the cave;
I could have easily satisfied them of the escape of the two women,
and have convinced them of the reality of the circumstance, when
they would have agreed that I had done my best. They being
satisfied of this, would have rewarded me, and let me into more
of their proceedings, wherein I could either have aided or counter-
acted them as I thought proper.

I now began to think I could not do better than return and
release them. It was but two days ago that I had immured them,
and they could not in so short a time be starved to death, having,
as I knew, rice sufficient left to last them at least for that period of
time. Yet, what would be my reward for emancipating them but
certain death for my treacherous intention of destroying them.
To retrace my steps, therefore, for the purpose of setting them
free, involved my own safety, and would be little short of madness.
To advance to the town of Asseerghur appeared useless; and to
trace Sagoonah, a task utterly hopeless, seeing I had not the most
distant cue to the road she had taken. To stand in the open
plain undetermined, seemed the excess of folly; but on former
occasions, when similarly circumstanced, I invariably met some

person or persons who, though strangers, said something, or proposed some scheme, which induced me to accompany them. At this moment, I saw not a living thing, and darkness was beginning to spread over the plain. Would there be any risk in entering Asseerghur? In favour of so doing, there was the consideration that I knew no one there, and could not be recognised ; but they might discover the silver chains of the unfortunate hircarrah, where he must have been so well known, and from whence he had started on his fatal errand. It would be rashness to attempt concealing these ornaments about my person ; for, if discovered, as a thousand accidents might occasion them to be, suspicion must attach itself to me, and occasion my ruin. Thus pondering some time as to what it was most advisable to do, I at last made up my mind to await till morning near where I then was, and after daybreak find out some spot which I might easily recognise, where I might bury the silver articles securely, and afterwards enter the town.

CHAPTER XX.

HAVING come to the resolution mentioned in the preceding chapter, I lay down under a tree. To sleep was impossible, agitated as I felt by doubts and fears, both on Sagoonah's account and my own. The singular conduct of the goatherd also haunted my mind, and I gave up all idea of obtaining even a moment's repose. While I lay ruminating on these things, I fancied I heard footsteps approaching towards me, and, listening more attentively, I found I was not mistaken. To remain where I was would expose me to robbery, perhaps to death. Seeing no other resource open for safety, I resolved to climb up the tree under which I had been lying. I knew that I must not lose a moment; but, on attempting to mount, I found it was too large to climb. The voices came nearer, and compelled me to relinquish what seemed my last hope. I hastily raked up the earth near the roots of the tree, and buried my silver chains, concealing the ring given me by the goatherd in the folds of my turban. I then went a short distance off, and laid myself flat on the ground, trusting to the darkness of the hour for preventing my being observed. The voices seemed by this time to be very close to where I lay—they were near the tree; and I heard one of them say, "It is strange! we agreed to meet at the fort, yet there are no tidings of him. What can have detained him?" "Oh, he has been smoking ganza, I suppose, and is fallen into a two-days' slumber." "It cannot be," said the first voice; "something unexpected must have happened at the cavern." "What, think you the idol has visited him with his vengeance?" said the second. "Nonsense," said the other. "This will turn out to be something very serious, depend upon it ; Kokoo never failed in this way before." "But he would be of no use were he here now ; the she-devils are fled, and how they got away is a mystery." Here the voices seemed retreating from me, and I could catch nothing more than detached expressions, such as "Trimbuckje," "old woman's business," and others of a similar nature. The direction taken by these persons was towards the road conducting to the glen.

I now arose and returned to my old place near the tree, leaving my treasure still buried. I had no doubt but one of the men who had passed so near me was the same whom I had heard in Sagoonah's dilapidated dwelling appoint Asseerghur as the place where he was to meet his mysterious companion, who, it seemed, was also named Kokoo. Whether Kokoo meant the tall or short man whom I had barred in the cave I could not tell, and I sat waiting impatiently for the dawn of day. As soon as it had dawned I set out, and in an hour arrived at Asseerghur, where I found every one busy in preparing to garrison the fort, as war had commenced with the Peeshwa at Poona,—Scindea, as well as the Berar Rajah, having combined to overwhelm the English troops. The cause of this war was the murder of the holy Shastree, on his way from Guzerat, by the relentless Trimbuckje, the agent of the cruel Peeshwa Badjerao. The British Resident at Poona found it impossible to pass by this flagitious act unnoticed, and, as before related, insisted on Trimbuckje being delivered up to the English. Since his escape from their hands, the Peeshwa still continued to befriend him ; and, deaf to all the remonstrances of the Resident (with whom he professed amity, as well as with his Government), involved himself in hostilities against the English, in concert with Scindea and the Rajah of Berar. He felt confident of success, and, calling Mahratta ingenuity to his aid, caused a report to be circulated that a large body of Pindarees were within two days' march of Poona. The whole of the British force was instantly marched against them, and the opportune moment chosen for striking an exterminating blow against the few British troops left in the city. These the Peeshwa imagined he should destroy very easily ; but a regiment of Europeans arriving from Bombay, he became alarmed, and sent a vakeel to the Resident, requesting they might return to Bombay. This request was not attended to. The vakeel again visited the Resident, and conducted himself with great insolence; and at last, half unsheathing his sword, bade him prepare for war. This was not unexpected, and the Resident immediately quitted his house for the camp. He narrowly escaped; for the Mahratta rabble attacked, and, setting fire to his house, completely demolished it. The main body of the English army was at this time far distant in pursuit of the pretended Pindaree force, and only about one thousand men were left with the Resident, to make a stand against the almost innumerable forces of the Peeshwa. The people of Asseerghur were astonished at the valour of the English at the battle of Kirkee, where, with only two guns, they gained a decided victory over the tens of thousands of the Mahratta horse and foot, drove the Peeshwa from his capital, and took possession of his palace. These events had damped the courage of the people of Asseerghur, who, while lamenting the fate of the Poona Peeshwa, expressed their persuasion that Scindea, their master, would show the conquerors a very different kind of game. I, however, who had seen him in the field, had my doubts upon this subject, the expression of which I took good care to keep in profound silence.

Penniless as I was, the idea of again entering the military service, of which I before thought I had enough, came into my mind. It was true that my duties would interfere with my search for Sagoonah; but it was equally true that, destitute of money, I could not, if I remained as I was then situated, follow up the pursuit. The chances of my military avocations might give me some direction, or lead me near the spot where she whom I loved had found a refuge. Those only who know what it is to be in an agony of doubt, such as I then was, can appreciate my sufferings. A female whom I tenderly loved was pursued up and down by powerful and violent men, while her fate was unknown to me, aad I could gain no trace of her footsteps; one who was a most ardent lover, and devoted his life and soul to his mistress, was even ignorant of her resting place, and unable to afford her protection, even if he discovered her! What, then, could I do?

What resource was left me? Was not my situation the most cruel on the face of the earth? Could I be blamed for my resolution? Bitter thoughts also hinted to me, that the enemies of Gunput Rao might even now have traced Sagoonah. Might she not at last accept the hand of his son, should he be discovered? Reflections like these almost drove me into madness. Others might be more fortunate in the circumstances of life than myself, but whose heart could be more devoted to the object of its regard? I lived but for Sagoonah; and, though poor in fortune, I was rich in stored-up love—in the fortune of the heart—and in the pure ore of a constant and boundless affection.

While I was thus ruminating on my unhappy destiny, I saw a party of English sepoys led prisoners by some of Scindea's soldiers. One amongst them had his arms tied behind him, a circumstance for which I could not account. On going up to the culprit, what was my surprise on recognising Fuzl Khan, the second Pindaree, and son of the sword-grinder and kabob-fryer at Broach. He did not appear to recognise me. On inquiry, I found he had been seized as a deserter from the English, and the sepoys were leading him away, when a party of Scindea's soldiers took both captors and captive prisoners, and were then conducting them to Asseerghur. Having made up my mind to try a soldier's life again, it appeared to me that Scindea's service was as likely to answer my purpose as any other, and that promotion was almost certain, either by my past experience and consequent merit as a soldier, or by intrigue. With the intention of entering myself, I proceeded up the hill on the summit of which stands the strong fort of Asseerghur; and I reached the gates just as they were flung widely open to admit the prisoners and their guard. Admittance was readily given to the captives and their guard, but it was surlily denied to me. I was obliged to submit to numerous interrogations; and, after waiting an hour, was only allowed to seat myself in the inner chowkee or guard-room. As soon as I was able, I made my wish known of being admitted as a soldier into the garrison; and I was conducted to a jummahdar of foot, who, being informed of my desire, accepted my services, and settled my pay. The former were likely to be very arduous, and the latter trifling enough. I was told, however, that I might scrape together by plunder a round sum of rupees. I was glad to hear this, not so much for the sake of pecuniary benefit, as because I should have a chance of being employed at a distance, and not be confined to garrison duty, which would entirely preclude the possibility of my discovering Sagoonah.

The jummahdar had a deputy named Nagoo. This fellow's real business was to deliver necessaries and pay, and to settle disputes between the soldiers; but, as Mahrattas are not over-nice in fulfilling the services with which they are entrusted, this Nagoo made free with the pay of the men, and was always creating, instead of settling disputes. Nagoo was anxious to enlist in his master's corps as many simpletons as he could, "because," he observed, "your writers and readers foment quarrels, and know too much; so that one cannot act as one chooses by them." No sooner did he hear my name announced (which seemed very high-sounding) than he summoned me to him. I had carefully predetermined to appear ignorant of reading and writing, because I feared that, by making myself useful, I might be detained in the fort, either in the treasury or arsenal. The before-mentioned disposition of Nagoo, of which I had been acquainted, induced me to adopt this course. I followed his messenger, meditating all the way how I could, most advantageously to my own objects, affect the numskull.

It struck me that I might stumble upon some one of my former acquaintance in the person of Nagoo, and I begged the messenger, in a careless manner, to give me some idea of his person—this I said in the most careless way. The messenger told me he was a Mahratta. I asked if he was tall or short; and found he was a very short man. "Fair?" I asked, with no little peturbation. "Yes, fair." "And not much hair?" "Not much," replied the messenger. "Light eyes?" "Very light." "Pray, is there a doctor in the fort?" "Oh yes!" "Do send him to me, then, for (pressing my hand on my stomach) I have the cholera morbus coming upon me so bad, that I fear I shall die." So saying, I leaned against the wall, and off went the messenger for the doctor. What would I not have given in the interval to have been out of the fort, that I might have escaped meeting Nagoo or the doctor! From the description, I apprehended Nagoo was the short man whom I had immured in the cave; and, from my knowledge of doctors, I had reason to apprehend little less than actual torture.

The doctor soon came, attended by a boy carrying medicines, and what he called instruments. These, in reality, were only an iron salamander and a keen knife. He ordered me to be taken to the hospital. An attendant lifted me up, and flung me across his shoulders as a butcher does a sheep. I was thus hurried across the fort to the hospital, a long building, without a single comfort of any kind. It sent forth the most disgusting effluvia I ever experienced. This horrid place, with the way in which I had been carried, my head hanging down in the midst of the burning sun, added to the expected torment from the doctor, was very likely to bring on the disease I had only pretended had affected me. I now considered also that an interview with Nagoo would ultimately be unavoidable; and I began to repent very bitterly my feigning sickness. I was first flung down upon a wooden bench, with a violence that, had cholera really been on me, would have relieved the doctor from further trouble. A dreadfully nauseous mixture was next poured down my throat through a horn. No mortal was ever before so dozed: they poured on and on, as if they were filling a cask. Of course, they no sooner withdrew the horn, than the most terrible nausea caused me to eject its contents again. Then they poured away, and the same result was attained. The doctor shook his head sagaciously, and declared that he had never seen, in the whole course of his practice, so obstinate a case of cholera. The violence of the retching was so excessive, that, completely worn out, I closed my eyes almost in a state of insensibility. I was soon aroused from my rest by feeling the most excruciating pains over the stomach, proceeding from the doctor's infernal salamander, red hot, drawn over my irritated and half-exhausted stomach, with as little concern on the part of the operator, as a farrier would feel when he was branding a horse. I roared with pain; and, being vexed and maddened at what I had undergone, and enraged at the ignorance of the doctor, I sprang up, and seized him by the throat. I verily believe he would have tortured no more patients, had he not received assistance from the attendants in the hospital. I was now bound down to the bench by cords, and pronounced mad. Cold water was flung upon me, and barbers ordered in to shave my head, while the doctor prepared his salamander once more to inflict fresh tortures, by applying it to my head—a very judicious method of curing madness![1]

How bitterly I repented the deception I had practised! The short man whom I feared could not have tortured me more than this accursed doctor, whom I heard boasting of the skill with which he had treated my cholera; though, owing to my impatience, I had brought on a temporary insanity, which, Ishwur being favourable, his salamander would speedily remove. His assistant at this moment whispered in his ear something, which I supposed was a proposal to await a little time, and see how the disease turned; the doctor seemed rather unwilling to assent, and I was left for an hour undisturbed. At the expiration of that time the doctor returned, and I endeavoured to convince the idiot of my sanity, by saying to him, "Ah, doctor! but for your profound skill, I must have died! I am relieved from the horrors of the cholera! Can I ever be grateful enough to you for it!" This flattery I thought would be grateful to the fool —all fools love it—and I did not think wrong. He ordered me to be set at liberty immediately. I never forgave myself for using flattery to this fellow, except by reasoning that it, perhaps, saved my life. I am certain, indeed, that I could not have survived his cruel treatment much longer; and yet this consideration will frequently, when I think of the time I was under his hands, hardly make me justifiable in my own eyes for the adoption of it.

As soon as I could do so, I set off towards the guard-room or chowkee; but, near the door of the hospital, I saw the messenger of Nagoo the deputy. "Come," said he, "as your cholera and your madness are now over, Nagoo will be happy to see you."

---

[1] Hot irons are substituted in the place of blisters, by the eastern native practitioners.

I said that it was late in the day, and I had had neither food nor rest. I urged the man to postpone the audience until the morning, or obtain Nagoo's consent so to do. He replied that he dare as soon propose delay to a tiger. "What!" I exclaimed; "is the deputy so fierce a fellow?" "Indeed he is," answered the man; "and he has met with something very unpleasant lately, which has terribly ruffled his temper." This was almost sufficient to convince me that Nagoo was, after all, the man I feared; and that his recent incarceration in the chamber of the cave was the cause of his present irritation. I followed the messenger like a criminal going to the tree: every limb trembled as I approached the residence of the tyrant. There was just light enough to discover the features of some one in the room; and what was my joy at beholding, not the mysterious short man whom I feared, but a perfect stranger to my eyes!

"Come hither, fellow!" was the first address of the self-important deputy. "So you have had a touch of cholera, I understand?" "I have," I replied; "and but for your learned doctor, I must have died." "Well, we could have spared you, I suppose; we have dunces enough in this place: to have lost a scholar would have sadly grieved us!" It was fortunate I knew the real character of Nagoo, and his views in so addressing me; for any one who was not in the secret would have fallen into the trap laid for him, and have boasted of his learning. "I wish I could read and write," I replied; "for then I should not be under the necessity of carrying a match-lock." "Then you don't read, eh? but you wish to learn, do you?" "Not I, now," was my answer; "I am too old to begin." "Perhaps it is as well you should remain in ignorance; you will find you can do better than a scholar. A soldier does not need a head to understand: ears to hear orders, eyes to see an enemy, and hands to fight him, are all he wants. What is the cause of a war to him? he must fight, be it right or wrong." Nagoo then asked if I should like to be employed outside or inside the fort? Of course I chose the outside service, giving as my reason, that there was greater pay and more variety in that service. "And greater risk, too," said Nagoo. I replied I could fight; and as to risk, I ran no greater than my comrades.

He then said I might draw upon him for my pay whenever I wanted it; and that he would advance any moderate sum for me, and draw my pay monthly himself. I thanked him, though I would have been gladly excused this kindness, as I could get my money through the regular channel; for I saw Nagoo intended to cheat me, and involve me in pecuniary obligations. I then took my leave.

I next proceeded to the guard-room, where the havildar demanded what he called tobacco-money—customary when a recruit entered the garrison. This demand I paid. Soon after, sundry other fees were required of me on different pretences, which I was obliged to give my consent to pay at some future period, not having a rupee left in my possession. I was exceedingly angry with myself, for allowing my fears to master my judgment as I had done, and for submitting to be blistered and physicked when there was no occasion for it. Though the description of Nagoo did correspond with that of the short man I had immured, and whose fate involved me in a horrid uncertainty; yet, had my fears allowed me time to reflect, I must have felt that Nagoo and the short man could not have been the same person; because I had been employed to gain admittance to the fort, which neither of my employers was daring enough to attempt. Moreover, had the short man been the jummahdar's deputy, he would have been, of all others, the best calculated, from his situation, to have liberated Sagoonah and her aunt. Some apology, however, I may claim, when the manner in which I left the men at the cave is considered; and what would have been the result of their finding me, should they, by any chance, have escaped death, and have fallen in with me.

CHAPTER XXI.

IN the fort, I met, as might be expected, with Fuzl Khan, with whom I claimed acquaintance. He was astonished at seeing me there; and I longed to hear his adventures, and how he escaped from the Pindarees and fell into the hands of the English sepoys. Having got leave of absence for a few hours, to go to the town below the hill, we entered a liquorshop, where Fuzl Khan told me that the Pindarees, having been defeated and driven in every direction, he, with difficulty, got away. I then asked after Mahadeo. Fuzl said he was a pious Pindaree—heart and soul in the cause—and that he had kept a very sharp look-out after the new comers; that he grew enraged beyond bounds, when he found that Nanna and myself had fled; and, suspecting that Fuzl Khan would do the same, he narrowly watched until he put spurs to his horse, and then fired his pistol at him; but the ball passed over his shoulder, and left him untouched. What his fate was afterwards, Fuzl could not tell, but concluded he fell in the general massacre that followed; for, as he had since heard, the whole horde was neatly cut to pieces. I was disappointed in being thus left in a state of uncertainty respecting the son of the pretender to the Sattarah throne; though I took care not to let Fuzl Khan know the cause of my anxiety respecting him. Fuzl had fallen in with a havildar's party of the regiment of sepoys from which he had deserted, and being recognised, was instantly seized; but Scindea's soldiers had taken the whole party, and rescued him, and finally brought them to the fort, where he was released by the killehdar, and taken into Scindea's service, in which he was happy in calling me comrade.

Fuzl was still the same sort of fellow as before. He indulged in repeated glasses until the fumes got into his head, and then the events of his former life all crowded upon him. He imitated the rage of the old cazee, who had eaten the dog's-tail soup; then he would turn grave and play over again his old agonies at losing his money, falling upon me as if I had been the boy who won it from him at eki beki; next he would laugh heartily, and cry out, "grind! fry! fry! grind!" as if his father and mother were actually present, and carrying on their old altercations, as he had detailed them in the fort of the Pindarees: all this ended in ?... falling down insensible. I left him at the liquor-shop and returned to the fort, where I learned that Nagoo had been inquiring after me. I thought it my duty to proceed immediately to his house, and I was instantly admitted. He seemed pleased to observe my ready attention to his wishes; and beckoning me to him, said, "Pandoo, I have work for you; can you be secret?" "Speak," said I, "and behold your slave." "So you all say," rejoined Nagoo; "but you must keep my secret as close as the oyster does the pearl." "I will keep it closer," I replied; "for the pearl is often, by the indefatigable fishermen of Ceylon, wrested from its innermost cell. From me, neither artifice nor violence shall wrest your secret." He was greatly pleased at this speech, and even condescended to present me with betel-nut and paun-leaf. Calling me into an inner apartment, and desiring me to sit down, he began by saying, "Pandoo, there is a woman"—(oh, how my heart beat!)—"there is a woman on whom I have bestowed thousands of rupees in golden ornaments." This woman I thought must be Sagoonah. "Sagoonah!" I exclaimed, completely forgetting myself. "No, no," said he, "her name is not Sagoonah; but no matter—this woman is my wife." What a cruel disappointment for me! "Yes, my wife; why do you stare so? is it wonderful I should have a wife?" "Oh no," I replied; "but it seems strange you should want to get rid of her." "No, no, Pandoo, I did not say anything of the kind; I only repent having given her so many ornaments, and I want to get them back again—that's all I mean: there is nothing strange in that, you know." "No, but why not demand them of her?" This, he said, would look shabby, and he should be laughed at; he wanted to get them all back, and not let her know who it was had them. This is not shabby at all, I thought to myself. The narrow-minded wretch then told me he had a plan in his head which might succeed for doing this : that she was going a short journey, and would take her ornaments and money with her; I was to enact the robber, and strip her of all her gold and jewels to the last grain, and bring them to him, and I should be well rewarded. I promised obedience, though secretly determined to disobey. Nagoo told me, that though obedience was my duty, he would merely wish that I should act as his friend in the present affair, because it was one of secrecy, and strictly confidential. This I admitted; but still I requested a companion or two, because a robbery such as he requested was seldom performed by a single individual. Nagoo hereupon observed, that he had no intention of trusting me alone—that he had a young man devoted to his interest, and he designed he should accompany me.

Having finished his nefarious business, as he thought, in the most advantageous manner for gaining his object, he arose and issued some orders to a servant who waited without; and in a short time this able assistant made his appearance in the person of my friend, Fuzl Khan, scarcely recovered from the effects of his yesterday's debauch, though doing the best he could to conceal them from observation. "Come hither," said Nagoo.— "*Ram, Ram, M,ha,raj,*" replied Fuzl Khan, bowing to the earth, and nearly falling on his nose. "Why, how now, friend !" exclaimed Nagoo, "that was indeed a low bow: what is the matter with you?" "Oh, my lord, I have—I mean, I am delighted with your summons, and cannot contain my joy." "Well, then, here is a young man," pointing to me, "who pants for employment, and also for a clever companion, and I know no one more able than yourself to effect the object I have in view." Here Fuzl Khan exhibited enthusiastic joy, and bowed again, until his nose almost came in contact with the earth. Nagoo then whispered to Fuzl his base plan respecting his wife; and Fuzl, who did not, it was evident, comprehend a single syllable of the conversation addressed to him, once more made his extravagant salaam. Our employer first whispering to me, bade me keep a strong check upon Fuzl Khan's conduct; and then whispered to him, no doubt, nearly the same thing respecting me. We were next furnished with passports to carry us from the fort and through the town. Nagoo told us that his wife would set out on the following evening, and we took leave. When we were fairly out of the house, Fuzl Khan came close to me, and asked what the old fool had been talking about all the time we had been with him. I told him he was about to seize his enemy's wife. Fuzl Khan observed, he had heard something said about a wife, and inquired if he did not also talk about her ornaments. I replied, that he said she would be an ornament to the fort, as she was very beautiful. Fuzl Khan then reeled home to his lodgings, and I walked to mine.

At this time I lodged at the dwelling of an old camel-driver, and expected I might gain some valuable information from him respecting Sagoonah and her aunt. The old fellow had appeared very cautious, and only answered my distant questions by a surly grunt, something like that of one of his own camels. I ventured to say I had met with an old goatherd, who had informed me that the women had come to his cottage in the glen. I thought this piece of information might have drawn out the old fellow, and made him communicative; still he replied only by his usual grunt, nor did it seem possible to render him conversable upon any point. Being heartily tired, I went to my mat immediately on my return from Nagoo. Just as I had fallen asleep, I was suddenly awakened by hearing a number of voices near me; and the old camel-driver entered my apartment, accompanied by several soldiers, who desired me to get up and follow them. I turned to mine host and asked an explanation of this unlooked-for affair; the only reply I could obtain was the old rascal's usual grunt. I made up my mind, therefore, to go with the soldiers, as resistance was fruitless. They took me to the killehdar of the fort, who told me he had sent for me in consequence of hearing from the camel-driver that I could give positive information respecting the two females who had escaped from thence. I was aghast at being questioned so suddenly on the subject, and assured the killehdar that he had been misinformed; that if I could give him any information, I should be happy to do so. I related what the goatherd had told me, from which the killehdar was not an atom the wiser, and I was dismissed with an half-angry, half-disappointed look. On returning to my lodgings I passed a bastion of the fort, where I heard persons conversing hard by. The moon broke forth just at the moment from behind a dense cloud, and I distinctly saw two men on the spot whence the voices proceeded. Determined to listen to what they said, as it seemed that something of more importance than usual must have brought them together at such an hour and in such a place, it being close to a lonely tower, I turned back, and reached the rampart over their heads by a circuitous route. I was soon within hearing of them again. One seemed to be in a great passion, whilst the other laboured to soothe and tranquillise him. "Who could have fastened the door?" said the more irritable of the two. "That I know not," replied the other; "but I found it so, and on opening it "—— "Well, well, you told me that before, why repeat it?" "It is useless, it is true, to do so; but I have no doubt Kokoo will re-appear, though the other will never see the light again." "But are you sure it was he?" "It is impossible I can be certain; but the place is known only to those two persons, and one is a corpse." "And a corpse shall he be who deprived me of his services." "Who," said the other, "was it that left him there?" "I know but one fellow, he who thwarts all my actions—Pandurang Hàrì." "Indeed! why then he is in your power; he is at present a soldier of this garrison." "Of this garrison!" said the other with surprise; "you deceive me: let me be certain of this ere I rest." "It is very certain, for I swear I saw him but yesterday at Nagoo's house; but how can you tell that it was Pandurang who locked the secret door?" "It is no matter whether he did it or not—he is my enemy, and stands in my way, and must "—— Here the voice died into a whisper, and I could hear no more. What was my agitation and alarm, however, at discovering that one of the two was Gabbage Gousla, for it was almost impossible to mistake his voice. This fortunate discovery enabled me to prepare for my safety. I went home to bed, and called Fuzl Khan very early, desiring him to accompany me, without loss of time, in pursuit of Nagoo's wife. He got ready immediately, and I quitted the fort, much to my gratification. It formed no part of my plan to suffer Fuzl Khan to aid in rifling the deputy's wife, nor in allowing him to see I did not rob her. On our way, we passed near the liquor-shop where Fuzl Khan had before been, and I took care to purchase two bottles of arrack and carry with us. As soon as we entered the jungle leading to the goatherd's glen I feigned fatigue, and sat down under a tree. I then produced the liquor; of which Fuzl Khan had no more objection to partake than I had to give, and he soon began to talk and laugh as usual. At length he fell down insensible, and I was left to my own reflections. My first was, how it would be practicable for me to escape Gabbage; the next, how I should explain to Nagoo's wife the nefarious scheme of her husband, and yet not make him my mortal enemy. At length, I was obliged to leave the matter to chance, and quietly await the approach of the ensuing evening. It was sunset when Fuzl Khan awoke, quite recovered from the effects of the arrack, which I had given him too early in the day. He was almost as sober as if he had taken nothing, and perfectly recollected, to my disappointment, that we were to make a woman prisoner. Finding it impossible to quiet him, I was obliged to offer him fifteen rupees to act exactly as I should direct, and assure him there would be no risk in deceiving Nagoo. He objected, however, that he should get only fifteen rupees, and I should make perhaps five hundred; for, of course, he supposed I meant to rob the woman of her ornaments, and he should expect half of whatever was taken. I assured him he should have half of whatever I took from her, and this pacified him. We now pushed on our way, determined to await the coming of the woman on the other side of the second jungle, not far from the fatal cavern in which the secret chamber was situated.

We reached a spot near the entrance of the cave, and soon heard the sound of a tattoo's feet, and the jingle of bullock's bells. It was, as I expected, Nagoo's wife and attendant. Notwithstanding my entreaties to Fuzl Khan to keep quiet when we came up with her, he rushed upon her, and began to threaten her, draw his sword, and swear. He then seized the gold ornaments on her neck with a savage eagerness, of which I had not before supposed him to be capable. I saw it was high time I should interfere, and coming up with my sword in hand, I told him to desist, or I would sever his head from his body. The poor woman shed tears of gratitude, and threw herself at my feet. I raised her up and restored her ornaments. Among the hair was some braided up with silver wire. This singular ornament struck me immediately, and I determined to inquire the means by which it came into her possession. At present there was no time for this. I therefore begged her to be composed, and offered to conduct her to a place of rest. I led her into the cavern, followed by Fuzl Khan, whom I represented as my servant, and for whose ruffian-like treatment of her I made many apologies. The gloom of the cave did not permit me to behold the face of the lady; but her voice was exceedingly melodious and sweet, so much so, I felt that the lips that uttered them must be beautiful. Having spread a mat in a retired corner, I called her attendant, who followed her on a bullock, and bade him cook some rice, and pay her every attention. I found the old rascal, to my great surprise, whispering with Fuzl Khan. By this time I had concluded he had been bought over by Nagoo, and that the conduct of Fuzl Khan was no more than he had expected; besides I observed he had kept aloof and never offered his assistance. This circumstance alone was sufficient to prove to me that the fellow was a villain in league with his master. The whispering I have mentioned continued until I went up to them with my sword in my hand, and declared if they touched the person of the lady, or approached her with a hostile intention, I would run them both through the body. To my amazement Fuzl Khan turned round and demanded who I was that pretended to dictate to them; called me a traitor for promising to serve my master Nagoo, and then to thwart him as much as lay in my power. "What, villain!" cried I, "would you rob a defenceless female?" "You are wonderfully considerate," he replied;

"what else are we come all this way about? what reward shall we get for not robbing her?" "The reward of a quiet conscience," I answered. Fuzl Khan and the old attendant upon this burst into a loud fit of laughing; and the former at last said, "By Allah and the holy Imam, those trinkets shall be mine," pointing at the same time to the ornaments of the terrified woman, who sat in inexpressible terror. I then told Fuzl Khan he must first pass me, and I put myself in an attitude of defence. He did not lack courage, though he never showed it but in a bad cause, and drawing his sword he made a lunge at me, which I parried with difficulty. It was so dark we could scarcely see each other, and before we had made more than two or three passes, the attendant came into the cave with a lighted torch, which he held up on high. We fought desperately, and the old villain taking advantage of my being fully occupied, stuck his torch in a fissure of the rock on one side the cavern, and falling on the woman, began to plunder her. I did not hesitate a moment, but, leaving my antagonist, rushed on the old miscreant, and with one blow felled him to the ground. Fuzl Khan returned the compliment by cutting me over the shoulder; fortunately it was the left, and he did not thereby disable my sword-arm. Furious with pain and anger, I turned upon him, and cut him over the wrist of the right arm. His weapon fell to the ground, and I made him beg for mercy, which he did without delay. I tied his hands behind his back, and proceeded to pacify the lady, who was screaming dreadfully. Having done this, I turned over the body of her old attendant, whom I had well punished for his villainy in attempting to rob his mistress. He was a corpse; not a pulse in his body beat; his jaw was fixed, and death was in his countenance; in short, he was past all power of doing ill again in this world. I felt no remorse for what I had done; for how could I take to heart the exit from the world of such a treacherous wretch, even though it was by my own hand.

Fuzl Khan lay groaning with pain, as he well might; for I found that, in my hurry, I had placed the rope which tied his arms, in the wound which he had received from my sword. I now removed the cord, and then began to think of the state of my own wound. Nagoo's wife applied water and bandages, and dressed it in the best way it could be done under existing circumstances I next took the torch, and approached the secret chamber-door which was behind the idol. The bolt was drawn back, by which it was clear some one had visited the place. I attempted to open it without success, until I remembered there was a secret spring, which I searched for minutely in vain. I despaired of obtaining an entrance, and returned to search for some instrument whereby I might force the portal, though it was very unlikely I should find one. I was obliged to break off the bough of a tree hard by, which cost me some labour, and I returned and battered the small door with it as violently as I could. It remained immove able until I had nigh given up the attempt; when most likely a fortunate blow touched the secret spring; the door flew open, and, grasping the torch, I entered the cell, from whence a most noisome stench proceeded, which, however unpleasant in itself, was grateful to me, when it convinced me that my enemies were no more. Still anxious to have ocular demonstration of the fact, I entered, but saw the mouldering body of only one person; it was that of the tall man : the body of his companion was nowhere to be seen. How could the short man possibly have escaped? I asked myself a hundred times; and how could the tall man have remained behind? Who liberated him? I could discover no hole in the roof, floor, or sides of the chamber, so that the door must have been the place of escape. To ruminate long was useless : I was glad to leave this chamber of death, and just as I came to the door, what was my surprise at seeing a man's hand on the bolt, in the very act of closing it, and thus consigning me to the doom to which I had left others. The horror of my situation came upon me in a moment, and I thrust the blazing torch on the hand that was thus ready to seal my destruction. The pain made the fingers let go their hold; and throwing open the door, who should stand before me in the cavern but Fuzl Khan! He it was, indeed, who had so nearly sealed up my life for ever. He had freed himself from his bonds, and having watched my motions, very cunningly hit upon the expedient of locking me in the chamber, and thus of having everything his own way. He saw that the plunder of the female must be his own. The pain he suffered from the burning torch was more than equal to that from the cut of my sword on his other arm. He groaned bitterly with his sufferings, and I was about to inflict instant death upon him, when he cried and prayed so hard for mercy, that I contented myself with again binding him, and, for greater security, fastening him to the idol's leg. Leaving him there to his meditations, I sought the poor woman, who could hardly yet believe herself secure. I succeeded in tranquillising her mind, and then proceeded to dispose of the body of the old man whom I had slain. About this there could not be much difficulty : and lifting up the torch in one hand, I proceeded to drag it to the secret chamber by the leg with the other ; where, before I safely bestowed it, I examined afresh the cords with which I had bound Fuzl Khan. I then entered the cell, and placed the body by that which lay decaying, and closed up the portal.

On approaching the woman, I entered into conversation with her, and she requested me to accompany her to the end of her journey. This I could not undertake to do ; but I informed her of the plot which had been got up against her, in a quarter from which she had little right to expect such an attempt to be made. I told her that the object was solely the ornaments which she carried about with her, and I advised her to be upon her guard for the future, as some stratagem would no doubt again be had recourse to for a purpose similar to the present. I now took an opportunity of remarking to her the singular trinket to which I have before alluded : I begged her to allow me to see it. She immediately complied ; and, on examination, I found the workmanship delicate and handsome, having six silver knobs very conspicuous upon it. I begged to know how she obtained the ornament, and she informed me it was a present from a female with whom she became acquainted in the fort of Asseerghur. "Poor creature," said she, "she was a prisoner there, and had no friend but me." Her name I eagerly asked ; and she replied it was Sagoonah. How I felt at the hearing that name again, and in having tidings of her so lately ! "You did, indeed, befriend her then ?" said I, "and have now tenfold reason to thank heaven for having enabled me to befriend you—to serve one who has showed kindness to her, who is so dear to me!" "You then are no doubt the Pandurang Hàrì of whom I have heard her speak?" I replied that I was, and would give worlds, did I possess them, to know where I should again meet with her; but that I began to fear she had forgotten me. "Very far from it," said the wife of Nagoo; "that hair entwined with silver, was studded as you see with six knobs, intended to denote the six happy months she spent with you at Kandeish, in peace and comfort." Upon hearing this, I pressed the precious relic to my lips and kissed it with rapture. I was so pleased, that Nagoo's wife begged my acceptance of it, and I with eagerness took it and deposited it next my heart.

I learned that both Sagoonah and her aunt had been very cruelly treated when in the fort; that they were nearly starved, and had no clothes save an old blanket each: that she herself taking compassion on them, had sent them food and clothing, the latter of which, she since learned, had never reached them, having been intercepted or stolen by those who guarded them. At length she obtained permission to visit them, and having compassion on their misfortunes, aided them in effecting their escape. When I inquired if she knew whither they were gone, she told me it was doubtful, though she had good reasons to imagine they had taken the road to Guzerat, as they felt certain that tranquillity nowhere awaited them in the Deccan. I next inquired if she knew to what part of Guzerat they intended to go, and she said she thought to Baroda, but that it was not their intention to remain there long. She, moreover, said that, as they had no means by which to live, they purposed to procure work if possible as a means of subsistence.

This was indeed opportune and valuable information. Guzerat was indeed an enormous distance; but what was distance in the way of true love? Nagoo's wife now begged me to accompany her a few coss on her road, until she was clear of the jungles. This I agreed to do, and nothing more remained than how to dispose of Fuzl Khan. Approaching him, therefore, I said, "Listen, Fuzl Khan; it would be much more to your advantage to be my friend than my foe, and now I give you a final moment to decide. If you do not choose to do so sincerely, you had better make peace with the idol, for I promise you enough of his company shall be yours. If, on the other hand, you are sorry for your past conduct, and swear to behave as you ought to do in future, I will release you, and give you one hundred rupees in consideration of your disappointment in not getting your ornaments—that is, provided you will accompany me to Guzerat." "What!" he exclaimed, "to Guzerat? to my own country? then I am your man for ever; release me, and I will swear to be faithful to you." He then reiterated his promises. His weakness prevented his accompanying us through the jungles, and it was arranged that I should return and call for him in the evening. The morning dawned, and though fatigued for want of sleep, I set off with Nagoo's wife from the cavern, and proceeded to escort her through the jungles. Having cleared them and arrived on the wide plain beyond, I took my final leave of her. and returned.

CHAPTER XXII

ON my return to the cavern, I was met by Fuzl Khan, who had been eagerly looking out expecting my arrival. He informed me he had been witness to a most singular scene since my departure—a scene that would astonish me. I begged him immediately to make me acquainted with the particulars. Feeling weak and exhausted, he said that he retired to a remote corner of the cavern, and lay down to try and obtain the best repose his wounds would allow him. He had scarcely closed his eyes, when he heard a gruff, coarse voice say, "It is impossible, you must have deceived me." "I swear," answered a second voice, "I did not deceive you; I liberated Kokoo myself, and left him weak and faint in the cavern awaiting your arrival." "Well, well," said the first, "I can see for myself." Both then proceeded to the little door leading into the secret chamber; "and I suppose," said Fuzl Khan, " they entered it immediately ; but they soon came out. One was in a violent rage, and said to the other, 'You are a vile liar, you have deceived me ; how should both bodies be at this moment rotting in the chamber, if what you say be true? Did not you tell me you saw but one, and that you yourself liberated Kokoo?' The other man replied he knew not what to say, but that if they found Kokoo where he had left him, he hoped conviction would follow. 'Show me the fellow, then,' said the first speaker. They both now proceeded towards the corner of the cavern where I lay. There was little or no light in that part, but still there was enough to discover a human figure reclining upon a mat. ''Tis well,' said one of the men; 'he sleeps; but how came there to be two bodies in the chamber?' This was a difficulty they could neither of them solve. The man who appeared to be superior, then came up to me and cried out,

'What, ho! Kokoo! asleep while there is so much work abroad? Awake! thou lazy varlet. Come, come, the birds are flown towards Guzerat; be quick, and follow them.'

"It may be easily imagined that I lay in no very pleasant state of feeling. I did not dare to confess I was not Kokoo, nor could I give any satisfactory account of myself, or how I came there. The man shook me by the arm, and cried out, 'Come, Kokoo; surely thou art not as dead as thy friend!' I started as if from a sound sleep, not wishing them to believe I had overheard any part of their conversation. 'Who in the name of Ishwur have we here?' said one of the fellows; 'bring me a torch!' One was lighted, and they held it close to my face. 'Why, you miserable, half-starved, Musselman dog!' cried one, who was in the garb of a gossein; 'where did you come from? and where is Kokoo?' 'Who is Kokoo? I don't know anything of a person so named. I never heard of the man you ask for before.' 'Come, come, my friend,' said one of the men; 'you must not feign ignorance; I left him here, and now I find you in his place.' The gossein then got into a violent rage, and began to accuse his companion of having deceived him. A violent altercation ensued, which ended in the gossein stabbing the other man in the side, after which he went away, muttering curses and imprecations upon him. I have been very anxiously waiting your arrival," continued Fuzl Khan, "as my situation was not a very agreeable one. I wonder who this Kokoo is?" I replied that I believed he was the devil, for it seemed impossible to get the upper hand of him. I described his person to Fuzl Khan, and told him to be on his guard, and give me immediate intelligence should he ever chance to fall in with him. He promised me obedience in everything, but did not fail to remind me of the one hundred rupees I had promised him.

I desired him to accompany me immediately, and took my way towards the tree where I had buried the silver ornaments. It was necessary to go through the glen where the goatherd's cottage was situated; and, before we reached it, the darkness of evening came upon us. As we passed the cottage, I fancied I saw two men enter it. I had little doubt but one of them was Gabbage Gousla, while the other in all probability was Kokoo, whom he had somewhere fallen in with. If I could have depended upon Fuzl Khan, I would not have hesitated an instant in entering the place and watching their motions. As I was circumstanced, I thought it better to pass on a little way, conceal myself, and watch, by which means I might learn something to my advantage. I desired Fuzl Khan to proceed, and await my coming at a place which was easily recognised. He instantly obeyed, and I continued in ambush, watching the door of the cottage, from whence the two men soon came out, taking the road to Asseerghur. They passed the tree near which I had concealed myself, and I could clearly hear Gabbage's rough voice cry out, "The old villain is fled, but I will ferret him out. Foiled in all my plans! I will not be so much longer. Curses on that Pandurang Hàrì, the sneaking rascal! It must have been he who locked you up in the cave. What idiots you were to let a stranger into our secrets!" "It was all Salla's work," his companion answered, "not mine." "Well," said Gabbage Gousla, "he has paid dearly enough for his rashness and folly. What we now have to do is"——

I could hear no more of the conversation of these men; but I was in great fear lest they might overtake Fuzl Khan, and, recognising him for the man whom they had left in the cavern, use him ill, or probably question him too closely, when he might inadvertently bring up my name as his fellow-traveller. I kept, therefore, as close as I could in their rear, only allowing them time to get a small advance of me in the road. I then proceeded towards the place where I had appointed to meet Fuzl Khan. On arriving there I could not find him, and began to conjecture a thousand things, and to despair of doing so at all; when, looking over the plain, I saw a man approaching me at a distance, seemingly in full speed. On his coming nearer I saw it was Fuzl, who told me he had been overtaken by two men, one of whom answered the description I had given him of Kokoo. He said they had very closely questioned him as to his business in the jungle, but had not recognised him as the slumberer in the cavern. Not knowing what reply to make to their questions, he told them he was about to join his master, Nagoo, in the fort. They asked him if he was acquainted with a person of the name of Pandurang Hàrì? He replied that he was, and said Pandurang was at present in the fort, where he had left him only the day before. Upon this the two men hurried on their way, muttering together. He heard them say, "This time he shall not escape!" Fuzl Khan immediately hastened to communicate the information to me. I then thanked him for the adroit way in which he had deceived the two men, and proceeded to the tree where I had buried my treasure. I thought it best, however, to await the dawning of day before I searched for it, and proposed to my companion to rest ourselves awhile. In the morning I went to the tree, and, digging, soon discovered, to my great joy, that the ornaments were all safe. I gave my companion the two silver bangles, with which he was highly pleased; and by thus keeping my promise, I attached him more strongly to my interests than I could have done by any other method, and I hoped to find him a useful person in pursuing my future objects.

I was strongly impelled, on a sudden recollection of what took place at the cavern during Fuzl Khan's absence, to return, and try if I could discover who it was had been the victim of Gabbage Gousla's revengeful passions. I therefore proposed it to Fuzl Khan, as there was reason to think the unfortunate man had not been killed, but only severely wounded, though there could be little doubt but his death was intended. My companion replied that he had seen quite enough of that dark and horrible place, and had no great inclination to set his foot in it again. I would not go alone, and Fuzl Khan seemed determined not to accompany me. At length I prevailed upon him to go as far as the entrance with me, and to leave me the task of looking for the wounded man. We set off, my companion being somewhat in a surly humour. We had the whole day before us, and there was nothing to be apprehended from thieves in the jungles, all of which we cleared in good time; so that a large portion of daylight remained after we had reached the cave. Fuzl Khan still determining not to enter the gloomy place, I went in, and groped in every corner a good while, but found nothing, and returned to my companion, who advised my lighting a torch, as so much of the cavern was impervious to the light of day. We had no torches with us, but we set fire to some sticks that afforded but a bad substitute for them; and Fuzl described the place where the man had been stabbed, but refused to enter and assist me. I now recommenced my search, and was at the point of giving it up, when, my light being extinguished in a dark part of the cave, I stumbled over something which I soon found was a human body. Whether it was dead or alive, I had no means of ascertaining. I called to my obstinate companion in vain, being determined to be satisfied. I therefore took the body by the leg, and drew it as gently as I could to the mouth of the cave, and, in so doing, fancied I heard a deep groan. This gave me hope that I might yet be of some assistance to the unhappy object of Gabbage's vengeance. On getting into the air, I found that the wounded man was suffering more from loss of blood than the depth of his wound. The latter had, however, ceased bleeding, and we contrived to bind up the wounded side with the sufferer's turban. The air, and a mouthful or two of fresh water, seemed to revive him. He opened his eyes heavily, as if with effort, gazed vacantly around him, and then shut them again, seeming as if he was in some horrible dream. Fuzl Khan did not scruple to render every assistance in his power now we were outside the mouth of the cavern; and by his care and my own united, we at last contrived to infuse a little more life into the object of our solicitude. Of speech he was not yet master; sustenance and unremitting attention seemed indispensable to restore it to him. Where we then rested nothing could be procured; and I proposed to Fuzl Khan that we should construct a litter, and lay him upon it, by which means we might convey him to some village, and obtain for him the necessaries, without which his recovery could hardly be calculated upon. My companion immediately assented to this proposition. We went to work, and, in a very little time, completed our task.

We lifted our patient on the litter, and slowly took the road towards Kandeish. The nearest village was that in which the durhm sallah was situated, where I first saw Gabbage Gousla's two men. We reached it before dark, and deposited our burthen there; and while Fuzl Khan went in search of rice, milk, fire-wood, and other necessaries, I remained by the wounded man. Fuzl soon returning, a fire was made, and provisions cooked; but, unfortunately, the object of our care could not raise his head, much less swallow food. We therefore covered him securely, and ate our own rice and milk, expecting to find him a corpse by the morning. The thought of this disappointment prevented my closing my eyes all night; but my companion, whom nothing could ruffle, lay snoring in perfect oblivion of everything, and utterly indifferent as to who might live or die.

CHAPTER XXIII.

THE following morning I heard, or fancied I heard, a rustling proceeding from the corner where the object of my care on the preceding day was reposing. I crept softly towards the place, the light not being yet sufficient to distinguish objects at a little distance, and, to my surprise, found the wounded man sitting upright. I lost not a moment in awaking Fuzl Khan, and desiring him to get a fire and warm some milk. He immediately attended to my first request, but hesitated about my second; when I discovered that he had drunk all the milk the preceding night. This being the case, I despatched the greedy rascal for more. The wounded man seemed as if he wished to articulate; but I desired him to desist, lest the exertion should bring on a relapse and bad symptoms. I washed his face, arranged his hair; and, on the daylight coming full upon his countenance, being now cleaned from the dirt and soil of the floor of the cavern, what was my astonishment on recognising my old companion, Nanna, who had been Trimbuckje's servant, and was taken prisoner with myself by the Pindarees! I was now more than ever anxious for the return of his health and speech. I longed to know how he could have become an instrument of Gabbage Gousla's. He did not seem to recognise me, nor could it, in his present deplorable state, be expected. On the return of Fuzl Khan with milk and provisions, I desired him to approach the wounded man, and see if he could not call his features to recollection. He replied he had seen the face before, but he did not recollect where or when. I reminded him of our being taken by the Pindarees, and that the present helpless object of our care was my companion at the time, and had been one of the audience when he, Fuzl Khan, told his own history in the ruined fortress. Fuzl observed how much he was changed, looking attentively at him, and thought it would be a miracle if he ever recovered. I had strong hopes of seeing him reinstated again. We washed his wound, and bound it afresh with the best cloth we could obtain. We gave him the warm milk, and soon found that these little offices contributed to benefit our patient, who by and by dropped into a profound slumber. I now went to the potail's house, and related to him the deplorable state of the wounded man, and how we had accidentally discovered him in the solitary cavern. I stated that, as the durhm sallah was a public place, I feared it was very ill calculated to afford him the quiet necessary in his situation. The potail offered me a room in his own house, and I very thankfully accepted it. When Nanna awoke, we lost not a moment in removing him thither. The potail placed him in a comfortable bed, and his wife promised to pay him every attention in her power. The truth is, we produced an impression of our consequence on the potail's mind much to our advantage. Fuzl Khan strutted about with his silver bangles, affecting an air of great importance; and I thought it not amiss to wear some of my ornaments,—all which made the potail judge it right to treat us with every attention and respect. The first day of his removal to the potail's, our patient did not utter a word, the effort seeming to be still far too great for him.

In the meanwhile, I found the potail a very communicative person, and well versed in public affairs. We entered upon politics and the state of the war. "Ah!" said he, "poor Badjerao is like a hunted hare. He never sleeps two nights in the same place. The very idea of the Toope Wallas being near him, makes him issue orders for marching; so that his men, cattle, and elephants are jaded to death." I inquired where Trimbuckje then was. The potail called him a scoundrel, and wished he had been dead before the Peeshwa knew him, for to him he owed his downfall. "Downfall!" I inquired, with surprise; "do you imagine him to be indeed ruined, and that all hope is past of his being reseated on the musnud of Poona?" "He is ruined beyond redemption," said the potail. "Trimbuckje has deserted him, of course, and is anxious only for his own safety. Poona is wrested from the Peeshwa; Scindea is defeated at Aheidpoor; and Asseerghur is about to be stormed. We must all now become ryots[1] of the Toope Wallas." "We must then do the best we can," I replied; "we shall find ourselves more peaceable, and they who will labour will have their reward. The thieves and turbulent will be kept quiet. We must submit to what we cannot avoid. The spear of the Pindaree will be changed into the ploughshare of the *coombie*."[2] "This is very true," said the potail; "but what is to become of our venerable Brahmins, and our men of rank? What will they say to lose their offices, and be circumscribed in their power? Their pensions, their profits, and *jageers*,[3] will be curtailed and regulated, if not taken away. The Toope Wallas may manage tolerably well as governors; but the worst thing is, they will never allow any bellies but their own to be filled." "You potails, coolcunnies, &c., will no doubt, even under your new masters, contrive to reap tolerable harvests." "It is true, we may for a year or two," said the potail; "but after that time I fear the ryots will begin to lose their respect for our authority, and to comprehend that they can have their complaints attended to. Farewell, then, our ancient and established usages —our golden times of prosperity! There will be no farming out of districts then; no agreeing with a coombie for half his produce, and getting three-fourths; no fees; no fines; no bargaining with soucars and bankers, to keep the coombies eternally in their books. We must not flog them, and torture, after the manner of our fathers, those who are obnoxious to us. It will be a new state of things; I think the oldest always best." "I have learned," I replied, "that there are people who have other opinions upon those subjects; but I confess I am not competent to enter into an argument upon them. I wish you success most heartly, my friend. May your undertakings flourish, and your country also!"

I had scarcely uttered these words, when an unusual bustle

---

[1] Subjects.   [2] Cultivator   [3] Grants of land.

was heard in the village, and an hircarrah on a camel rode up to the potail's house, calling out, "The Peeshwa! the Peeshwa! Provisions, provisions! or your heads shall answer!" The potail was in great consternation, and promised to do all in his power towards assisting the fugitive prince. A sumptuous palanquin, borne by eight bearers, who appeared ready to fall to the earth from fatigue, came up directly afterwards. The Peeshwa alighted from it, and rushed into the potail's house. He threw himself in despair upon the ground, wailing bitterly. How different from his appearance when I last saw him in his palace, surrounded by Brahmins and officers, train-bearers and courtiers, in all the insolence of power! Then, indeed, I trembled in his presence. And well I might tremble, for I was assuming a character, the discovery of which would have annihilated me. Now I looked upon the once awful Peeshwa with pity and contempt, and thought how a little time since he strutted in his kinkobs and diamonds, like a gaudy peacock. He was deeply humbled, even to the very dust, watering the cow-dunged floor of the potail's house with tears of repentance and distress. His few attendants, as miserable as himself, were worn out with long marching. They came, however, to his side, imploring him to arise and rouse his spirits, puffing up the valour of his troops, his own greatness, and whispering hopes that could never be realised. Badjerao then assumed the monarch once more. He arose and issued some orders with a heavy heart. The camp lay without the village, and was well provided with rice and necessaries. The Peeshwa went through his ablutions, put on the silk vest in which he uniformly dined, and was monarch once more, until a courier galloped into the village, crying, "The Toope Wallas! the Toope Wallas!" Badjerao forgot his dinner, and bade his palanquin be off directly. His followers, unfed and unrefreshed, were obliged to resume their duties; and in half an hour the whole aswarry, with horse and foot soldiers, camels, elephants, and bullocks, were clear out of the village.

The potail came to me when they were gone, wearing a face of mirth, and well satisfied with himself. From this I judged that the Peeshwa had rewarded him for his trouble and provisions. I congratulated him, therefore, on his good fortune, asking him the amount of his present. "Present!" said he, "no, no, I have received no reward; that is a part of his business Badjerao never remembered in his life." I then observed it was fortunate the English were so near, as their approach had rid him of so many troublesome guests. The potail smiled, and said, "The English are far enough off, my friend. This was all a contrivance of my own. I foresaw ruin to us all, when the runaways came to my village, if I suffered them to stay long; and instead of procuring a stock of provisions for so many hungry mouths, I sent a fellow a few coss off, with orders to ride into the village furiously just as the soldiers were eating their dinners, and give the alarm which you have heard. I knew the name of Toope Wallas would scare the poor Peeshwa out of our precincts, and set him flying again; and, considering the road he has taken, it is ten to one but he will fall in with them. He has gone towards Ashtee, to which I have heard the English are approaching. Did you ever see such a pusillanimous man calling himself a fighting king?" I observed he did not bear his misfortunes with either manly or kingly fortitude; and I inquired where Gokla, his great general, was. The potail said, "Gokla is a brave man, but must persuade his rabble followers to fight before he can do anything; and without a few thousands like himself, he can do nothing for the Peeshwa's fortunes. We shall soon hear of some battle; and rely upon this truth, it will be the last Badjerao's troops will ever fight." I could not but admire the potail's ingenuity in getting rid of so many hungry vagabonds, who never dreamed of remunerating him for the expenses they heaped upon him.

All being again quiet in the village, I visited my patient Nanna, and found he was mending fast, though still very feeble and ill. He asked me where he was. I assured him in very good hands, and that he should be taken care of. He seemed sensible of the kindness shown him, and said he had nearly given up all hope of being restored to life. His wound was deep, and well aimed by the villain that gave it; but, when he next met him, he would convince him that there was another dagger more unerring. "This is my reward!" said Nanna. I desired him to be composed for the present, as he could give me an account of his disasters when he was better able to converse. He thanked me, and said he had but little to tell. "I served one villain," said he, "whom I deserted to follow a greater; and my wages have been a stab in the side, which but for your kind aid must have been my death. You shall find, however, that your kindness shall not be forgotten; for I swear to serve you, whoever you may be, provided you are not engaged in murder or other bad deeds, which I now from my very soul abhor." I assured him I was not engaged in any such schemes, and that possibly he might have it in his power to aid me materially. He squeezed my hand, and fell into a deep slumber. I left him, and, on going away, met Fuzl Khan, who said, "Who do you think I have met? Mahadeo, the first Pindaree, who is at this moment actually an officer in the Peeshwa's army." I asked him if he was certain of this. He replied he was; hat he made himself known, and should have had more conversation with him, but for the peremptory orders of the Peeshwa to march without a moment's delay. This was very satisfactory intelligence to me; because I felt certain Mahadeo was in the land of the living, and I knew where, though I had hoped he was no more.

The next time I visited Nanna was on the following morning. He had not yet appeared to remember me. Finding him much refreshed by sleep, I begged him to tell me the particulars of his history, as far as the time when he was left wounded in the cave. He accordingly began—"You have, no doubt, heard of such a man as Trimbuckje Danglia?" "I have," I replied; "and know him to be a sad villain." "He is indeed bad; but there are even worse men than he—for instance, the fellow who wounded me in the cave. But to proceed. I served Trimbuckje Danglia." "And so have I," was my observation. Nanna hereupon said, "Ah! I know that voice;—let me look full in your face. Thou art indeed Pandoo! Didst thou but know how I have been hunting after thee to work thy destruction, thou wouldst not save my life! But, henceforth, I am thine for ever! Listen, then; Trimbuckje, although we aided him in his escape from Thannah, never gave us the stipulated reward. This I did not so much

Q

grieve about; but he intrigued with my wife; so that I became
the laughing-stock of all his household. Full of indignation,
I vowed revenge; and he shall find I can remember my vow.
In the moment of my highest rage, I was met by Gabbage
Gousla, a hanger-on in Trimbuckje's train. I related all my
injuries to him. The watchful and cunning Gabbage blew the
sparks of vengeance which lurked in my bosom into a flame.
Listening to his artful incitements, I grasped the dagger which he
wore, and half presented to me, and swore I would plunge it
into Trimbuckje's heart. Gabbage grinned a horrible smile of
triumph, and bade me be sure of my blow. I was to meet him
at a particular spot as soon after the murder as it was possible for
me to reach it. I reiterated my promises of punctuality, and we
separated. At the hour of twelve, I ascended cautiously the narrow staircase leading to Trimbuckje's apartment. I opened his
door, and entered the chamber. He slept soundly. My dagger
was raised for the blow, when a noise in an adjoining chamber
awoke my victim, who turned round just as my weapon descended
upon his breast. The point only grazed his arm, upon which he
awoke, and cried out for succour. I had not a moment to lose,
but rushed down the staircase, and gained the street. I was soon
joined by Gabbage Gousla, to whom I related my ill success. He
bade me secrete myself in his house, and await until he could find
out what steps would be pursued to apprehend the murderer. On
the following day, he told me I was suspected, and that persons
were on the search for me. 'Save me! save me!' I cried to
Gabbage. That, he said, depended upon myself. 'Serve me,
and I will save you,' said this arch-fiend. I inquired how I was
to do this. Gabbage told me that he demanded my services;
but, if I failed to obey him, he would give me up to the enraged
Trimbuckje. I observed I was indeed in his power, and that if he
spared me I would serve him. 'Then,' said he, 'you must again
grasp your dagger, and take care this time that it strike home.'
On asking whom I must strike, Gabbage told me Pandurang Hàri.
I asked if he meant my old fellow-servant. 'The same,' growled
the villain. 'Go to the village of which Trimbuckje is master,
and, at an uninhabited mansion near the great tank, you will meet

with persons who will instruct you how to act. The least deceit or deviation from your duty will cost you your life! Come, disguise yourself!' Having said this, he brought me the dress of a Jungum priest; and, being equipped in a perfect disguise, he sent me to the village before mentioned, where I arrived in safety. I found the house, and two ferocious-looking fellows in it. One was a very tall man, the other short and thick. They led me, by a secret passage, into a room on the ground floor, the windows of which looked into a court-yard, and were very small. They soon proceeded to business, being well apprized of the orders which I had received from Gabbage. They told me I was fixed upon to murder you, because they themselves were ignorant of your person, and were besides too much engaged in other matters. These they communicated to me to be the apprehension of two women who were in custody at the fort of Asseerghur. Money was then given to me, and I was informed that you had actually been seen in the village that day, and in all probability would be at the collector's office on the following morning. A knock at the door of the room alarmed my companions, and one of them, the tall man before mentioned, went out by a secret passage, which led by a staircase to the upper rooms. He fired his pistol, but all was silent." " I know that very well," I observed to Nanna; "and he very nearly saved you the trouble of using your dagger." "Then it was you who knocked at the door?" continued Nanna. "It was, my friend," I replied. "Had my companions been aware of this, you would have been sacrificed to their vengeance," said Nanna. "I fear nothing could have preserved you. I would have tried to screen you from their fury; for my promise to obey Gabbage was only a subterfuge, by which I hoped to escape from immediate ruin, being, as I was, completely in his power. As I live, I would not have harmed you, nor, to save my own life, imbrue my hands in the blood of an innocent and unoffending man, who had, moreover, been my friend. As soon as we were convinced all was quiet, we separated. I was to dog you to a convenient place out of the village and murder you, my companions promising to meet me at Asseerghur, where I was afterwards to assist in liberating and carrying off the two women, that they might be delivered from the clutches of one tyrant to be thrown into the power of another. Gabbage himself was expected to meet us there, with proper persons, to whom the two women were to be given in charge. I was unable to find you in the village, though I remained two days searching for you; and I finally proceeded towards Asseerghur, as I was promised a reward by my employer, if I was faithful to his interests. At Asseerghur I saw you, just as you came from under the hands of the doctor. Before I could determine what step to take, Gabbage Gousla made his appearance. How he gained an entrance into the fort, I cannot conjecture. I did not know whether he was aware of your being there also; perhaps he might himself have seen you. I dared not conceal my knowledge of your being so near; and, meeting him by appointment under one of the bastions, I informed him I had seen you, but that the fort was not the place to commit the deed in, and that I was determined to await his arrival. He grumbled his displeasure at my not having effectually prevented your appearance there at all; and insinuated that I had either betrayed or neglected his interests. He dismissed me with an imprecation, but not before I had acquainted him with the fate of my two associates, whom, I should have told you, I met with again, in a very singular manner. Passing the cave which, but for you, would have proved my sepulchre, I heard the most piteous yells and cries, as if some dreadful crime was perpetrating. I entered, and distinctly heard sounds proceeding from behind the idol, then the fall of a heavy substance, and all was silent. Shortly after commenced a knocking, as if some one was endeavouring to get out. Cries and groans began again, and I approached close to where they seemed to issue from, and calling out aloud, asked what was the matter? 'Oh, let me out!' cried a faint voice; 'I am famished!' I withdrew the bolt, but the door would not open. The captive, whom I knew by this time to be Kokoo, instructed me to press one of the knobs under the bolt—which I did, and the door flew open. Kokoo rushed out, nearly overcome by weakness and hunger. I asked him where his companion was, and he told me his dagger had done the business for him. I shuddered at the coldness with which he related this. He explained the circumstances to me, which were matter of great astonishment, relative to the way in which he and his companion had been imprisoned by a fellow whom they had trusted with their secrets. Kokoo remained in the cave, being too weak to leave it; I proceeded to Asseerghur, and requested Gabbage's immediate presence at the cave. Kokoo said that the scanty provisions they had in the chamber were soon expended between him and his companion, and that then they began to quarrel, and drew their daggers, and he, Kokoo, being quickest, thrust his into the tall man, who fell. Hereupon I hinted the possibility of his not being dead. Kokoo bade me go and see, if I pleased, but that neither man nor devil should ever tempt him to enter that infernal place again. I then went myself into the stone room, and found the man quite gone. Gabbage was pleased to learn that one of his vile instruments was living, and desired me to accompany him, and bring Kokoo to the fort, and afterwards to take measures for putting you out of the way. On our arrival at the cavern, Kokoo was not to be found; and, on going into the inner chamber, behind the idol, how was I surprised, to find two bodies in the place of one that I had left when I set out! Gabbage was in a violent rage, and swore I had deceived him throughout. I begged him to search the cavern minutely; and I thought we must meet with Kokoo, and thus it would be proved I was sincere. In the place where I had left Kokoo, we found another man, who had been somehow wounded. Here Gabbage lost all self-command, and stabbed me in the side; then muttering imprecations over me, took his departure. In the state in which I was left, you found me; and to your exertions I owe my present renovation to light and life."

I now informed Nanna that I had immured the two slaves of Gabbage in the chamber. On hearing this, he applauded me for my promptness, and regretted that he had been the instrument of effecting the liberation of the most formidable villain of the two. I then told him that the man he found in Kokoo's place was Fuzl Khan, the second Pindaree, whose tale had so amused us in the ruined fortress. Nanna wished immediately to see him, and Fuzl Khan came. Nanna immediately began to thank him for lending his assistance in preserving him. Fuzl candidly confessed he did not merit them ; for the horrors of the cavern were so strongly impressed upon his mind, that he would not venture in again, and refused to accompany me. I told Nanna that his wound was partly owing to me, as I had placed the other dead body in the chamber, and related what had taken place to induce me to do so. We were both struck with the wonderful coincidences which had again brought us together, and at the recollection of the events which had occurred since we met before.

Among the other questions which I put to Nanna in our various conversations, while he was in a convalescent state, I asked if he knew why Gabbage sought my life? He told me that Gabbage was aware of my affection for Sagoonah ; but that, while I lived, he could scarcely hope to accomplish his purposes, whatever they were. Nanna said he was ignorant of the objects of Gabbage; but that, since he had been at Sattarah, he was more than ever desirous of destroying me. Upon expressing my wonder at his hearing anything at Sattarah that could affect me, Nanna said he did not know what ; but I ought, he thought, to keep out of his way. I knew this was not an easy thing to do, for he was everywhere in an incredibly short space of time ; and that were I to change my name, walk naked, or be clothed like a sultan, he would unerringly recognise me. Nanna remarked, however, that, except Kokoo, all his agents were ignorant of my person ; but that Kokoo must remember me as long as he lived, and be incited to find me out, to revenge my having locked him in the chamber, besides the motive of the wages promised by his iniquitous employer ; these were strong inducements to a man so bloodthirsty to hunt me down. I told Nanna that I intended to go to Guzerat. He immediately said that our meeting Kokoo there would be certain, as he was going after the women, who had fled thither. I observed that he could not be of much use there, as he did not know Sagoonah's person ; but Nanna contradicted me, and stated that he was one of the persons employed to murder her. I now informed Nanna of all that had taken place at Poona, and of my adventures as a magician; of my taking Sagoonah under my protection, and the subsequent incidents I had met with, at which he was astonished. He could hardly believe I was the person who had caused so much noise there in my disguise, and ruined Habeshee Kotwall.

There was one thing for which I could never account in my own mind, and that was, the reason that induced Gabbage Gousla at first to seek the destruction of Sagoonah, and afterwards to try to preserve her life. This Nanna cleared up to a certain extent by desiring me to recollect, that when Gabbage sought to assassinate her he was in the interest of Trimbuckje Danglia, and had no knowledge who or what the girl was. He was fully aware of the imposition practised upon the Peeshwa relative to the pretended guilt of Habeshee Kotwall, as he was in the confidence of Trimbuckje. He also guessed (knowing the affair of the girl) that the pretended magician must have obtained his knowledge from some authentic source. The girl had escaped his clutches, but she might somehow or other have fallen into those of the magician. I found from Nanna that I was very closely watched, and traced to a village about a coss from Poona. On receiving the report of his spy, Gabbage himself repaired to the village, and returning in great perturbation, set out immediately for Sattarah, from whence he quickly returned, and gave orders that the girl at the cultivator's cottage should be seized. It was discovered that she had fled, and his rage knew no bounds. All the information that could be obtained was, that she had taken the road to Seroor. Little was said before Trimbuckje's servant, whom Gabbage had employed as his spy, because he wished Trimbuckje to imagine Sagoonah really dead. A person was despatched after the fugitive, but Nanna never heard the result of the pursuit.

This result I told him, and also how narrowly Sagoonah and her aunt had escaped. On expressing my wonder that Gabbage, with all his art and his numerous agents, had never yet succeeded in entrapping Sagoonah, Nanna said it might be accounted for by Trimbuckje's servant, who had acted as a spy in watching me, having informed his master that the girl was living, and that Gabbage had some particular views respecting her. Trimbuckje seized a favourable moment to quarrel with Gabbage, not allowing him to know how well informed he was regarding Sagoonah's existence. They separated, and Gabbage then discovered that Trimbuckje was aware the girl was alive,—for he found all his craft and cunning opposed by Trimbuckje's power,—and that, although the latter was a prisoner in Thannah, his influence in Kandeish was such, that measures were taken at that very time to seize the girl and her aunt. I was summoned away to attend Trimbuckje immediately, not for the value of my services, but that I might thwart Trimbuckje's scheme ; for he had begun to think me a very shrewd kind of fellow, and clearly saw that I had advanced my own ends, and made a tool of him first, by getting away Sagoonah from him, and, in the second place, a situation and reward. He retaliated, however, by condescending to affect a particular predilection for me, and I in return planned his escape from Thannah, which, when effected, he not only failed to be grateful for, but sent expresses to Kandeish to deprive me of my place.

In this way things, until now unaccountable to me, were cleared up. I recollected the warning of danger given me by a soldier at the guard-room in Kandeish, and that after this I went to the deserted mansion, where I was so near being shot. Nanna could not inform me how it was that Gabbage and Trimbuckje became reconciled to each other, but supposed, being both involved in schemes of villainy, it was not worth while for them to counteract each other any longer. It appeared that the sun of Trimbuckje's power was for ever set, and the Peeshwa crushed, past all hope of again governing. Gabbage, therefore, had latterly found it no longer his interest to adhere either to one or the other, and having nothing to fear from their power, relied at present upon his own cunning and a few hirelings, ready instruments of his designs, to get Sagoonah into his hands. "You," said Nanna, "are one great obstacle in his way, and you he is determined to remove. Kokoo is his head assassin, and he it was who cut to pieces the Shastree from Guzerat. This shameful murder was planned by the Peeshwa himself, aided by Trimbuckje, and executed by

Kokoo." I could not help observing, here, how unfortunate for me Nanna's arrival at the cave, and the release of Kokoo, had proved. "It proved also very unfortunate for me," said Nanna; "where he went I cannot guess, but had he remained where he proposed, I should not have been wounded, and been brought to the brink of the grave." I asked if there was no way to escape the villain's fury, in case I fell in with him. Nanna seemed to think a bribe would have done it, had I not drawn the fatal bolt upon him, but that no money would purchase his good-will under present circumstances. He advised me to go well armed, and be very circumspect in my movements at all times; that if I went to Guzerat, or remained in the Deccan, he would be there also. I asked Nanna if he would accompany me thither, and told him my design was to get into some employment, the profits of which I would share equally with him and Fuzl Khan, and we should then be better able to provide for our mutual security. Besides, Nanna might obtain some place in the service of the English Government, and thus we should live in quiet. Nanna promised never to desert me, as I had preserved his life. He considered himself bound to do what he could for me; and we agreed to go well armed, and never to be farther apart from each other than we could possibly avoid. This would be some security against Kokoo and his employer, whose open attacks were least to be feared. Fuzl Khan swore to be faithful to us, and to travel with us wherever we might direct our steps; and we promised, in return for his sharing our hazards, that he should partake in our comforts. He possessed animal courage, and though his honesty was not the most pure of its kind, and his youthful propensities still had a fast hold upon him, we had no reason to think he would turn out a traitor to our cause. I now felt my mind more at ease than it had lately been, and anticipated a joyful interview with my Sagoonah.

On consideration, it appeared dangerous for us to remain much longer where we then rested. Gabbage was too near us, and I recollected that his son Mahadeo was also at hand. They might chance to meet, and unite their forces against us. I deemed it prudent to keep my knowledge of the real designs of Gabbage to

myself, and to seem ignorant of his views towards the musnud of
Sattarah, because the remotest chance of a man being in power
secures to him money and followers. After all, Nanna was a
Mahratta, and it is a peculiarity in the character of this people,
that the hope of being provided for, even at a future time,
operates very strongly upon their minds, though I had no reason
to think such would be the case with Nanna. As to Fuzl Khan, I
knew he would set off in a moment, on the shadow of such a hope.

On inquiring for my friend the potail, I found him busily
employed in indemnifying himself for the losses he had sustained
by the passage of the Peeshwa's army through his village. He
was screwing the cultivators and villagers to the last pice;
taking money from one, cattle from another, and had actually
in pawn the wives of two poor fellows at once, while the hus-
bands were endeavouring to borrow money to satisfy his
rapacity. It was not my business to interfere, though I with
difficulty beheld the scene unmoved. I informed my host that
we intended to quit him immediately, and begged him to furnish
us with a tattoo to carry the wounded man. He did so very
readily, and I paid for it with some of my silver ornaments,
presenting him with an ankle-chain as a remuneration for his
hospitality. Fuzl Khan, who was possessed of great ingenuity,
told the potail, on setting out, that he had better take good
care of his money, as he had overheard a plot to deprive him of
it. He described to him very accurately the persons of Gabbage
Gousla and Kokoo, as the conspirators. This he did to prevent
the potail giving them any information as to our movements,
should they come to question him about us. Knowing their
persons, he would naturally refuse to admit them under his roof,
and they would go away just as wise as they came. I highly
approved Fuzl Khan's trick, and we set off, intending to take the
short way to Guzerat through the Kandeish jungles.

Our first stage was to Trimbuckje's once flourishing village,
where I had held a situation, and where stood the house in
which Sagoonah had resided, which was now inhabited by
soldiers and all classes of people. We alighted at a durhm
sallah, where several horsemen were assembled. These were

in the service of the English, and were conversing very freely on the affairs in which they were engaged. We soon found that they were in search of Trimbuckje, and that considerable rewards were offered to any one who would give information whereby he might be apprehended. Upon finding this to be the case, Nanna called me aside, and said, "Now is my time for revenge; I know where Trimbuckje is concealed, and I will unkennel him from his hole, and take good care he knows who it is that ruins him." "Are you certain?" I asked him in return. "Can you be sure of pointing out the place?" He assured me he could, but that he was not yet strong enough, and would wish to enjoy another night's rest before he accompanied the Toope Wallas to the place. He remarked that if he gave information that night, the English would not rest until he delivered the villain up to them. At this moment the public crier came by, offering a reward of five thousand rupees to any person who would bring information to the English resident at Kandeish where Trimbuckje Danglia might be found. Nanna, confident the secret was in his bosom alone, apprehended no danger by waiting until the morning. We ate our supper, threw ourselves upon our mats, and enjoyed a sound repose

CHAPTER XXIV.

THE next morning, Nanna, being refreshed by an unbroken sleep, called me over where he was lying, and told me he was determined to proceed immediately to the tent of the English Resident, and demand an audience. He had reflected upon the step which he proposed to take, and found his resolution rather strengthened than weakened, in consequence of what had presented itself to his mind upon the subject. It appeared to me highly necessary that he should first ascertain whether Trimbuckje was actually at that moment in the hiding-place he suspected, as otherwise we should appear in a very ridiculous light before the English commandant. This I stated to Nanna, who, being of the same opinion, proposed he should start alone towards the place where we suspected our enemy was concealed; and I promised to await his return at a particular spot, which I indicated to him. He departed accordingly, and promised to be with me again before nightfall. During Nanna's absence, I strolled with Fuzl Khan into the neighbourhood of the village, and seeing the English horse formed in a line, and an officer examining the horses and accoutrements, whom I had seen at Bombay, I approached pretty close, and found him to be the man whom I supposed at this time to be the husband of Jane Bebee. He did not seem to recollect me, and I was not very anxious to attract his notice. He had since become a cavalry officer, and I have no doubt was a very active one.

In the evening Nanna came back, and told me Trimbuckje was in his secret abode. He made sure of this, because he had watched several men into the building, of whose faces he had a perfect recollection; and he thought, from the preparations and bustle he observed, that matters were arranging for his removal. This being the case, not a moment was to be lost ; and we proceeded to the tent of the English Resident, and obtained an audience. I desired Nanna to enter, awaiting myself the result of the conference on the outside. He very soon came back, and the Resident immediately began to issue orders. The cavalry officer was sent for, and a second came with him. After a short conversation, they went away, and quickly returned at the head of two hundred men, accompanied by *mussalchees* or torch-bearers. Nanna was mounted, and desired to lead the way. We followed him across ravines and broken ground, until we came to an ancient stone building in a ruinous state, and thatched with straw. Nanna now advised that half the men should dismount, and that twenty of them should endeavour to obtain an entrance, by a way he would point out, into the courtyard of the place. The officers declared if he played any tricks with them, he should be shot through the head on the spot. Nanna vowed fidelity, and led the way. Not a torch was yet lighted, though care was taken to be ready to do so at the moment the word was given for the purpose. We passed through a cow-shed, the wall of which, being of mud, was broken down in a moment. We were now in the yard, where we heard the bells of bullocks jingling, a sign that the inhabitants of the place were upon the point of decamping. Proceeding straight forwards, we came up to an elephant, whose keepers were fast asleep. The sagacious animal, aware of strangers being near him, rattled his chains and set up a tremendous yell, which awoke his keepers, and gave the first alarm to the inmates of the place. The torches were now lit up at once, and the consternation of the inhabitants at the blaze may be easily anticipated. Some of Trimbuckje's men resisted our advance, and an obstinate battle ensued, which ended in their speedy destruction ; others, throwing open the great doors, attempted to fly, but were cut off and killed by the English horse stationed without. Still no Trimbuckje made his appearance. Nanna then led the way to the interior of the building, where we found the wives of Trimbuckje, and many other females, all of whom begged for mercy, which was extended to them. They swore, however, on being questioned, that Trimbuckje had departed from them two days before. We were not to be so easily deceived. Nanna still led on, through passages and dark rooms, until we came to an iron door, which was forced open; but Trimbuckje could not be found. Nanna himself was now at a loss, but we determined on searching every hole and chamber; and, ascending a small narrow staircase leading to a tower, we were opposed by a single man armed with a spear, who prevented our going higher. Sounds were heard from above, as if some one was attempting to break through the wall, and we had no doubt it was Trimbuckje himself. The English officer got impatient, for every knock seemed as if it brought the object of our search nearer to freedom. The spear, however, effectually prevented our ascending, and it was so rapidly thrust down and drawn back again, that we could only see the hand that guided it at considerable intervals. At length one of the troopers rushed forwards, and received the point of the weapon in his breast. The man who held it having some difficulty in extracting it speedily from the trooper whom he had trans-fixed, exposed his person to the view of one of the English officers, who discharged his pistol at him, and he fell dead instantly. The trooper having been removed out of the way, we were enabled to push forward into a stone-room above, where we could see nothing but straw upon the floor, with several heaps of charcoal and fire-wood. Not doubting but some one lay concealed there, the officers gave orders to set fire to the straw, upon which a groan was heard from under it, and the once formidable Trimbuckje Danglia made his appearance. Finding that resistance was vain, he quietly surrendered himself. Nanna was the nearest person to him when taken, and cried out, " Trimbuckje, I am avenged—if you ever again climb into power, make your dependants your friends, and not your enemies!" The fallen man spoke not a word in reply, but suffered himself to be led down the staircase. Having joined the troops without, we went back to the village by torch-light, and reported our success to the English Resident, who con-sidered Nanna fully entitled to the reward offered for Trimbuckje's apprehension.

I hinted to Nanna my fears that, now he was so enriched, he

would leave me to journey alone to Guzerat. He appeared to feel hurt at my surmise, and said that I mistook his character greatly. **Part** of his reward he received down; the remainder he left in the hands of the Resident, which he begged to be allowed to draw for by a bill of exchange from Guzerat, or elsewhere. He was fixed in accompanying me still, because I had saved his life, and he had promised to serve me in return; and also out of regard to his own safety, for he could not deem himself secure in the Deccan, especially when it was known that he had betrayed Trimbuckje to the English. This man had many adherents, and his wife would very probably urge them on to revenge. All that Nanna required me to do, was to carry some of his rupees that he meant should be expended for our mutual benefit. I could not help expressing my admiration of his conduct to this noble-spirited fellow, and declaring that I had never set my eyes on a fellow-being before who would act so kindly towards me. Trimbuckje little knew the value of the dependant he had ungrate-**fully** requited. "None of your flattery, Pandoo," cried Nanna. "Mahrattas use it when they are most bent upon mischief; and, if you continue in this strain, I shall fear you are plotting something against me. Enough of this. Now, as to our companion Fuzl Khan; you remember his own history of himself, and the depravity he makes no bones of displaying. His inclination seems naturally bent upon grasping what was not his own. Do you think we can safely trust him?" I answered that I feared he was an incorrigible fellow, and I had never seen him exhibit signs of amendment; but were we to dismiss him at that place, I was well aware, from his disposition, I should bitterly repent the step. I proposed taking him with us to Guzerat, his own country, where, being once more arrived, he would not evince a desire to return to the Deccan; the company of his Mohammedan friends would so occupy him, that he would quickly cease to be anxious for ours.

I could not help asking Nanna what had made him thus suddenly think of Fuzl Khan. He told me that, on returning to **the place where we put up** the preceding night, he found Fuzl **Khan busily ransacking** his bag. He might have saved himself that trouble, as it appeared there was nothing in it, being as empty as when first made. I could not help admitting that he was an incurable knave, and hoping that he would not be quite as familiar with our bags on the road we were going. "I shall take good care of mine," said Nanna, "for I will not leave it in his power! I abhor such pitiful practices; and, if I were to catch him doing so, he should suffer for it. If we were enemies, and he sought to overreach us that he might ruin us the more certainly, one might call him a clever fellow; but to filch from companions and friends is contemptible!" The conversation ended by our both agreeing to keep a sharp look-out after his conduct.

In the morning we set out, giving Fuzl Khan to understand that Nanna only was purse-bearer, and that we had but little in the bag. "Little!" ejaculated Fuzl Khan; "come, that will not do for me. You forget I heard the reward cried for the discovery of Trimbuckje; and you have not received it? Not that I can claim any part of it; but to tell me you have got but little, that won't do, my friend." "Why, Fuzl," said Nanna, "do you suppose I would carry five thousand rupees through the Kandeish jungles?" "No," he replied, "I am not such a fool as that either; but I may fairly conjure you have a thousand at least, between you both." "Curse the fellow," said Nanna, "he is a conjuror in reality; well, I call one thousand rupees little enough." "Do you, indeed?" said Fuzl Khan; "I do not. That's all—a thousand rupees!" "Listen, my friend," said Nanna; "whether we have one or five thousand, you will make yourself content. We shall give you your rice, and pay your travelling expenses, and no more. By Ishwar, if I discover you peering into my bags again, I will run you through the body!" "I peer into your bags!" said Fuzl Khan, as if surprised—"I attempt to rob any one! By Allah and the twelve Imaums, it is false! It is true I looked into your bag; but it was only in search of a mouse, which I saw take shelter among your things. My rice having been devoured by these vermin, I determined on catching the first I saw. Me a thief, indeed! Recollect, I am one of the faithful—*Allah howul!*"[1] We could not help laugh-

---

[1] God forbid.

ing at the rogue's ridiculous subterfuge about the mouse. Nanna observed, "What you have told us, Fuzl, may be very true, but recollect, the next time a mouse runs into my bag, he is safe under my protection; and you will, therefore, await my presence before you molest him." "By all means," answered Fuzl Khan, "as it is your wish. I have no desire to be rat-catcher to the party." "Your actions belie your speech, however," observed Nanna; "but remember that in travelling with us as our friend, let neither mouse nor rat tempt you to become our enemy, or you shall repent it!" Fuzl Khan made no reply, and we proceeded on our journey.

The only circumstance which gave me any regret on quitting the Deccan, was the not having time to gain any information respecting the goatherd of the glen, to whom I determined to write, under cover, to Shewdhut Wanee, informing him I had gone to Guzerat; but that, previous to my departure, I had learned nothing of importance to communicate to him. The first place of any note we arrived at on our journey was Nasik, from whence I despatched my letter to Indore. I trusted it to a soucar of Nasik, who promised to forward it by his own messenger. In passing through the jungles, Nanna was obliged to hire a palanquin and bearers, the fatigue being otherwise too great for him. We heard at Nasik that Badjerao had fallen in with a part of the English troops at Ashtee, and not being able to escape fighting this time, a desperate battle took place, in which his general, Gokla, was killed. Badjerao, taking advantage of the confusion, as usual, decamped, closely followed by his enemies. His name was detested by the Brahmins of Nasik, as being both weak, wicked, and cowardly. Every one was glad he was defeated; but all were sorry the English were the conquerers. The capture of Trimbuckje Danglia was also known, and had given universal satisfaction.

Everything being arranged for continuing our march, and having hired tattoos and bearers (the latter not much relishing the passage through the jungles), we set out. The bearers grumbled, and seemed to feel real alarm lest the fever should attack and carry them off on their route; no one, according to them, had

R

ever escaped it, and it was going into certain destruction. They asserted, also, that the jungles were haunted by Bheels and tigers, and that if we valued our lives we had better not venture into them. We were deaf to all their remonstrances. On our journey, and during the very first evening, Fuzl Khan began to be alarmed, mistaking the trees for Bheels, and every solitary bush for a tiger. The first day neither Bheel, fever, nor tiger arrested our progress ; the second was also free from interruption, and in one day more we should have cleared this dangerous tract of country. We were congratulating ourselves in the evening at our good fortune in having got through them, or very nearly so, when we were surrounded by Bheels armed with bows and arrows, who began at once to rifle us of everything we possessed, making us all prisoners together, lest we should inform against them to the authorities at Guzerat. Nanna parted with his money very reluctantly. Fuzl Khan, who had nothing to lose, met his fate with the most cheerfulness. The palanquin-bearers were escorted back to Nasik by the Bheels, while we were conducted to the haunts of these remorseless robbers. Why they detained us so long, and took us with them, I cannot tell, unless they imagined Nanna to be a person of rank, for whom they might obtain a ransom. Our arms were tied behind us, and we were led through the thickest part of the jungle, across ravines, and down precipices, through bog and water, until we came to a cave of extraordinary size. There one of the Bheels gave a loud whistle, and lights were seen emerging as if from the centre of the earth. A trap-door had been raised, and two tall black men appeared, to whom we were given in charge, and by whom we were thrust through the door with brutal violence, and led down stone steps to a second door, which opened into a long, damp passage. "Surely," I exclaimed to Nanna, "they mean to bury us alive in this dismal hole!" Neither Nanna nor Fuzl Khan uttered a syllable in reply, terror had so overpowered all their faculties. We proceeded until we came to a second passage branching off from the main one to the right hand. Into this last we went about twenty yards, when a strong door being opened on one side of it, they forced us into a dark and damp cell, and, shutting the door, left us to our reflections.

We had been in the cell about an hour, when a man opened the door, and thrust in to us some dried grain and plantains, which we eagerly devoured. Water was also given us, of which neither Nanna nor myself could partake, not knowing who might have drunk out of the pot containing it. We passed a most miserable night, anxiously hoping that the coming day would restore us the blessing of liberty; for more we could not expect. The prison door was opened early in the morning, and we were told to arise and follow our gaoler. We readily complied, and were conducted through the narrow passages, and up the stairs leading to the trap-door. At length we found ourselves in the cavern, in which twenty Bheels were assembled, before the chief of whom we were led. He called to us, and bade us approach, and we obeyed. "Well, how like you your prison? What think you of our caverns above and below? What, silent! They are to be your apartments until death release you, without you furnish us with another thousand rupees; you may then proceed, promising not to reveal our retreat." We assured the chief we had no more money, as he must know that we were only poor travellers. "Very poor indeed!" said the chief; "only a palanquin and a thousand rupees! Not much like poverty either!" Nanna then confessed that he had rendered the English a service, and that this money was his reward. "What was the service?" inquired the Bheel. Nanna, not knowing whether Trimbuckje was not a friend to the band, was at a loss what answer to make, until, risking everything, he let out the real secret. "So, then, your reward was five times greater than we discovered about your person? Down with the other four thousand, or you return to the dungeon!" Nanna said he had not got it with him. "You did not throw it away?" said the other; "you know where it is to be had?" "No," Nanna rejoined; "it is in the hand of the English Resident, to be drawn by bill." "Well, then, you must give me a bill for it, made in my favour, my good friend, before you stir a step from hence." This was a sad blow to us all; but our lives were dearer than the treasure, and they would have been sacrificed had we refused. "This is but just," said the chief; "for Trimbuckje would have been under our protection, which we agreed to afford him for five thousand rupees; and as you prevented our getting it from him, we must get it from you. Ho! bring paper, pens, and ink. You, prisoner, frame your draft in favour of Gondia Bendage Punumchund, at sight, and I will myself be the bearer." Nanna drew the draft, and demanded to be released. "Not so fast," said the other; "you must await my return. All you have been telling me may be false; and then how foolish shall I be not to find you here on my return! No, you must remain; but it shall not be in your dungeon below, but in this apartment; and be careful how you attempt to escape."

I now supplicated the chief that I might be allowed to prosecute my journey, having nothing to do with the money-transaction. After some consultation, my request was granted, on promising not to betray the Bheels to any Europeans in Guzerat. The chief now led us to comfortable chambers, not, however, remarkable for over-cleanliness. Some papers lay about on the ground, and he sat down to finish a letter. When he had done, he gave a loud whistle; an attendant answered the call, and he inquired if Sumboo was returned. A reply in the negative made him seem angry, and he petulantly thrust his papers into a box in the corner of the room, the lid of which he closed with great violence, crying, "When the tardy scoundrel comes back, tell him his delay may be attended with serious consequences. Yet stay! I will await his return." He then paused, and, reflecting a little time, said, turning to Nanna, "When does the English Resident leave Kandeish?" "I believe immediately," replied Nanna. He then desired that two Bheels might get ready to accompany him, and that if Sumboo arrived while he was absent, he should not stir from the cavern until he, the chief, came back. He next gave orders for our being strictly guarded. I reminded him of his promise to myself that I should depart. He replied, "True: you may go; and the next time you pass this way, bring no money with you." I bowed in silence, and he quitted the cavern.

When we were left to ourselves, Nanna reproached me for being so anxious to depart, leaving him behind. "My dear friend," I said to him; "who knows what may happen if I go away? It is possible I may be of material benefit to you, though it is hardly probable that such will be the case. I deemed it prudent to secure the chief's consent to my departure for this reason; but, if you don't agree in my views, I will most readily remain with you, and await the result." Nanna, convinced I had no intention of deserting him, or acting unkindly towards him, began to consider how our temporary disunion might be conducive of mutual benefit. All that we could arrange was, that I should prepare some place for him at Baroda. As this was not of sufficient moment for causing a separation, the arrangement was cancelled, unless some accident should eventually render it necessary to put it in practice. This evening we enjoyed the privilege of cooking our own rice, and drawing water in our own pots, from the cavern well. The room we occupied being quite dry and comfortable, compared with that in which we had passed the preceding night, we enjoyed a sound sleep.

Early on the following morning, I awoke, my fellow-prisoners being still asleep; and, not knowing what to do for amusement until they joined me, I employed myself in examining the room in which I was, and everything around it. There was nothing worth notice, except the box in which I had seen the Bheel fling his papers. It was of very curious workmanship, apparently formed out of the root of some species of tree, of a very hard wood. I tried the lid, which, to my great surprise, I found unfastened. The inside was lined with iron. The papers very naturally attracted my chief attention. These I set about examining; but they were very difficult to decipher, being ill-written in a most barbarous kind of Mahratta. They contained nothing of any interest to me in my present circumstances; and I was about to close the box again, when the newly-penned letter of the Bheel chief caught my eye. It seemed written with great care, and I contrived to decipher it without much difficulty. Its contents were as follow :—

"To his highness, the all-powerful Guicowar, lord and sovereign of Guzerat, Mulharia Bheel sends his faithful brother,
Sumboo, to the throne of excellence, claiming from thence the
promised reward for services performed by the Bheels, whose
words are sacred. For this purpose, Mulharia Naique begs his
highness to consider his promises and the Bheel's services, and
give to his trusty servant and relative the sum of six thousand
rupees, as agreed upon by his highness. On failure, Mulharia
Naique promises his highness not a village in his dominions shall
enjoy quiet for a single week together. The enraged Bheels are
already dissatisfied at the money not having been paid them
through the two messengers which have been already sent to
demand the same. No bills will be taken; the ready money is
demanded, and if not sent, will be collected by force from the
villages in Guzerat.

(Signed) "MULHARIA BHEEL NAIQUE."

Upon the perusal of this insolent letter, a thought struck me
which might be productive of great advantage to us. As I was
to have my liberty, could I not take it with me, and, on my
arrival at Baroda, personate Sumboo, and gain the rupees myself?
I communicated this scheme to Nanna, as soon as he awoke and
Fuzl Khan could be got out of hearing. Nanna was as cunning
as myself, and suggested the same plan, before I opened mine, as
soon as he read the letter. Our only fear was lest the chieftain
on his return should discover the loss of the letter before Nanna
could get clear off. It struck me it would be better to copy the
letter; but, on reflection, this did not appear safe, as it was evident this was not the first application of the kind, and the
difference in the handwriting would be very readily seen. Nanna
agreeing with me in this, we arranged that he should not lose a
moment in quitting the cave, as soon as the chieftain would grant
him liberty. It was very natural to suppose that the Bheel would
call for his rice after his journey; so that Nanna would be out of
his reach long before the loss of the letter could be discovered.
I folded it up, and directed it, imitating the writing in the inside
as well as I could. Not finding any gum to close it with in the

room, I determined to do that at Surat, which was the first place I should arrive at in journeying. I made a hearty meal, and then reminded the Bheels of the permission given me by their chief to depart. They demurred, and made a good deal of difficulty about it; but at length I succeeded. Before my departure, I had another conference with Nanna regarding the place of our meeting. This was to be at a durhm sallah known to Fuzl Khan, who directed me how to find it; and calculating the time which the Bheel chief might take in going and returning, and the time necessary to be consumed in travelling to Baroda, we hoped to meet on the sixth day from our separation. I cautioned Nanna against inquiring for me in Baroda, in case I might not succeed; for his enquiries would only show the people he was connected with me, and might involve him in difficulty. I gave the same caution to Fuzl Khan, who was instructed to search for me, but on no account to describe my person, or ask any one about me. The next thing was how to dispose of the money, in case we should obtain it; and it was agreed I should deposit it with a banker at Baroda, giving him one per cent. for taking care of it.

I now set out and reached the opening of the cavern, when it struck me that the person of Sumboo might be known at Baroda. I wished to consult Nanna upon this point, but the Bheels would not let me go back. "Well, Pandoo," thought I to myself, "you must rely upon your own wits should any suspicion alight upon you." I was now in a hideous jungle, alone, and opposed to the two powerful enemies of man—tigers and fever, and with only a little raw rice and grain in my bag. How could I reasonably expect a fortunate issue to my business? or rather, how could I, at present, make certain of my life? In respect to Nanna and Fuzl Khan, I gave up every hope of again effecting a junction with them, or even beholding them any more! and how slight was my chance of ever seeing Sagoonah again! Thus, uneasy in mind and body, I continued to follow the track towards the main road, from which the path to the cavern of the Bheels deviated. With some difficulty I found the right track, and, to my indescribable joy, cleared the jungles before night came on. A vast plain lay before me, and before complete darkness set in, it was quite impossible to guess the way before me. It appeared my wisest plan to remain in the place I then was until morning; yet the heavy dews alarmed me, especially as I was hourly expecting an attack of fever, which, if it did not carry me off, might retard the objects I had in view, or delay me so long, that I should not dare to show myself in the character of a Bheel demanding money. It was likely Sumboo would have anticipated me, in which case detection would be certain. I went on, therefore, right or wrong, leaving it to day to discover which. A light soon appeared; it was a most welcome sight. I proceeded at a double rate towards it. I made no doubt it was a hut, where I might find shelter; but was sadly disappointed to discover I was on the banks of a river, and that the light proceeded from the dying embers of a funeral pile,—some corpse having been just burned, according to custom.

I approached nearer the spot, and something close to the fire attracted my attention; it appeared dark, and almost shapeless. Presently I saw it move. "What can it be, that, at such an hour, hovers round the ashes of the dead?" I eagerly called out. A hoarse and hollow voice cried, "Who speaks?" It was a female, and I went up to her, saying, "Why, good woman, what can bring you here, at this hour, to watch the dead?" She replied, "To watch the dead!" concluding with a sort of laugh; "watch the wood you mean!" "What, wretched creature! art thou stealing from the dead?" I exclaimed; for I perceived by this time that she was a low-caste Dheeria, who make a practice of picking up the half-burned pieces of wood from funeral piles, and carrying them home to their own fire-places for domestic uses, even cooking their victuals with them. "Rob! no; I rob not the dead! The corpse has done with the wood now. Here is all that remains," said she, holding up the skull; "wood won't burn that!" Here the old creature went on raking the wood together, which she tied up in a coarse cloth. "It is a rare time for us now; the cholera morbus has sent me wood from twenty funeral piles! I have collected a stock that will last me a good time." Disgusted with the hag's remarks, I begged her to tell me where I was, and how far from any village. "Follow me!" she exclaimed, kindling a torch at the almost expired flame; "follow me, and I will show thee." I obeyed her, and soon saw the lights of a large village, where, on my arrival, she directed me to a durhm sallah, into which I entered with a pleasure I cannot describe. I ate my dried grain, and some rice which I cooked, and, laying myself down soon fell into a profound slumber.

 AROSE early on the following morning, and attended to make pùja to a deity hard by, where I found a number of persons assembled for the same purpose. Being a stranger, the eyes of all the inhabitants of the village present were directed towards me, and more than one of them was exceedingly anxious that I should give some account of myself. I refrained, however, from satisfying their curiosity, and they suffered me to return to the duhrm sallah unmolested. I there inquired the way to Surat, and was little pleased to find that I could not travel thither in less than two days. Not intimidated by the intelligence, and firm to my object, I set out with a good resolution, and had not gone far when I overtook several bullocks with their drivers, employed in the conveyance of grain, and found, like myself, they were bound to Surat. These drivers very readily gave me permission to accompany them ; and, as we proceeded, we grew more friendly, until one of them offered me a seat upon his beast, and thus saved me many a weary footstep. I reached Surat about the time I expected ; and, contrary to my former custom among bullock drivers, met with no adventure on the road.

Surat was crowded with ships and vessels of all kinds. I found it a great place of traffic, and frequented by most of the merchants of the East, as well as the West; rich, populous, and busy. I took the first opportunity of examining the city, as I had never before been within the walls. It bore the remains of its former grandeur, though the principal streets, or what had once been so, in the Moghul Serai, were narrow and exceedingly dirty. This was the first time I had ever been in a city, the inhabitants of which were principally Musselmen. The filth of these people around their habitations struck me very forcibly, and made me thankful I was among the followers of Brahma.

After rambling in the Moghul Serai, I entered the common bazaar, which is on the outside of the old city wall. The misery, dirt, and stench I encountered there was the most disgusting sight my eyes ever beheld. Kabob frying (which recalled Fuzl Khan's mother to my recollection) was carrying on in every corner. The numbers of old women roasting and frying, polluting the very atmosphere with their abominations, would almost exceed belief. The meat at the butcher's-stalls, the bread at the baker's, the very sweetmeats, were covered with impurities. The men were one-half of them drunk, though, as Mohammedans, they were forbidden strong liquors—so much for their imperfect obedience to an imperfect religion! How far more exalted and sincere are the followers of Brahma! The women were bold, carried themselves coarsely, and seemed to be all slatterns. Quarrelling was heard from morning till night in every corner of the place, and the followers of the Faithful in Surat appeared to me the vilest class of men I had ever sojourned amongst. The English, to whom it belonged, seemed either incapable of enforcing cleanliness by their authority, or had given the object up as a hopeless task. Leaving the bazaar, I saw not far off a large building, which they informed me was the jail, and that it was only just erected. The adawlut, or court-house was close by, and again recalled Fuzl Khan, and his troubles there, to my recollection. The judge was considered, on the whole, to be a fair sample of the profession everywhere, having his prejudices and sympathies as well as other men. Woe to those, however, who fell under his dislike, and still more under the hatred of a vagabond Parsee in authority beneath him, but a much greater man than his master. By superlative cunning and hypocrisy, this Parsee had the good fortune to persuade men that he was as truly honourable and just as he appeared. He had filled several situations in all branches of the service—in the revenue, justice, customs, police, and commerce. With his long experience in so many departments, and without the inclination, who could be more honest? The English were either aware of this, or in ignor ance of the character which really belonged to the fellow—the reader must decide which of the two was really the case. During my residence here, this obsequious and artful knave gave a grand *nautch*, or dance, to which the heads of the different departments were invited. The use of these invitations was, not to pay a compliment to the English, which they were silly enough to imagine, but designed to add to his own importance by the presence of the strangers, which fully compensated for the expense incurred in their company, as they seldom remained more than half-an-hour. The influence acquired in consequence, was used in facilitating the extortion of money from the inhabitants, or in evading the payment of their just debts. In either case, who would dare grumble, when the judge himself was the intimate friend of the party against whom complaint was to be made? The judge came to his dance, ate his sweatmeats and conserves, praised his children, and returned his embrace. Would any one be fool enough to complain against him? Such was the result of the feeling in the place; and whether the reasoning was false or true, the poor people dared not run the risk of making the attempt. Thus, as usual, the great ends of justice were defeated by the means taken to dispense it.

I remained no longer at Surat than was necessary for recovering myself after my journey; I left so thoroughly disgusted with all I heard and saw there. I journeyed on until I reached Broach, the birthplace of Fuzl Khan. If I found Surat a filthy residence, how much more disgusting was this place! It seemed the concentration of all the dirt in the country, the centre of every beastly and disgusting habit. A native-born individual not only ruled or managed the people, but his superior also. It was painfully ludicrous to hear how the wise and proper regulations of the Government were constantly evaded or set at nought, by the very person employed and paid to see them enforced. The confidence reposed in vagabonds with the high-sounding names of sudr aumeen, foujdar, sheristadar, vakeel, &c., exhibited a great degree of folly. Whoever has attained one of these titles is very certain to make his fortune quickly; and I longed for one of the appointments where ease, and comfort, and competence were insured by a little address in screwing the people. But I must pass over other particulars of my journey, and take up my story from the time I entered Baroda, this being an interval of some days from my leaving the den of the Bheels.

The English Government was just at this period very suspicious of the Guicowar, having reason to fear he would join the confederated powers of the Deccan. Not thinking news of this nature could be of any moment to me, I neglected to make particular inquiries respecting any change of affairs that might have happened in the court, and made my way directly to the palace. At Broach I had taken care to provide myself with the bow, arrows, and garb of a Bheel, and took the character as well as I could, covering myself with a cloak, that I might not be known for one in the streets of Baroda. On entering the palace, I solicited an audience of the Guicowar, which was refused until I stated my errand, and the object of my visit. This I whispered in the ear of an attendant, and the name of "Mulharia Bheel" acted like magic. I had an audience immediately; but when in the presence of the Guicowar, my courage very nearly failed me. All the horrors I felt when personating the magician before the Peeshwa at Poona now came upon me again. It was impossible, I knew, to recede; and therefore I mustered courage to present the letter of the Bheel chief, saying that Sumboo having expired suddenly, and Mulharia being pressed for time, I had been deputed to convey the letter. The Guicowar upon this called in his secretary, who with difficulty made out the contents of the epistle. After it had been read, both of them eyed me in a very pointed way, and retired into an inner apartment. I would have given double the sum I came to demand, had I possessed it, to have got clear out of the palace. In about an hour's time the Guicowar returned, and desired me to await his reply a little longer. Hearing an unusual bustle in the court below, I ventured to peep through the window, and, to my consternation, beheld the British Resident there, whose arrival caused the guard to be turned out, and I witnessed the pomp with which he was received upon his entrance to the palace. Something now struck me that this visit was connected with my demand for the money;

and on the Resident entering the room in which I was, and looking me very hard in the face, I was confirmed in the truth of my conjecture. "Well," thought I, "my doom is fixed!" The Guicowar having called me to him, the carpet was turned back that I might not pollute it, and I approached him. "Listen," said he; "your master has taken a most unlucky time to make his demand upon me." Thinking his highness was going to plead his inability to pay, or frame some excuse to evade doing so, I plucked up courage, and said, "And most unlucky it will be for you and your villages if the demand be not complied with. You have read the letter, and must be aware of the consequences of non-compliance." "Insolent scoundrel!" cried the Guicowar; "I will not only not comply with the audacious demand, but will make the bearer of it shorter by a head. Guards, seize that contumacious rebel!—confine him in the lowest dungeons of the palace, and await my further orders respecting him!" I was instantly disarmed, and dragged down to the dungeons. A pretty business have I made of it, I reasoned to myself. All is now over! They brought me such provisions as a Bheel would not have refused, but which it would have polluted me to touch. Such was the consequence of my assuming a false character. The bearer of them appeared inclined to be communicative, though in a sarcastic way. He cried, "Thou great deputy of Sumboo, and ambassador of Mulharia, eat thy fill to-day, to-morrow thou wilt die. What an idiot you were to come and thrust your neck under the axe in the way you have done! Did you not know that the Guicowar and the English are now become sworn friends, and have entered into fresh treaties, in which they jointly engage to put down you rebel Bheels? The Guicowar now does not heed your threats—you can no more intimidate him. O you ass! if your master had not known this, his ambassador should have had wit enough to have discovered it in Baroda, before he rushed into the very jaws of his enemy." I now saw how needful it was to have inquired into the state of political affairs before I rashly made my demand. "My friend," said I, "is it certain I am to die to-morrow?" "Ay," he replied, " and ten thousand more of your gang, if we could lay our hands upon them. I always thought the Bheels were cunning fellows, but you are no specimen of their superior sagacity; Ram, Ram, thou Bheel ass!" On so concluding, he left me, as may be very easily guessed, in no enviable state of mind. There seemed no hope for me, either of mercy or escape. The next day came; my gaoler appeared again, but did not open his lips to me. Another and another passed away, in solitude and suspense. At length I was summoned to appear in presence of the Guicowar and his ministers. The English Resident was present; and I made up my mind, should they sentence me to die, that I would fall at his highness's feet, and relate the whole affair as it really stood. To my indescribable joy, however, the Guicowar began by saying he would spare my life upon one condition, namely, that I should accompany the soldiers to the haunt of the Bheels as a guide, by which means they might be surprised and taken. "I know," said he, "that some of you thieves will often prefer dying to discovering the haunts of your associates; but do you be wise, and you will preserve your life; be foolish, and you perish." The English Resident repeating the promise that my life should be spared, I fell down and related all that had befallen me: how I had been robbed by the Bheels; in what manner I had gained my money (taking on me the name of Nanna), and the scheme I had planned to get reimbursed. I concluded my relation by stating that I would with all my heart conduct the troops, as far as I could recollect the road, to the haunt of the robbers. All who were present were astonished and amused at my tale, and at the attempt to deceive both the Bheel and Guicowar. The Resident, hearing I was the man who caused Trimbuckje to be apprehended, instantly became my friend.

I was now sent back to my dungeon, and ordered to hold myself in readiness to march with the troops in two days' time. I rejoiced in this delay, as I thought it would give my companions time to be off from the cavern before the soldiers surrounded the entrance, otherwise I feared they would be put to the sword with the rest. I enjoyed a sound sleep on the ensuing night, though the harassing and pain of mind I had undergone did not lead me to expect it. My gaoler came to me on my return to my prison, and said, "So you are no Bheel, after all? Well, I thought as much; a Bheel would have been a little more circumspect in presenting such a letter to the Guicowar. You are a shrewd fellow, though, for all that blunder; by Ishwar, you were very nigh pocketing the cash. A week earlier, and the Guicowar durst not have refused your demand. Come, as you are a Hindoo, you shall, if you like, cook your own food. Never counterfeit a Bheel again; it is a most hazardous character—scarcely safe in the jungles, much less within the walls of a palace." I thanked him for his advice, and promised to regard it as long as I lived, in which it may be taken for granted I was sincere, as I bitterly repented my late exploit. When the fellow left me, I began to fear that my chance of meeting Nanna again was very little, unless he should hear a rumour of the events which had occurred at the palace. In that case, I conjectured he would wait in Baroda my return with the soldiers; for I most anxiously looked forward to the day when I should again see my friend, and tell him from what cause our plot miscarried.

Two days had elapsed, and on the third I was ordered by my masters to get ready for setting out. I replied that I had no preparations to make, and that I was ready on the instant. I added that I only waited their pleasure, and that they would have no difficulty in finding me at my post, for being found at which I must confess my obligation to them. At length I was led out, placed on a horse, and ordered to proceed, and lead the way at the head of a strong detachment of horse and foot soldiers, commanded by European officers. These very civilly informed me on starting, that they had orders to shoot me through the head, if I failed in my promise to conduct them to the right place. I told them I was certain I could take them within a coss of the spot; but I could not answer for my memory explaining to me every turning and winding of the jungle, as if I had been an old inhabitant of the place, and that I trusted they would not expect me to do things that might be impossible. I swore I would do what I could to lead them direct to the spot, and assist them all in my power. They bade me lead on, and I set forward. We were followed through the city by crowds of inquisitive persons eager to get a sight of the sham Bheel, as they denominated me. I felt so much shame that I covered my head with a cloak, so that my eyes only could be seen, and thus proceeded beyond the city walls. Every house and window was filled with females anxious to get a sight of me. It was nearly at the limits of the city, and as we were emerging from a narrow lane, in which a dwelling stood solitary and detached, when, going towards the gate, I cast my eyes to the upper windows crowded with females, all laughing at the cavalcade, and (what language can describe my astonishment!) I beheld my dear Sagoonah, who was one of the anxious and inquisitive spectators awaiting the arrival of the sham Bheel. I could scarcely keep my seat on horseback at the discovery. To see her, under such circumstances, for the first time after our separation, and to be unable to approach her and fold her to my bosom!—that she should see me thus a prisoner, dependent only on the will of others, and doing only what they commanded me to do, cut me to the heart. My consolation was, that she could not possibly recognise me, and my hope that, in a day or two, I might return again to Baroda and behold her free. I was happy indeed when I reflected that I was forced to conceal my person, and that she could not witness the degradation to be mine. I grew so dejected in a little time, that my escort began to think me an impostor. Why did I not push on with spirit? they repeated to each other; I must therefore dread the termination of the journey. "Well may he be afraid," said one soldier. "for the idea of a brace of bullets through his head cannot be a very cheering one." "Oh, he will not be hurt," said another, "if he lead us to the place and perform his promise" "True," replied the first speaker, "but I will wager a rupee he is leading us"——— "What?" said a third. "Why, where he does not know himself." "We shall see," cried another voice, "if we are to be made fools of, and led through those unhealthy jungles for nothing; if we are, I hope I shall be employed to blow out his brains." These observations, or similar ones, were constantly making, and I was forced both to hear and to bear them in silence. I was in no very enviable situation, for I might easily go wrong through the difficult, narrow, and overgrown paths which we had to pass along. This, as if to inflict still more torture upon me, was happening, just as I got a glimmering of hope and happiness once more, by the discovery of Sagoonah. My thoughts added to my pain;—the shadow thus cast over my dream of bliss, the miscarriage of my plan, no friend near me, and scarcely able to congratulate myself on my escape from the jungles and fevers, before I was again compelled to breathe their pestiferous atmosphere, with a brace of pistols close to my head, ready to be discharged whenever the caprice of the holders should be inclined so to do. I had just escaped from the hazards of the wild beasts, to fall into the hands of men far more savage ! Could I forbear from appearing dispirited?

We continued our march, until, in due course, we reached the jungles, in which, after we had proceeded for two days, we arrived at the place where Nanna, Fuzl Khan, and myself had been captured by the Bheels. To the right of the spot lay the narrow path by which we were led, and I headed the soldiers in that direction. The underwood thickened, and the path became every step more difficult. I could not see an inch before me. The vegetation rose far higher than our heads, and was very dense, and in some places united above us. I was still tolerably confident we were in the right way; yet I was not without my fears upon the subject, for we passed several turnings to the right and left. At length we came to a gentle ascent, which I remembered I had gone over, not far from the cave. My spirits rose, though I feared what might be the fate of my old companions during the attack, should they by any chance expose themselves; but I thought my own safety was now secured. I bade the soldiers be on the alert; and I had scarcely so cautioned them, before we were involved in the gloomy shadow of the rock in which the cave was situated. It towered high in the air above us, rough and craggy; at the base was an arch which spanned the entrance to the stronghold of the Bheels. A party of the soldiers dismounted, and drew up in a crescent around the entrance, while another forced its way in. The alarm was speedily spread to the inmost recesses of the hold. The Bheels resisted valiantly, and the work of death began. Mulharia, with his powerful arm, made wonderful efforts to cut his way through the party that first entered, and succeeded; but he was shot outside the cave. The whole band were speedily overpowered and slain, except two, who were badly wounded, one of whom informed me that there were two prisoners in the vaults below. I there found Nanna and Fuzl Khan. It appeared that the British Resident, suspecting the bearer of Mulharia's forced draft, refused to pay the money; and the latter, enraged, had subjected them to a severe imprisonment, and threatened their lives. Nanna inquired how he saw me there with soldiers; but I told him it was no moment for explanation then, and bade him follow me to the daylight. I led my two friends forth to the officers commanding the detachment, introducing them as my companions in misfortune, and begging they might be allowed to accompany us back to Baroda. My request was immediately acceded to; and all being anxious to quit the jungles, we set out for Guzerat on our return. The officers commanding told me I was at liberty to go wherever I pleased, they having no orders to take me back with them, in the event of my performing my promise. I begged, however, to be allowed to proceed with them, to which they agreed.

Nanna, Fuzl Khan, and myself brought up the rear of the party; and the soldiers being a little in advance, Fuzl Khan said, "Nanna, after you went, told me of your scheme. How have you succeeded? Have you secured the money of the Guicowar?" "Let us hear all about it," said Nanna; "how came you here with soldiers?" I speedily satisfied their curiosity, and related the danger I had encountered. "If," said Fuzl Khan, "you had deigned to consult me on the subject, I could have told you how the affair would terminate. These Guzerat rajahs never come down with cash; nothing but mortars and nine-pounders can extract it from them. Mulharia, of course, tried all he could to frighten the Guicowar out of his money; but he knew there was little or no chance of succeeding; and for you two fellows, who pretend to be so sharp and cunning, to be entrapped by a Bheel's paltry scrawl, I am surprised at you!

Consult me the next time, I pray you. I am not such a fool as
to have acted as you did, and can see as far forward as any one.
But you are a bold fellow, I must allow, to enter a palace, and
act the part of a Bheel there ! I wonder your head was not
struck off on the spot !" There was much good sense in Fuzl
Khan's remark, and both Nanna and myself found, on reflection,
that his observations were unanswerable.

We at length reached Baroda in safety, and put up at a comfortable durhm sallah. I now informed Nanna that I had seen
Sagoonah looking from a window in the part of the town which I
have before mentioned. He advised me to lose no time, but to
repair thither at once, and make inquiries, offering to accompany
me. I accepted his offer, and we proceeded together to recon-
noitre the house. I cannot describe the transport I felt when we
set out, and I hoped to clasp my beloved girl once more to my
heart. What was my disappointment on finding that Sagoonah
and her aunt had set out four days before, and taken the road to
Surat ! that they lived with a rich old grain-dealer, who provided
for them—Sagoonah's aunt acting as his housekeeper. Having
nothing more to detain us in Baroda, I determined to follow
their steps. Fuzl Khan was charmed at the idea of once more
seeing Broach, which lay in our route ; for, in returning from the
jungles, the soldiers took a nearer way back to Baroda than by
passing through Surat and Broach—so Fuzl Khan had missed
seeing his native city. Before we set off, Nanna wished to
obtain some money by drawing a bill on the British Resident ;
but not one of the sahoukars or bankers would cash it unless he
found security for its payment, or until a reply could be got from
Kandeish. This he could not do ; and thus every chance of
getting money at Baroda vanished. It was possible I might
overtake Sagoonah at Broach ; and therefore I went to the
house where I had seen her, and inquired the name of the
grain-dealer with whom she was travelling. They told me he
was called Hurrychund Doolabdass, a very infirm old man,
whose love of money was so great, he would not leave off trade
while he had an eye left, or leg remaining to stand upon. In
consequence of his age, he travelled very slowly, and there was

every reason to think I should overtake him at Broach. If we were fortunate enough to do this (which Nanna agreed to try by forced marches), there could be no doubt the old merchant would advance the cash upon the draft of Nanna on the Resident, as Sagoonah would, no doubt, answer for our characters. We accordingly set out, without a single rupee in our pockets. Fuzl Khan was the first to complain of hunger, and declared he could not walk another coss[1] without something to eat. Just at this moment we met some bullock-drivers, and begged a little rice or grain of them, which they kindly gave us on explaining our necessities; and thus we contrived to reach the end of our first day's march, very much fatigued.

[1] About two miles.

CHAPTER XXVI.

E arrived at Broach without any incident of note occurring to us, and entered safely into that sink of filth and abomination. I made inquiry at the grain-dealer's bazaar for Hurrychund, the merchant; and, to my great joy, heard he was then sojourning at the house of one of the principal grain-dealers. I lost not a moment in going thither; and at last, folded Sagoonah in my arms. Her joy at seeing me was excessive. She thought I had forgotten her, or deserted her for some other girl. "At one time I would doubt your constancy," she said; "and then I thought you might be a prisoner, or, perhaps, no more. Tell me all—tell me where you have been, and why so long separated from us?" I observed to her that my sufferings had been great, but that I had abated nothing in my affection for her, and had vowed to find her out if I searched the world over for her; that now I had succeeded, and we would part no more. Her aunt was also overjoyed at seeing me, and immediately cooked a very comfortable repast for me, a luxury I had not enjoyed for many a day before. I begged leave to introduce Nanna, and went and fetched him. I found him in the house, endeavouring to negotiate his draft with old Hurrychund, who refused to make him an advance, until assured by Sagoonah that we were not swindlers, and that he might rely upon my word. Nanna gave a bill upon the British Resident at Kandeish, but took only one hundred rupees. Nanna came to dine with us; and, on introducing him, I pointed him out as being one to whom we were indebted for the removal of one of our foes, Trimbuckje Danglia. "Thank Heaven!" said the lovely girl; "he is no longer to be dreaded; he has, indeed, been an inveterate enemy!"

We had finished our conversation, and were just going to dine, when a sudden dizziness of head came over me, and my brain seemed to whirl round. Fever succeeded, and I found the pestiferous air of the jungles had begun to act upon my constitution. My late march on foot, joined to my anxiety of mind, had, no doubt, contributed to increase its virulence. Instead of enjoying the company of Sagoonah, I was doomed to toss on a bed of fever, and to writhe in delirium. Day after day the fever continued to visit me. Sometimes the cold fit would make my jaws chatter, and seem to freeze my blood; then a burning heat would parch up my mouth, and bring with it temporary madness. How long I continued in this state, I cannot tell; but I found myself one morning in a violent perspiration, and felt better. The first person I knew was Sagoonah, watching me like a Peri —anxiety in her countenance, and her tenderness standing in her eyes. The sight almost repaid me for my sufferings; and I was about to speak, when she anticipated me, by desiring me not to make an effort too great for my strength, and, pressing my emaciated hand, bid me be composed. At the foot of my bed was an Englishman, who, I learned, was my doctor, and that his skill had brought me back from the brink of the grave. As soon as I was well able to converse, I inquired for Nanna, and found that he was also slowly recovering from the fever. Of Fuzl Khan nothing was known, though it appeared he had escaped it, as a Mohammedan had, I found, called daily to make inquiries after me. I requested the next time he called I might see him. The doctor soon pronounced me out of danger, and I thanked him most gratefully for the care he had bestowed upon me. He asked if I could account for the attack—if I knew any cause? I thereupon gave him the history of my visit to the jungles, and my return, and advised him, should duty or inclination lead him to visit the Deccan, by all means to avoid the jungles of Kandeish. He assured me he should do so most scrupulously, for he had never, or rarely, witnessed a species of fever more violent than that from which I was recovering. He told me that Nanna's restoration was certain, but slow, he not having had attentions bestowed upon him similar to those on me by

Sagoonah; nor had he taken his medicine regularly, or he would have been further advanced in a state of convalescence than he then was. From this, I learned the additional value of female kindness. Again and again I thanked and blessed the girl to whom I owed so much, and whose unremitting attention had rescued me from the grave.

I now gained fresh strength daily, and had a great desire to hear from Sagoonah her history while we were separated from each other; I therefore besought her to give me a minute detail of her sufferings and adventures, promising to relate mine in return .

She thus commenced :—" After your departure, we resided in the village, and nothing interrupted our peace for a considerable time. At last a religious old woman called on my aunt one day, and endeavoured to persuade us to visit the temple to perform our devotions. My aunt consented to go on the following day. The woman said that there was the same night to be a grand ceremony, when every one should attend, and advised us to be there at an hour she named. We agreed to this, and she left us, evidently much pleased at getting our consent. After she was gone, I ventured to hint my suspicion to my aunt that all was not right, and that I distrusted this old hag. I called to her recol- lection the warnings you gave us against admitting religious mendicants into the house, and declared my determination not to go to the temple, either by day or night. My aunt now began to open her eyes, and suspect all was not correct, upon calling to mind several things in the woman's conduct which had not struck her at the time, particularly a suspicious anxiety on the subject. In consequence, we did not attend the ceremony, but stayed at home. On the following day, the old woman called again; but we had previously given orders that she should not be admitted, and she went away highly incensed. A gossein next tried to gain admittance, but without success, as we were of course on our guard against the whole tribe. We now never ventured to stir from home, and admitted no strangers. All our precautions, however, were useless; for violence effected what fraud had been unable to perform. Our house was one night surrounded by armed men, and we were dragged from our beds, and borne off on horseback at a rapid rate. The persons who committed this outrage were in the employ of Trimbuckje, and we had no power to do anything but submit to our lot. In due time we reached Asseerghur, into the citadel of which we were conducted, and locked up for the night in a narrow cell. In the morning we were taken before the killehdar, who was smoking his hookah. He asked me if I was not a fool to refuse the brilliant offers of Trimbuckje Danglia. I told him that as I had refused the still more brilliant offers of the Peeshwa, it was not probable I should accept those of his slave. The killehdar then said, " Insolent girl ! you shall repent this contumacious conduct. Remember, in a week's time I shall call again upon you for an answer ; and, if you still remain an enemy to your own happiness, we must try other means to force a compliance." We were now dismissed, and again locked up in the cell, and fed upon the coarsest grain. Our guards were sullen, or I should have asked why we were not at once conveyed to Trimbuckje Danglia, and what necessity there was for detaining us longer in Asseerghur. In the course of a week, a compassionate woman, the wife of the jummahdar deputy, visited us, and we learned from her that Trimbuckje was involved at that time in much difficulty, and could not at the moment receive us. In fact, we found that he was actually a prisoner, though he hoped soon to be set free, when he would no doubt turn his thoughts towards me. We lingered in our cell week after week, almost starved, and clothed with miserable blankets. At length we found that Trimbuckje had escaped, and would soon appear in the Deccan again. We now thought that if there was a possibility of escape we should try it now ; for, should Trimbuckje arrive in the fort, we should be irretrievably ruined. The only thing was how we could effect such a thing, confined and watched as we were. We could come to no determination, until the female who had before taken compassion on us came again, and gave us provisions and sundry articles of comfort. We lamented our hard fate to her, and she pitied our sufferings. This led us to indulge the hope that through her means we might con-trive some mode of escape. Our intimacy increased daily, and we at length ventured to hint our wish that she would assist us in obtaining our enlargement. She lent a favourable ear to our applications, but declared her inability to be of service. We acknowledged our obligations to her for her repeated kindness; and, as a token of remembrance, I presented her with some of my hair braided with silver wire, which she said she should carefully preserve for my sake." Here I interrupted Sagoonah, by telling her I had seen the trinket, which was very dear to me, and I wore it next my heart until the Bheels robbed me of it. I now explained how it came into my possession, relating my adventure with the very woman to whom she was under such obligations, and my having preserved her from being plundered; which she was overjoyed to hear. Sagoonah then resumed her story:— "One day the wife of the jummahdar's deputy communicated to us a plan by which we effected our escape. My heart beat with joy at the idea of getting beyond the walls of the fortress, and I fell at the feet of our deliverer, kissing them with rapture. She raised me up, and bid us be cautious, stating that she had obtained permission for us to visit her at her house that day, and in the evening she intended going down the hill to pay her devotions to her god, when she was always attended by two of her retinue, whose clothes she proposed we should wear, and thus pass the gates without suspicion. Her own servants were to take our characters, and be conducted to the prison in our stead. As soon as the affair was discovered, and the servants were found not to be what they represented, they would be discharged. If the mistress was suspected, her husband would only be fined, and she herself come off with a scolding. This plan was duly carried into effect. We paid our visit to the lady, who took us through the gates in safety. How my heart beat when I found myself outside the fort! We took a hasty and grateful farewell of our kind friend, thanking her with tears of joy. She advised us to fly from that part of the country with all expedition. We followed her advice, and made for the jungles, near which, at a late hour of the night, we came to a glen, where was the habitation of an old goatherd. We knocked at his door for admittance; but when he found we had escaped from the fort, he was very anxious for our departure,

fearing he might suffer if it were known he had afforded us shelter. **Very early** the next morning, before he arose, we again set off, and **struck into** a road on the left, among ragged pathways and water-**falls.** Whether we were travelling on the right road we could not **tell;** but trusting to fortune, and being sensible that every step **took** us farther from the place of our captivity, we kept on until **we came** to a river, so shallow as to allow us **to** ford it. Here my aunt became so much fatigued, she could proceed no further. We therefore **sat down** under a tree, **and ate** some dried grain **which** the goatherd had given us, and drank water from the river. When somewhat refreshed, we renewed our journey until evening gathered in around us. We fortunately met some bullock-drivers, and my aunt asked the men if we were on the right road to Guzerat, and how far we were from Nasik. To **our great** disappointment, we learned that Nasik was three days' journey from the spot we then stood, and that there was only one **village on** the way. I **called out in** despair to my aunt, 'Arry Mousee, what shall **we do?'** 'By Ishwar,' said one of **the** drivers, 'I have heard that voice before;' and coming up to me, rudely uncovered my face, saying, 'Ah! my little traveller; what, **is it you** again? Where is your protector now?' You may con-jecture what my fears were at the moment, when I state that this fellow was the impertinent bullock-driver who accompanied us from **Poona** to Seroor, and pretended you were gone forward. 'I have got you now,' continued the scoundrel, 'and shall take the liberty of carrying you with me as far as Asseerghur. 'Tis strange if I don't turn a penny of you some way or another.' On hearing Asseerghur named, my aunt screamed; upon which the driver **said, 'I see how it** is—you have escaped from thence. **This is** **fortunate for me;** I **shall** be sure of a reward for bringing you **back** again. **So** come, mount my bullock, my pretty girl, and make up your mind **to** return whence **you** came.' So severe a disappointment quite overcame me, **and I** fell senseless to the earth. At this moment a man **on** horseback came up, desiring to know **the cause** of the delay. He was a grain-dealer, accom-panying **the** laden beasts. I begged him to interfere and release us, saying we **were** unfortunate women seized by the driver; upon which the latter declared I was his wife, whom he had lost for a long time, and that now, having found me, he determined upon never quitting me again. I declared it was all false, and fell at the merchant's feet, as did my aunt, telling him the fellow wanted to get a reward for bringing us again into a captivity from whence we had escaped, and that we preferred death to returning to the fort. The merchant, fearing we should delay his cattle, and he lose his market, ordered the fellow to let us go immediately and to proceed. The driver, though very sullen, was forced to obey, grumbling to us that he would be even with us yet—some one should soon be after us. We thanked our deliverer, who recommended us to call on Hurrychund Doolabdass, in that place, who was about to proceed to Surat, and he probably would allow us to follow in his suite. He also directed us on the way to Nasik. We begged his name, by means of which perhaps Hurrychund might sooner notice us. He told us he was called Toolseram, and so bade us farewell.

"Being now free of the impertinent driver, we once more indulged hopes of a safe arrival at Guzerat, and made use of every effort to gain the first halting-place, which was a miserable durhm sallah, without a village near it, or any kind of comfort whatever. I need not tire you with a detail of our sufferings on our journey, but merely state that, after encountering the most severe hardships, we reached Nasik. Our first care was to find out Hurrychund, in which we succeeded. We communicated to him the circumstances by which we became known to Toolseram, the grain-dealer. He congratulated us upon our escape, and offered us lodgings for the night, stating that, in a day or two, he should proceed towards Guzerat, and if we pleased we might accompany him. We cooked our rice, and my aunt, out of compliment, sent the old merchant some *sheeree pooree* (a dish in the making of which she excelled). Hurrychund was so pleased, that he declared no one else should cook for him in future but my aunt, and she has ever since superintended his household affairs, and cooked his victuals herself. We reached Baroda in safety, travelling by easy stages, not through the jungles, but by a more circuitous route. At Baroda we lived in a narrow lane "——

Here I interrupted her by saying I knew that, for there I saw her. "Saw me!" said Sagoonah, "and would not come to me! O Pandurang!" I said I would have given worlds to have flown to her arms; but when she heard the circumstances under which I was situated, she would acquit me of neglect. I inquired if she did not remember the sham Bheel, and informed her that I was the person—the very sham Bheel whom she laughed at from the window. Sagoonah hereupon made me relate all the circumstances that had taken place since we met before, which I now found myself strong enough to do.

Sagoonah was much struck with the history of Mahadeo, the first Pindaree, and made me relate it over again to her aunt. The latter declared her firm belief that Gabbage had murdered his nephew, to whom Sagoonah had been betrothed. "Ay," cried I, "and his brother also, the poor boy's father." She said she very much doubted that, for she had heard from good authority that he had escaped the vengeance of Gunput Rao. I then continued my history, and made them laugh heartily at the tale of Fuzl Khan. When I stated that the plan of old Gabbage was to force Sagoonah to marry his son Mahadeo, the women were both astonished at the old scoundrel's knavery and art. Sagoonah declared she would die sooner than be wedded to the son of such a fiend, though he were to be crowned king of the world. They now more valued the state of security in which they found themselves, and congratulated one another on their lucky escape from Asseerghur. The women were also rejoiced to find that their rich relation was at present in existence at Sattarah, though the belief of his having entered deeply into the views of the pretender to the musnud, Gunput Rao, greatly embittered the pleasure they would otherwise have felt, as it was impossible, under such circumstances, that they could ever approach him. We talked over the mysterious appearance of the old goatherd of the glen; and from the words which I had overheard Gabbage use, it struck us as very probable he might be that villain's brother, and the rightful successor to the musnud of Sattarah. This surmise gathered strength from the concern he displayed when I informed him that Gabbage still lived, and from this information it was that he gathered he was not in security where he then resided. The rest of my adventures amused the women much, but they censured me severely for acting the part of the Bheel at Baroda, and were astonished how I could present the letter, without first seeing my way clear as to the state of matters at court. The certainty that the bullock-driver would give information to Gabbage respecting the women greatly annoyed us. He would be sure to find the gossein at Asseerghur, and Kokoo we were certain would be after us, whether the driver gave information or not.

Our conversation was concluded by our receiving a message from Nanna, whom I was able to inform that I was much better, and hoped soon to see. The fever had not yet left him altogether, and he was still very low. Fuzl Khan also called to learn how I was: and when Sagoonah saw him, she could not help smiling at the recollection of his extraordinary adventures. I had now been nearly twenty days on the bed of sickness, and Nanna very nearly as many. Fuzl Khan had no money, nor any means of subsistence. He succeeded pretty well at first among his old Mohammedan acquaintance. His father had gone to Surat, and had set up a grinding-shop there. Nanna advanced him a few rupees, as he was useful to us on many occasions. One particular duty we assigned him, which was to watch all strangers, and see if he could discern Kokoo or Gabbage in the town. We accurately described their persons to him, and he promised to use his utmost vigilance. I also made him promise he would not engage either in puchees or eki beki, but keep quiet until we could get him some situation. At length, I found myself perfectly recovered, and thought it was become time to seek out the means of obtaining a livelihood. Sagoonah spoke to Hurry-chund for me, who in a little time procured me the situation of a writer under the Nazir of the udalut or court of justice at Broach.

The Nazir is a perpetual sheriff, and executes writs and summonses to all the parties required to attend in civil and criminal cases. Nanna contrived, by paying enormous fees, to get employed in the police department, so that thus, doubly armed with authority, we conceived ourselves a fair match for Kokoo, should he venture to appear at Broach with any hostile intentions. Fuzl Khan was made a peon in the udalut, and thus we were all provided for.

The system adopted by the English government for the administration of justice, however admirable in theory, is in many respects liable to perversion by those who carry it into effect. The artful agents of the court-house were perpetually on the look-out to take advantage of every new regulation or decision of the judge. My duty was to make out the summonses, and copy papers of importance. Nanna was also fully employed, and for three months we enjoyed uninterrupted peace. News reached us from the Deccan that Badjerao had surrendered to the English, who were now its sole masters. Broach, and all the stations in Guzerat, continued in their usual quiet state. The deposed king of Sattarah was once more placed upon his musnud by the all-conquering English; but his health was in such a precarious state, it was supposed he could not enjoy his newly-recovered power for any length of time. I heard also that a person named Gunput Rao, attended by his son, had openly declared himself successor to the throne, and that on the demise of the present rajah, there was no doubt but the English would acknowledge his claims, no one appearing to dispute them. This intelligence was of great consequence to Sagoonah, who now more than ever wished to keep out of her uncle's reach. We still remained in peace at Broach, and I will now take the opportunity of letting the reader know the nature of the duties which my new situation required, and give a brief account of the manner in which the English organised our court.

CHAPTER XXVII.

THE court of Broach consisted of the judge, a registrar, and an assistant-registrar—all Englishmen acquainted with the native languages. The first, of course, from a longer residence in the country, was the most experienced man of the three, and was accordingly at the head of the department. Before the judge, suits involving any amount were tried; before the registrar, only those which did not exceed five hundred rupees. Independently of the decision of civil suits, the registrar's business was to register all bonds and deeds of importance, receiving a fee of two rupees for every bond so registered. The assistant-registrar was generally a young man, lately arrived in the country, to whom the management of a few easy suits, of small amount, was intrusted, upon each of which a regulated fee was paid. The registrar also received established fees, in proportion to the amount of suits decided by him; but the judge received a regular income, and had no fees of any description. The judge also decided criminal as well as civil causes, and was consequently employed every day in the year. Some of my countrymen, who knew nothing of the true state of things, imagined these officers had nothing to do but 'amuse themselves, and make money—they were greatly in error; the duties were most laborious, and the pay scarcely adequate to the labour performed. Two days every week, suits were filed, numbered, and distributed to the persons authorised to decide upon them. In a city like Broach or Surat, the file was never clear, although the judges worked hard every day. New cases constantly poured in, much faster than the old could be got rid of; and without the greatest attention and regularity, the file would accumulate so great a number of causes for hearing, that no judge could get through it. A reader and writer belonged to this court. The first read the plaintiff's petition. The judge then called for the defendant's reply; which, being read, was entered, as well as the petition, in the record book by the attendant's writer, whose business it was to number and enter every document read before the judge. After the answer of the defendant was read, a second statement was heard from the plaintiff, and then a rejoinder from the defendant; but no other documents were admitted. The plaintiff was then called upon to prove his assertions, which he did by parole or documentary testimony, and after him the defendant was called on to disprove them. The judge then gave judgment.

Supposing the parties involved in a suit are not confident in their own skill and management of their affairs on the trial, the government vakeels, or pleaders, natives of the country, were ready to plead for them, and conduct their cases through. Everything was done with the greatest order and regularity: no confusion, no squabbling, or pulling off turbans, or coarse abuse was allowed. All had equal access to the judge in his regular and appointed turn. O my poor countrymen of the Deccan, I used to think, how differently these matters were managed with you! No feeling or bribery was allowed at Broach, no gratuities to greedy arbitrators and potails, &c. But, with all its excellences and advantages, the good intentions of the government were too often perverted even there, and unsuspicious judges imposed upon. Still, such cases were rare, and, if detected, were severely punished. The mode thus adopted at Broach, and the wish to render strict justice to all, were so much approved by the people, that they contrived to keep the files of the respective courts crammed full. There were not persons wanting who urged this as as an argument against the very way in which the English administered justice, urging that it promoted litigation, and advising that the people should keep to the old rules of their fathers. Such a class of fatuitous reasoners is never wanting in any country, to fling dirt upon improvements, and extol custom beyond common sense. The old system of arbitration, which I may hereafter touch upon, being the institution of past times, was that which those who did not take the trouble to examine into the reason of things extolled to the skies. The singular circumstance of my life threw me into many situations, wherein I had opportunities of making my observations on both systems. But I must first mention here, that the inhabitants and subjects of the government at Broach, and the neighbouring places, were in general very well satisfied with the dispensation of justice made for them. Trade flourished, and each individual felt secure in his property. That the establishment of the udalut, or court of justice, was the reason that causes were increased, is very incorrect. Justice had not before been attainable, and the people were obliged to endure wrong, for which they had no redress. When they found that injustice could no longer exist with impunity, they poured their grievances into the court. It might, therefore, as well be asserted that the erection of an hospital was the cause of an increase of sickness, as that giving the people an opportunity of gaining justice was the cause of the increase of applications to the courts. From the judge at Broach, an appeal lay to the superior court of Surat, called the court of appeal, and from thence to the sudr udalut at Bombay; what more could be wished or desired? The criminal code of regulations was equally good. The judge, though he had the power of committing a felon, did not try him. A circuit court was established, and one of its members went round to the different stations and held a jail delivery; so that the committal by the resident judge, was frequently no more than for safe custody till trial, when the prisoner was set at liberty.

Through the interest of Hurrychund, I at length obtained the situation of pleader in the court of udulat, in the registrar's department, and was now quite a man of consequence. Nanna continued attached to the police, and Fuzl Khan was still a peon, and carried a sword. Old Hurrychund had a nephew, who was lately married at Surat. The new-married couple arrived at Broach to visit him, and I was invited to dine with them on the first day of their arrival. The bride was accompanied by her mother; the former named Beema Bhae, and the latter Anundee Bhae. Beema was in height and figure very like Sagoonah.

Nanna was invited at the same time, and we had a very pleasant party. Before we separated, Hurrychund proposed giving a dinner to the caste of Marwarrys, of which he was a member. His nephew having no objection, invitations were sent out the following day, and the dinner was fixed to take place in four days' time. All the caste, save one individual named Premje, were invited. This person was considered an outcast, for some cause which I never heard explained. The dinner was accordingly given, and about one hundred and twenty Marwarrys partook of it. In the middle of the dinner, a man entered the room among the guests, and demanded why he was excluded, saying, he was a Marwarry, and would come also. All was immediately bustle and confusion, and the party demanded that he should be excluded or turned out. Poor Premje seemed in a dreadful passion, but it availed him little; he was turned away by the company unanimously. Temporary booths are erected before the doors of persons giving entertainments at Broach; and, indeed, in many other parts of Hindustan, and the street is for the time blocked up. Premje, though ejected from the booth, would not go away, but stood on the outside, grumbling, and asserting his right to be invited to the dinner. At length, some of the guests were favourably inclined towards him, and said that Hurrychund had treated him harshly; that since the alleged charges (for which he was now excluded) had been made against him, he had been seen at dinner with Gopaldass, the banker; and that was precedent enough for giving him an invitation on the present occasion. Being myself seated near the entrance of the booth, I heard Premje declare he would bring an action against Hurrychund, for fixing such a stigma upon his character; and with this threat he departed. The entertainment being over, I acquainted Hurrychund with Premje's threat; who laughed, and said, "Well, Pandoo, if he does bring his action, recollect I retain you for my counsel, and hope you will get him worsted." I thanked him for his good intentions towards me, and told him, if Premje did put his threat into execution, I would do my best in his behalf. The following day was the first filing day in the court; and, true to his threat, Premje thrust in his petition, or rather declaration, against Hurrychund—which was admitted and numbered in the usual way, and a day was appointed for hearing the cause. Premje's vakeel was a clever fellow, named Atchoo Bhae, who, as soon as he knew his opponent was to be Pandurang, the Mahratta pleader, snapped his fingers exultingly, and declared he would beat me so hollow, that I should be ashamed ever again to show my face in court. In the evening, I visited Hurrychund, my client, and informed him that Premje had actually commenced proceedings against him, and begged him to furnish me with materials for his defence. The first question he asked me, was the amount of damages laid; and I informed him that the sum was five hundred rupees, and that the cause would be tried before the registrar. "'Tis a large sum," said Hurrychund, "and you must speak loud, Pandoo, and do your best." I promised him I would exert myself to the utmost; and was beginning to take down the heads for the defence, when one of the Nazir's peons entered, bearing a summons to Hurrychund, who was obliged to accompany him, to put in security for his appearance at the day of trial. This having been accomplished, the old merchant returned, and duly instructed me how I was to proceed, and conduct the defence. My attention from the civil side of the court was drawn away, just as I had left Hurrychund, to the criminal department. As I quitted the door I met a mob approaching, and heard a voice calling out (which I knew to be Fuzl Khan's), begging me to save him and his friends from ruin. On inquiry, I discovered that he and two of his Mohammedan acquaintance had committed a theft, and were all apprehended, and expected to find bail in Hurrychund's house; in which they were disappointed, as I refused to interfere with the old man in their behalf—they were, I knew, such determined reprobates. Fuzl and his companions were consequently led away to prison. These true believers had for some time carried on a system of gambling, and were at last reduced to the extremity of committing a theft to raise funds for the support of themselves and their malpractices. The words of Fuzl Khan's mother, that eki beki would be his ruin, were thus verified. I immediately repaired to Nanna, and informed him of both these affairs. That of Premje he considered of most importance; as to the second, he contented himself with the observation, that Fuzl Khan ought to have been hanged long ago! I replied, as to that, it was not for us to pass judgment upon him, as we were far from being immaculate ourselves. Nanna did not much relish this remark, though he could not deny its justice; and he therefore turned off the conversation, and began to inquire particulars concerning the action with Premje. As I was pleader on the side of the defendant, I deemed it prudent to say as little on the subject as I could, and carefully to avoid letting out any part of the defence. I contented myself, therefore, with re-marking, that I was confident of success; and I left him, expressing a hope, that as Fuzl Khan came soon under his department, he would try and do all he could for him. He nodded assent; but Nanna was too much of a Mahratta to take trouble without a fee for any one; and as poor Fuzl could not bestow one, I was pretty certain no one would care a rush about him. For my own part, however willing I might be to serve him, I dared not risk offering a fee to carry into effect my good intentions respecting him, holding the situation I did; he was, therefore, left to his fate.

The day of the trial of Hurrychund's cause came on. The court was crowded; even the windows were filled with spectators of all descriptions, anxious to see the new pleader, and hear the arguments used to exculpate Hurrychund. The moment the opening of the cause took place, Atchoo Bhae, the pleader for the plaintiff, came forward, holding his client Premje by the hand. I approached alone, Hurrychund not choosing to be present. We stood in front of a large desk, at which the registrar sat. He was a little mean-looking man, very ill tempered. I never saw a more strange mortal. He looked like some of our deities, red-haired, with gooseberry eyes, and a great belly. He was so sour, that I was half afraid to address him. The declaration against the defendant was read. It complained that Premje Bohun, a Marwarry merchant, and inhabitant of the city of Broach, where he had resided for many years, gaining an honest livelihood by trade and fair dealing; had ever adhered to the rules of the caste to which he belonged, and had been admitted to all assemblages of caste, within or without the city walls, until the fifth day of the current month, when Hurrychund Doolabdass invited the whole of the Marwarry caste to a dinner, in celebration of the marriage of his nephew, Goolchund. In consequence, the whole caste assembled at Hurrychund's house; and, in booths erected for the occasion, partook of the entertainment so given; but that he, Premje, was excluded, as he did not receive any invitation; and that his character was much injured, and he was much aggrieved in consequence. That, hoping the omission was unintentional on the part of Hurrychund, he proceeded to the place of feasting, and entered the booth; from which he was rudely turned out, and ordered to go away. That he, therefore, sought compensation in damages for the injury sustained by him in loss of character, to the amount of five hundred rupees. This sum, if recovered, he intended to expend in giving a dinner to his caste, and in promoting every object that could tend to reinstate him in his former place in society, and thus remedy the injustice done him by the conduct of the defendant.

To this allegation I answered as follows :—" First, that he set forth he had ever adhered to the rules of his caste, and had been admitted to the assemblages of the Marwarry tribe on all occasions, until neglected by Hurrychund. Now, as to this point, no reply need be made, as the dinner was one, not given by Hurrychund, the defendant, to celebrate the marriage of his nephew: the dinner was not a caste dinner given by Hurrychund, but a private feast, given and paid for by his nephew, Goolchund; consequently, the present defendant could not be called upon to pay damages for a neglect of which he had not been guilty. This assertion could be proved by witnesses. It is admitted that Premje was not invited; but, if he had sustained any injury, he must sue the nephew and not the uncle:" I consequently prayed that the plaintiff might be nonsuited. I next called my witnesses, who were persons present at the dinner; and they proved that the invitations sent to them were not in the name of Hurrychund, but of his nephew. Other witnesses proved that Goolchund paid them for the various articles supplied to the entertainment.

The above was a defence which the plaintiff was not prepared to meet. The ugly little judge, after asking a few questions, non-suited Premje, adjudging him to pay all costs. Premje went away, determined to commence an action against Goolchund, the nephew: an arrangement we were not sorry for, as it would bring more fees into court. Hurrychund was pleased at my having put Premje to so much expense for nothing, and richly enjoyed the fellow's blunder. Sagoonah, too, congratulated me on my success in my first attempt; and the pleasure it seemed to give her was a spur to further diligence in my professional exertions.

Before the second suit was commenced, Fuzl Khan was brought to trial. He had been imprisoned from the moment he was apprehended. The circuit judge arrived, and held his court at the udalut in great pomp, attended by the registrar and the moulavee, the cazee,[1] and two shastrees.[2] It appeared that Fuzl Khan, in his capacity of peon, was employed to attach the property of a cloth-merchant, and ordered to keep guard over it. They who ordered him on this service little knew his character, or they would not have employed him on such a duty. Instead of guarding the property, he admitted two of his gambling associates to the warehouse, and all three helped themselves to the choicest muslins, kinkobs, and other fine articles. They were detected by one of the party wearing a rich muslin turban, and the other disposing of a shawl for half-price at a pawnbroker's. Fuzl Khan's house was searched; and stolen property being found there, he was apprehended immediately. All three were found guilty, and sentenced to be imprisoned and kept to hard labour on the roads for one year. The next time I encountered my friend Fuzl, he was working in the registrar's garden, with irons on his legs. The fellow was singing away very merrily; but, when he saw me, he stopped and began conversation, reproaching me with having abandoned him in the needful moment. I satisfied him it was out of my power to have assisted him, or I should have rejoiced

---

[1] Mohammedan law-officers.   [2] Hindoo law-officers.

in being able to do so, and thus prevent his becoming the sad spectacle he now was. I gave him a few pice and went my way.

The time for the new trial of Premje against Goolchund drew near. I was prepared to defend the cause. At the hour fixed the court was crowded, and the windows filled with people. One of these windows looked into the yard, and being open, a number of persons stood on the outside, and thrust in their heads. The window was exactly opposite the place in which I stood to plead. Goolchund himself was present, and full of anxiety lest he should have to pay five hundred rupees. He repeatedly prompted me to speak loud and to the purpose. The declaration was read, and was the same as the first, with the alteration of the name of the defendant. I had to prove that the dinner was not a marriage-dinner; because that must, according to rule, have been given at Surat, where the ceremony took place. It was, moreover, necessary to prove we were fully justified in not inviting the plaintiff, even if it were considered a caste meeting. To do this, I could prove the plaintiff had, on a former occasion, been overlooked at a great meeting of the caste at the house of a principal Marwarry, who give a dinner on the death of his father. Moreover, I could prove the plaintiff an outcast, having committed some fault which rendered him unfit to be admitted among the good and correct men of his tribe. The plaintiff, on the other side, was prepared to rebut this evidence respecting himself. The witnesses on my part were sharply cross-examined by Atchoo, the pleader on Premje's behalf, and we all eyed each other as if life and death depended on the issue of the trial. Goolchund was constantly pulling my sleeve, and proposing many silly questions to be put to the plaintiff and his witnesses. At length we got so far that I rose to address the court. I stated that I could produce a witness whose testimony would not leave a doubt on the mind of the judge as to the character of the plaintiff; and having heard him, the issue of the trial could not be otherwise than favourable to us. Having spoken to this effect, I cast my glance towards the persons who were looking in at the window, purely from accident; but how can I express the agitation and alarm I felt when, among the group, I recognised

Kokoo, with the ass-driver by his side! My papers fell from my hand—I stood without motion. A trembling came over me; and, notwithstanding my client, Goolchund, pulled my sleeve nearly to pieces, my eyes remained fixed on the window, from which I had no power to take them. At length I saw they were gone, and picked up my papers; but I still gazed around me bewildered, until the registrar demanded what was the matter. Goolchund replied, the people at the window disturbed me; upon which they were ordered to retire, and the window was closed. The registrar then called on me to name the important witness I stated I should call. Goolchund named him to me, but I pronounced the name in a most confused manner. He appeared, however, and was sworn in; but I had not a question to put to him—all had been driven from my recollection. I confounded Premje with Goolchund, and *vice versâ*. Of these things Atchoo took the advantage, and urged the badness of my cause from the ill way in which I was able to support it. He pulled my poor witness so to pieces, that he deposed things the very opposite to what I intended he should have done. Goolchund endeavoured to speak, but was not allowed, as I was his vakeel, and only one of us could be heard. At length the judge, tired at the delay and confusion which I had caused, decided in favour of Premje, and ordered Goolchund to pay the sum of five hundred rupees, with costs of suit. After this decision, we of course could not be heard there, but we were told we might appeal to the judge's court if dissatisfied. Thus ended a cause which, had not my attention been called away by the sight of an object so terrible to me and mine as Kokoo, I felt certain I should have gained. I had now to submit to the ill-humour of Goolchund, who hinted I had been bought over by the opposite party. Hurrychund also looked very cool upon me, and was extremely dissatisfied.

On my returning home, Sagoonah inquired what, in the name of Vishnu, could have so paralysed me; how I failed, and what was the cause of my agitation. She besought me to tell her what it was that struck me speechless in the court. I said, "When you are in danger, my dear Sagoonah, it is impossible I can attend to anything besides." The frightened girl now inquired how she could be discovered in danger in the midst of my pleadings. I communicated to her the cause of my alarm, and that I had recognised Kokoo, and his companion the driver, at the window of the court-room. I entreated her to keep within doors, and never to exhibit herself in the streets. I also begged her to explain to Hurrychund how I had been alarmed, and the cause of it, which occasioned the loss of his nephew's suit. She promised me I should be reinstated in his favour, for she had great influence over him; and before night came, I found she had performed her promise successfully, for old Hurrychund became as affable and good-natured as before. Goolchund, however, still continued to wear a long face, which he altered a little upon my talking to him respecting his cause; repeating my regret at its failure, which could not have happened under any other circumstances than those which I related to him. I advised him by all means to appeal against the decree of the registrar; for although it was not common for the judge of the upper court to hear fresh evidence on a cause, yet, upon my representing how I had been interrupted in my defence, it was probable he would waive the general custom, as an exception, owing to very peculiar circumstances, and grant the admission of fresh evidence. Goolchund shook me heartily by the hand, and declared he would give notice of appeal on the following day.

When Goolchund quitted me, Nanna came in, full of anxiety, to hear the cause of my failure in court. When I told him, he said he was not surprised at it, for the sight of such an inveterate foe seeking one's life, at all times appalling, must have been particularly so at such a critical moment, and was enough to bewilder the strongest and most courageous man. Nanna advised me never to go out after it was dark, or venture at any time beyond the city walls. Day after day passed away, and all was quiet: neither Kokoo nor the driver appeared. The appeal case was heard in due course; I having furnished affidavits, stating how I had been interrupted, and that important evidence, which would have decided the cause the other way, had not been heard, the judge granted the request. I was not permitted to plead, because I belonged to the lower court ; but the cause was ably conducted. After a long hearing, the decree of the court below was reversed, and Goolchund was successful, to the inexpressible chagrin of Premje and his friends. Old Hurry-chund was so pleased at the issue of the appeal, that he gave a nautch [1] on the occasion, to which all the most respectable of his caste were invited.

[1] Dance.

CHAPTER XXVIII

T the nautch mentioned in the last chapter, an excursion to the island of Kubbeer Burr was proposed. This place is situated some way up the river Nerbudda, and is remarkable for being entirely covered by one large banyan tree. The branches of this tree growing downwards, take root, and become each of them a distinct trunk. From these, other branches droop in like manner to the ground, and thus traverse over and shade from the sun an immense space of ground, nearly two thousand feet in extent. It is deliciously refreshing, during the hot weather, to walk under the green arches formed by this tree, and enjoy the shade and coolness. Walk joins to walk, among green festoons, and a labryinth of leaves and branches. Nothing could be more agreeable than parties made to spend the day on such a spot. The distance was but a pleasant sail, and the relaxation from business, and a due attention to the important duties of eating, drinking, talking, and smoking, were anticipated by all who were to join in the excursion with no small delight. As there was but little preparation necessary, matters were speedily arranged for starting. The women were to accompany us—a measure which I opposed in vain, dreading the machinations of Kokoo, who, I was convinced, remained lurking in the neighbourhood, waiting a fit opportunity to consummate his nefarious plans. Sagoonah was extremely desirous of seeing the island, and endeavoured to persuade herself there was no danger in going thither, protected as she would be by us and two or three udalut peons. Goolchund's wife and mother were to accompany us, and therefore Sagoonah was determined to venture. Finding argument of no avail, I gave up the point, and prepared for the excursion. It was fixed to take place on the

304

third day after the appeal cause came on. Hurrychund sent everything we could need to the island the day preceding, and spared no expense to render the whole party as comfortable as possible. At an early hour in the morning, we set out on our excursion. It happened to be an Hindoo holiday, and no business was transacted at the court-house; so I requested Nanna to accompany us, and we both went, well armed, and, each attended by two armed peons, escorted the females to the boat. It was at the hour of five in the morning, it being necessary to go up with the tide. Owing to the darkness of the hour, which the morning mist increased, it was impossible to distinguish Sagoonah from Beema, Goolchund's wife, their figures were so much alike, and both enveloped in dark shawls. After a few hours' sail we saw the island, to the great joy of Beema and her mother, who were both ill from the boat's motion. It was agreed that those who were tired of the voyage should land at once, and ramble about the island, or enjoy themselves in the shade. On landing, I was much struck with the remarkable tree, having never seen one half its size in any part of the Deccan. There seemed to me to be a thousand trunks, supporting an immense roof of foliage of a deep green. Not a ray of the sun could penetrate through it; all under it was in shadowy silence. The great drawback to our pleasure was, that the place abounded in snakes, so that we were ever in fear of trampling upon them, and of getting bit. This would not have been the case, however, without frequent warnings, as the boat-men and servants enchanced the danger by marvellous stories of the venom of these reptiles, as proofs that it was more powerful here than in any other part of India. One of them related a tale of a person struck dead at encountering the fiery eyes of an immense serpent covered with hair, that reached in length from one side the island to another. As if to help out the marvellous narration, a large *cobra di capello* brushed away from us among the underwood at the moment, and so alarmed the females, that we moved in another direction, taking a different path, and one more beaten. Our presence in this unfrequented place seemed to cause great consternation among the monkeys and birds, which haunted it in vast numbers, and of all varieties. The screams of the disturbed and affrighted fowls as they flew off, and the chatter and grin of the monkeys, that, peeping amid the branches of the trees, seemed mocking our power to take them, were highly amusing. Though all creatures besides seemed to flee us, the bat hung by his enormous wings in certain dark hollows of the trees and densely 'shaded boughs, apparently insensible of our presence. The coolness, and the additional feeling of gloom thrown over the deeper recesses of the foliage, were far from being agreeable on this account. The bats differed much from those which visit our streets and houses in the city, being immensely large, and measuring three or four feet from wing to wing when extended. They call them in the Deccan *wur wagool*. In all my wanderings, I never before saw such a sight. They hung with their heads downwards in every direction by hundreds, suspended from small hooks at the extremity of their wings. After a short ramble under this magnificent tree, we found our-selves almost close to the landing-place where our boat lay. Some of the party, while we took rice for our first repast, proposed remaining on the island, and others were for sailing a little further up the river and returning to dinner. Those with whom the water disagreed, naturally were for keeping upon the land. Sagoonah and her aunt were so much pleased with the sail to the island, that they expressed a wish to proceed a short way up the stream, and rejoin their female friends in an hour or two. Sagoonah, her aunt, Nanna, two peons, and myself, therefore embarked to take a little more pleasure on the water. The time passed so pleasantly, that we did not reflect upon the dis-tance the wind and tide were carrying us. At length the tide turned, and the boatmen advised us to avail ourselves of its assistance, and return to the island. Unfortunately the wind was full in our teeth, and we could make no way but with the oars ; our boat also was large and heavy. Not being prepared for this disappointment, and having but three sailors and two oars, one of which afterwards snapped in using it, our progress was very slow. Sagoonah's aunt had fortunately a little dried grain and bread with her, of which we partook. Without oars,

we were obliged to hoist our sail, and tack and wear, hoping to
reach the island before the tide again turned; but in this we
were disappointed. We made no distance, and were tossed
about to no purpose. The females became ill, and our party was
miserable enough. When the tide turned, we were obliged to
take down our sail and anchor, to prevent being carried back
again; this we did pretty near the shore, and then we consulted
what was best to be done. It was now six o'clock in the evening,
and we seemed without a possibility of reaching the island, where
the rest of our party must be anxiously awaiting us—for await us
they must, as there was no other boat to convey them home. I
now proposed sending the two peons on shore to procure oars,
and four stout fellows to row us to the island. The peons set
off, while Nanna and myself guarded the females, who were
alarmed, and stood much in need of rest. Hour after hour
passed away, and it was ten o'clock before the peons returned,
bringing with them only three oars, but no men to assist; they
reported that it was with great difficulty they procured these.
There being no remedy, we determined to make the best
use of the oars we could, and, weighing anchor, pulled with all
our strength against the tide. With every effort we gained
but little, till the tide again turned in our favour. This
was at twelve o'clock at night. A miserable day of pleasure
we had, toiling at our oars, and Nanna vowing he would never
go boating again for pleasure. At length we saw lights at the
island, and the men set up a loud shout, which was answered by
our friends, who were no doubt tired enough. About two o'clock
we set our feet on shore, and found all wailing and lamentation.
The first person we saw was old Hurrychund, beating his breast
and tearing his clothes, at the same time crying, "Oh, my
nephew, wife, and her mother, all gone!" I demanded whither.
The old man exclaimed, would to Ishwar he knew—"Some
villains had borne them off." He then demanded where I had
been so late, exclaiming every moment, "What a day of pleasure
—misery, misery!" I begged him to explain himself, but
the old man could only weep and beat his breast. One of the
peons whom I had left with the party on the island, to whom I

appealed for information, told me that, hour after hour passing by, and not seeing anything of us, they went in parties round different points of the island, to see if they could espy us coming. About six in the evening Hurrychund's nephew, with his niece and her mother, being absent, he bade them go in quest of them. He did so, and on arriving at the end of the island, was just in time to see a boat push off, well manned, and to hear the screams of the females on board. The boat went against the tide to Broach, but, owing to the number of hands on board, it moved away rapidly. He returned immediately to Hurrychund, and told him what he had seen. The old man was struck dumb with terror and alarm. Pursuit was impossible, for there was no boat, and they became more anxious then ever for our arrival. Hour after hour passed, till it was too late to pursue them, if there were hands and oars to overtake them. Nanna, during the recital, declared his belief that Sagoonah, her aunt, and myself, were the persons whom the villains intended to seize ; but that, it being dark, they had not been able to distinguish the one from the other. I fully coincided with Nanna in opinion, and rejoiced at our escape, though I sincerely bewailed the fate of our friends. Hurrychund ordered the boat to return to Broach, as the tide would soon again become adverse, and not a moment should be lost. Having embarked, we rowed, fatigued as we were, and reached the city by five o'clock in the morning, having had twenty-four hours of everything but pleasure. Application was immediately made to the police to pursue the villains who had carried off Hurrychund's relatives. Parties were despatched by land and water to endeavour to obtain tidings of them. Leaving Nanna to watch over Sagoonah and her aunt, I embarked with a strong party to scour the river, entertaining but a faint hope of success. Well knowing the sanguinary disposition of Kokoo (who, I felt certain, was the agent in the affair), I feared that, finding he had missed his prey, it would instigate him to commit violence on the unhappy persons who had fallen into his clutches. We made inquiry of every boat which came up the stream if the people had seen an open boat well manned, or had heard the screams of women proceeding from any vessel on the river. We were uniformly answered in the negative, and began to despair of obtaining any tidings of Goolchund and his wife. At length we found ourselves opposite a bungalow, or house, built by an English gentleman, who resorted there when sickness rendered a change of air useful, the sea breeze being very sensibly felt at that place. We could not return to Broach until the tide changed, and I determined to go on shore, and wait its turn at the bungalow. We accordingly anchored; but no sooner was the anchor dropped, then we were hailed from the bungalow by a voice which I recognised to be Goolchund's. We immediately landed, and joined him at the front of the house, expressing our pleasure at meeting him once more. He bade me come in, and he would tell me all that had happened to them. I eagerly inquired if his wife and her mother were safe; and he answered me by throwing open the door of a room, where I saw them quietly seated on the floor, eating dried grain. They were much pleased at seeing me, and begged me to sit down by them.

Goolchund now proceeded to relate the circumstances of their capture. They had gone round the island to see if they could find us, or rather to look out for us returning down the river, when they were suddenly seized by a number of men, who bore them to a boat, and put off from the shore. The thing was so sudden, that they were all astounded, and it was some time before they could recover themselves. The men rowed with all their force for some miles, until they were past Broach; having taken the precaution to gag the women, and thus prevent their screaming while passing the city walls. A small boat now met them, from which a shrill whistle was heard, and answered by those who were in the boat with us. The little boat then ran alongside ours, and two men came on board us, having a lantern. One of them was a short man, with light hair; the other taller, having a dark complexion. As the light flashed across the boat, I could distinctly perceive our late opponent in the law-courts, Premje, who instantly ordered the light to be put out, and began a very earnest conversation with the short man, who had just entered the boat. Goolchund was seriously alarmed to find himself thus in the power of an enemy, of whose resentment it was impossible

U

to foresee the extent. At length they reached the bungalow, and cast anchor opposite to it. They were then landed, and compelled to walk up the bank to the house, in a room of which they were locked. The villains who had taken them off prepared to sleep in the hall; their prisoners also lay down, but could obtain no repose, for Goolchund heard one of their guards say, "Do? why, kill the fellow, to be sure! Did he not try to subject me to the most cruel and lingering death—even to starvation?" "Impossible!" said another voice, which was Premje's; "he has never been away from Guzerat in his life." "Aye, aye! but I know better," replied the first speaker; "he shall be food for fishes, on our way to Bombay." Goolchund here made a violent knocking at the door, and two men entered the room in which they were confined; one of them was Premje, and the other a shorter person. They inquired the cause of the uproar. Goolchund informed the short man he had heard their conversation, and was anxious to convince him of his error. He desired him to look in his face with the lantern close, and say if he had ever seen him till then. He did so, and in a moment exclaimed, "Death and fury! have we had all this trouble for nothing? What fellow have we here?" Goolchund then told him his name, and he said, "You will soon, perhaps, be set at liberty;—but, though disappointed in my man, the women are in my power." Goolchund assured him that one of them was his wife, and the other her mother, entire strangers to him. Upon this the short man called out, "Rajoo! get up, you lazy rascal! and come hither instantly!" Upon this the taller man of the two, who had come on board us from the little boat, came in, rubbing his eyes. The short man whispered something to him, and then bade him approach the females, and say if the young one was not Sagoonah. Goolchund then saw through the whole affair, and comprehended the mistake which had been committed; and that Sagoonah, her aunt, and myself, were the persons they intended to carry off. The man who had been sleeping approached the females, and after a minute inspection, cried out, "Alas! we have caught the wrong birds!" The short man's rage knew no bounds; taking Premje by the collar, he dashed him with violence against the wall, and hurried out of the bungalow, summoning together his men; and, going on board, they weighed anchor, and were far away before the morning dawned. It was clear Premje was the agent in this affair, he having a grudge against Goolchund; and, conceiving him and his wife the persons wanted, he was, doubtless, active enough in his exertions to effect the object in view. Though sorely bruised, he fled from the house, and was not seen there afterwards, nor was it likely he would venture to enter Broach again.

I then explained to Goolchund who the short man was, and that his face had prevented my succeeding in court in gaining his cause; that I had no doubt of his object being myself; and that, had he succeeded, I should have been food for fishes too certainly. Goolchund thought I had had a narrow escape, and then bade me explain the cause of our absence from the island, which I did in every particular.

The whole party now embarked in my boat, and one tide carried us back to Broach. We reached the city about six o'clock in the evening. Crowds of persons were in waiting to receive us. The whole city had heard of the outrage committed, and every one was anxious to know where the missing persons had been discovered, and who took them away from the island. I had previously advised Goolchund not to say a word about Premje being concerned, until we had communicated with old Hurrychund; we therefore reported to the multitude, that we were ignorant of the persons and motives for committing the outrage upon us. This only increased the public curiosity, and many false reports were circulated respecting the affair; at length the people, by some accident, hit upon the truth, or so much of it as established, that as Premje had been an opponent of Goolchund's in court, and the latter having gained the cause, the former had hired persons to carry off and murder his antagonist and wife. Premje's disappearance from the city at the time caused this statement to be believed. The Marwarry caste crowded around Goolchund, and desired him to swear by the holy cow whether or not Premje was in the plot. Goolchund acknowledged that he had seen Premje in the party which carried himself and his wife away from the island. The Mar-warrys, upon this, combined, and surrounded Premje's house, which they would have razed to the ground, had not a strong body of police been sent to protect it from their rage. It now became necessary that Goolchund should proceed to the police court and formally depose against Premje; this he did, whilst I escorted home the females, and hastened to relieve the anxious mind of old Hurrychund. Thus terminated our pleasure-party to the island of Kubbeer Burr.

CHAPTER XXIX.

IN human life one misery is certain to be followed by a train of half a dozen. The discomfiture of our excursion to the island was followed by the illness of old Hurrychund, who had been too long exposed to the night air for one of his advanced years. He caught from the damps a severe fever, which in three days carried him off. A funeral, instead of a wedding, was now ordered to be prepared in booths in the front of his house. The sudden demise of the old man was a sad blow to us all. I had myself been fanciful enough to suppose he would recover from the attack; but, on the third day after it took place, on returning from the court, I saw the kind and emaciated old man stretched on the fatal bed of *cusa* [1] grass, and I was convinced no hope of his recovery remained. The old man was, in fact, deathstruck, and had no more time allowed him than was sufficient to make a few donations to his surviving friends and relatives. Among the former was Sagoonah's aunt, to whom he bequeathed five hundred rupees

None of the sacred water of the Ganges being at hand, the ceremony of sprinkling his head was omitted from necessity, but the *sála gráma* [2] stone was placed near him, and all the ceremonies performed which the friendship of his relations could prompt, and had the means of executing. Holy strains were chanted, and sacred hymns poured into the ear of the dying; leaves of hallowed trees were scattered over his head, and every attention

---

[1] When the death of a Hindoo is certain, and no hope remains, he is laid on a bed of grass, called *cusa*.

[2] A small black smooth stone, perforated by worms, or, as the Hindoos believe, by Vishnu, in the shape of a reptile.

religiously paid him in his expiring moments. As soon he as was dead, the body was washed, perfumed, and decked with flowers; a ruby put into his mouth, together with coral, and small pieces of gold thrust into his nostrils and eyes. Goolchund, the nearest relative, as usual, brought the cloth sprinkled with fragrant oil, and threw it over the corpse. Two hours afterwards they conveyed the body to the funeral pile; it was raised up by his relatives, and placed on a wooden bier for the procession. It now moved slowly on, with fire and food borne before it in an unbaked earthen vessel, accompanied by the sound of drums, cymbals, and wind and stringed instruments. The funeral passed out through the eastern gate of the city to its place of destination. The corpse being laid upon a bed of cusa, with its head towards the south, the relatives of the deceased bathed in the river, on the banks of which the funeral pile was to be prepared. They then began to mark out lines, upon which the wood was placed. The pile being ready, they washed the body, clothed it in clean linen, rubbing it with perfumes, and then placed it on the wood with the head to the north. Goolchund then threw the cloth over the corpse, and taking up a lighted brand, invoked all the holy places, saying, " May the gods, with mouths of fire, consume this body !" He then walked three times round the pile, looked towards the south, and dropping on his left knee, applied a torch to the wood near the head of the corpse, while the attendant priests recited the proper prayers. During the time the wood was consuming, several of the relations of the deceased having taken seven pieces of the wood, walked slowly round the pile and threw them over their shoulders upon the fire, saying, " All hail to thee who consumeth flesh !" All who had followed or touched the body were obliged to walk round the pile, keeping their left hands towards it, but not looking at the fire. They then proceeded to the river, bathed, and returned home in procession, having performed many minor ceremonies, such as sipping water, &c., too minute to mention. On arriving at the house of the deceased, the funeral cakes were baked, and food put aside on a leaf for the crows. Cake was thrown into the water, and milk and water were suspended at the door of the house in earthen vessels every evening, until the time of mourning expired. This endured for ten days, and mournful days they were to us all.

Sagoonah and her aunt lived with Beema, and Anundee her mother, but as the latter intended to go to Surat, it was necessary to make some new arrangements. At length, Nanna procured lodgings for Sagoonah and her aunt in a very retired quarter of the city, and Beema and her mother took leave of us, and proceeded to Surat, leaving us melancholy enough at their departure. The uncertainty we were in respecting Kokoo, was a great drawback upon our comfort. Sagoonah, knowing the imperious necessity for concealment, resigned herself to the alternative of close imprisonment in her lodgings, with a placidity which more than ever incensed me against her persecutors, and raised her still higher in my esteem. Business had become scarce at the court, and I consulted Nanna as to whether we had not better proceed elsewhere to some other court where the Mahratta language was used, whereby we should gain many advantages that Guzerat did not afford us. Nanna being of my opinion, I informed Sagoonah that we intended to proceed to the Northern Concan, in hopes of obtaining practice as pleaders in that court. Neither Sagoonah nor her aunt were particularly desirous of remaining in Broach, and they both acquiesced immediately in our plans for the future. Whether we should proceed by sea or by land was the next point ; and we finally fixed upon the latter mode, hoping we should not be molested by Kokoo or his agents. I informed the judge of the reasons which induced me to quit his court. He approved of my plans, and gave me a letter to the judge of the Concan, in which he also re-commended Nanna. Just as we were taking leave, the nazir came running in, reporting that a prisoner had escaped who was employed in working upon the roads ; he had knocked down the guard, and disencumbered himself of his irons. The judge inquired the name of the man ; and, to my surprise, I found it was Fuzl Khan. "Where did this fellow come from ?" inquired the judge. "He came with these two Mahrattas," was the reply of the nazir, pointing to us. "Indeed !" observed the judge ; "and these two are just going away, and their friend is departed? It appears very suspicious. I fear you have aided the fellow in breaking prison." We were much hurt at such a suspicion, though we could hardly wonder at its being entertained. We most earnestly assured the judge we cared nothing about the fellow, and had taken no interest in his affairs. The judge said there was certainly no proof of our conniving at or assisting in his escape, and he would not detain us. He advised us not to be seen in the fellow's company again on the English territory. We bowed, and retired. On the outside of the court we saw the guard whom Fuzl Khan had knocked down. The poor fellow's teeth were literally driven down his throat. Fuzl had used his irons as the weapon of offence. Nanna observed that he was a desperate man, and I agreed that he was more so than I had apprehended; but I said I thought he must be speedily retaken. Nanna imagined he was too clever a fellow for that; but we both agreed never more to have anything to do with him if he came in our way.

Everything being in order, we set out on our journey. Sagoonah and her aunt were seated in a small covered cart drawn by bullocks; Nanna and myself were mounted upon tatoos. We started at an early hour in the morning, that we might reach Surat at night, resting an hour or two at Khim to refresh our cattle. From the latter place, where we enjoyed a comfortable meal, we set forth again for Surat. The bullocks being knocked up, our journey was delayed so much, that darkness came on before we arrived near Surat. We had passed two travellers on the road on foot, who now overtook us, so slow did we proceed. These two men seemed very suspicious characters; if we stopped they did the same, and sometimes they kept up with us by running. Nanna was convinced they were not common travellers, but had some sinister motive for thus following us. We watched them narrowly; but as they did not offer to molest us in any way, we took no other notice of them, and soon entering Surat, we hoped to lose sight of them entirely. In this, however, we found ourselves mistaken; for while we were assisting the women to alight from the carriage at a comfortable lodging which Nanna had procured, the two travellers posted themselves one on each side of the door, and having seen us enter, hastened away down the street. "Who can these fellows be?" inquired Sagoonah. "They once opened the cloth which covered the carriage, and peeped in." I swore, by Ishwar, had I known this before, I would have prevented their ever attempting it a second time. I requested her not to be alarmed, as we should keep a good look-out. I endeavoured to persuade her they would probably cease to follow us any further, as Surat might be the place of their destination. Notwithstanding all I said, Sagoonah was evidently alarmed. Nanna and myself agreed to keep guard by turns outside her chamber, and to strike down any one who might attempt to enter or to molest us.

After we had dined, Nanna went out to hire fresh cattle for the ensuing day; and, on his return, the females retired to their apartment. Nanna took post at their door for the first half of the night. At one o'clock he awoke me, saying all was quiet. I took his place, and remained there until morning; but nothing occurred to disturb us. The cattle were ready; and, having taken breakfast, we once more set out, unattended by any prying travellers, so that I began to hope we had rid ourselves of them entirely. Nousarry was the first stage, and there we thought of remaining all night, the females complaining of fatigue. What was my surprise, on alighting, to find the two mysterious travellers posted there! and before I could demand the reason of their thus molesting us, they were off. This conduct was now a subject of serious alarm to us all, and I determined, should they follow us to Damaun, to take some measures for eluding them. We also thought it prudent to travel only by short stages in the day, so as not to run the risk of being benighted. In this manner we proceeded, and were sure to behold the travellers posted at the durhm sallah where we alighted. At length we reached Damaun, a large fortified place belonging to the Portuguese. As before, the two men were watching our arrival there. On seeing this, I thought it high time to consult on some method of eluding their watchfulness, and therefore determined on taking a boat, and proceeding by sea the rest of the distance. We could never have a better opportunity than at Damaun, for it was a seaport, and boats of all sorts were riding in the harbour. The travellers, conceiving we should still proceed by land, would set out before us, as they had hitherto invariably done, and would be at a loss when they missed us at the following stage. This plan was agreed to. Nanna went and hired a boat as secretly as possible, and early in the morning we went on board and set sail. The boat we had hired was called a pattamar: it was a large one, and had a cabin for the females. On the third day, we saw Bassein, the chief place in the Northern Concan, whither I determined on going. A better boat than ours for sailing came after us, as we supposed from Surat, and hailing us, asked whither we were bound? I desired the tindal, or steersman, to answer, "Bombay." The strange boat now ran so close to us, that I could recognise the faces of all on board; and what was my vexation in discovering the two men who had before followed us, muffled up in dark shawls! It thus seemed impossible to avoid them. Nanna proposed shooting them; but, aware of the consequences of such a proceeding on the territory of the English, I begged him not to think a moment of such a step. The strange boat now passed us, and I desired the tindal to put into Bassein, which he had no sooner done, than I had the mortification to see the strange boat put about, and run for the same port. "We must submit," I observed; "let the fellows follow us if they will; we must be prepared for them; and what more can be done?"

We landed at Bassein, procured lodgings, and, as early as convenient, I presented my letter to the English gentleman there, who, on perusing its contents, advised me to proceed to Thannah. The court was held there, and he was going to that place in a very short time, and would then do all in his power for me. In consequence of this, we left Bassein, and reached Thannah by water, seeing nothing of the two men, who, I hoped, had departed. At Thannah we waited until the judge arrived, when I made my salaam to him; and he promised me a vakeelship as soon as a vacancy occurred, which he daily expected. It happened, unfortunately, that an old inhabitant of Thannah was candidate for the place also, and in consequence, I was regarded with an evil eye; and I even heard that some plan was on foot to ruin my expectations. One day the judge sent for me, and said, "So you wish to be a pleader, do you?" I replied in the affirmative. "Why," said he, "you must be the most impudent fellow in the world! I understand you were once a common peon in Bombay, engaged in a dreadful conspiracy to murder the treasurer, and was, in consequence, expelled from the island!" I denied it stoutly, and said it was all a base fabrication of my enemies, and the man who was a candidate for the pleader's place. "Well," said the judge, "we will see; call in the man who says he will swear to this would-be vakeel." A man now came forward, whom I knew to be one of the mysterious travellers; he was wrapped up in his coarse black shawl. On approaching the judge, he uncovered himself and made a salaam, which afforded me an opportunity of seeing his face. The features were familiar to me, but I could not call to mind where I had seen them, or on what occasion. The judge asking his name, he replied it was Gumbia. This was enough to enable me to remember that he was the very man expelled from Bombay with myself, and who left me to return thither and search for my treasure. I now felt that my hopes of the place here were frustrated. The fellow deposed to a thousand falsehoods; swore he himself was in the plot, and was expelled Bombay at the same time that I was, and for the same crime. The judge said he also conceived it his duty to send me from Thannah, and desired me to go in two days' time, or he should be forced to compel me to do so. This was a fatal blow; but what was to be done but to obey? I returned home, and as I entered the house the traveller Gumbia overtook me, and, giving me a fiendish grin, hurried away. I did not relate to Nanna or to the females the reason of my failure; but informed them the judge had preferred another man, and it was desirable we should all proceed to the Deccan once more.

After my failure, I had some conversation with Sagoonah relative to my hopes respecting herself. I told her, on our arrival in the Deccan, I was determined to discover whether the boy to whom she had been betrothed was living or not. If I could satisfactorily prove this, I demanded whether she would longer refuse me the right of affording her legal protection.

She put her hand into mine, saying, "But prove he is no more, and this hand is yours." I then told her we must proceed to Sattarah, for there only could anything be learned that was satisfactory upon this subject, so important to us both. "What!" cried Sagoonah, "to Sattarah? to my rich uncle, who will take me from your protection?" "Not so," I said; "he must not be acquainted of your being there." "He will—he will know!" replied Sagoonah; "I must not even accompany you to the Deccan. My aunt and I will proceed to Bombay, and await tidings of you there." I could not but acknowledge the good sense of this arrangement. To prevent their being followed to Bombay, Nanna hit upon a most ingenious scheme, by which the two spies, cunning as they were, must be infallibly deceived. His plan was to procure two other women for hire, and get them into the house over-night. In the morning these women, muffled up, were to accompany us across the river to the Mahratta country. The travelling spies would follow us as usual, imagining the women to be the same who accompanied us from Guzerat. Sagoonah and her aunt might then set off for Bombay, where they might provide themselves lodgings; for it would occasion suspicion were he or I to go there for that purpose, and return again. We all thought this an admirable plan, and agreed to adopt it without delay. Nanna procured two women, as like Sagoonah and her aunt in figure as possible, and got them slyly into the house. They willingly engaged in our service, when we imparted to them the business for which they were wanted, and accepted our terms; but they could not help expressing their wonder at the reason of our taking them to Sattarah with us, merely to send them back again. We promised to explain the why and wherefore at some future time; and we kept them shut up for the night, so that they might not guess there were any other females than themselves in the house. Nanna proceeded to the bazaar, and openly demanded bullocks and tatoos for the following morning. On returning, he informed me that one of the spies was at the kotwall's office when he gave orders for the beasts; and that we might rely upon it, they would be near us on our march next day.

This was the last night of my being happy in the presence of Sagoonah; for all I knew, it might be the last time of my life! The next day we were to be separated from each other; and who knew but it was for ever? We neither of us closed our eyes until the hour of parting came. I agreed to let her hear from me by a messenger, so as not to trust to letter-communication; and the more, as she could not read, and must get that done for her, which might put others in possession of our secrets. She desired me to send the messenger to Sunkersette Baboolsette, the great goldsmith at Bombay, and inquire for her under the name of Beema Bhae, and the messenger would receive proper directions where to find her. I thought this method the best that, under the circumstances, could be devised, as I could thus, at any time, be certain of her being concealed, and yet communicate anything I wished to her. Not liking that we should be seen taking leave of each other, we parted at daybreak, with heavy hearts. I then threw myself for a few minutes on a mat, endeavouring to compose myself, before **Nanna** called me to set out upon our journey.

CHAPTER XXX.

NANNA soon came to me, and bade me get ready to start. We set off on foot, with the two women muffled up; and crossing the river, found bullocks and tattoos in readiness on the opposite banks. The drivers led us through passes, over hills and rugged places, till, after a fatiguing journey, we reached Campowley—a small village at the foot of the Ghauts. The heat here being intolerable, we determined to set off again as early as possible the following morning. The spies had not made their appearance during the whole of the preceding day. This gave us considerable alarm, fearing our plot might have been discovered, and the women were still watched by the villainous agents of our foes. I began to fancy Sagoonah and her aunt pursued by them to Bombay, or, what was even more to be feared, prevented from reaching that place. Our fears on this head were fortunately groundless; for, in the morning, when we arrived on the summit of the Ghauts, we saw the two spies in conversation together. Turning round, and seeing us approach, they walked forwards at a rapid rate. We congratulated ourselves on the success of our plot, and cautioned the two women, should we pass the men who had gone forward, to muffle themselves up carefully, and with evident fear and perturbation. They promised obedience; and, having baited our cattle, and taken some refreshment ourselves at Candala (a village on the summit of the Ghauts), we once more journeyed onwards. The fresh breeze from the Deccan was most exhilarating after the heat of the lower land, and both Nanna and myself were charmed at once more setting foot in our own country. Before we reached the next stage, we passed the two travellers, who were sitting under a tree eating dried grain. The women, as they had promised to do, muffled themselves up in apparent haste ; and we saw the men cast very significant glances at each other as we went by. I now imagined Gumbia's companion to be the mischievous ass-driver, as, from his height and figure, he very much resembled him.

We reached Poona on the following day, and the two spies were, as usual, posted at the door where we alighted. The women entered the house, well muffled up, and then the two scoundrels went their way. On my way to Sattarah, I had no occasion to visit Poona ; but I thought it prudent to ascertain, in the best way I was able, the state of affairs at Sattarah before I went thither. I found that the rajah was still very ill, and that the pretender, Gunput Rao, though he was acknowledged by the English, was opposed by another man, who declared himself to be his elder brother, but who had not yet appeared publicly in that character. His name alone, it was reported at Poona, had enlisted many persons on his side ; and that, in consequence, Gunput Rao had been raising soldiers to crush the elder brother as a pretender. The latter had assembled a valiant body of troops to support his own cause ; but the two parties were not likely to come to blows until the decease of the present rajah. The name of the claimant to the Sattarah musnud, by right of his seniority, was Sevaje ; and the people guessed he was concealed somewhere near Sattarah. I was advised, if I went to that place, to be as silent as possible in regard to political affairs, as there were many bloodthirsty villains abroad, who found means to get rid of all who spoke adverse to the party they supported, whenever opportunity was favourable for it. I pretended everywhere at Poona the utmost indifference as to the different claimants to the musnud. I stated to those of whom I made inquiry, that I was going to Sattarah merely to seek employment, and that I should enter into the service of neither of the parties striving for the mastery. Nanna advised me not to proceed to Sattarah, because Kokoo was no doubt there, with Gunput Rao ; and his disappointment again respecting the women would cause him to seek me out more perseveringly, and to sacrifice me to his vengeance. This advice was worth regarding ; and, having made Nanna fully acquainted (as his conduct warranted me in doing) with the circumstances of Sagoonah, I begged him to go to Sattarah, and make every inquiry possible respecting the youth to whom she had been betrothed. I agreed to remain in Poona, and await his return.

The foregoing plan being fixed upon, Nanna prepared to set out. He proposed that we should start together; and when the two spies were some way on the road before us, I should suddenly return to Poona with one of the women. Nanna, when he overtook the travellers, was to cry aloud to them for protection, declaring a gang of rogues had forcibly taken away his companion and one of the females. The woman with Nanna was to play her part, by crying, tearing her hair, and other symptoms of grief. By this means there could be no doubt but the spies would be deceived. The travellers would not think of returning to Poona, but would imagine the pretended ruffians were some of their own gang, employed by Gabbage or Kokoo. If that should be the case, they would most likely proceed to Sattarah at once; and should they seize the woman, it was time enough then for them to find out their mistake, and let her go again. The plan appeared to me useful for confusing the two emissaries; and we all left Poona the following day, concluding the travellers, as usual, were on before us. At the part of the road agreed upon, I turned back with the youngest woman to Poona. Unfortunately, this day the spies were behind us instead of being in front, as we made sure they were. After travelling a few coss back, we met them face to face. The woman muffled up, and so did I; but they recognised us, and stood and looked after us for some time. The separation seemed to confuse them, and they appeared to hesitate which party they should follow—Nanna's or mine. I left them, however, in apparent uncertainty; for both the woman and myself being mounted on tatoos, we flogged the animals, and set off in good speed to Poona—the beasts quickening their pace, as they knew it was their road home. By this means we left the travellers a good distance behind us in a few minutes after we had started. On arriving at Poona, I dismissed the woman, after paying her the stipulated reward. She was a stranger to her companion who had gone forward to Sattarah; and I was careful to recommend her immediate return to Thannah, in order to prevent any intelligence being obtained from her respecting myself, if she remained in Poona, where I designed to sojourn for a short time. The woman took my rupees gratefully, and we parted.

The first step I took was to change my appearance as much as possible. I got shaved, and disguised myself as well as I could, and then sought a very retired lodging. In the house in which I fixed myself, lived a hanger-on at the court of the English collector. This collector was an officer of the army; collector and judge at the same time. A desire from my past experience and knowledge of the law at Broach, led me to examine into the state of its administration at Poona, upon finding I possessed such an opportunity, and having, moreover, little or nothing else to occupy my time. My fellow-lodger, like many others, gained a livelihood by knavery and chicanery in the arbitration suits; he held his nocturnal meetings, and met his arbitration-gangs at all hours of the night. His name was Loochajee, and he managed to be concerned in almost every cause. His intentions in this respect were admirably seconded by the prevailing system of administering justice by arbitration. He contrived to enrich himself by plundering both plaintiffs and defendants. I will endeavour to give my readers an account of the system of punchayet or arbitration, said to be far superior to the system of justice enforced in Guzerat, which I have elsewhere explained. It will then be easy to judge which of the two systems is best adapted to afford real and substantial justice. At Poona there was no regular judge, as in the courts of Guzerat;—a collector of the revenue, with two assistants, was expected to do everything. In the administration of justice he obtained the assistance of a punchayet, consisting of five arbitrators—a plan said to be highly approved of by the natives, it being their own customary mode of settling disputes; but, if a better mode were pointed out, it does not seem to me that they would despise it. Trials by punchayet flourished most during the power of the great Poona minister, Nanna Furnavese, when no files of undecided suits were ever heard of. The difference between that time and more recent ones was, that then three-fourths of the declarations of suits were never allowed to be put on the file—a very simple method of keeping it clear. Under the English, almost every plaint was admitted and referred to arbitration: the consequence of this being, that a sufficient number of persons to sit on arbitrations could not be found; and those who did sit had no pay, either from the litigating parties or from the Government. A few respectable merchants and others had no objection to sit now and then upon a punchayet; but it could not be expected that such would sit every day in the year, and leave their own concerns entirely, to settle the business of others gratis. Even supposing they were paid for their services, the fee would most likely fall short of the profits arising from their own exertions in their daily avocations. A marked man, or having the reputation of ability, would be constantly called upon. The punchayet consists of two persons named by the plaintiff, and two by the defendant, the Government nominating the fifth or umpire. The latter I never could discover to be of much use. He was designed to see fair play, and prevent delay; but in the event of two arbitrators being for the plaintiff and two for the defendant, the case could only be settled by the umpire, who was always expected to decide it one way or another. If he allowed an award that was unjust, he was called to account for it. If he reversed or interfered with the opinions of the two arbitrators, either for plaintiff or defendant, he was severely censured for so doing. His office was thus completely neutralised. At length, no respectable natives would sit as arbitrators; and the court was, in consequence, haunted by fellows like my fellow-lodger, Loochajee—men who could write and read, and were respectable, as far as external appearance went, but in reality were depraved and unprincipled. By such men came, at last, to be decided the claims of the inhabitants of Poona for justice. The method by which they turn their trade to account is, by first securing a large retaining fee from the disputants who nominate them, and then they contrive to follow up the first fee by numerous others; so that the richest man is almost sure to win his cause. Oftentimes the arbitrators are all in league, and divide whatever comes to the net in equal portions—in this case they apply themselves to *sumjao*, the defendant. In Poona this word has several meanings—such as, to buy a person over, to talk over, or to persuade; but it is meant also to threaten an individual, and in that sense it is generally used by the arbitrators when in combination. The different arbitrators come to the defendant, and state that they have determined he shall pay to the plaintiff a certain sum of money. He objects, and they tell him he had better comply, and say before the umpire that he is satisfied; for, if he does not, they will fix the sum to be paid at double the amount, and then he must pay, or go to a gaol by their decree. This is denominated the *sumjaoing system;* and the poor defendant has the option of paying a comparatively small sum of money by his own free-will and consent, or of agreeing to be ruined by a decree of the court. The arbitrators having been well fee'd on both sides before they read a paper in the cause, put on their lawyer-like looks, and lead the unlucky defendant before the umpire in the court-room. The foreman of the party presents the decree, and the umpire asks if the party is satisfied. The poor devil, knowing the power of the arbitrators, joins his hands, and answers, " Ho,m,ha,raj,"—yes, my lord. He is then ordered to pay the money forthwith, and the arbitrators, like my fellow-lodger, retire to hunt down fresh game. Should these men be at any time detected in their malpractices, it is a matter of indifference to them, as they have no character to lose; and, should they be marked out and never employed again, they think themselves lucky in having made what they have contrived to secure.

Another class of persons who, I found, turn a penny by the sale of justice, are the hangers-on of some inferior offices of the courts, who just cook up cases, and then make the disputants believe that, through their interest, their cause will be admitted without delay. The Mahrattas, well aware of the difficulty that existed under their old government of getting heard, think that the same difficulties exist under the new, which is contrary to the fact. An agent sat daily to receive petitions, not one of which was presented without a gratuity being paid to some hanger-on in the court, who had pretended to the petitioner he either will or has spoken to the officer of justice in his favour, and that he may advance and lay his document safely on the table, and rely it will be received and attended to in consequence of their interference. In Guzerat, where the Government receives all fees for admitting suits according to the amount sued for, every one knows what he has to pay on filing his suit; and, at all events, feels confident it will be attended to in turn. Notwithstanding all the pretended advantages of the arbitration system, the files of causes were soon found swelling to a prodigious size; for, though there were two or three gangs of arbitrators appointed, they were so dilatory, that business accumulated faster than they despatched them. But, though little was effected in the way of despatch, these judges were ever ready to take a fresh fee or a new cause. Thus, my fellow-lodger had twenty cases on hand at once, on all of which he had taken care to pocket the money. Should he be detected, he well knew he was safe on the credit side of the account, while his clients would have to fee his successor, and be duped twice over. At length, a gentleman was appointed to the office, who saw into the devices of this class of men. They determined, however, to get rid of him at all hazards. They collected together charges against him that were groundless in themselves, but which they offered to substantiate; and he was recalled, for their benefit and his own ruin.

A military individual was placed at the head of the civil department at Poona; another of the same profession at Sattarah, Ahmednugur, and Kandeish; these were selected for their knowledge of the Mahrattas and their language. Yet this could hardly be true; for I heard of far better scholars in the two Concans, who could write a Mahratta letter and read an answer in that tongue; whereas not one of these military Englishmen in the Deccan could understand the contents of a letter, unless it were read to him by an attendant clerk! In consequence, the latter might read whatever he pleased to make the contents of the document in his hand to be. In the Concan, gentlemen not of the military profession conducted all their business in the Mahratta tongue; while those of the Deccan transacted theirs in bad Hindustanee, so as not to be comprehensible to either Deccan Brahmin, or Deccan Coombie. The former were therefore infinitely better fitted for the purpose of judges than the latter, and it seemed to me bad policy in the Government not to see this. As to the punchayet system, it will not do, if the English wish to distribute justice to the inhabitants, and do not wish to discourage applications for redress, and thus force the people to settle their own differences among themselves. I found those civil-military men so eager to call in arbitrators, that they proceeded to try criminal as well as civil cases by them. The folly of this, however, became too apparent to be long allowed, and the Government issued its orders to discontinue the trial of criminals by this method.

CHAPTER XXXI.

AFTER remaining in Poona some weeks, and hearing nothing from Nanna, I became very anxious respecting the future, and finally determined to set off for Sattarah myself. I was convinced something very unexpected had occurred, to prevent my receiving tidings from that quarter. Delay, too, was prejudicial to my future views; and therefore, muffling up myself one dark evening, and taking my sword and dagger, I left Poona, travelled all night for better concealment, and in the morning crept into a shed, eating only bread and dried grain. I left my hiding-place at night, and again proceeded onwards, thus effectually concealing my movements. On the morning of the third day I reached Sattarah, where I found everything quiet. One evening I went into a temple to make pùja to the god; I stayed a much longer time than was customary, because I imagined I might hear something interesting respecting public affairs from the people who repaired thither. In this expectation I was disappointed, as I heard nothing that could be of the least service to me. The bell tolled before I prepared to leave the consecrated spot, and the small lamp burning before the image expiring, all was darkness. I groped my way towards the threshold, and had just crossed it, when the sound of voices struck my ear. It was evident the persons speaking intended to enter the temple, not to make pùja to the god, but to discuss some secret transaction. As I imagined their conversation might relate to politics, I became anxious to gain some information; and having just sufficient time to do so unobserved, I re-entered the temple and concealed myself in a corner. The two persons entered, and seated themselves in the centre of the building. One of them began by

330

exclaiming, "So you are just as clever a fellow as your companion; you have been all this time at Poona, and have not found out that Pandurang Hàrì!" "What could I do?" replied the other fellow, whom I knew to be Gumbia; "he eluded me, as I before explained to you." "Shame on you," observed the first speaker, whom I knew to be Kokoo, "to dog them all the way from Guzerat, and then to lose sight of them within two days' march of Sattarah! Then, again, your sagacious companion, the bullock-driver, to bring us a woman no one ever saw or heard of before—an old hag, that it would be common charity to drown! Sagoonah is no doubt in Poona, and that devil Pandoo is with her. You say you met them returning thither, and pursued them, and that your companion pursued the other man and woman, whom nobody knows or cares about. However, I shall take good care of the man, and will not release him until he gives me information whereby I may secure his friend and Sagoonah." "We shall get them yet," said Gumbia; "there is plenty of time yet to "—— "Dolt, idiot!" cried Kokoo, "there is not a moment to be lost. Who knows but the rajah may die to-morrow? and has not Sagoonah's uncle declared he will not advance a rupee to Gunput Rao until the latter shall produce his niece, and she is married to Mahadeo? This Sevaje is also supposed to be in Sattarah, ready to produce his claims to the throne; how, then, is there time to spare? Now, what stupid wretches have you two been!" "Not so fast," cried Gumbia; "did you never miss catching the birds yourself at Broach?" "Yes," said Kokoo, "because I depended on that sneaking villain Premje. Would I had knocked out his brains!" "Perhaps you have," observed Gumbia. "I fear not," said Kokoo. "Have you any tidings respecting Sevaje, or his place of concealment?" "None," was the reply. "That is the old answer," said Kokoo; "done nothing, and know nothing, and still expect to be paid! I see it is useless to trust such scoundrels as you are. Gunput Rao must be independent of the rich banker, and strike a blow with the means he already has in his possession." "He will fail then," said Gumbia. "Scoundrel! say that again," retorted Kokoo, "and it shall be your death.

He shall not fail; though we wade through rivers of blood, either he or his son shall sit on the Sattarah musnud." "But Sevaje has a party also," said Gumbia. "He has," replied Kokoo, "and they march to-morrow night for a stronghold to the southward, and will be cut to pieces on the way. Do you know the fortress where they now are?" "Yes," replied Gumbia, "on the high hill, eight coss from hence." "Well, then," observed Kokoo, "they quit that place, and must pass through deep ravines. Our troops will meet them hemmed in there, and annihilate the presumptuous followers of the unwary Sevaje. Hasten you to Hossein, my brave Mohammedan lieutenant, and bid him prepare and meet me on the open plain at noon to-morrow." The two villains then left the temple.

I determined, as soon as I could, to proceed to the hill-fortress, and apprise the garrison of the designs of Kokoo. I left my hiding-place much grieved at finding Nanna had fallen into the hands of our enemies. It was more than probable Gabbage would again see him, and, remembering his former conduct towards him, complete that which it was not his fault was not finished when he stabbed him in the cave. I should have been most happy to overhear the place of his confinement; but Kokoo did not mention it, and it was impossible for me to make the discovery without some cue. I felt sure Nanna would never betray me or Sagoonah. I could only hope that chance might conduct me to the place where he was detained, and that I might, by some means or other, be enabled to effect his liberation. I was not at an equal loss to know where the troops of Sevaje were posted, and I accordingly hastened to the hills, on the summit of the highest of which stood a strong fortified tower. I ascended the rugged path that led to the gates of the fort. On arriving at them, I knocked for admittance, and an old man thrust out his head from a loophole over the door, and inquired who had disturbed his slumbers. "Slumbers!" I answered, "who would expect to find any one asleep within these walls? If this be the case, awaken the garrison, and let me have an audience of the commandant." "That thou hast already," said the old man, "and for one very good reason—I am the only person it contains."

"What!" I cried, "are not the troops within?" "No, I tell you," said the old fellow; "they left me in the dead of night." "Then all is safe," I exclaimed; "I came to apprize them of their danger on their march through the ravines." "They must, then, by this time, have met with it or avoided it," observed the old man : "but who are you that appear to be so vastly knowing, and unaccountably kind to our troops?" "Hush!" I replied, in a whisper; "this is no place for politics. If you will admit me into the fort "——— "Stay a minute," cried the wary old fellow; "you do not take me for such an ass, do you? Get you gone from hence instantly, or you shall have a matchlock bullet or a Bheel's arrow after you! Ho! begone." So saying, he pointed the muzzle of a matchlock through a loophole towards me, which caused me to use no little expedition in getting away. I made the trusty old guard a salaam when I got at random-shot distance, and soon reached the plain.

Whether the troops had left the fortress or not, I could not presume to decide. It was probable the guardian there had mis-informed me on purpose, conceiving me a spy in the employ of Gunput Rao. Knowing Kokoo was in Sattarah, and seeing little chance of obtaining intelligence respecting the youth to whom Sagoonah had been betrothed, I determined upon taking advan-tage of the present moment to proceed to Indore, in hopes of once more falling in with the goatherd of the glen, or of gaining some intelligence respecting him from his friend Shewdhut Wanee, to whom he had before referred me. It was the current report that Sevaje (whom I had strong reason for believing to be my old friend the goatherd) was concealed at Sattarah. This, however, was but report, and there was no chance of my arriving at a certainty upon the subject, without proceeding to Indore and making the needful inquiry, and learning, if he were really at Sattarah, how I was to discover him. I had no time to lose, and therefore I travelled as fast as I could towards the city, for I had no money to hire tatoos; and, after a six days' laborious march, I entered Indore. I had expended my last rupee; and, hungry and wretchedly fatigued, I presented myself before Shewdhut Wanee. A thousand times I regretted having fallen in with the Bheels, and being plundered of the silver ring given me by the goatherd. I felt that the friends of the old man were obliged to be exceedingly cautious respecting the knowledge of him, circumstanced as he must be; and that, without some undeniable proof of my acquaintance with him, I should not be trusted even by Shewdhut. Upon my requesting an audience of Shewdhut, a lean meagre form lifted up his head from his account-books, and said, "I am Shewdhut Wanee, brother; what do you want?" I replied I came in search of an old man, for whom I had a sincere regard; who bade me, should I wish to communicate with him, apply here. "Old man! apply to me!" cried Shewdhut; "why, I don't keep old men!" "You are right," said I, "to be cautious; but, rely upon it, I am no deceiver; for this old man gave me a ring (which I described to Shewdhut), and said that, upon showing it, you would conduct me to him." Upon my saying this, he shut his book, and, looking me very closely in the face, beckoned me to follow him into the interior of his dwelling. I obeyed, and Wanee, upon our being seated, held out his hand for the ring, which he bade me produce. I was now compelled to relate by what unforeseen accident I had been deprived of this valuable token of my identity. I ended by expressing my hopes that my description of the old man, and of the ring he had given me, would be a sufficient proof to him that I was no deceiver, but a sincere friend, who panted to serve the recluse with all my heart. The Wanee would not refuse me his confidence, but he gave it me very warily and cautiously. He said he recollected the recluse had mentioned to him something about a young man whom he was anxious to see; but that, it being a long time ago, he had quite forgotten what he said. "You must know, young man," continued Shewdhut, "that the person you seek is not in Indore." I told him I expected as much; but I asked if he was not at Sattarah? Wanee said he was, and he was about to join him there; and, if I would go also, he would be my guide. This was singularly fortunate for me, and I expressed my readiness to attend him thither immediately. He proposed to leave Indore in two days, and I promised to be punctual in my attendance upon him for that purpose.

Before I rose to depart, I begged Wanee to inform me whether the ralations of Sawunt Rao, my old benefactor, were still in Indore. "They are," said he; "but how dost thou know these people?" "I knew Sawunt Rao," said I, "and served in his army." "Indeed!" observed Wanee, "and what is your name?" I replied, "Pandurang Hàri." He then asked if I was Sawunt's adopted son, and if he left me any money when he died. I answered according to the facts, adding, that I must except a kurdoorah chain found on me when I was a child. Wanee then inquired where the chain was, and I told him it remained with the relatives of Sawunt. "It must be!" said Wanee to himself, musing as if about some mystery. "Young man, you must possess yourself of this chain, and take it with you to Sattarah. Ask me no questions. But stay—it may not be! yet it is strange—an embossed chain, say you?" I nodded in the affirmative, very naturally wondering at the same time to what all the mystery tended. He then bade me describe the clasp. I replied it had a snake's head, with two rubies for eyes. "It is what I thought!" said Wanee; "we must be off to-morrow, my young friend. He who first bound that chain round your loins pants to behold you." I asked who that was, with some eagerness. Wanee answered, "He whom you seek, the recluse of the glen—your father!" "The recluse, the old goatherd, my father?" I exclaimed. "O good Wanee, bring me to him; let me clasp him to my heart! Have I, indeed, found a parent? Say, is it Sevaje?" "Silence! let not that name pass your lips. Walls have ears," said Wanee, "and whispers are often carried upon the air: silence alone is security. It is the same whom you knew—the goatherd, the recluse; and ere long he will welcome you as a king and a father!" "Then Ishwar be praised!" I rejoined, "and nerve my arm to crush all his enemies. Has my father given up every hope of finding me?" I inquired. "He has long since despaired of doing so," said Wanee: "often has he conversed with me upon the fatal events which tore you from him; and has frequently alluded to the embossed chain, which he himself fastened around your waist on the dreadful night of your separation." I then demanded if Wanee had all along been the friend of my unfortunate parent. He answered in the affirmative, and that he saved my father's life; but bade me seek to know no more at that moment. "Yes," I cried, "I must hear more. Did my father mention a girl who was betrothed to me?" Wanee replied that he did. I eagerly demanded "if he knew her name?" "This," said Wanee, "I never heard him mention. But from him you shall yourself learn more, if, indeed, as you appear, you are in reality his son. Let us hasten to regain your chain, and then push on to Sattarah, where your father now sojourns." "Thanks," I cried, "my best friend! and may the great Dum reward you for all your goodness!"

We set out accordingly for the house of Sawunt Rao's widow, and, being introduced into her apartment, I made myself known to her. She arose immediately, and welcomed me with much sincerity. After I had made inquiries respecting the health of her family as well as her own, I asked her respectfully for the silver chain left me by her husband. She desired us to seat ourselves, and withdrew, saying she had not forgotten her promise to take care of it for me. In a few minutes, she returned with it in her hand. Shewdhut examined the silver kurdoorah minutely, and declared openly his opinion it was the identical chain he had so often heard spoken of before. He desired the widow to tell him what her husband said when he presented me with the chain. The widow replied, that he said he bequeathed the chain to me, because it had been found on my person when a child, and he had preserved it in the hope it might lead to a discovery of my parents. Shewdhut observed that he was now convinced all his surmises were correct respecting me. The widow expressed her hope I should soon discover my friends, and was curious to learn whether I had already found any clue to my parents. Wanee said he hoped we had, but that it would be wrong to be too sanguine, and that she should in due time be made acquainted with the result of our inquiries.

Wanee now requested me to return with him to his dwelling to sleep that night, saying he had a comfortable apartment for the accommodation of his friends. Sleep, as it may naturally be supposed, was a stranger to my eyes; and I lay all night restless, and haunted with reflections on the strange disclosures which that day had brought to light by means of Shewdhut Wanee. I could not believe it possible that I, a poor houseless wanderer, could be the lawful successor to a musnud; that in a short time I should clasp a father to my heart, when I had been so many years a desolate outcast. This was a happiness which I never could have conjectured to be in store for me! I moreover reflected that it was probable I was the being to whom Sagoonah had been betrothed; for though Wanee did not recollect the name of the girl, I felt almost convinced it could be no other. This idea was the source of infinite delight. Was it a delusion? It might be, but it was much more probably a reality, than my being the son of Sevaje, and a prince. When I reflected upon my affinity to Gabbage, I shuddered at his crimes, and thought how little I imagined, when listening to Mahadeo's tale in the Pindaree fort, that the relater was my cousin, who had sworn to persecute me. These reflections kept me awake during the whole night; and, as soon as it was morning, I went to the door of Shewdhut's room. Not hearing him stir, I called out, and was answered by his wife, of whom I demanded whether her husband was ready. She replied he had been gone out an hour before. "Gone," said I, "and not called me? Impossible!" "He went to the temple," replied the woman, alarmed, "to make pùja, intending to return and summon you to attend him on his journey to Sattarah." I inquired how long it was since he left his chamber; and she answered, "a full hour." I ran immediately to the temple. The morning was clear and beautiful; and with breathless haste I entered the edifice—but I could find no Shewdhut there; and I was leaving the place in despair, when, to my surprise and horror, I discovered spots of blood upon the pavement. Some one, it immediately struck me, had murdered him, and carried off his body. How was I doomed to bitter disappointment! The motive which led to such an act could not be plunder, it was evident; for at such a time it was not likely Wanee would have had money about his person. I searched everywhere around the temple without effect. The traces of blood disappeared at the entrance of the building, so that on the exterior there was no mark or track to direct the pursuit. I hastened back to Shewdhut's wife; and, with tears in my eyes, related what I had seen, and my fears of the worst having happened. I bade her hope, however, that it might not be the blood of her husband, and that he might still return. She began immediately to beat her breast and tear her hair, screaming in so frantic a manner at the same time, that her neighbours rushed in from all quarters to demand the cause of her loud lamentations. "Oh! my husband, my husband!" were the only words she could utter; while I informed the by-standers of the event which we had too much reason to fear must have happened, requesting some of them to accompany me, and try if we could get any further tidings of Wanee, who, if alive, it was reasonable to surmise could not be very far distant. All bewailed the fate of their late neighbour, but not one volun-teered to accompany me in search of the lost man—so very careful was each individual present of his own security.

Disgusted at such conduct, and impatient of delay, I sallied forth again from the house with my sword in my hand, and once more entered the temple. I saw no one there, and then I pro-ceeded to search a small grove at the back of the building. The grass was trodden down apparently by several footsteps; thence I tracked feet to the open plain, where I entirely lost the marks. I continued my search until evening unsuccessfully, and I then returned to the distressed wife of Shewdhut, disconsolate and unhappy. I found the poor woman stretched on her bed, almost exhausted by weeping and sorrow. I feared to disturb her; as, by having nothing comforting to communicate, I should but add to her sorrow. I sat down on the threshold of the door, meditat-ing on Shewdhut's disappearance, and thinking that my hopes of beholding my father were now almost annihilated. Still I deter-mined to proceed to Sattarah, and spare no labour, when there, to find out Sevaje's present concealment. Having the kurdoorah in my possession, I could not fail of being acknowledged by him as his son, if I really were so, although the presence of Shewdhut would have facilitated the means, and hastened the time of inves-

tigation. Fastening my turban under my chin, **and** putting **on** my shoes, I was leaving the street in which the house of Shewdhut was situated, when, to my astonishment, **I was** surrounded by a crowd of Wanee's friends, who made **me** their prisoner, calling me Shewdhut's murderer. It was in vain that I endeavoured to convince them of their mistake: they hurried me to the police-**office, where, the whole affair having been investigated, I** was fortunately released. **I** call **myself** fortunate, because, on being charged with such a crime by a mob, **I did** not get more ill-usage, and was suffered to depart. **I did not go in peace** notwithstanding, although the kotwall **released me; for the people** still maintained their first opinion of my being, directly **or** indirectly, concerned in Shewdhut's murder; and I was hooted, hissed and pelted out of the city, as if I had **been the greatest criminal** that had ever been within its walls.

CHAPTER XXXII.

BEING once clear of the people and in the open fields, to which I had run until my breath began to fail me, I was surrounded by night, which had begun to close in before I was clear of the city. I still, however, continued my journey towards Sattarah, until I was overcome with weariness and fatigue. I threw myself down under a tree, and sank, almost worn out, into a sound slumber. I was awoke by the loud snorting of an elephant, which, with its driver upon his neck, was proceeding along the road. As I was rousing myself, the mahouhut called out, "Hollo, brother! what—asleep in the jungles at this time of the year! I replied, travellers wearied by long marching had no choice left, and the shelter of a tree must, in such cases, be put up with. "Whither art thou going?" asked the driver. I told him to Sattarah. "Well, that is fortunate," rejoined the mahouhut, "for I am bound there also, and will give you a ride upon the elephant." I thanked him, and tapping his animal upon the head, he cried, "Kneel down." The huge creature obeyed, and I clambered up his side, and when seated, the animal arose with us at command. It was the first time I had ever rode upon one of these sagacious beasts. The elephant was sometimes troublesome, in which case the mahouhut thrust his goad into the hole of a wound behind the animal's ear, which he said he never suffered to heal, and it instantly had the good sense to become submissive. The mahouhut observed, that he had another sore place which he probed when he wanted the animal to quicken his pace, and another when he wanted to make him scream, or utter a salaam in praise of his lord and master. I inquired his master's name, and he informed me it was Holkar's dewan, or prime minister; adding, "and a good master he is, for we all act as we like, and fill our bellies by doing the people to the extent of our fancies." Thus the mahouhut scarcely ever ceased chattering about one thing and another every minute of the journey, except when he called out to his elephant, *Chul, chul,* or "walk on quick," accompanying the word of command with a kick behind the creature's ear. The beast went along snorting and puffing at a brisk rate, and the driver would begin to talk to me again. I inquired what news there was at Indore. "Oh, nothing particular," replied the fellow; "an old wance,[1] they say, has been murdered (chul, chul, Baba!), and it is supposed a stranger, who lodged in his house, is the guilty person; but our kotwall could see no ground for the charge, and released the stranger, who was no doubt very glad to get off. For my part, if he really did kill the old grain-seller, I think he did a good act; there are too many of these miserly old rascals in Indore, and the grain is so dear, a poor man must almost starve." I remarked, I did not think that was his case, for he appeared in excellent condition. "Me? no. no, old *Futteh gudge*[2] here gives me half his flour and ghee daily, and he must be fed, let grain be at what price it may. You know it would little redound to my credit to mount my lord on a lean brute." I observed that what he said was true, nor would it redound to his lord's credit to be driven by a lean mahouhut. "Exactly thus," replied the driver; "and thus Futteh and myself are, you observe, in condition, not among the spare creation.

This mahouhut was a merry good-natured fellow, and at any other time I should have entered into and enjoyed his jokes; but now, recent events, and my anxiety for the future—the idea of finding a father, or of being crossed by some mischance in my endeavours to penetrate to his retreat, pressed upon my mind. I could not long continue to feign an enjoyment of the fellow's wit, and to put on a jocularity that must sit but very awkwardly upon me. The driver soon perceived I was not his match in spirits, and that I often relapsed into silence and thoughtfulness. He would then console himself with a song, stopping frequently in the midst of his ditty to cry out to his elephant, "Chul, chul,

[1] Or shopkeeper.
[2] Epithet applied to the elephant, meaning "victorious."

Y

Baba!" The last halt we made, before reaching our destination, was at a small village, where the driver purposed to dine, together with his beast. He being a Mohammedan, I could not dine with him; but he said he would give me some raw rice, if I would accompany him to the grain-shops in the small bazaar. Having fastened the elephant's hind leg by a chain to a tree, and put a rope round his fore legs, we entered into the bazaar. To observe the airs the fellow put on, he might have been taken for the dewan himself, instead of his mahouhut. He twisted his mustachios, and cocked his turban on one side, folding his arms akimbo before a grain-shop, where, in the midst of a few half-filled baskets of grain, sat crossed-legged a starved meagre Marwarry, the owner of the shop. "Ho! you skin and bone Marwarry," cried the driver, "up with you, and supply my lord the dewan's elephant with rice, ghee, flour, and *jagree*.[1] Be quick, I say, or, by Allah, I will show you how my elephant serves those who will not feed him." "*Arry deo, hoi, hoi*,"[2] cried the grain merchant; "I have no rice, no ghee, no flour, no jagree. Your beast would eat up all in the village." "Silence, you rascal," cried the mahouhut, "or I will report you on my return." "Indeed," said the poor devil," you must go to the potail; I have no supply of what you demand. Good driver, don't distress me; go," added he, in a low whisper, "to the shop of Laldass in the next street, his granaries are full of everything you want." "Well, well," answered the mahouhut, "if he has not any, I shall return to you." We then went on to Laldass; but he having probably heard of the great devourer that was come into the village, and knowing that if he parted with his grain he would never be paid for it, had carefully shut up his shop. In a violent rage, the mahouhut returned to the Marwarry; but he, taking advantage of our absence, had done the same thing before we could return to him, and most carefully secured the avenues that led to his rice and flour, in the midst of which he had no doubt taken up his quarters. The mahouhut then went to the potail, saying, "Here I am; do you choose to feed us?" "What can I do?"

[1] Coarse sugar. [2] An exclamation.

replied the poor fellow; " I cannot make grain." " Very well, my friend," said the driver, " you know the consequences!" The potail shrugged up his shoulders, and said he was helpless; for the grain-dealers had shut up their shops. " Then, by Allah," said the mahouhut, " they shall soon be opened." Having said this, he went to the place where he had left his beast tied up, and roaring for his food. Loosening his chain and ropes he scrambled upon his neck, and rode him up to the shop of Laldass, which was merely the verandah of a house, closed up with a number of narrow planks that served for shutters. The elephant stood close with its enormous head touching the shutters, and his rider called out, " Ho! within there, I want rice." " *Chawul nu,hue*,"[1] cried a voice from within. " Bring flour then," said the mahou- hut. " *Attah nu,hue*,"[2] was the reply. " Ghee then." " *Toop nu,hue*,"[3] answered the shopkeeper with a hearty laugh, as if it was a good joke. " Give me jagree then," said the driver. " *Gor nu,hue*,"[4] responded the shopkeeper. " I will see if you tell truth then," answered the mahouhut; and placing his heels behind the ears of his elephant, and goading him in one of the sore places he had before mentioned, he exclaimed, " *Tor dallo, Baba, zoor se*."[5] The cunning animal, as if it knew the flour was behind the shutters, butted at them with full force, and crash they went to pieces in an instant, and discovered Laldass in the midst of plenty, tumbling affrighted over his baskets of grain. " Oh, mercy! mercy!" he cried; " here is flour, ghee, rice, and sugar, good mahouhut, take what you want." " Rascal," cried the driver, " I have a great mind to make the elephant squeeze the breath out of your miserable body, for giving me so much trouble. Come, fill my sacks, or I will not spare you." The women of Laldass now came forward, and filled the bags with everything he wanted, for which they did not get a single rupee in return. The bags being placed on the ele- phant's back, the animal walked majestically away, the mahouhut saying to the poor devil of a grain-dealer, " Perhaps I shall not report you on my return to Indore, provided you have a second

---

[1] No rice.   [2] No flour.   [3] No ghee.
[4] No sugar.   [5] " Break it to pieces, old fellow, with all your might."

supply ready for me as I come back. Don't give me this trouble again." The family bowed in silence. We now sought the potail, who had provided wood for us, and some sugar-canes for the elephant to eat while the bread was baking; and we once more secured the animal, and left him to munch them, while we attended to our own cookery. "Did you ever see such rascals?" said the elephant-driver. "They would no more mind seeing me and my elephant starve, than you would mind seeing them hanged." "Not they," I replied; "but, it is well we are not out of Holkar's dominions; for, were we in those of the English, we should, I fear, be made to repent our feat." "Perhaps we should," answered the fellow; "but as the case stands, we have nothing to do with the Toope Wallas, and I heartily wish they were driven out of India." "We must fight harder than we have yet done to accomplish this," I rejoined; "but were it not for the bad management of your master and the other rajahs and rulers, these foreigners would never have done what they have. Holkar, Badjerao, and Scindea, are always ready for war, and when it begins they run away from it. This is the way the Toope Wallas have got so firm a hold among us, and we shall, I fear, never live to see the end of it." "What you say may be very true," answered my companion; "but hang me if I know anything about the matter; but I do know that, as long as I drive an elephant, he shall not starve, come what may." We pursued this discourse no further; and as soon as the elephant had devoured his bread, rice, and sugar, we continued our journey. Nothing more occurred until we perceived the hill on which the seven-towered fort of Sattarah[1] stands. I then deemed it prudent to alight, and thanking the mahouhut for his kindness, I walked, well muffled up, into the city.

In the streets I saw groups of ill-looking fellows conversing, and their appearance convinced me there was something of importance about to take place. In one part two men passed me at a quick pace; one of whom I felt certain was Gabbage Gousla. They were out of sight in a moment; but, from their hurried

[1] Called Sattarah, or Sath-Istara, or the Seven Stars, or Pleiades, from its seven towers.

manner, I had a conviction that mischief could not be far off;—perhaps some plot was on the eve of explosion, as my intelligence respecting the state of affairs gave me good reason to surmise would be the case. Having no money and little food, I determined to fast until the next day, and I rambled about until I reached a durhm sallah, which was, very fortunately, unoccupied. Here I took my silver kurdoorah, and secured it about my person. It was too small to go round my waist, but I wound it twice round my arm, getting the snakes' heads to meet with some difficulty, and fixing them by the small screw attached to the ornament. I had scarcely done this before I heard voices approaching; and presently some men entered, carrying spears and matchlocks. Seeing me sitting unemployed, they cried, "Ho, brother!—do you want a job? if so, come with us, and load yourself with some of these weapons." I inquired whither they were going;—they told me where pay was to be had. I asked who were their employers; and they said they were persons who would either be kings or beggars; but upon my questioning them further, they told me that was neither here or there, but bid me jump up and assist them, for it was no time to be idle. I desired them first to tell me whom I was to serve; and one of them cursed me, and said, ' Shoot him! he is one of Gunput's spies!" "Hold!" I cried; "I am not inclined that side the question, anyhow." The men then bade me come along. I piled several matchlocks on my shoulders, and followed them through ravines and over hills, until we came to a very considerable cavern. Here one of them gave a loud whistle, which was answered by one more shrill, and of longer continuance, from within. Not a word was spoken by my guides, until a light gleamed from a recess of the cave. One of the men then said, taking my wrist, "Come on, but utter not a word." The bearer of the light now approached us; and, seeing me, asked me who I was. One of my companions answered that the load was too heavy for them, and they had therefore hired me. Some whispering then took place between the men who arrived with me and the person who bore the torch, which ended in the latter addressing me nearly to this effect:—" Stranger, you

are at liberty to return from whence you came, or to enter
the cavern. If you choose to go away, here is your hire;
if you prefer to remain with us, you must not depart until
certain circumstances dissolve our band, in which, provided
you will enlist, we shall be happy to accept your services; but
you must not flinch from the cause you have embraced, you
must bind yourself by a solemn oath to be faithful to our cause,
and to promote our objects even to death." I begged him to
admit me, and to state to me the nature of the service in which
they proposed I should embark. I said I was fearful lest I
should enter a den inhabited by Gunput Rao and his party, in
whose cause I would not engage; but if I did so, and found after
all that I was admitted of a party I could not support,—how
could I retract? To suppose no worse, after what I had said,
the cavern must be my prison until the present disputes were
settled. I said I had no objection, should an opportunity be
afforded me of so doing, to take a conspicuous part in fighting
for the unfortunate Sevaje, whom I had every reason to suppose
I was bound in honour to serve; but to fall into the hands of his
opponent would, indeed, be a dreadful thing for me. The torch-
bearer, seeming to feel my embarrassment, desired me not to act
in too great a haste. "No deceit is ever practised here," said he;
"the troops of Sevaje fight in open and honourable warfare, for
no guile is suffered in his name; and it is the same in all other
matters in which his followers engage." The name of Sevaje and
these statements (which I was conscious no agent of Gabbage
would use or make), determined me how to act. I made a
motion to the torch-bearer to lead me on, and delivered to him
my sword, as a sign I submitted to an engagement on his side of
the question. He then led me, with the other men, over several
rugged places, until we came to a wide stream that flowed subter-
raneously through the cave; across this a door presented itself,
studded with iron spikes of enormous dimensions. On a signal
being given from without, the door was gradually lowered, until
it formed a bridge across the stream. We passed over, and
entered a spacious place—so much so, indeed, it seemed as if
the whole hill had been excavated to form the apartment. In

this excavation there sat twelve men, partly in armour, and before
them were provisions of all kinds. A hum of numerous voices
was heard, proceeding from different passages on the right and
left hand of the hollow or great chamber, which I immediately
conjectured to be Sevaje's stronghold. Who knew but he might
himself be there, or one of the twelve men before me? I was so
intent in regarding their features, and so occupied with my
thoughts, that I did not hear one of them address me, until I
was pulled by the sleeve by the torch-bearer, who stood at my
side. Having satisfied my **own** mind Sevaje was not among
them, I craved pardon for my abstraction; and **one of** them
repeated his question, demanding my name. I determined to
use no deceit, lest, on being discovered, I should not be trusted
in their affairs; I therefore replied, "My name is Pandurang
Hàrì." Several voices spoke at once—"Is it possible?" cried
they. "Am I known, then," I responded, "by any of this
gallant band?" "Your name," said the first speaker, "is familiar to us;—you have enemies, but your lucky star has led you
here. We have certain information of persons lying in wait for
you at Poona, where, it is reported, **you** have concealed a girl
named Sagoonah. Not being acquainted with your person, we
deemed it fruitless the attempting to find you out, and warn you
of your danger and of the secret attacks of your enemies. But
how did you come from Poona hither, and escape the assassins
that lurked about for you?" I informed them in return that I
came not from Poona, but from Indore. They inquired if I
came alone. I said an unhappy man, who I feared was no more,
was to have accompanied me. They asked his name, and I told
them Shewdhut Wanee. "By Ishwar! the very man," cried the
chief of the party. "But say, how know you he is no **more?**
How were you acquainted with him?" I told him my life had
been one unfortunate scene of disappointments and hardships;
that I had been hunted through the world by an unrelenting
enemy, who had sworn to take my life. **I** had fled to Guzerat
from the Deccan, but **I was** allowed no rest; my enemies followed
me closely, and dogged me back to my own country. I had been
tricked by knaves, robbed by Bheels, and pursued by assassins;

that it so happened, as I was flying from the latter, I fell in with
an old man, a goatherd, in a glen near Asseerghur, whose life I
by chance discovered was in jeopardy. I made this circumstance
known to him; we conversed together, and were mutually pleased.
I thought his resignation, and manners, and hidden misfortunes,
most touching; I swore to serve him, should it be ever in my
power to do so. He told me he should quit the glen, and proceed to Indore, where lived a Wanee, named Shewdhut, who, on
my producing to him a silver ring which he left with me, would
conduct me to the place of his retreat. Circumstances afterwards made it necessary for me to visit the goatherd, from whom
I conceived it possible I might learn something regarding an
unfortunate and persecuted girl already named; that I went to
Indore for this purpose, had an interview with Shewdhut, whom
I convinced I was no impostor, and he, at length, told me that
the goatherd was not at Indore, but at Sattarah, whither he was
himself proceeding. I then mentioned the disappearance of
Shewdhut Wanee, and the reasons I had for believing him to
be murdered.

The chief of the party heard me conclude my story, with
melancholy in his countenance at the fate of Shewdhut. The
whole twelve now whispered to each other in so low a tone, I
could not catch a single syllable of what they said. The chief at
length begged me to retire for a short time, but to await their call.
The torch-bearer arose, and, opening a little side-door, desired
me to follow him. I then entered a small square chamber,
covered with mats, on which he bade me be seated, and left me
to reflect on my singular adventure. In about an hour I was
summoned again into the presence of the council, the chief of
which desired me to be seated in front of him. I obeyed,
and he then commenced by stating that they had resolved to
ask me a few questions more, which I might or might not
answer, as I saw fit; but that, in answering them, there was every
probability of benefiting myself. Moreover, having heard my
answers, they could better determine how far to intrust me with
the secrets connected with their cause, and the object they had
in view. I bowed assent, and they proceeded:—"Have you

any reason to believe that the goatherd you mentioned is any other than a private individual?" I answered, "I have every reason to believe him to be Sevaje, the lawful successor to the musnud of Sattarah." They then bade me state my reasons; and, fearing to hint at the chance of my being his son, lest it should not be so after all, and I should be esteemed presumptuous, I answered, "that Shewdhut had dropped some pretty strong hints to me, and some expressions had escaped him, from which I gathered that such was the case—indeed, I felt certain of it." They then inquired who Sagoonah was. I replied, "A girl betrothed to a young man who has never been heard of." "How came she under your protection?" I answered, "She is not under my protection; she lives with her aunt. I am acquainted with them, and wished to marry the girl; but the uncertainty as to the fate of her betrothed husband prevents our union." They then inquired where I first knew her, and I told them how I had rescued her from the hands of murderers, and had aided in concealing her from them to this day. They next questioned me if I knew any of the murderers, and I told them that one was named Gabbage Gousla, who was also an enemy of mine. "Indeed," cried the chieftain. "Know you aught of this Gabbage?" I replied, "Yes, that he was Gunput Rao, the pretender to the musnud of Sattarah." "Has he a lawful right?" inquired one of the twelve. "None," I answered; "he is a villain and a murderer!" "How can you speak so positively?" questioned the chief. I replied, "Because I heard his history from the mouth of his own son, Mahadeo." "This is very strange!" exclaimed several of the council at once. "It is so," I remarked; "for, at the time I heard the son say this, he had no idea he ever should meet his father again, or be in any condition to aspire to the throne—he was then a roving Pindaree."

After this I was desired to withdraw again to my seat in the small chamber. I remained there another hour, when I was again summoned. "Young man," said the chief, "knowing so much of the history of Sevaje and Gunput Rao as you do, whose cause will you espouse?" I replied that of Sevaje, and that I would serve him honestly and faithfully with all my heart;

that he should have no more devoted adherent, no stauncher supporter. "You see, then," he added, "men before you now who will die for Sevaje; if you are sincere, will you enrol your name among ours, and take the oath we shall prescribe?" I answered that I would. Upon this a naked sword was presented to me, and I was desired to repeat the following words :— "I swear by the holy cow, by fire and by water, to aid and assist Sevaje Owdhut in his attempt to reign in Sattarah! I devote my heart and body to his cause, and I will oppose and contend, even to death, with his enemies, on water or land; that neither cold nor heat shall deter me from pursuing them, nor mountains nor rivers be obstacles to turn me aside from this my purpose; that neither rewards nor threats shall bias me to the cause of the traitor Gunput Rao, or his son Mahadeo; but that the last drop of blood in my veins shall be to Sevaje! And I bind myself also to obey his officers, and aid and assist them in battle and council, should my services be so needed; and if I fail, or act contrary to this advice, may Ishwar judge me!" I then touched the sword, and was allowed to retire.

No great while after this, the chief, or he who seemed to lead the council, came to me, seated himself by my side, and entered at once into conversation. Among other things, he told me he thought I must be curious to know how my name became so well known to them, but that the fact was their spies had overheard a man named Kokoo, a chief of Gunput Rao's force, propose my assassination. From the conversation of this man and of others, it was evident I was considered a person of some consequence, whom it was very desirable to remove out of the way; hence the surprise of the council at hearing my name. I observed that Kokoo had an enmity to me from a private cause, and wholly independent of his zeal for the cause of his employer. I then narrated my adventure at the cavern. The conversation finished by my receiving the offer of the command of fifty men, who were trained to the duty of both horse and foot soldiers that they might act as circumstances should require. I accepted the command with gratitude, and requested his name, that I might acknowledge his commands as my superior. His name,

he said, was Naroba Taitia, a jagheerdar, who had been deprived
of his estates unjustly by the present rajah of Sattarah. Seeing
no chance of obtaining justice by supporting Gunput Rao, he had
linked himself with the other side, and would stand or fall with
it, as he could rely on Sevaje's justice.

I now ventured to inquire a little how our public affairs stood,
and what were our resources. I found the troops were more
numerous than the money at hand would maintain, and that the
death of Shewdhut was a loss in this respect, as he had always
supplied Sevaje with cash. How Gunput Rao could discover
this was a mystery; but there seemed little doubt he had been
murdered by Gunput's agency. The chief of the council left me
soon after this, hoping I should attend them on the morrow. In
the meantime, I had an opportunity of observing everything that
was going on in the cavern, and that there were nearly three
hundred men scattered about, all cheerful, confident, and to
appearance very well appointed. I found that an equal number
were assembled at another stronghold a few miles off, and that
as Gunput Rao was known to have no more than four hundred
followers, we hoped to profit by our superiority in numbers, as
well as in valour. I inquired where Sevaje then was, and found
he was in Sattarah, though Gunput Rao believed him in one of
his strongholds. I found orders came from him daily, and that
a despatch was then hourly expected from him. He had very
fortunately a sincere friend at the court, who held the office of
dewan, and daily informed him of every proceeding known there.
By this means Sevaje was aware of Gunput's intentions, as the
reigning rajah was no stranger to any of them, and befriended
Gunput.

The next morning, on the assembling of the council, a shrill
whistle was heard from without. All were eager to learn what
orders the messenger had brought. The draw-bridge being
lowered, an hircarrah appeared, and taking off his turban, produced a sealed roll. The chief of the council took it, and
reading the contents, first dismissing the messenger from the
chamber, he told us that if ever we struck a decisive blow, now
was our moment. It appeared that Gunput Rao had for some

time been petitioning the rajah to restore him his estate, which had been long ago sequestrated upon his disappearance. Not content with doing this, he had also successfully claimed his brother's, on pretence of his having been murdered. Moreover, on giving, or promising to give, to the minister of the rajah an enormous sum of money, he had obtained an order on the treasury for the arrears of both estates, as annually collected from the time of their sequestration. This money was to be issued to him the next day, at the hour of five in the evening, and he would no doubt convey it immediately to his stronghold, and thereby raise an overwhelming force, which it would be madness in Sevaje to resist. The latter therefore wished, as the despatch stated, that the band assembled in the cavern should march against a fortified village, which was named, on one of Gunput's estates, and destroy it while the troops at Sevaje's other hold should lie in ambuscade for the treasure of Gunput on the road from Sattarah. If these two attacks succeeded, the followers of the party attacked would be paralysed, and a favourable reaction be thereby produced in favour of Sevaje. The chieftain concluded by requesting us all to arm. This was received with cheering, and the cavern rang with the animated shouts. The despatches further stated that Canooje, who commanded at Sevaje's other fort, would be with us on the morrow to arrange the plan of attack. Orders were then given to afford him the most rapid access, and the council broke up. All now prepared for the events of the next day; the arms were put in order, the ammunition examined, and every heart seemed elated with the prospect of being actively employed, some perhaps with the hope of plunder as well as of glory.

CHAPTER XXXIII.

BEFORE the day broke, I was awoke by a sentinel, who called me to attend the council, for Canooje had arrived. I hurried to the great chamber, and was introduced to this chief, with whose courageous and lofty presence I was much struck. His deportment was noble, his air military, and his countenance elevated and pleasing. I found that the determination to place Sevaje upon the Sattarah musnud had originally proceeded from him, and that it was by his interest and efforts all the principal jagheerdars, of whom the council consisted, had joined to aid in the cause. It was now settled that, at four o'clock in the afternoon, we should storm the fortified village belonging to Gunput Rao, whilst Canooje's division was placed in ambuscade among the ravines, within five miles of Sattarah, through which the treasure of Gunput Rao must pass; and, having made themselves masters of it, bring it to the stronghold as the nearest place of safety. Our division was ordered to despatch intelligence to Canooje, while he remained in ambush, of the result of our attack on the village; at the same time, if we failed, we were to remain and blockade the place, to prevent the garrison having a communication with the detachment that escorted the treasure. Thus the corps that formed the escort could not be increased in strength, and the chance of the discomfiture of our design was more remote.

The plan of attack being thus finally arranged, Canooje left us to return to his troops. When I found that the whole of our strength in the cavern was ordered to march on the village, I suggested the prudence of leaving a party behind to protect it. I observed that the enemy would hardly omit to attack it in our

353

absence, for we should not have marched far before Gunput Rao's spies would convey to him intelligence that the cavern had been vacated, and that on our return we should run the chance of seeing it occupied by the enemy, which would be an effectual damper to our successes elsewhere. This suggestion was properly weighed, and ordered to be carried into effect by a majority of voices. Fifty men were left with a jummahdar for this purpose. If we arrived before the village at the hour of four, we should probably prevent the garrison from sending out a reinforcement to support the treasure party. In case the party had marched, we could then attack it in the open plain on our advance towards the village, or leave a party for this purpose concealed in its line of march. We determined therefore to move forwards directly. All became bustle and preparation. I collected my men, saw that they were properly armed and accoutred, that their swords, shields, daggers, and matchlocks were in order, and that they were well supplied with ammunition, scaling-ladders, and ropes; for we had no cannon to breach the village walls. When we mustered and marched away, I was much pleased to see the regularity and sobriety of our brave comrades, many of whom had been soldiers under the fallen Peeshwa Badjerao, and were happy to be employed on the present occasion, when their pay was punctual, and they were well supplied with the needful munitions. Those on the side of Gunput Rao were men of the same order, but not headed by officers as experienced or respectable as ours, but by desperadoes like Kokoo, who looked to future reward and aggrandisement from him whom they supported, but were themselves among the unprincipled and dishonourable. Upon our arrival at a deep hollow, we halted and concealed ourselves in it, sending out scouts to watch the motions of the inhabitants and garrison of the village against which our operations were directed, and which was only distant from us about two miles. Our spies soon returned, and informed us that one hundred men had left the village, and taken the road to Sattarah, which passed by the place where we lay concealed. We observed them approaching; and, with a jummahdar and about a hundred men, I rushed from our ambush upon the unprepared soldiers of Gunput. Though taken completely by surprise, they recovered and ranged themselves in fighting array, keeping up so constant a fire from their matchlocks, that we could not attack them sword in hand as we intended. Their commander, however, having made them fire a volley, thinking to terrify and disperse us, our jummahdar ordered us to charge the instant their pieces were fired, and before they could reload, or even draw their swords, we were on them. Nearly every one of them was cut down, and our victory was complete. We learned from the prisoners that the village contained about one hundred and fifty men, who were entirely unprepared for a hostile attack. Naroba, in consequence of our success, was in high spirits, and gave orders to march directly upon the village, which we did at once, compelling the prisoners to guide us with their arms tied behind them. On our arrival before the gates, we summoned the garrison to surrender. A shower of arrows was the only answer we received, upon which, placing our ladders against the mud wall of the fort, we mounted to the attack. I led the storming-party sword in hand. We found a number of Bheels had been mustered for the defence of the place, whom Gunput Rao had but lately taken into his service. These fellows galled us dreadfully with their arrows ; but as our plan was to close with them, we gave them few opportunities, after our once effecting a lodgment on the walls, of using their fatal weapons. The fort of the village was very small, and the garrison, taken by surprise, was cramped for room and in confusion. Part of them made a sortie, some for the purpose of fighting, and others of running away. Naroba at the head of his corps met them, and having borne down all opposition outside the walls, was coming up as I pursued the enemy out at the gate. The Bheels stood outside inactive, fearing to discharge their arrows, and wound their own men, intermingled with ours. I now attacked the Bheels, who, with the party that had been so anxious to make a sally from the fort, attempted to return and enter it again ; but I placed my men before the gates, ordering them to resist to the last any body of the enemy that should attempt to force an entrance. The enemy seeing this, with great alertness ran to the scaling-ladders, which still remained against the wall, and tried to force an entrance by their means. These intentions were quickly seen by Naroba, who sent round fifty men to keep a flanking fire along the wall as they descended inside, while another party performed the same manœuvre on the outside. By this means they were tumbled headlong down in every direction. The Bheels, finding their own party worsted, sought for safety in flight to their native wilds. The other soldiers without the walls, seeing there was no hope of success, fled for their lives. Everything being thus in our possession, and not an enemy left before us in less than an hour after we began the attack, we proceeded to plunder. But we could discover only a few pots and pans. There was, it it true, a good supply of grain, of which we carried off all we could find the means of conveying away.

Whilst some of the men were hunting for plunder, they reported that they had found a prisoner in a subterraneous cell, and bound to the wall by a strong chain. Thinking the unfortunate being was some enemy of Gunput Rao, I obtained permission from Naroba to release him before we quitted the place to march back. I thought it possible he might perhaps give us some information of importance, and I went myself to his place of confinement, which was dark and damp. Not a sound save the clank of the unfortunate prisoner's chains could even be heard in it. A soldier was sent for a torch to show us the way, and soon returning we reached the spot. On placing the torch so as to see his countenance, what was my surprise at observing my old and tried friend Nanna. "Nanna! my dear friend, is it you, indeed, that I behold in this horrible dungeon? Speak! you cannot have forgotten me." In a voice feeble and faint, he replied, "What, Pandurang! is it you—a friend, and here?" "It is in truth," I answered; "thanks to the gods who conducted me hither." I bade them break his chains, which was soon done, and Nanna and I were speedily in each other's arms. "Am I in a dream?" said Nanna. "How came you here—can it be real?" I told him this was not a time or place for explanation, that I must lead him to my comrades, who would rejoice with me in the preservation of a friend. Nanna was weak, and it was with difficulty we got him to walk up into the air, the sudden effect of which made him faint. A little of our attention speedily recovered him, and I related to Naroba the friendship that had existed between us. He congratulated me on the event, giving his hearty assent to Nanna's accompanying us to the cavern. I confess I longed to hear the particulars of his captivity. Curiosity was a leading characteristic in my disposition, and I thought he must also feel not a little curious to know how I came into my present situation.

The total destruction of the fort would have required more time than we could spare, or safely afford to remain while our other detachments were in the field, and their operations a matter of uncertainty to us. We contented ourselves with demolishing the gates, and as much of the walls as time allowed, and then returned to the cavern, having lost ten men, and others of our number being badly wounded. I myself received a sabre cut, which, though not dangerous, gave me great pain. It was late before we reached the cavern, and upon making the well-known signal, we were admitted once more. We found, as I had apprehended, that during our absence a party of the enemy had attempted to carry the place, but had been repulsed by the guard, which but for me would not have been left to protect it. The detachment which had gone in search of the treasure had returned, not so successful as we hoped it would have been. Canooje stated that he had lost twenty men, and that, although he had seized the money, to his great disappointment there was not half the sum he expected. He had learned from the prisoners, however, that the bulk had been conveyed away in a different direction ; and that, his men not being in a condition to pursue it, they had returned with about seven thousand rupees in their possession. The money was well escorted, and it appeared that if we had not cut up the intended reinforcements, Canooje would not have attained his purpose as easily as he did, perhaps not at all. The news of our victory was no small thing, however, in our favour, and tended much to lessen the consequence of Gunput Rao, and to damp the spirit of his followers. Our wounded having been attended to, and every care in our power shown them, we stretched our fatigued limbs on our mats, and sought a refuge in sleep from our past labours. In the morning a council was held, to consider what steps had best be taken in pursuance of out objects. Canooje first proposed sending out spies to obtain intelligence of the movements of the enemy; but this was overruled until the receipt of another secret despatch from Sevaje. It seemed necessary, as we had lost so many men, to send our considerate agents to obtain recruits for our detachments. This was immediately done; and Canooje, after giving a full account of our recent proceedings, and the capture of the treasure, in a despatch to Sevaje, marched away from us with his well-appointed troop.

There being nothing of moment to occupy me, I hastened to Nanna, who was already showing he made progress in his recovery from the effects of his barbarous imprisonment and accompanying starvation. I related to him the particulars of my history since we quitted each other, and with which the reader must be already so well acquainted as to be able to recall them to recollection. Nanna in his turn informed me that, on arriving at Sattarah, he lodged the woman who accompanied him in an obscure house, which was the same night surrounded by the agents of Gunput Rao, who forcibly carried her off; but the next morning she returned, saying the people who took her away had released her. Nanna stated that, being intent upon finding out whether the boy to whom Sagoonah had been betrothed was living or dead, he lost no opportunity of inquiring into the matter; but finding it in vain, he left Sattarah for the purpose of joining me at Poona. In his way thither, he was surrounded by ruffians, who bound him fast, and conducted him to the fort from whence we had rescued him. There Kokoo examined him, and desired him to tell where Sagoonah was concealed; he also made strict inquiries respecting myself. Nanna would answer none of his questions, but remained silent; upon which he was sentenced to imprisonment in the dungeon, and *natchne rotee:* [1] this was to endure until he should betray his friend. Having said he was determined not to do so, he was in addition chained to the wall

[1] Bread made of the coarsest grain.

where he was found. I hereupon pressed this trusty friend to my heart, and related to him all I had formerly omitted in giving him a sketch of my history. I also let him know the probable situation I stood in with Sevaje, the lawful successor of the Sattarah musnud. Nanna was struck with wonder on hearing this part of my history. After standing with his mouth wide open, he said, " I always thought you were a great scholar, but never dreamed of your being a prince at the same time—let me fall prostrate ! " "Not so fast, my dear friend," I cried ; " it is not quite so certain I am a prince ; and, if I should be, it is more than probable I shall never be in a situation to receive the homages of my friends in the way you would deliver yours." " You shall be, though," said Nanna ; "and may I live to behold you on a throne, and to say another star is added to the Pleïades, and that Sattarah shall henceforth be Atarah ! " [1] I could not help telling Nanna he had already made great progress in the language of a courtier ; that he perhaps acquired it from his enemies while a prisoner, and they had been practising flattery, and the arts of rising at court, upon the strength of their expectations. " I shall need," said I, "a deal of polishing, my good friend, before I can be compared to the dullest star in the heavens, as you would agree with me in thinking, were you acquainted with the whole of my history, which perhaps I shall one day unfold to you. Predjudiced as you are in my favour, you would shake your head upon me were I seated on a musnud, if you knew everything. Nanna was going to reply by a second essay in courtiership ; but it was so disagreeable a thing to my ear to be addressed in this gross way, that I thought, if ever I reached such high honour, it would then be full time enough to suffer the infliction of its hollowness, as some balance for the glory of the situation. Besides, I really felt conscious of my demerits, and all the flattery in the world could not make me change my opinion of myself ; for I knew what my own conduct had been in numerous instances. It is true I was brought up and educated by menials and base wretches of every description ; I had been cast upon the stream of life to float along by myself, as necessity or fancy directed ; I had

[1] Atarah, or eight stars.

been persecuted wrongfully, and obliged to resort to mean artifices oftentimes for existence itself. This had been the case in youth, when passion is warmest and reason possesses but little influence. I knew that the few good actions of my life were overborne by the many bad ones. Still I was comforted that I had bought experience, and been enabled to see the advantages of a steady, correct, and uniform line of conduct. Villainy, I was convinced, had but a short day, and upright intention would ultimately triumph in every circumstance of life. Mahrattas are for the most part bad men—cunning, insidious, and self-interested; but they were ever unfortunate enough to be badly governed. The bad examples of their kings and rulers were ever before them; and the corruption and vices of lesser persons in authority contaminated the people, who are always profligate or virtuous according to the way in which they are governed. I observed to Nanna that I had a deep dread at the idea of being called upon to govern; and the only chance I should have of success would be to follow the example of my father, who I hoped I should see for many years fulfilling his duties, and thus I might become his scholar. My friend Nanna, upon this, observed that I talked like a book, and that what I said must be true. He would only ask me, ignorant as he was, to be allowed to bask in the sunshine of my favour. I could not help laughing, but told him he might rely upon it, I should never forget him. I said he must not be too sanguine; that I intended the same day to consult with Naroba upon this subject, and upon the propriety of my making a visit to Sevaje, as I felt unhappy at being kept so long in suspense. I desired Nanna not to let a word drop upon this business in the cavern, as he respected my friendship, and, anywhere else, not to let a word respecting it escape him. He promised me all I required, stated his determination to be faithful to my cause, and left me.

There were many solid reasons why I did not wish to make public that it was probable I was so nearly related to Sevaje. One reason was, that it seemed to me possible Gunput Rao might be induced to consent to a public inquiry, or an arbitration of the question between my father and himself, and that the right of the lawful successor might be settled this way; for he would perhaps be induced to abide by such a decision as long as he thought Sevaje alone was living, as, after his death, Mahadeo would infallibly succeed to the musnud. On the other hand, were Gunput Rao to discover I was living, nothing would induce him to abide by any decree excluding him and his son. With these notions on my mind, I went to Naroba, and earnestly requested I might be allowed to visit Sevaje, having matters of importance to communicate to him. Naroba replied that he himself could have no objections, but that he considered it his duty to mention the request to Sevaje, in the first instance, and then he would immediately communicate his answer to me. I was of course obliged to consent to this step being first taken, and I patiently awaited an answer from Sevaje, which could not occupy a long period of time in communicating. Naroba and myself, in the interim, made the best use of our leisure. We had the sword-practice among our soldiers every day, rendering them as expert as possible in the use of their arms. I afterwards found the benefit of these lessons, as will be seen in the sequel. I also exercised myself in every possible way; but, from the exertion, I found the wound in my arm inflame, and become exceedingly painful. At the time an answer arrived from Sevaje I was in very great pain; but the reply being such as was consonant with my wishes, I determined that even the serious appearance it had begun to put on should not deter me from my visit to him, whom I had so much reason to believe was my father. I stated my readiness to depart, and Naroba procured me a guide, desiring me to put on an appearance as unsoldierlike as possible. The first guide was to conduct me to a second person, through whose means I should gain admittance to Sevaje, unsuspected by the enemy. I obeyed every suggestion made, and followed my guide with a palpitating heart to a small wood, at a considerable distance from our stronghold. My guide tapped at the door of a miserable hovel, which was opened by a lean, tall, emaciated old woman, who instantly admitted us upon seeing the person of him who conducted me. There was something in the appearance of the old hag which at first led me to suspect treachery, and my suspicions were not laid asleep on my seeing the guide and old woman, head to head, in a close whisper. I thought this was unnecessary, where all present were friends, and my bosom became filled with vague suspicions everything was not right. The guide now went away without uttering one word to me, and the old hag seated herself opposite to where I sat; but no effort of mine could induce her to enter into conversation. She mumbled unintelligibly to herself until I began to get impatient, and begged her to lead the way whither I designed to go. She turned her head round and pointed to the sun with her shrivelled finger, and then to the western quarter of the heavens, from which I judged we must not set out for Sattarah until after the sun had set. It wanted full three hours' space of it yet, and being fatigued, and my wound very painful to me, I spent my time in no very agreeable way; for not a single word could I get in the way of conversation from this mysterious old woman. I threw myself on a mat to try and sleep; but sleep fled far from me, and I could only indulge in dreams of what the future might have in store for me, and fall back upon my own thoughts for a means of employing a short period that passed away slow as ages.

CHAPTER XXXIV.

T length, the sun having gone down blood-red, and left that tranquil gloom which so quickly covers the earth on the departure of an Indian day, the old woman tapped me on the shoulder with a long stick. I arose and followed her. Age made it necessary for her to proceed slowly, and a complete ignorance of the point to which she was leading me, impelled me to keep pace with her. My impatience could ill brook the tediousness of such a mode of travelling. A man just hoping to behold his parent, from whom he had been separated nearly the whole of his life, might be excused for an anxiety to press onward and realise his anticipated hopes; I therefore offered to procure a litter for her, or even carry her on my back, so that we might not linger away all night in our march to the city. The woman made no reply to my offers, but merely shook her head; and I was compelled to proceed at a snail's pace coss after coss, so that it was past eleven o'clock ere we entered Sattarah. My conductress took me through the principal streets, until we came to a shop where they sold sweetmeats, and there she purchased several bits of burnt sugar. We then visited a baker's, where she bought bread; and the fruit bazaar, where she obtained cocoa-nuts, betel-nuts, and pomegranates. In the last place she purchased a basket to hold what she had bought, and placed it upon my head; so that, in my present dress, I had exactly the appearance of a cooly or porter, and was completely disguised. I followed her still in silence as before, and she led me, to my great surprise, towards the hill on which stands the seven-towered fort of Sattarah. Observing my astonishment, she for the first time told me to address her as mother, but not utter a single syllable to any one I might see in her presence. The

363

old creature clambered the hill with difficulty; and when we arrived at the gate of the fort she knocked with her stick, and a sentry opening the wicket demanded who was there. She replied, "Only old Bhowance and her son." "Ah! mother," said the sentry, "I thought you had forgotten us: how do you sell your sweetmeats? Come in." So saying, we entered; the basket was taken from my head, the contents examined, and some purchases made. We were then allowed to proceed to the house of the officer who had the charge of the arsenal, an octagon building in one of the seven towers. The old woman was admitted immediately, and a whispering dialogue began with the officer, which convinced me they were well acquainted. After some little further delay, I was beckoned into an inner room, and the officer resident in the house began to remove a large ammunition-box which stood in the centre of the chamber. I was wondering what could be the meaning of this, and to what it all tended, eagerly looking out for the end of the mystery, and almost suspecting foul play, when, I imagine, the man touched some secret lock or bolt, for a door in one of the corners of the room flew open, and discovered a flight of stone stairs, which my conductress descended, motioning me to remain where I then was. The resident in the house retired, and I was left in a most uncomfortable solitude, not wholly divested of fear, when I recollected many circumstances in my past life that, less suspicious in appearance, had led me into trouble. It was not without pleasure, therefore, that in a short time I heard the old woman returning, and greeted her haggard face at the top of the staircase. From thence she beckoned me to follow her, and I found myself quickly in a very comfortable square stone room. She then opened another door in the wall, through which she disappeared, and again left me in solitude. I now threw off my coat, and lay down upon a mat, the wound in my arm torturing me severely. I had not been reclining many minutes before the door through which my conductress had passed opened, and she again entered, followed by a venerable old man, who bore a lamp in his hand, the dim radiance of which did not suffice to give me at first a correct view of his features. Before he noticed me he whispered something to the woman, who reascended the staircase, and closed the trap-door, as I judged from the sound.

I was now alone with him who was most probably my father. **What** my sensations were at that moment can I ever forget? Hope, fear, pleasure, pain, seemed to have possession of me at the same instant: filial awe, reverential regard, a respect for royalty, came upon me, and robbed me of all power of utterance! One minute would decide my fate, and cast the die of my life— raise me to honour, or dash me into the lowest deep of misery! The old man, turning towards me, now said, "What, young and valiant man, wouldst thou with me? I have heard of thy bravery in my cause, and I cannot fear treachery from a brave man! I **have,** therefore, admitted thee to my seclusion. What wouldst thou, young man, with me?" As he spoke, the light flashed upon his features, and I recognised the old goatherd of the glen. "I would claim acquaintance, my lord," I observed; "we have met before." "Ah! where, where?" he hastily inquired, stooping at the same time to examine my features, as I was sitting cross-legged on the mat. "Truly," continued he, "I have seen that face before; come to the light, let me be certain." So saying, he bade me arise, and I obeyed. "Yes," said he, "I have seen that face before." "I think in the Asseerghur glen," I responded. "In the glen!" said he. "What! art thou the youth to whom I gave a ring?" I told him I was the same; and, mindful of my promise, had sought him in Indore in vain, and had now sought further, and found him in Sattarah. "And dost thou then take so great an interest in my fate as to follow me from place to place? This is kindness I have been of late little used to. But your arm bleeds! I fear I am the cause of much bloodshed. Say, where got you that frightful wound?" I observed, it was a mere scratch, the consequence of my own rashness. "Rather of your valour," said he; "for I guess how it is; but it must be bound up, and thus the blood staunched." So saying, he drew my coat, which I had taken off, over my shoulders, and began to bind it round my wounded arm. This sudden and unexpected act made me bare my right arm, on which was fixed the silver kurdoorah. He started, and exclaimed, "What! what do I see? Nay, I am blind—my eyes are old, and fail me! It cannot be!—let me look again. It is the same! Where got you that chain?—speak! torture me not a moment longer!" "It is my own," I replied, "and I feel I am in the presence of him who first bound it round my loins." "My son, my son!" cried the old man, as I fell upon my knees and called him father! A moment was passed in deep silence, which ended in a shower of tears, that, streaming down my father's venerable beard, fell warm upon my head. I can make no attempt to describe my feelings at that moment, or to do justice to the scene. It was a feast of unspeakable joy to my heart—a moment worth years of adversity!

As soon as the old man was more composed, he requested to know by what accident I had learned that his recognition of the chain would warrant me in concluding I was his son. I related to him all that Shewdhut Wanee had informed me of. At the name of Wanee he wept aloud, and desired me to state the particulars of his disappearance, as he understood from Naroba I could give him every particular respecting it. I then entered into the melancholy detail once more. It was frequently interrupted in the recital, by his tears and bitter invocations against the perpetrators of the deed. He then referred to the kurdoorah, and exclaimed, "Oh! that was a night of horrors, when I put this chain around thy infant body; it was a bloody deed, my Jeoba!" "Is Jeoba, then, my name?" I eagerly inquired. "It is thy name, my son, and happy was the day to me that gave thee birth; for, notwithstanding the machinations of my most deadly foes, Heaven has brought thee to my arms!" "May you be successful against your enemies!" I now observed, in order to lead away the conversation from myself. "Your claims to the musnud of Sattarah are just, and you have stout hearts devoted to you, my father, among your troops." "Ah, my son! would this dispute might be settled amicably! Would that Gunput Rao, your unnatural uncle, could be induced to acknowledge my claims, and forego further bloodshed!" "As long as he believes I am not forthcoming," I replied, "he might show a readiness so to do, and waive his claim until after your decease, when Mahadeo, his son, would succeed to the musnud." "Then must our present relationship remain a secret," said my father. "I have applied to the English Government to interfere and adjust our quarrel : or, if they refuse to do so, that they will allow their agent here to appoint an arbitration, and see that all is fairly and honourably conducted. Thus Gunput will not dare to commit any outrage, should the decision be given in my favour ; although, by his intrigues, he will endeavour to effect all that bribery and influence can accomplish, to secure in his interest the persons to whom the settlement of the cause is entrusted." "Justice, however, must prevail," said I ; "and, when you are acknowledged the real successor, then will I openly, and not until then, address you as my father."

Sevaje assenting, we turned to other matters ; and he demanded how it was possible I had been preserved, amid the perils I must have undergone, and then miraculously appeared at so critical a time ? I replied that no one but he who sought for my destruction could account for my escape in infancy, and that in due time I would relate to him all my history, and the minute events of my chequered existence, which had so singularly brought me into the arms of a father and a king. I remarked that of the particulars of his quarrels with his relentless brother, Gunput Rao, I had also acquired some knowledge. My father was in amazement, and could scarcely credit this. I observed also that I had it from the best authority—no less than that of Gunput Rao's own son, and my cousin Mahadeo, at a time when neither of us had a knowledge of our affinity. I now related to my father all I had heard from Mahadeo respecting the conduct of his brother, and he proceeded to inform me of the earlier part of my history. He told me that after I was betrothed (here I interrupted him, to inquire to whom, and whether to a girl named Sagoonah ?) to one who was now no more, or, if alive," fallen into the hands of Gunput Rao. I again proceeded, "Oh, say not so ! she is safe ! We love each other with a fervour equal to that of Leila and Mejnoun,[1] though little did we imagine we had been betrothed in our infancy." "This is indeed extraordinary," observed my father. "Where could you have met her ?

---

[1] The Romeo and Juliet of the East.

How could you have fallen in with her?" I said I would unfold all to him when he had done relating his own history.

"The will of great Dum be accomplished!" said my father, who then proceeded:—"After you had been bethrothed to Sagoonah, the rage of Gunput Rao, your uncle, knew no limits, and put on such a deadly appearance, that I conceived it prudent to quit my place of residence, and retire with you (then an infant, and my only offspring) to a small estate which I possessed in the Chandore territory. Having some business to transact previously at Indore, I visited it for the purpose, and left it one rainy evening. With the ready money I had about me, I purchased there for you the silver kurdoorah, which I thought remarkably elegant, and fastened it around your waist myself. Proud of the ornament, you frequently tottered beside me, until I feared you would be fatigued before you would let me take you up in my arms again. After sunset, about the space of an hour had elapsed, when we were surrounded by armed men, among whom I discovered your revengeful uncle. 'Seize the miscreant!' he cried; 'bear away that child—obey your orders!' At that moment you were forcibly taken from me, and your uncle's dagger entered my body. The ruffians departed immediately when I fell, to satiate themselves (so I reflected, for I had full possession of my senses) with your innocent blood. I shortly became insensible, and knew nothing more, until I found myself stretched upon a comfortable bed and watched with great solicitude. I shall pass over the many days that elapsed before I recovered, and merely inform you that the kind man to whom I owe my life was Shewdhut Wance, of Indore. He told me he had been to Oogein, and on his return found me weltering in my blood. Discovering signs of life, he placed me in the hands of two coolies who were attending him, and despatched his servants in search of the assassins. It need scarcely be repeated that all search after them proved ineffectual. You may now not be surprised at my sorrow on hearing of the fate of Shewdhut, and that for his interference in my concerns he lost his life. He knew my rank and expectations; he was well acquainted with my misfortunes, and promised to afford me all the help in his power, on his return from Marwar (for which he shortly set out), provided I had not succeeded before that time in obtaining justice on my enemies. As the rajah of Sattarah was deposed, it did not then seem the most eligible time for asserting my claims; and, not wishing to criminate my brother, or try to gain redress against him or security for the future, while the issue of my application might be doubtful, I determined to live as a recluse, until affairs at Sattarah became more favourable to my views. Should such a time arrive, I thought I might intimidate Gunput, by threatening to expose him and bring him to justice if he threw any obstacles in my way. Alas! I little knew the implacability of his disposition, the desperate daring of his character!

"After living some years in retirement, I visited Shewdhut, who told me he was going to Sattarah on his mercantile affairs; and I requested him, at the same time, to try and gain intelligence of Gunput and his plans, and particularly to discover, if possible, whether you were alive and with him, and what were the reports that had been circulated respecting our disappearance. He promised to use his utmost exertions to discover what I required. On his return, I once more emerged from the woods, and went to his house. He stated that his brother had placed himself upon a litter, and had been thus conveyed to Sattarah, pretending he had been waylaid while in company with me, that our lives had been attempted, that, in defending myself, I had held up my child, which was stabbed to the heart! In short, that he himself was left for dead, and plundered of everything valuable about him! It appeared that he acted his part marvellously well; every one gave him credit for shedding tears of genuine sorrow; especially as he exhibited a letter, purporting to be written by his 'dear brother' at Indore, inviting him thither for the express purpose of settling all their disputes, and arranging for ever the causes of the unhappy differences that had subsisted between them, and stating his own claims to the throne to be false. This letter, Shewdhut told me, bore my signature; and so well was it imitated, that no one doubted its being a faithful document, and none, therefore, were likely to dispute the tale my brother had imposed upon them. That he might the better deceive the people, he gave out that it was his determination to resign the world; and with his son Mahadeo, he had left Sattarah, and not been heard of there from that time.

"Such was the account which Shewdhut brought me, and which, I must confess, struck me with amazement. Why Gunput should resign the world, possessing the ambitious views he did, was a problem beyond my power to solve, even by conjecture. In all likelihood, finding he could not succeed whether I was living or dead (there being no hope of the rajah again sitting on the throne at that time), he made up his mind to quit Sattarah, lest some unforseen event should develop his ferocious attempt on my life and on that of my son. Shewdhut could tell me no more of you than what I have stated already; namely, that having used you as a shield to cover my own body, you had been stabbed, and thus perished. Nothing new occurred to me for some time. I selected the glen of Asseerghur for my place of retreat, known only to Shewdhut. One day a gossein begged admittance to my cottage, and ever ready to shelter a weary traveller, I admitted him. He told me his name was Gabbage Gousla. His manners were singular, and, to me, unaccountably strange. He did not remain long, and I thought little about it, except that he disguised his features as much as possible, and spoke a very few words, and those apparently in a feigned voice. It was not until conversing with you on the same spot, and your informing me Gunput Rao walked the earth in the disguise of a gossein, and with the name of Gabbage, that I knew it. The truth then flashed upon my mind; I felt certain that he must have recognised me, and this at once accounted for his constrained and odd manners."

After mentioning that nearly about the same time two females had taken shelter in his cottage, who, I informed him, were Sagoonah and her aunt, my father continued:—"Feeling certain," said he, "that my cruel brother meditated a fresh attack upon my life, I left my place of refuge, and once more bent my steps to Indore; there my friend Shewdhut concealed me. The war was then raging, and I felt assured that, if the English were disposed to act with justice, they would not fail to reinstate the deposed rajah of Sattarah. It turned out that they did so; and I therefore requested Shewdhut to gain for me some intelligence upon which I could rely, respecting the plans and objects of my wicked brother. He confirmed me in the surmises that I felt, in consequence of your information in the glen. Shewdhut went further than I had commissioned him to do; for, learning from some disaffected jagheerdars at Sattarah, that there was much doubt as to the truth of my being really dead, and they evincing great partiality towards me, and equal abhorrence at the idea of my brother becoming king, he told one of them, named Canooje, that I was then alive at Indore. Canooje, much pleased at this intelligence, left Sattarah with Shewdhut, and presented himself before me, urging me to come forward, and assert my right to the musnud; he assured me that there was a powerful party ready to support my cause. Thus encouraged, I consented to make the attempt; and, finding the present rajah was in a sickly state, and that no time must be lost, I promised to enter Sattarah in secret; and, when a sufficient number of men were raised and organised to support me, I agreed that I would openly declare myself.

"A curious circumstance occurred about this time, which tended strongly to confirm me in my new resolution. It was during Shewdhut's second absence at Sattarah, that an old woman came to Shewdhut's house. She perceived that I avoided her, as I necessarily did all strangers. She called out after me, saying, 'Why fly you from your friends, my lord, the king?' 'King?' I ejaculated. 'Ay, king!' she replied; 'for he who claims a throne shall not succeed, and who has not claimed, may; I shall follow you.' After she was gone away, I heard she was considered a witch at Indore, and that her name was Dhankin Bhowanee." Here I interrupted Sevaje by saying, " Bhowanee! why that is the name of her who conducted me to these chambers!" "The same," said my father; "and a most useful channel of communication I have found her, between myself and the band in the cavern. I am at a complete loss to discover what her motives are for serving me so zealously; but there is no doubt we shall one day discover. Her appearance removes suspicion; no one suspects her of being a messenger of mine, and her services have been most important." I then remarked upon the strangeness of the circumstance, and inquired how my father himself obtained admittance to the fort. He said, "By chance : a relation of my wife's was the officer in charge of the arsenal; and Bhowanee, assuming the character of a dealer in fruits and vegetables, introduced herself to him, and informed him of my existence; also requesting him to aid in secreting me for a short time. He readily gave his consent, and I followed the old woman in the character of a porter to this place. To deceive the sentinels, my friend here sent another man down the hill with the woman, dressed much as I was; and thus my presence is not suspected, and I am, perhaps, in a place of greater security than elsewhere. By means of Bhowanee, I have been enabled to convey my wishes to Canooje, Naroba, and my other brave friends and officers. Your stay here now must be short; but we may soon hope to meet again under better auspices. Before you depart, however, you must inform me of everything respecting Sagoonah; for she has an uncle, a rich banker here, who has engaged himself on the side of Gunput, and is determined to bestow her hand on his son Mahadeo." "My dear father," I answered, "be assured she is in safety, and beyond the reach of both Gunput and her uncle! She is now in Bombay, and I am anxious to send her intelligence respecting myself; for it is long since I have done so, and her bosom is torn by a thousand conflicting doubts and apprehensions respecting my safety." My father then said he would procure me a trusty messenger, who would safely take what I had to communicate; but that, not being present nor within call, it would be better I should give him my message, and he would take care it was forwarded, instructing the hircarrah himself. I consequently gave my father the necessary information to convey. I was about to depart, when I heard that the old woman was gone, but had left word she would await my arrival at her lonely hut. Dressed as a servant of the keeper of the arsenal, with whom I set off, I accompanied him as far as the city, and then, bidding him adieu, hastened to Bhowanee's hut.

I now felt like a new man; my spirits were raised and my

heart lightened by my interview, so that I was almost a different being. I was no longer fatherless, but had become of importance in society! I felt that happiness might yet be mine, and I bounded over the road with astonishing alacrity. Just as I reached the wood in which the hut of old Bhowanee stood, a *cassid* or letter-carrier passed me. Knowing he was the bearer of the English post, and on his way to Poona, I hailed him, and asked what the news were. "The rajah is dead!" he replied; and continuing his pace too fast for me to keep up with him, I could learn nothing more. I now felt that this was to me a most awful crisis. Now must we either stand or fall for ever! and the importance of this intelligence so occupied my thoughts, that I was close to the old woman's hut before I imagined I had gone half the distance. I found her within, and communicated to her what I had heard from the cassid. She told me she had heard the evening before that the rajah was not expected to live many hours. I begged her to proceed, and show me the way to the cavern. She said, in reply, that she must hasten away to Sattarah, lest Sevaje should wish to communicate with Naroba on the affair, and that I must patiently await her return. This was a delay I little expected, but to which I was obliged to make up my mind. It was evening before she returned; and then she bade me follow her, and she would conduct me to the guide who would see me safe to the cavern. She led the way to a rude hovel; and knocking at the door three times, a man appeared, to whom she gave her despatches, and, pointing to me, turned away towards her own habitation. On my arrival at our place of security, I informed Naroba of the death of the rajah. He observed that the time was now come to bestir ourselves, but first proceeded to read the despatches from Sevaje, which he found contained the same intelligence. Sevaje also acquainted him that he had prepared a document to be presented to the ministers and the British Resident, claiming his right of succession to the throne, and adding that he hoped Gunput Rao would be prevailed upon to submit the dispute to arbitration, and thus prevent tumult and bloodshed. He further required us to remain in peace, and we should receive early intelligence from him of the result of the requisition which he had made. He further stated that, if his proposal were agreed to by the opposite party, he should nominate Naroba as one of the punchayet, to which his claims should be submitted. In order to induce Gunput Rao to come more readily into the measure, Sevaje had pledged his word to bury in oblivion the attempt that had been made by Gunput upon his own life, and the murder of his child. He concluded by saying that he eagerly awaited the reply of Gunput, and that he had every hope the dispute would be terminated without further bloodshed. If it were not, he had left no means untried towards its being done peaceably; and he was clear of all the consequences that might arise out of a different line of conduct on the part of his brother. Upon receiving Gunput's answer, Sevaje promised to forward another despatch.

CHAPTER XXXV.

SHALL henceforth relate the progress of events as they unfolded themselves. The reader of these my memoirs will understand that all which I detail as having taken place before I again meet my father, I glean from the despatches which almost daily reached us from Sattarah, or from the direct communications of those concerned, unless it may be anything in which I was personally concerned. Gunput Rao took several days to consider the contents of my father's communication. With the conviction of my non-existence, he at last consented to an arbitration, relying on my father's promise of not divulging, either on the trial or afterwards, the attempt made upon his life; and further, that as my father's troops had deprived him of great part of the arrears of the estate, that he should not be called upon to refund any money that might appear to be against him and in my father's favour. This being agreed to on the part of Sevaje, the preliminary conditions were signed by both parties. Naroba was nominated on the side of my father, and the rich banker, Sagoonah's uncle, on the part of Gunput Rao. The two others next named were my father's friend, who filled the office of dewan at Sattarah, and Lucknuchund Baboolchund, the farmer of Gunput's estate. The British Resident presided as umpire. This last arrangement was vehemently opposed by Gunput; but the Resident declared no arbitration should take place unless he were present as umpire, and Gunput was obliged to submit. Naroba now prepared to leave us to proceed to Sattarah and sit in the court of punchayet, and I requested leave to accompany him part of the way thither, as I was now able to find my way back to the fort or cavern without a guide. Unwilling to make any display of pomp or parade, Naroba determined to proceed on foot. We set out accordingly one morning very early; and just as we were entering a deep valley, which led by the shortest cut into the main road, old Bhowanee appeared, spreading wide her shrivelled arms, and crying, "Stop, stop! there is danger in the glen—advance, and you die!" I observed to Naroba, "Can this be possible? Can Gunput Rao act so treacherously as to murder one of my father's arbitrators in so public a manner?" "I tell you true," said the old woman; "hasten round yonder hill. From thence there is an open and safe path; 'tis a long way round, but delay not a moment." We thanked her, and offered her a present of some gold; but she turned away from it, saying, "Away!—avarice guides not my actions—away, away!"

"This is a strange being," I remarked to Naroba, as soon as we were out of her hearing; "what is the reason she takes such an interest in Sevaje's affairs?" He said, in reply, no one knew, but the time would probably soon arrive when she might be brought to explain her motives. He commented severely on the treacherous act of Gunput Rao to waylay him, and observed that it must be noticed; for he had no claim now to be treated with like an open and honourable disputant, but to be crushed and put to death for an assassin. I observed that this was very true, but we could not prove anything against him beyond the words of the old woman, and they would have but little weight in the court. Naroba seemed convinced I was right, saying nothing in reply, moved forward in silence. On arriving at the hill on which Sattarah stands, I bade him farewell, hoping he would let me hear from time to time how the business proceeded, which he promised to do, and we separated.

Our band in the cavern was now commanded by a sirdar named Jysing, a Rajpot of great valour and personal strength. Nothing occurred for two days after my return from Naroba. At length a despatch came, announcing his safe arrival, and that the arbitration had sat once upon the cause for which they were summoned, and that both disputants had entered into an engagement to abide by the judgment given. It appeared that Gunput had brought up the old story of the washerwoman again, and endeavoured to prove my father basely born; so that, from the nature of the investigation required, the business was likely to continue a long while in hand. At length the conclusion took place, and the award was made out; but the umpire, aware of the hostile forces of each party being in the vicinity, declared he would not announce it until the armed bands of both parties appeared before the palace gates, and surrendered their arms. In the despatch which communicated this intelligence, Naroba mentioned his having written to me expressly some days before, and given me joy on the event of the trial. It was therefore clear that my father had made known to him the relation in which we stood to each other, conceiving, as the matter at issue was nearly concluded, there could be no danger in so doing. I was at a loss, however, to account for the non-receipt of such a letter. I feared, as it had miscarried, it had fallen into the hands of Gunput or his party. Still I apprehended no danger, even if this ferocious man should discover my near connection with Sevaje, as the business was settled, and he had bound himself to abide by the decree of the arbitrators.

At last the day that was fixed for our marching upon Sattarah, to deliver up our arms before the palace gates, arrived. The award was still a secret to all but the arbitrators; and they had been kept in the palace, lest through their means it should by any chance be made public. The anxiety manifested by the people was at its highest pitch of excitement, and crowds awaited the arrival of the hostile bands with great anxiety. Jysing, although about to surrender up his arms, determined to keep up the dignity of the soldier to the last moment, and ordered every man to be prepared as if going to battle on the morrow. In consequence of these orders, swords were sharpened, horses caparisoned, and armour examined and securely buckled on; so that we made, on the whole, a very imposing show. Two hundred of the number were mounted, and the remainder acted as infantry. I was mounted on Naroba's Arab war-horse, and never felt so proud and elated in my life. At length I thought my miseries were over; I was no longer to be a wanderer over the country—an outcast, without a place to repose in; but I might look forward to quiet and enjoyment. We proceeded to the open road by the hill, where I had last parted from Naroba; the spot was about four miles from Sattarah. When we had got round the hill to a place where we could command a view of the road, we saw the corps of Gunput Rao proceeding slowly towards Sattarah. On seeing us approach, they halted, and held out a white flag as a token of amity, and we did the same. We naturally imagined from this, that they were anxious we should all arrive together, and at the same moment, under the gates of the palace, and we accordingly approached them, greeting them as friends. When we were nearly close to them, however, Jysing, whose eye was upon the slightest movement among them, espied the sword of their commanding-officer or chieftain half unsheathed as it were impatiently. Convinced there was treachery before him, he gave his men the word to halt, and draw their swords, but not to advance, acting solely on the defensive, and awaiting the intentions of the enemy. Nanna was close by my side, and said, "Pandoo, we shall have hot work—we shall be attacked!" The words were scarcely spoken before the conduct of Gunput became clear, by his cavalry forming, and charging us with great fury. Our men were dreadfully exasperated at such unheard-of treachery. They received the charge like well-trained soldiers, furious as it was; and our detachments were so nearly equal, for Canooje's corps had no yet joined us, that we were horse to horse in the cavalry and nearly man to man in the infantry. The latter having discharged a volley at each other, flung away their matchlocks, drew their swords, and fought hand to hand. At a distance, giving his orders, stood my treacherous uncle Gunput; while his son Mahadeo, and Kokoo, his chief officer, led on his men. Nanna speedily got engaged with Mahadeo. Both were mounted, and fought with deadly anger. Nanna was an excellent swordsman, and Mahadeo had acquired no small dexterity among the Pindarees. While they were in the height of their combat, Kokoo observed me near, and singling me out, made a furious charge upon me. He sat his horse firmly, and approached, shaking his two-edged sword, and gnashing his teeth with passion. When he came up to me, he cried, "I have found thee at last, thou would-be king!" His horse was tall, and my little Arab wheeling at the instant he came up to me, to avoid the shock which would have overturned us, he passed me with the impetus of his horse's motion; and before he could wheel round to face me again, I was close in his rear. This gave me a great advantage. I had now reason to rejoice at my good sword practice; for whatever skill I possessed, I knew I should have occasion for it with Kokoo, who was a skilful swordsman and a bold enemy, but rather too forward and choleric. He cut at me with such fury at first, I could do little more than parry his blows. Of the state of the combat around me I knew nothing. Kokoo's violence, however, got the better of his skill; he began to strike slower, and give me the opportunity of cutting at him occasionally, though without effect. At length we ceased, as it were by a tacit and mutual consent; and while thus taking breath, I perceived a reinforcement of the enemy approaching. My heart sickened at the sight, and I made up my mind not to perish unrevenged: when I heard the cry of "Canooje!" from our own men. This revived me a little. "We shall still retrieve our fortune," thought I; and raising my sword, I became the aggressor in attacking my antagonist. Kokoo's eyes flashed fire; he defended himself dexterously, and soon converted my attack into a defence, by severing the reins in my left hand, so that my well-trained horse was no longer manageable. I saw my danger, instantly dismounted with a spring towards the rear of Kokoo's animal, and thrust my sword into its flank at the same instant, and all as it were by one effort. Horse and rider both fell; but Kokoo was on his legs before I could touch him, and being both now upon an equality, we hacked away without mercy. I had the advantage in height, and my antagonist in strength. At last he wounded me in the left shoulder by a slanting blow, and at the same moment I succeeded in cutting the cloth that fastened on his turban, just grazing his chin. The turban soon fell off; while, enraged beyond measure, he dealt a blow at me which had settled for ever all our enmity, had not I luckily contrived, more by chance than design, to receive it on my shield, which it penetrated half through, though made of rhinoceros' hide. My next cut, however, made at his bare head, before he could recover his guard, told home. My superior stature gave me more power in striking that part of the body than any other, and my sword entered his uncovered skull with such violence that it snapt in my hand! From Kokoo I had no more to dread; and taking up the weapon that dropped from his unnerved and yet quivering fingers, I was enabled to breathe a moment in comparative safety again.

Nanna, who had been as obstinately engaged as myself with my cousin Mahadeo, was the first object that caught my view. He was standing with his uplifted sword over Mahadeo, who lay stretched on the ground, mortally wounded. The combat still raged around me, save in the immediate spot where Nanna and Mahadeo had fought. Resting on my sword a moment, ere I went to the assistance of my friends on the other part of the ground, I saw old Bhowanee rush past me towards the spot where lay the fainting Mahadeo. She uttered something which I was too distant and too much occupied to hear; but Nanna told me afterwards that she screamed out, "Thou art there— thou art dying! Thou knowest me (which it appeared Mahadeo did, by his horror at her presence). Did I not tell thee I should exult over thee one day? Did not I tell thy father the sod should be thy only crown—the grave thy palace—the dust thy bed of state? Govindah, my son, thou art avenged!" She was the same hag whom Mahadeo described he had encountered amid the terrors of the pit, where he buried the carcoon. The dying man seemed as if he would have answered her, and muttered something which could not be understood; while, having spoken the foregoing words, Bhowanee walked as quickly away as her aged and shrivelled limbs would allow.

But to return to the battle, which still raged with great bitterness. Gunput Rao finding Kokoo had fallen, rushed among the combatants, and incited his party to fresh exertions. Age did not seem to slacken his courage, nor remorse to make terrible to him the prospect of danger. Just at this period, and before victory had declared itself for either party, a strong body of English cavalry came down upon us and, commanding us to desist, made us all prisoners, with Gunput Rao at the head of his party, who seemed mortified to the quick, and bit his lips with rage. Canooje was killed, and Jysing. was badly wounded; I had received several slight scars, besides that which Kokoo inflicted upon me. Nanna escaped unhurt; but almost all our jummahdars were badly wounded, and we had seventy men killed. Our antagonists also suffered severely; Kokoo and Mahadeo, with four of their chieftains, were killed, and sixty men, besides twenty badly wounded. Thus terminated this bloody conflict, so wickedly planned by my cruel uncle, who had no doubt obtained a knowledge, by some secret means, of the result of the arbitration being in Sevaje's favour, and also of my being in existence. What his ultimate object was in thus attacking us I could not conjecture, unless he was actuated by revenge alone; for, if he had succeeded in annihilating our whole force, my father was still safe in Sattarah. Gunput Rao would not, therefore, have been one step nearer a throne; for had Mahadeo survived, his father's conduct, after our destruction, would have operated to prevent his succession. The violation of his word to the English Resident, and his attacking us so close to Sattarah, would have been sufficient to effect this.

The officer in command of the English troops would not be supposed to know which party were the aggressors. We were all obliged to submit to be his prisoners, until he received orders from the Resident how to dispose of us. Gunput Rao marched at the head of the whole party, guarded closely; behind him were Nanna and myself; and then came the other officers indiscriminately. In this order we arrived at the city gates, and were just entering, when Bhowanee crossed our march, in front of Gunput Rao, and pointing at him, set up a hideous scream, between a laugh and a shriek, and mingled among the crowd. My uncle's countenance saw her not unmoved, but he uttered not a syllable. The multitude followed us to the durbar, and the whole city was in the utmost consternation.

It appeared subsequently that Gunput Rao's plans extended beyond the attack of our party. We learned that Sevaje, deeming it proper he should appear at the head of his friends, as Gunput

Rao was to appear with his followers in person, had left Sattarah, and was proceeding to meet us on our road, when he was surrounded by ten men of Gunput's corps, who were taking him off, when the English came up with them, released him, and sent him back to Sattarah with a guard. How the British troops came so opportunely to the spot where we were engaged, I did not at first discover. It appeared afterwards that the Resident, in order to give all the effect possible to the development of the award to the parties and people, and to confer all the dignity he could upon the proclamation of a successor to the musnud, had ordered the troops out accordingly, and they were under arms, waiting the arrival of the hostile parties. The delay in our appearance occasioned a strong suspicion that everything was not correct, and that, on the part of Gunput Rao, there was some foul play. Apprehensions were also entertained for the safety of my father, who had been seen to set out alone to join his soldiers. The Resident was deliberating on what step he should take, when intelligence was brought to the durbar that Gunput Rao's troops had attacked those of Sevaje on their march. A strong detachment of cavalry was instantly sent off, with orders to protect Sevaje, who was on his way to meet his troops, unsuspicious of treachery. The English cavalry soon came up with Sevaje, who had been made prisoner by Gunput's party, freed him, and sent him back to the city, escorted, as before stated, by a guard. The remainder arrived in time to prevent further bloodshed, and to make all on both sides prisoners.

Upon our arrival at the mansion of the English Resident, we were ordered to lay down our arms; and, as soon as it was discovered that we were not the aggressors, we were all released, both officers and men. Gunput Rao was kept a close prisoner, and his men were marched off to a distance in separate parties, so as to disperse them as far from each other as possible; and then, after being warned not to be found again in arms, they were set at liberty. My father was sitting near the Resident when I entered the hall, and on seeing me, rushed into my arms, exclaiming, "My son, my son!" The Resident had heard of me before, and was consequently not unprepared for what he saw.

He congratulated my father upon once more beholding me. Faint from fatigue and loss of blood, I was obliged to retire, and was conducted to my bed. The proclamation of the true successor to the Sattarah musnud was deferred until the following day, that I might not be excluded from a participation in the ceremony.

Gunput Rao, in the meanwhile, was outrageous at being deprived of his liberty. He demanded to be set free; but no attention being paid to his requests, he at last maintained a sullen silence. Unfortunately for him, another cause had arisen to add to the heavy vengeance that hung over his head. A conspiracy was detected at Poona to excite a rebellion, and induce the inhabitants to throw off the British yoke. The conspirators also were discovered to be carrying on certain treasonable practices beyond that city. Several of the ringleaders, among whom were a Brahmin and a goldsmith, were blown from guns, by the orders of the British Resident. Some of the conspirators could not be found. One, however, was known to be Gunput Rao, the aspirant to the Sattarah throne; and his friends at Poona only awaited the tidings of his success at Sattarah, to carry into execution the most violent of their measures. Such was the state of affairs, when an express arrived from Poona, on the day my father was to be proclaimed, ordering the Sattarah Resident to arrest and detain Gunput Rao, until proof could be produced against him. The Resident, upon this, had my uncle brought before him, and openly charged him with malpractices at Poona. Gunput, seeing all was known and concealment useless, boldly acknowledged his share in the plot, and that he was one of the conspirators. He was remanded to prison, and his confession reported to the Resident at Poona; while a separate despatch announced the decision of the arbitrators respecting my father, and the outrages of Gunput, together with his attempt to murder us many years ago. The Resident communicated this part of the despatch to my father, demanding if it were the truth. Sevaje replied he would rather be silent upon his brother's crimes, and most particularly upon those he now alluded to; but he was compelled to acknowledge the report was but too true.   The Resident urging him still further, he related the whole affair.

The royal succession was announced with great pomp.   I was just able to go through the ceremony, seated by my father's side, though the proclamation was not long in reading.   It was read in the Mahratta and English languages; after which discharges of cannon and volleys of musketry resounded on every side.   My father held a durbar the same day, and all the principal natives, with most of the English officers, attended it, and offered my father their congratulations upon this happy event, which had thus put a termination to his long sufferings, and placed him at last upon the musnud.

CHAPTER XXXVI

N the following day, the English Resident requested an audience of my father. He appeared before him with a melancholy countenance, and, after the customary compliments had passed, informed him that the fate of Gunput Rao was decided, he having received instructions to cause him to be blown from a gun within twenty-four hours after the receipt of the order. My father shed tears at hearing the sentence which was to be executed upon his enemy. Still he felt that enemy was his brother, connected with him by the closest ties of consanguinity, which, though the other had outraged, it became him not to forget. He could scarcely repress his grief within proper bounds on perusing the order, and, with a fervency of manner that did honour to his heart, he implored a commutation of the sentence. I seconded the petition ; for, independently of a wish that his life might be preserved on my father's account, I was very anxious to learn from my uncle a full and true account of his crimes. By this means the world must be convinced of the injuries we had individually received, and of our indisputable claims to the throne. I mentioned the different characters in which I had encountered Gunput Rao in the strange vicissitudes of my past life ; and also that he had been the agent of the murder of the shastree, at the instigation of Trimbuckje Danglia, this being a point which I knew the British Government was most desirous of casting some light upon. The Resident conceived that a full and clear elucidation of this affair would be a plea that might possibly preserve my uncle's life ; and in case Gunput would make a full confession, he promised to bring the consideration of the matter before the Poona Resident, upon our petitions in the culprit's favour. There was also this advantage attending the preservation of the criminal's life—namely, that the English would thus become masters of the full extent of the treasonable conspiracy at Poona in all its ramifications, and be thereby the better enabled to crush any minor associations to which it might have given rise, and to which they had no cue that would open a discovery. In the meantime, sentence of death was pronounced upon Gunput. The effect it produced upon his mind baffled all our previous calculations respecting him. We had expected an exhibition of that callous indifference to danger, that disregard to consequences and recklessness of the future which had always seemed to form a part of his character. The very reverse was the fact. Perhaps the constant state of excitement in which he had lived, and the high hopes cherished by ambition, had kept up his fierce spirit through his long career of guilt and wickedness. Baffled at last, and no longer stimulated by the prospect of success, his spirit had given way; he was unable to rally, and sank into despondency. However this might have been, upon his being brought up before the Resident, he seemed overcome with the horror of his situation. Pale and trembling, a cold perspiration crept over his frame; his knees tottered, his lips shook, and the agitation he evinced on hearing his sentence, showed that he was no longer an object of fear. He with difficulty kept himself from falling to the earth; and, when ordered back to his cell, he was obliged to be supported. My father was not present; but I attended the scene, and shall never forget it. The mind that outrages every human obligation, that has smiled at murder, and followed the dreams of a flagitious ambition; the hand that has been dipped in blood, and the heart fertile in the conception of crime, has in this life but one step to sink, but one moral degradation more, and that is, that it should meet the evil it has often inflicted upon others like a coward, when it falls upon itself. Seeing me, the offender meanly supplicated my interference to preserve his wretched life, and I more than ever despised him for it; yet I was not unmoved, particularly on account of my father. I turned away my head, and made the miserable wretch no reply. On retiring, I reflected upon my present situation compared with that of my uncle. The vindictive, relentless Gabbage

Gousla was changed indeed; he, who had so long, so mercilessly persecuted me, now sued me for his life! Alas! what mercy did he ever extend to a victim? Nevertheless, I determined to do all I could to preserve him. I went to my father, whom I found closeted with the Resident, prior to sending off the despatches for Poona, in which our prayers and requests were to be transmitted. As soon as my father saw me, he said, "He will be spared, my son; I feel that he will be saved, if his proud spirit will allow him to make a full confession of all his enormities."

The event showed that my father was correct in his opinion. The English Government took up the subject in the view I had formed, willing to oblige a brother, and to develop secrets which Gunput only could unfold concerning their own affairs. The sentence of death was commuted into imprisonment for life, provided a true and ample confession was forthcoming on the part of the culprit, to commence from the day he quitted Sattarah for the purpose of destroying my father and myself, to that of his imprisonment. My father thanked and embraced the British Resident for his kind intercession, and said, with tears in his eyes, that, had his unhappy brother met the fate to which he had been sentenced, his own remaining years would have been passed in unremitting sorrow. The Resident now put an end to the subject, by saying that he felt confident this act of mercy conceded to his wishes on his ascending the throne, would be an earnest of his future clemency to his subjects, and that he hoped his highness's reign would be a long and prosperous one.

The confession of Gunput Rao was to take place in public, in the event of his accepting the conditions proposed to him. The Resident sent for him under a strong guard, and the hardened sinner approached with the full idea of meeting his sentence. The gun which was to blow him to pieces, and scatter his mangled remains over the earth, was loaded before his eyes. The match was lighted; and slowly, and with trembling knees, he drew near the fatal instrument. His countenance was haggard, his eyes deeply sunk; fear made rigid every feature, and his pale and dry lip told that the fever of his soul had dried up all the moisture from his tongue. On being brought before the Resident, and informed of the conditions of his pardon, he seemed overcome by the unexpected event; and at length, clasping his hands in agony, he exclaimed, "Spare my life, and I will confess every act and deed in which I have participated!" Methought at that moment he appeared more hideous than I had ever before beheld him. He was informed that though his life was spared, he would be imprisoned in the fort of Ahmednugur for the remainder of his days. He bowed very low, even to the earth, and was then taken back to recover himself, having been informed of the day he was to make his confession, and unfold the dreadful catalogue of his enormities.

By this time I was become very impatient to hear about Sagoonah, and to clasp to my heart one who had shared with me in many of the vicissitudes of my adverse days. I despatched a suitable escort to Parwell to meet her, having first sent a message to Bombay to apprise her of the joyful news of my unexpected elevation, and to express my anxiety that she should participate with me in the prosperity that attended my steps. She arrived at the time I expected her. Our meeting was too full for description; it was steeped in a joy that can be felt but not described—it was a sort of ecstasy, which is too like delirium for sober language to paint. Sagoonah was struck with no less wonder than pleasure, to find that I was the youth to whom she had been betrothed, and that her spouse was a prince. Women love show and splendour, and she was almost bewildered with delight. She put a thousand and a thousand questions to me; her eyes, brilliant and deathly dark, sparkled, to think she might be ere long a queen! Never before in Hindustan did man and wife meet as we met. Now were all our troubles and escapes rewarded, and become but subjects to jest upon, or beguile an idle hour in relating! In the meanwhile, our fondness increased every hour; and I should occupy time and space to little purpose, were I to attempt a relation of all we said and promised each other. My father was highly gratified by the beauty of Sagoonah, and not less by her modest good sense. He gave his blessing, over and over repeated; and an early day was appointed for our nuptials, provided the Brahmins gave their consent, as they are so tenacious of their rights of nominating the time of all weddings.

While my father and I were awaiting the hour to proceed to the durbar, and hear the confession of my uncle, I could not help asking him how the arbitrators on the other side came to decide so suddenly in our favour. He informed me, that, finding Sagoonah's uncle to be one of them, and that he adhered to Gunput Rao solely in the hope of marrying his niece to Mahadeo, it was quietly hinted to him that I was yet alive, and the betrothed spouse of Sagoonah. The banker finding this to be really the case, like a genuine trader, thought it more to his advantage to affect a show of his sense of justice, and serve his views and credit with the public at the same time. He did not, indeed, care which married his niece, provided a prince was secured, and he therefore veered round to the party likely to be strongest. Thus the other arbitrator of Gunput was left in a minority at once. The solitary arbitrator, not wishing to stand alone, or side with a falling cause, signed his name to the award, without remark or observation.

Sagoonah was introduced to her rich uncle, who made her a number of complimentary speeches on her approaching nuptials. I left her at his house, the durbar being assembled to hear Gunput Rao relate his confession; and I promised Sagoonah to give her every particular as soon as it was concluded. The Resident, many officers, men of rank, sirdars, jagheerdars, Brahmins, and pundits, were present, assembled around my father. The latter entered, and I followed, both of us dressed in a rich suit of kinkob, with a string of pearls, and a diamond sprig in our turbans. We were preceded by chobdars and mace-bearers, who vociferated our praises in the usual strain on entering the court; and my father took his seat on a velvet cushion, embroidered with gold. I sat at my father's right hand, and the Resident on his left. When every one was seated, the culprit was sent for. In a few minutes, the door of a side-passage unfolded. There was a stillness in the durbar, as if the world were dead. Every eye was fixed on the culprit, who seemed confused at first by the number of the auditory, but soon recovered a little, and took the place assigned him, with a guard on each hand. His lip was wan, and his cheek withered by anxiety, age, and apprehension. He began the following confession, with a tremulous voice but strong accent, at times hurriedly, and then with great deliberation, as if he were fearful of his recollection failing him :—

"In what I am going to say, my interest cannot lie on the side of truth or falsehood ; for enough is already known of my actions to prevent my concealing any part of the scenes in which I have been an actor from motives of shame ; the worst, perhaps, is already known. I shall state the simple truth ; the fear of the world's anathema cannot affect me in a dungeon ; and the good appearance I once endeavoured to keep up, and the holy character I attempted to sustain, I even then used as subterfuges or cloaks for my deep-laid designs. I had flung everything on the hazard of a die, and fortune has betrayed me. I now, therefore, may well submit to my destiny ; and, where a knowledge of my life and actions may be useful to others, unhesitatingly reveal the secrets of my past years ; not that the advantage of others concerns me, but that, by so doing, I purchase life, which, in its very dregs, is dear to me, and the only thing that I can say I feel an attachment for in the world, now that my dreams of ambition are ended. Vain dreams, that dazzle to destroy ! If I have appeared overcome, subdued, humbled, it is because I feel I am worse than nothing ; that even hope has forsaken me, that the preservation of my life is all I have now to obtain, and that it only remains for me to spend my future hours in solitude and chains. Still, time may reconcile me to these. But, to die ! no, I could not die !

"They told me that in my infancy I was considered of a wayward and obstinate disposition ; yet I showed an aspiring temper. It may or may not have been so ; education and intercourse with the world change our natural dispositions. It suffices, that on my arrival at man's estate, my ambition and haughty conduct involved me in many disputes. One of these I will relate :—My estate lay close to that of my brother Sevaje ; and, being always anxious to increase my own property by any means, I claimed a piece of land belonging to my brother as my own. Sevaje refused to give it up to me. The cause was tried by a punchayet; and, by address and bribery, I got a decree in my favour, and secured the land. It was not long after this that my wife brought me a son, whom I named Mahadeo; but she died in childbed. I was exceedingly grieved at her loss, and had scarcely recovered a little from the affliction into which it had plunged me, when I found that my son was carried off from his nurse, and could not be found. He was, however, soon after brought to me, having been picked up floating down a neighbouring river in a basket. The person who found him was a young man named Govindah. Judging of my brother's disposition by my own, I readily imagined that this was his act, committed in revenge for the loss of his property. I therefore meditated a deadly retaliation, and consulted a friend how I should proceed to effect it. This friend it was who first conceived the idea of throwing a stigma on my brother's birth, and thus enabling me to lay claim to the right of the eldest son; by which means, should the deposed rajah be reinstated, I might, on his death, succeed to the musnud. Hence sprung all my crimes. This little seed of ambition, sown in a soil so congenial to its growth, rapidly sprung up like a rank weed, and I fed upon it to intoxication. Years passed away, and notwithstanding unceasing attempts to fix a blot on my brother's birth in such a way that it should be fatal to his rights, I could not succeed; he was still considered the eldest son, and everywhere respected and beloved. It happened that my brother had a son as well as myself, though considerably younger than mine, named Jeoba. The child was seldom seen by any one; and, deadly enemies as my brother and myself were, it was not likely he would ever come into my sight, unless by some extraordinary accident. My friend and adviser, whom I have before mentioned, informed me one day that my brother had sought the hand of a girl named Sagoonah for his son Jeoba. This information greatly enraged me; for, though the father of Sagoonah was poor, he ranked high in his caste, being no less than a Nagga Brahmin, and much respected by the people. Before my brother's proposals were accepted, I presented myself to the father of Sagoonah, and made an offer in behalf of my son Mahadeo. The father immediately mentioned to me the proposals made by my elder brother, and said that at present he could give neither of us an answer, as he must have time to consider well so important an affair. This reply did not entirely deprive me of all hope, and I remained quiet, determined that the father of the girl should not have any rational grounds for objecting to my alliance. I was, however, disappointed; the girl was betrothed to my nephew, instead of my son. This stung me deeply, my pride was wounded, and I vowed deep unrelenting vengeance on both father and son. I swore I would crush them, sweep them from the earth, annihilate them! Sevaje, knowing well my disposition, determined to quit his estate, and retire to Chandore, having occasion to visit Indore first, upon business. I obtained intelligence of his design; I knew he must pass through a jungle; and there, with two hired ruffians, I waylaid him and his child. The latter I wrested from him, and gave to my followers, desiring them to carry my orders into effect at a little distance; and, as soon as they had turned their backs, I stabbed my brother, who instantly fell. I was going to repeat my blow as he lay on the ground, to make assurance doubly sure; but, hearing a noise, as of persons approaching, I ran away, I knew not whither. In my path I saw something white, which I found to be the boy, whom my followers, probably also in alarm, had flung down, but had not destroyed, as I intended they should have done. I snatched up the child, intending to have murdered it in a deep ravine that lay at no great distance, when I heard voices and footsteps very near. I felt certain that my brother's body had been seen, and I was pursued. I ran, to get clear of my pursuers, without knowing whither, and found myself, at last, close to some bullocks, apparently harnessed for marching, though not a single attendant was in sight. My pursuers gained upon me; and to be caught with the child in my arms would be to make detection certain, while it also impeded my flight. I had scarcely time to throw the boy among the bullocks, which were standing together in a knot, there being no hedge, ditch, or copse near, where I could leave him, and recover him, so as to make sure of his death. The pursuit still continued, until I entered a village, where there was a well, a little out of the road. Some bushes hid me from sight a moment, and I went down the steps, and stood upon the lowest. My pursuers passed by into the village, and thus missed me.

"I remained in the well the best part of the night. All was quiet; and, as I knew if I delayed until the dawn I should be found by the people who would come for water, and thus the villagers suspect me, I mounted the steps before day, and, once more in the fields, retraced my road, thinking I might recover my nephew; but I either mistook the path, or, if I did not, I could discover no bullocks, nor even marks of their feet, the way I travelled. I was thus foiled in respect to the child, whom I long considered dead, or brought up in some lowly cabin, and ignorant of his parentage, and that, therefore, I should hear nothing more of him. My surprise was great, a few days ago, to find, by means of an intercepted letter, that he was in existence, and well acquainted with his parentage. I was still more struck, when I recollected how frequently I had fallen in with him, whilst wandering about as a gossein, in years past, and how I have persecuted and lain in wait for him. My reasons for having done this will be seen in the sequel of my confession; at present I will continue my history, from the time of my brother's attempted murder, and the loss of his son.

"I now began to fear that inquiry would be made into the sudden disappearance of my brother and his child. I knew I should be immediately suspected as an accessary to it; and therefore caused myself to be carried into Sattarah in a litter, having previously cut myself in several places, and having my garments stained with blood. I gave out that my brother and myself had been attacked by ruffians, that I had fortunately escaped, but that I feared my brother and his son had fallen by their hands. I had taken the precaution to forge a letter as from my brother, inviting me to join him at Indore; so that I fancied no suspicion attached itself to me. The father of Sagoonah, however, was by no means satisfied with my statement of this affair, and openly declared he would investigate the matter most strictly. I was in a great fury at this conduct upon his part; and I determined, as I had gone so far in the case of my brother, I would not hesitate to take my revenge upon him. My guilt in this case was never even suspected, so adroitly was the affair managed: I removed him out of the way by poison. His wife became a suttee, and I saw her ascend the funeral-pile of her husband; I saw the fire envelop her; and I heard her shriek of death pierce through the red fierce flames with inward delight, when I reflected that no one thing now stood in my way to thwart my projects!"—[Here the auditory of Gunput uttered a groan of horror, but no one spoke. He paused a moment, and resumed his narrative.]

"The orphan, Sagoonah, was left unprotected; but some charitable persons conveyed her to her aunt, at Poona. She had an uncle; but, as he resided in Marwar, and had never seen her, and she, perhaps, had never heard his name, the roof of her aunt was her only secure refuge. This aunt was a very poor widow; and, by a singular coincidence of circumstances, I was very nigh staining my hands with the blood of her niece, though at the time little suspecting who my victim was. By an event no less strange, the girl was rescued and protected by the very man to whom she was betrothed—by Jeoba, my nephew, whom I had often met under the name of Pandurang Hàrì. But to return to the regular chain of my history. After the funeral of Sagoonah's father and his wife, I saw no chance of our family succeeding to the musnud of Sattarah, and I repented deeply the supposed murder of my brother; for that he was murdered I had not the smallest doubt. Being looked upon with an evil eye by many persons in society, I pretended to bewail my brother's loss, and gave out my intention of becoming a sunyasse, and retiring from the world. I very soon afterwards carried my intention into effect, having farmed out my estate, which, however, the Government sequestrated, as soon as my absence and the course of life I had adopted were known. This act reduced me to real poverty, and I was also under the necessity of becoming a gossein. I caused my son Mahadeo to enter into the same mode of life, and we were regularily consecrated by a religious recluse, and duly commenced our wandering state of mendicity. Meeting with a set of gosseins, we joined them, and, conducting us to a cavern, they produced their ganga and opium, and began to smoke. The pipe was offered to me, and I inhaled the somniferous vapour until my head became affected, and I fell down insensible. On awaking, I found my son had departed ; nor could I obtain any tidings of him for many years, though I wandered everywhere in search of him. The prayers of the Peeshwa for a son being heard, he gave a grand feast to all the gosseins, from every part of India, who would come. I readily attended, and there first saw his confidant, Trimbuckje Danglia. He was then in the zenith of favour, and homage was paid to him by all present ; but whether there was more reverence in my manner of saluting him, or he discovered in my eyes a beam of wickedness that corresponded with his own, and a talent that might be useful to him, I cannot tell ; it suffices that, after the feast was over, he sent for me. I waited upon him, and he demanded my name. I told him it was Gabbage Gossein —this was the name by which I went, after taking up a religious habit ; but I was commonly styled Gabbage Gousla, from my supposed habits of avarice. Trimbuckje told me he was in want of a *gùrù*, a religious instructor, to his household, and made me the offer of the situation, which I gladly accepted, and took up my residence in Poona.

"I soon discovered that Trimbuckje was very careless on the score of his religious duties ; like many statesmen who keep up an hypocritical show of regard for their established creeds, but in reality are of no religion at all. It was an excellent plea, however, for my being closeted with him frequently, and thus I became a ready sharer with him in all his schemes of villainy. There being a great meeting of our tribe at Indore, I procured leave of absence, and proceeded thither. On returning, I entered the hut of a recluse whom I met at Indore, and who promised to join me the following day. In his hovel I smoked ganga, and fell into a deep sleep, from which I was awakened by feeling water flung in my face. When I came to myself, I found that a traveller had discovered the hut to be on fire, had removed me from danger, and extinguished the flames. This traveller appeared to me a young man without money or employment, and apparently of such a pliable disposition, that I conceived, with a little tutoring, he might become very useful to me at Poona. I persuaded him to turn gossein on the spot, and to follow me. His name was Pandurang Hàrì. In stripping him to besmear him with dirt and ashes, I discovered he had a long bag of rupees tied round his waist. I made no observation to him on the discovery, but secretly determined the money should be mine by some means or other. We sallied forth on the road to Poona, not now thinking it worth my while to await longer the owner of the hut, who had delayed beyond the time fixed for his return. On the road, I instructed my pupil in the art of raising money by begging. One method of extortion is by letting the blood flow from some part of the body, or by threatening to use a dagger; the person so threatened, knowing that ill fortune is the consequence if he causes the blood of a gossein to flow, is instantly alarmed, and pays his mite. Thus we impose on the public credulity, and thus the greater part of the religious mendicants gain their profits. Not in the present instance desirous to wound myself, I proposed to my pupil that he should undertake the ceremony, whilst I collected the money. Pandurang Gossein was not the soft fellow I expected to find him; for, on desiring him to cut, he drew the knife across my arm instead of his own. I raised a mob directly, and accused him of an attempt to murder me for my share of the money which he carried. His rupees were thereupon taken from him, and he was ordered to quit Poona. Having secured his cash, I had made the best bargain, and felt glad the fellow was gone, as he was much too sharp for an instrument such as I then wished.

"I now joined Trimbuckje again, and remained in his service some time; when a difference occurring between us, I quitted him and went to Bombay, where I gave out I was deeply skilled in magic. I had not resided long in that city when my services were required to conjure to death an Englishman in office there. The person who brought me the written proposals was a peon in the police office, who, to my great wonder and amazement, I discovered was my old acquaintance, Pandurang Hàrì. I owed him a grudge, and when the affair was discovered, which from the incautious conduct of the parties it was very soon, I did not hesitate to implicate him in the plot, and he was imprisoned in consequence. I was put into a room out of the common gaol, from which I contrived to escape in the night by bribing a police peon who had charge of the chowkee.

"I felt that Bombay was no place for me to remain in one hour longer, and I got clear off to Poona again. There interest induced me to seek a reconciliation with Trimbuckje. He became friendly again, and placed me once more upon his establishment. Nothing of moment occurred, until one day when the Peeshwa went to the Motee-baugh, when it appeared that he saw a pretty girl at a window. He became desirous of obtaining her for his harem, and Trimbuckje was despatched for the purpose of making her an offer to that effect, on the part of the Peeshwa. On getting a view of her features, Trimbuckje became enamoured as well as his master, and neglected his employer's interest for his own, proposing to take her under his protection. The girl refused indignantly, and threatened to make the Peeshwa acquainted with the way in which she had been treated. Had she done this, Trimbuckje must have been ruined; I was therefore employed to silence the girl effectually, and I engaged three gosseins of infamous character to assist me. We enticed her to a lonely house in the suburbs, where we prepared to stab her; but none had the heart to do it, and my companions seemed anxious to save her. Upon this I rushed into the apartment where we had secured the unfortunate girl, and grasped her throat with a violence I considered sufficient to occasion her death by suffocation. I then opened the window and we threw her out, purposing to go round and convey the body to the river, and there fling it in. Before we could get to the back of the house where the window looked, we were necessitated to make a circuit of some distance; and on our arrival under the window, what was our surprise to discover the body gone! We were now all of us terribly alarmed. We lit torches, and proceeded to hunt about, even to the bank of the river. We had distinctly heard a splash, and concluded that the girl, having recovered enough to get upon her legs, and run she knew not whither from her fright, had made off unconsciously in the direction of the water and fallen in, or plunged in upon seeing us in pursuit. Still we were in doubt whether she was dead or not. Upon returning to Trimbuckje, I told him his orders had been executed, and he liberally rewarded me, and hoped he should hear no more of the murder. On the following day, to my great dismay, the aunt of the supposed murdered girl, by some unaccountable mode, obtained admission to the palace, and to the Peeshwa's presence, to whom she related the circumstances of the death of her niece as far as she knew. The Peeshwa, finding the murdered girl to be no other than she whom he was desirous of placing in his harem, was enraged beyond measure, and pledged himself to discover the murderer of the old woman's niece. Trimbuckje was in great alarm, and I was in no less fright, and we were considering how we could best ward off the blow that seemed impending over us, when a stranger desired to be admitted to him. I was not then present, but what passed I knew from Trimbuckje. The stranger offered to criminate Habeshee Kotwall, a decided enemy of Trimbuckje's. He appeared to know every particular of the murder, and it must have been he, whoever he was, that carried off the body from beneath the window. I did not understand that he stated the girl had escaped death, by which I concluded she was really no more. I never saw the stranger until the day when, in the character of a magician, he entered the palace to accuse the Habeshee to the Peeshwa. I then determined to get a glance at his face, and going round by a private passage which led to the Peeshwa's closet, where the magician was seated, what was my surprise to discover, under all his disguises of paint and dress, my old acquaintance Pandurang Hàrì! I was so struck I could scarcely tear myself away, and I was, I believe, nearly discovered by the Peeshwa. Pandurang in this affair acted entirely on our side, and in our favour; it was not therefore my interest to thwart him. I awaited the result of his plans, which ended in the conviction and death of the Habeshee. Well, I thought to myself, this is a very clever fellow. How much was I mistaken in thinking otherwise of him! There remained some mystery about the affair to be fathomed still, and I determined to watch the steps of Pandurang very closely. Observing Pandurang frequently gain access to Trimbuckje, I caused a man named Suntoo to watch his steps, and report to me his place of abode, the houses he visited, and the individuals who resided with him. He obeyed my orders with great exactness, and one day informed me that he had watched Pandurang into the house of a poor cultivator at a small village near Poona, and also that two strange women were living in the same house. I instantly bade him conduct me to the place, and watching my opportunity, I appeared one day in presence of the women during the absence of Pandurang. Not having seen the features of the girl on the night of the intended murder, I could not be positive she was the person who escaped from me ; but having seen the aunt crying before the palace gates, I instantly recognised her. Appearing before them as a mendicant, I dared not ask any questions ; but, being presented with a handful of rice, I departed. On my return to Poona, I made the most minute inquiries respecting the females who lately resided near the Motee-baugh, and to my astonishment learned that the girl had come from Sattarah, and that the aunt was a poor widow woman who had resided for a long time in Poona. Could this girl be Sagoonah? If it were she, I rejoiced in her miraculous escape, for I had deeds of horror enough on my conscience, without adding the weight of the child's murder to that of the father !

"Anxious to know how affairs went on at Sattarah, I left Poona, and journeyed until I came to a large tank, in which I bathed and refreshed myself. The shades of evening now gathered fast around me, and, fully aware that I could not reach Sattarah that night, I began to look around for some place of shelter. I found a lonely cottage with a light in the window, and being attired in the habit of a gossein, I did not hesitate to request a lodging for the night. An old woman opened the door, and what was my surprise on recognising in her person the mother of a boy who saved my son from a watery grave ! I addressed her, saying I had seen her face before. 'Indeed!' she demanded ; 'where?' 'Near Sattarah,' I replied.

She looked, but did not recollect my features. I inquired after her son Govindah. She answered in a mournful voice, 'He is dead!' 'And so young!' I observed; 'surely disease could not so roughly handle him?' 'A villain handled him!' she replied. 'What, murdered!' I exclaimed, 'who could have had an enmity towards him? She answered, 'The wretch whose life he saved from the waters—he killed his preserver.' 'Speak! who mean you?' I asked. 'Your son, Mahadeo—your son,' said she, looking me full in the face; 'and art thou, indeed, Gunput Rao?—thou hast a son as great a fiend as thyself!' 'Dost thou know where my son is?' I eagerly questioned her. 'Canst thou tell me where he is to be found; years have passed since I beheld his face?' 'Question me not further about your miserable child; he lives, no doubt—where, or how, I neither know nor care,' she answered. I again urged her to explain to me where I should find my son, and expressed my belief he could not have committed such a deed. She told me to speak no more to her on the subject, for her brain maddened at the recollection of it; and she bade me quit the place before sunrise. Finding it impossible to learn anything more from her respecting him, I retired to my apartment, and in the morning pursued my journey to Sattarah. The distance being short, I arrived about noon. While in the city, I found that Sagoonah's uncle had returned from Marwar; but that he intended to go thither again in about a year's time with an immense capital. I contrived to get introduced to his notice, and found him a man of haughty and aspiring ideas; but before I mentioned to him my knowledge of his niece, I made more inquiries in the town concerning her, and the result was a firm conviction on my part that the girl I had seen at the cultivator's cottage, under the protection of Pandurang Hàrì, was the very same to whom my nephew had been betrothed. The report that the rajah would be reinstated on the musnud happened about this time, and kindled in my ambitious mind the desire of securing myself succession, though how to effect this object did not then appear by any means clear to me.

"My visits to Sagoonah's uncle at length became very frequent, and I at last ventured to mention him his niece, advising him to take her home and aggrandise himself and her by marriage. He assured me he was perfectly willing so to do, if he could find her out; but all attempts for that purpose had hitherto proved abortive. 'Could I but find her,' he said, 'some rich jagheerdar would doubtless seek her hand in marriage, on account of my wealth, and the purity of her caste.' I told him he might soar higher than a jagheerdar, for a prince might be proud of such a wife. 'Princes,' he observed, 'are not so plentiful, and it seems the relatives of the present rajah are all dead.' I told him not all, for the nearest of them stood before him. He inquired if I was Sevaje. I told him no—*he* was no more; but that I was his brother, Gunput Rao, and claimed the right of succession to the throne. The banker then asked if my son lived also. I told him he did, and, with his consent, should have his niece in marriage. He was much surprised at what I related, but told me I talked as if his niece were close at hand, demanding if I knew anything of her. I told him I did, and that I wished I had as accurate information respecting my son; but I pledged myself to find him out and deliver his niece to him, provided he pledged himself to compel her to marry my son, and aid us with his wealth in attempting the sovereignty. The banker, who looked no higher than a landholder for his niece, instantly agreed to my proposal, and promised his niece and his coffers should be at my command. He bade me first haste and secure his niece, giving me full authority to do so, and to bring her to Sattarah. After some other topics were touched upon, I took my leave and hastened to Poona, imagining I could pounce upon Sagoonah without much trouble. But in this I was mistaken; for Pandurang Hàrì, having obtained a situation under Trimbuckje Danglia in Kandeish, had left the cultivator's cottage, and proceeded to his station. I despatched a shrewd gossein after them; but, although he actually had them at one time in his power, he let them slip through his fingers, having been wounded by a bullock-driver, with whom he found it necessary to form an acquaintance. I employed divers stratagems to make Sagoonah quit her home in Kandeish; but, being now on her guard, she never ventured out.

"Trimbuckje requiring my presence about this time, I could not proceed to Kandeish, but was obliged to depend upon my hirelings. The business upon which I went related to the murder of a shastree, who was on his way from Guzerat to the court at Poona. The particulars of this murder I can state when required; I shall only now say that he was murdered; Trimbuckje was suspected, and his person demanded by the British Government. In this predicament he consulted me, and I advised a quiet submission to his fate; and that, as his life was not to be forfeited, there was every hope he might escape from his prison again. I recommended him to select the most cunning of his followers, amongst whom was Pandurang Hàri, whose name I mentioned, being anxious for his removal from Kandeish, to enable me to succeed in my plans relative to Sagoonah. Trimbuckje also appeared anxious that Pandurang should accompany him; and his anxiety was so evident, that I could not help mentioning it to several of his most confidential attendants. I learned, to my mortification, that Suntoo, whom I had first set as a spy at the cultivator's cottage, had recognised the parties, and made Trimbuckje acquainted with the existence of Sagoonah. Hence his anxiety to deprive her of the protection of Pandurang Hàri. I now saw plainly I should have to contend with Trimbuckje Danglia, and oppose my cunning to his force. During my last interview with him before his apprehension, he was pettish and quarrelsome, and I was haughty and insolent, which I then felt I might be, he being a fallen star. He resented my conduct, bade me depart and never appear before him again; and I withdrew in a rage. Pandurang Hàri arrived, and set off with Trimbuckje to Thannah; and, as soon as they were gone, I proceeded to Kandeish, where I found Trimbuckje's power had outdone my craftiness. Sagoonah and her aunt had been forcibly seized and conveyed to Asseerghur, the killehdar of which place was a sworn friend of Trimbuckje's.

"Nothing daunted in my determination, I returned to Poona, and once more journeyed to Sattarah, to report to the banker my failure. I said, 'Neither your niece nor my son are yet found; I hope, nevertheless, to recover the former very soon, and then deliver her into your hands.' The banker expressed his regret at the circumstance, saying he left it all to me, as he was about taking a second journey to Marwar; and, on his return, he should hope to find both the young man and woman awaiting his arrival at Sattarah. Pleased at finding the banker still confided in me, I promised to spare no pains to do as he desired during his absence, particularly as his niece was running up and down the country under the protection of a vagabond.

"I found it impracticable to get the women out of the fort, and therefore awaited very impatiently the deliverance of Trimbuckje out of the hands of the English, and his re-appearance in the Deccan; for I never doubted but he would contrive, in some way or another, to effect his escape. In this idea I found I was ultimately correct. Trimbuckje, requiring the help of a friend, sent a messenger to me, desiring I would procure horses to be ready near the Thannah river. Not understanding the message delivered by the men sent, I journeyed to Thannah as a gossein, where I soon found out the intentions of the captive. I determined to aid him, that I might once more get admitted to his houschold, by which means alone I should be able to fathom his intentions towards the women at Asseerghur. I was the more ready to aid in his escape, from finding that he only was to escape, and that his followers would remain prisoners; so that Pandurang Hàrì could not interfere with my future views respecting the females. Trimbuckje escaped, and fled to Kandeish. The Peeshwa corresponded with him; but Trimbuckje's day of glory was over, and I found it a useless loss of time to dangle after him, and mingle in his train; yet hardly knowing what step to take, I stayed with him until the sudden arrival of Pandurang Hàrì and one of his servants, who had been left behind at Thannah. The name of the servant was Nanna. He informed us of their having been seized by a horde of Pindarees, and of the events which occurred in a ruined fortress. The fellow related the story of a Musselman, named Fuzl Khan, which amused Trimbuckje highly. Finding this, he related the story of another of the band, who was a Hindoo, and, to my astonishment, proved to be my own son, Mahadeo, of whom

Nanna could give me no account, after his escape from the
Pindarees himself. Pandurang Hàrì was coldly received by
Trimbuckje, who viewed him as a rival with Sagoonah, and
wished him at the bottom of the sea. Not getting any reward
for planning Trimbuckje's escape, as was promised him, he quitted
us, and I have reason to believe, went to Kandeish, where he had
left Sagoonah and her aunt. Trimbuckje said, when he quitted,
'He will find what he deserves at the village.' I therefore felt
convinced orders had been sent there to put him out of the way,
if he appeared again. I felt great pleasure at this, because, in
that case, an obstacle in my way would thus be removed.

"I was so fully assured of the necessity of getting rid of this
Pandurang Hàrì, that I determined to have him assassinated myself, should Trimbuckje fail to do it. I was meditating how I
should best carry my intentions into effect, when Nanna, boiling
with rage, informed me that Trimbuckje, instead of rewarding
him, as he promised, for aiding in his escape, had repaid his
services by intriguing with his wife, and that he determined to be
revenged upon him at any risk. Anxious to secure such a tool
to aid me in my purposes, and to follow up my plans respecting
Pandurang Hàrì, I affected to enter into his feelings, and so blew
up yet higher the feeling of revenge that still lurked in his bosom,
until he swore to murder Trimbuckje, by stabbing him when
alone. I did not imagine he would succeed; but, whether he
succeeded or not, the attempt would answer every end I had in
view. He failed, and came to me for protection. I offered to
save him if he would swear to serve me. He dared not refuse
my terms; but consented, at my instigation, to murder Pandurang Hàrì. For this end I concealed him for the time, and
then sent Nanna, for the purpose of hunting him down, to Trimbuckje's village, in Kandeish, whither I knew he had proceeded.
At the village, I informed Nanna he would see two active agents
of mine—men of singular courage, and with hands that had much
blood on them—one a robber by profession; the other, named
Kokoo, not at all his inferior, having a head to contrive, and a
hand to execute any mischief. To these men I had intrusted
the rescue of Sagoonah and her aunt from the power of Trim-

buckje, and felt almost certain of success, anxiously awaiting intelligence from them. Trimbuckje Danglia's importance being gone, his friends and train fell off from him one by one, **and** by and by he absconded, no one knew whither. Not hearing from Kokoo or Nanna, I determined upon proceeding towards **the fort** of Asseerghur myself; in passing which, I found **the** women **were no** longer there, having made their escape. In going through a deep **glen,** where there was but **one small hut, being** thirsty, **I demanded** admittance. The door was opened by an old man, in whom I recognised my brother Sevaje, whom I believed dead long ago. I mentioned my name, received what I requested to drink, and departed. At **times I had wished the** blood **of a** brother lay not upon my head; now, when I saw him alive, a formidable obstacle to my views, I wished him out of the way most heartily; and hastening to Kokoo and his companions, I unfolded all my plans to them, and made them swear to murder the inhabitant of the glen as soon as possible. I thus buoyed myself up with the hope **of** learning that **Pandurang** had **been** despatched, the women secured, and my brother, the goatherd of the glen, as he was styled, really destroyed. On my arrival at Asseerghur, Nanna crossed my path, and we agreed to meet under the fort. Instead of hearing from him that my plans had succeeded, I was mortified at discovering that Pandurang Hàrì had not been found, that the women had escaped, and that Kokoo and his companions had been shut up in a cell, and left **to starve** to death. My anger knew no bounds, and it was some time before I could understand that Kokoo was living, but that his companion **was a** corpse. I immediately set out with Nanna **to the place** where this affair took place, because Kokoo **was** waiting **my** arrival there. **On** entering a dark cavern, Nanna led me **to a** small chamber, where he told me the body of Kokoo's companion lay, and that we should find him in another corner of the cavern. I entered, and, to my amazement, found two dead bodies instead of one. It struck **me** Nanna was deceiving me, and I looked upon him as a traitor. **Instead of** finding Kokoo, we discovered a sick man, a stranger. Upon this my rage rose to **madness;**

and, drawing my dagger, I struck Nanna with it in the side, and left him for dead. I now retraced my steps to Asseerghur by the road that led through the glen ; and, on looking into the hut of Sevaje, I found Kokoo there, the door open, and my brother, the goatherd, fled. Kokoo was overcome with weakness after his incarceration, and was resting against the wall. It appeared that, owing to Kokoo's want of caution, they had enlisted Pandurang Hâri himself to assist them ; who, having heard all their designs, had fastened them into the cell at the cavern, and left them to perish.

" Kokoo was in a desperate rage to be so duped, and he swore vengeance, while I encouraged his relentless humour. We proceeded back towards Asseerghur, where I intended to give Kokoo necessary rest. On our way we met with a gossein, whom I had despatched to trace out Sagoonah. He gave me information of her having been seen by a bullock-driver whom he knew, and that they were gone towards Guzerat. The bullock-driver stated that he might have brought them to Asseerghur, but for his employer, who, when he stopped them, released them, and suffered them to go their own way. This was two months prior to that day. Kokoo soon after volunteered his services to proceed after them to Guzerat with the gossein who hoped to overtake the bullock-driver in his return to Nasik. The latter was able to identify the persons of the women. I then bent my own steps towards Poona. The war was at its height; and, as the English had possession of Poona, the probability of the Sattarah rajah being reinstated became greater, and my hopes of success proportionably strengthened. On my arrival at Poona, I connected myself with several dissatisfied persons, and soon found myself involved in treasonable conspiracies. My amazement may be conceived, when the conspirators introduced me, at one of our meetings, to a young man, who, they informed me, was the successor to the Sattarah throne, and one of the most active among them. This young man proved to be my unhappy long-lost son, Mahadeo, who was equally surprised at meeting his father again. When the conspirators were made acquainted with our affinity, they became more sanguine than ever; for, on my succeeding to the throne, through the aid of the English, my first act was to have been to their injury, by an attempt to retake **Poona.** The particulars of this conspiracy are here." [Gunput now handed them in writing to the Resident.] "While we were arranging the proceedings in this conspiracy, Kokoo returned from Guzerat, informing me that he had been disappointed at Broach, by the seizure of two strange persons, instead of Pandurang and Sagoonah. He had left spies over them, being obliged to remove from the neighbourhood himself, from motives of personal safety. These spies followed a man and woman to Sattarah, and we secured them; but found we had obtained a strange female, of whom we knew nothing, and a man, whom I ordered to be imprisoned, until we could get from him some account of the motions of Pandurang Hàrì and Sagoonah.

"I had heard my brother Sevaje was in Sattarah, but where concealed I could never discover. It was reported he had assembled near six hundred men, determined to fight for the crown on the death of the rajah. I called a council, and it was resolved that we should also increase our numbers; for the pay of whom I proposed that I should, by some sacrifices, obtain the arrears of my estate-rents and of my brother's, from the time of their sequestration. We discovered that my brother received his money from Shewdhut Wanee, of Indore, and that the best method to cut off these resources was to despatch Wanee out of the way. This Kokoo did with his own hand. My brother's partisans, however, attacked my treasure, and deprived me of a great portion of it. I thus began to despair of weakening his forces, and at length acceded to his proposal of the trial by punchayet of our respective rights, not for an instant supposing he was aware of his son's existence. Finding matters, in this respect, the reverse of what I expected, I repented the giving my assent to this mode of settling our claims, and despatched a party to cut off Naroba, on his way to the arbitration. By some means my plan miscarried. Naroba was a shrewd and keen fellow, and I dreaded his influence and penetration. I had considered Sagoonah's uncle my staunch friend; but, to my suprise, he all at once became cool, and seemed to have no longer any zeal in my behalf. The decree, too, I found, before it was promulgated, was not in my favour. My troops also had captured despatches from Naroba to the commander in Sevaje's stronghold, and with them a letter to Pandurang Hàrì. What was my astonishment at discovering, from its contents, and the congratulations mingled up in it, that he was the Prince Jeoba, the son of Sevaje, and the successor to the musnud! 'Now,' thought I, 'the sovereignty is gone from me for ever! but, if I cannot mount the throne, neither Sevaje nor his son shall. I will strike a blow to effect this, if we all perish together!'

"I summoned Kokoo, and we arranged that, when our respective corps met to enter the city, we should charge Sevaje's troops. Understanding my brother would proceed to join his men in person, we waylaid him, and got him into our power. How he was rescued I need not tell. From the conflict I alone survive; my son, Kokoo, all my principal confidants, have fallen! I now stand alone. My dream of ill-starred ambition has vanished! That which cost me so much toil, anxiety, and crime, is as if it had never been! No longer excited by criminal hope, or supported by the perpetual attraction to the great object of my wishes, my spirit has fallen back upon itself. It is indifferent to any state of things with life, and henceforth it must be occupied by corroding reflections, and that bitter anguish of the soul which scorches, but consumes not—which tortures, but will not destroy! I bow, therefore, to that fate which it cannot be said I have left one effort untried to thwart; and, when I enter the dungeon where the remnant of my wretched hours is to be passed, I shall reflect that I am but another victim added to those who have been sacrificed in the pursuit of the objects of a criminal and too daring ambition!"

Such was the miserable history of my uncle's guilty career. The whole of it was reduced to writing, and the part which he gave in added to it, containing the details of the murder of the shastree, and the conspiracy at Poona. When the durbar broke up, I hastened to Sagoonah, to lay before her the particulars of my uncle's confession. I took the same opportunity of relating my own adventures, previous to the time when I rescued her from the hands of the assassins. My father, who was present, severely chid me for many of my actions, and read me a lecture on the crimes of my juvenile days. Except pleading the mode of my bringing up, and the people with whom I associated—the rabble of the camp, and the society of those who, like myself, were dependent upon chance for existence—I could offer no defence, and bowed to his censures. On his retiring, I remained alone with Sagoonah, both of us anticipating the pleasures of the future, and our union in those bonds which death, in Hindustan, can scarcely be said to break asunder.

In a few days, my father determined upon going in state to the Temple of the Preserver, to make pùja, and I prepared to accompany him. Crowds of his subjects were assembled to behold their new sovereign, and among those present I observed Fuzl Khan. How he found his way to Sattarah I could not imagine ; but, on my return to the palace, I sent for Nanna, and got him to make some inquiries respecting Fuzl. Nanna told me that he had been some days in Sattarah, and having heard that Pandurang Hàrì was a prince, determined upon getting a sight of him, hoping he should not be entirely forgotten. I sent for him, and the fellow came, making as many salaams to the very ground as he made to Nagoo in the fortress of Asseerghur, before he sent us out to plunder his wife. "How," said I, "came you in Sattarah ? " "Since your highness saw me at Broach, with irons on my legs," he replied, "much has happened to me. The dulness of a convict's life was by no means suitable to my disposition, a high-spirited Mussulman as I had always been. Your highness will not, therefore, censure me for having dashed out the teeth of my guard, with the irons placed on me for securing my presence, and then taking to my heels. I wandered about the country for some time, till I found myself at Jumbooseer, where a number of boats lay at anchor. I hired myself to the tindal of one of them ; and, in the character and capacity of a sailor, I arrived at Bombay. There I left my master, and wandered about the Deccan, until chance led me to Ahmednugur, where I was imprisoned upon a false charge. In the same gaol with myself were several Bheels, who were imprisoned for life. These men got hold of the muskets of the sepoys, and some cartridge-boxes of the sebundees, a militia corps, and by these means expelled their guards, and took possession of the gaol, amusing themselves with firing the muskets into the air. The magistrate of the place, however, becoming alarmed, surrounded the prison with troops, so that escape was impossible. No greater mischief had been done by this frolic of the prisoners, than the waste of a few rounds of musketry, which showed, if bloodshed had been intended, the unhappy prisoners would have known better than to destroy their means of defence for amusement. The officers on the outside called to them to open the doors; but the prisoners, enjoying their fun, paid no attention to the mandate. Horrible to relate! the doors were then blown open with a six-pounder, and a whole corps marched into the gaol, which corps was commanded to put the unresisting prisoners to death. I could not conceive such a dreadful example would have been made by those who pride themselves upon their humanity, as the Toope Wallas are accustomed to do. The poor, naked, defenceless men crouched up in one corner of the gaol, having thrown away the muskets with which they had been frolicking; and, never making a show of resistance, were fired upon, from the distance of a few yards only, as they were begging for mercy. I was, fortunately, perched upon a wall, and escaped the effects of this merciless and barbarous act. Twenty were shot dead, and twice as many wounded. The English Government, it was thought, could never sanction this inhuman act; but it appears that those in authority were very well pleased with the civil officer's conduct. It is strange that the Toope Wallas boast of their desire to do justice, but never take notice of complaints against their agents in cases similar to the present. The officer makes his own report of his own conduct; and this they take, in all cases, to be true, and boldly uphold it in the teeth of fact; because, if he had not been a true worthy man, they would not have employed him! Moreover, the prisoners in this case were but black rascals, and the gaol wanted thinning; so that the prisoners commenced their frolic at the most convenient time. As for myself, I descended from the wall, and was thrust into a cell, and deemed a lucky fellow to have escaped. A cart came the next day, and took away the bodies of the slaughtered men, as well those who had as those who had not to do with the tumult, and carried them to the place of interment, in which it was desirable to bury the recollection of these murders at the same time. My term of imprisonment having expired, I was set at liberty, and found my way to Sattarah, to throw myself at your highness's feet." Fuzl Khan having thus concluded his history, I observed to him that it was impossible I could employ one on whom no dependence could be placed; but I advised him to enter as a soldier, and if his conduct were correct, I would take care he should not want promotion and encouragement, for I should keep him carefully under my eye. He bowed and went away, looking sullen and disappointed.

I afterwards inquired into Fuzl Khan's extraordinary history of the massacre of the prisoners, and I found it was too correct. How the magistrate would have been enabled to justify himself to the Government, had he been accused, I cannot tell. The latter would have relied upon his official statement, perhaps, and the matter would have been just as it was. I mentioned it to one Englishman, who showed great reluctance to enter into any conversation upon the subject, or even to hear it mentioned, and many of his countrymen seemed equally indisposed to make it a subject of conversation. Hence I conjectured that this wicked deed was not thought much higher of among the Toope Wallas than by ourselves; and that it was not likely to add much to the reputation of their countrymen in the East or West. Perhaps the silence of so many upon this subject, should the foregoing surmise not be correct, may be attributed to the known modesty of our conquerors, who never indulge themselves in anything like a boasting, even of their most valiant acts! It would also, no doubt, be presumptuous to suppose that anything but dire necessity, and a wholesome regard for the security of the city and gaol (so deeply involved as they must have been!) could have led a magistrate to a measure of such unparalleled and monstrous severity.

The next step which I took relative to myself was the holding a consultation of Brahmins respecting my marriage, which, they were of opinion, should be celebrated as early as possible, with the same forms adopted on our betrothment. On the day nominated, I proceeded to the residence of Sagoonah's uncle, with whom she was residing; and having been welcomed in due custom as a guest, he presented me with the hand of my beloved, which I took with rapture. The priests then bound our hands together with grass, after the usual way, and I threw the cloth over my bride, which was, in the present case, of unusual richness; the corner of it was fastened to my garments, and I made the oblations to fire, while my bride dropped the rice into the flame as her offering. The bride having stepped upon the sacred stone, we both walked round the fire (I cannot help relating every particular of a ceremony, though so well known, because it was one so important to myself); and, before the ceremony was completed and irrevocable, the Brahmins made Sagoonah go through the tedious seven steps, the Brahmins using a text of the holy writings to each: the first step for food, the second for health, the third for religion, the fourth for happiness, the fifth for cattle, the sixth for wealth, and the seventh and last, for priests to perform sacrifices. I then approached my bride on the completion of her task, saying, "May none interrupt us!" Next, I was obliged to address the spectators, and say, "This woman is auspicious! approach, and view her; and, wishing her well, depart to your homes." The spectators being gone, I remained, as usual, three days in the banker's house; and, on the fourth, conducted my bride, in great pomp, to my own residence, where my father awaited her arrival, and received her with great solemnity, ending all with oblations to fire.

What more can I have to record, the perilous and varied years of my life being past, and having arrived at a tranquil and secure haven? I have performed my promise, as recorded in the first chapter of this my history. My readers now know my real birth and parentage, and the difficulties and troubles I had to encounter from my youth up to the present happy period. Should the reverses, which it is often the destiny of man to encounter, reduce me from the elevation of the musnud to private life again, or should my future years be filled with eventful circumstances of a public or private nature, I may once more intrude myself upon the world. For the present, then, my labours are over; I cease to write, and seek, in repose, to scrutinise my errors, and enjoy that peace which, at one period of my life, I thought fate had never destined to be mine.

I composed these memoirs of myself to leave behind me, for the benefit of my children, a testimony of their father's vicissitudes in life. Now, while I am writing, I have one child, a son, whom, in compliment to my early protector, Sawunt Rao, I have named Pandurang Hàrì.—Courteous reader, farewell!

THE END.

PRINTED BY WILLIAM CLOWES AND SONS, LIMITED, LONDON AND BECCLES.